Don'
The Way to

Brave New EARL

"**Absolutely delightful**…strong characters and interesting obstacles…a must-read."

—*Night Owl Reviews*

"Ashford exhibits her skill with creating complex, **intriguing characterization**…witty prose, and a message of redemption."

—*Publishers Weekly*

"Seasoned romance author Jane Ashford's **stellar writing** is on full display in *Brave New Earl*… Readers will be charmed…and will thoroughly enjoy observing these two honorable, wonderful people as they struggle to reach the happiness they both clearly deserve."

—*BookPage*

"Ashford begins The Way to a Lord's Heart series by, once again, expertly bending the conventions of Regency historicals to gift readers with a **refreshingly different**, sweetly romantic love story they will long remember."

—*Booklist*

"Jane Ashford writes a lovely story **full of charm and wit**."

"This sweet, unassuming historical romance was **a delightful surprise**."

Also by Jane Ashford

EARL to the Rescue

JANE ASHFORD

sourcebooks
casablanca

Published by Sourcebooks Casablanca, an imprint of Sourcebooks,
Inc.
P.O. Box 4410, Naperville, Illinois 60567-4410
(630) 961-3900
Fax: (630) 961-2168
sourcebooks.com

Originally published as *Gwendeline* in 1980 by Warner Books, Inc.,
New York

Printed and bound in the United States of America.
OPM 10 9 8 7 6 5 4 3 2 1

One

GWENDELINE GREGORY PUT HER PEN DOWN ON THE elegant gilt-inlaid writing desk and looked up, frowning; she brushed at the crumbs of muffin she'd let fall on her new black gown and poured herself another cup of nearly cold tea. This was her last breakfast at Brooklands, and there was nothing to be done about it, it seemed. She looked sadly around her parlor. The fragile straw-colored velvet and gilt furnishings, bestowed on her absentmindedly by her parents on her eighteenth birthday last summer, the figured wallpaper and pale blue hangings chosen by herself with such pleasure, the ormolu clock brought in from the unused drawing room, the flowered carpet—all these things would be offered to strangers at auction. For a moment, she felt like crying, then she shook herself and turned back to the list she'd labored over half the morning. Her seldom-seen parents were dead, killed four months ago in a carriage accident, and Brooklands was to be sold by her father's creditors. There would be nothing left, the lawyer had told her, but her clothing and personal jewels, so she had to plan for her future.

She picked up the list and scanned it. "Relatives" was the first item she'd written. Gwendeline frowned again. The usual recourse of young ladies in her situation was to take refuge with some member of the family. Unfortunately, Gwendeline's parents had no surviving family. Their parents were dead, and they had left no brothers or sisters; in fact, her father's solicitor was still searching for a male heir to take the title. He'd find one, no doubt, but Gwendeline didn't intend to ask a complete stranger for a home. She had no family feeling herself—her parents, having been utterly uninterested in family, had never instilled such an emotion in her—and she saw no reason why the new baron should wish to take her in. But that was beside the point; on the exceedingly rare occasions they'd noticed her, her parents had made no mention of relatives. She knew of none. Gwendeline sighed and drew a neat line through "relatives."

The same objections arose when she moved to the second item, "friends." Gwendeline had never been introduced to any of her parents' friends, and the neighbors here in Devonshire were distant acquaintances at best. Not having officially "come out" despite her age, Gwendeline had never been invited to their houses; and her governess had not permitted her to ride with the local hunt, as she had often wished to do. There were no family friends to give her a home.

"Guverness" was the third item on her list. Looking at it, Gwendeline wrinkled her nose and wondered about the spelling. Her education had been erratic. Though her parents had exerted themselves to the point of hiring an excellent governess to teach her,

Miss Brown had been too kind to resort to severe punishment, and in the end, Gwendeline had gotten little from their association beyond a clear sense of her governess's worth and a respect for her principles. Left mainly to her own devices in the great rambling house, Gwendeline had learned only what she chose—riding, a bit of French, drawing. She'd neglected the piano-forte and the more serious subjects, and since Miss Brown had left last year, she'd scarcely opened a book. No one would think of employing a girl to instruct others who'd been the despair of her own teacher.

Even had her schooling been satisfactory, every-thing else about her was unsuitable. She was too young, she exhibited far too much levity (or so she'd often been told), and her rank was a hindrance. Her clothes were all wrong for a governess, she concluded, smoothing the folds of her modish mourning frock. The fact that this final objection raised only feelings of complacency in her breast further argued her unfitness for such a post. I might sell my clothes, Gwendeline thought wistfully, and buy others with the money. But then she did not wish to do anything of the kind. And most likely, when she had done it and was supplied with a wardrobe of ugly, dowdy dresses, she'd still not be hired, and she would have lost her pretty gowns. She scratched item three off her list.

This left only "seamstress" and "actress" of her long-pondered alternatives, and she knew both of these to be entirely unsuitable, even had she been qualified or eager to try them. She put the list back on the desk and turned to butter another muffin. At least her last breakfast here would be a fine one, she thought rebelliously, putting out a hand for the pot of marmalade next to the teapot.

At that moment, there was a soft tap at the door and the butler entered. "Pardon me, Miss Gwendeline," he said, "but there is a gentleman to see you." The news barely ruffled the air of gloom that Reeves, and indeed all the servants, had exuded since the funeral, an air that originated partly from sympathy for Gwendeline and partly from disgust at their former masters' profligacy, which had deprived them all of expected pensions.

"One of the neighbors, Reeves? I thought all of them had called long since."

"No, miss," he replied lugubriously. "A stranger. He gave me his card." Reeves handed her the square of pasteboard with a gesture that conveyed his lack of faith in its genuineness. "The gentleman *says* he knew your father," he added with a touch of disdain.

Did this unknown gentleman have any idea, Gwendeline wondered, how poor a recommendation acquaintance with her father was in this house? The man who had squandered every penny of the Gregory fortune and estate was not popular or much respected in his former household. She glanced at the card. "The Earl of Merryn," she murmured to herself. The name sounded familiar; she almost felt she should know it. Had she met this friend of her father's? No memory surfaced, and after a moment, she looked up. "Ask the gentleman to step in, Reeves."

"Yes, miss," the butler answered doubtfully. "And shall I remain in the room while you see what he wants?"

Thinking of the final item on her list, Gwendeline was amused. A girl about to be thrown into the street was to be protected to the last moment, it appeared. "I see no need of that. You may bring some refreshment later if you wish to see that I'm all right. I'm sure the man hasn't come to ravish me."

Reeves looked shocked. "No indeed, Miss Gwendeline. It's just…the gentleman struck me as, well, formidable."

"Really?" Gwendeline paused. "Well, I expect Papa owed him some gambling debts or something of that nature. I'll have to speak to him, if only to tell him that there's nothing I can do. I'll ring if I need you. Send him in. And bring some of the good Madeira. We may as well serve it while we can. They mean to sell it all at the auction, you know."

Reeves smiled dolefully and went out. Gwendeline moved to the sofa under the long window overlooking the garden, puzzled and rather intrigued by this unexpected visit.

The latter emotion intensified when Reeves ushered the earl into the room. Alex St. Audley, fifth Earl of Merryn, was a striking gentleman, well above middle height, with the broad shoulders and powerful thighs of an athlete. He moved with unstudied grace and the air of one who knows his own superiority too well to require reassurance. His auburn hair was brushed into a fashionable Brutus, and though the points of his starched collar did not even approach his high cheekbones, the exquisite tailoring of his dark blue coat, the gleam of his tall Hessian boots, and his intricately arranged neckcloth proclaimed the nonpareil. His eyes, cool and gray, surveyed Gwendeline with obvious surprise, rapidly changing to approval. "Good day," he said when she remained silent. "I expected a child. It appears I was mistaken." He bowed, and when he straightened, a smile lit his features, quite transforming his rather austere countenance.

Gwendeline, dazzled, didn't reply at once. Her father, the only other gentleman of fashion she'd ever encountered, had been accounted very handsome and modish, but Baron Gregory's careless style of dress and heedless manners couldn't begin to match this stranger's elegance. But when her initial reaction passed, Gwendeline found herself assailed by another, less rational feeling. For some reason she resented this man. The unconscious assurance with which he strolled into her private room, the cool way he appraised her, as if amused by something she would never comprehend, and the general effect of his appearance, which fairly cried out his wealth and independence, set her back up. The charming smile somehow heightened the emotion rather than dissipated it. "How do you do," she answered him coolly. "I am not a child, as you see."

"I do indeed," he replied, taking a seat, uninvited, on the sofa beside her. "Most of Roger's acquaintances were astonished to hear that he had any children at all, and we simply assumed you must be still in the nursery. What an irresponsible pair your parents were. Did they mean to leave you rusticating here forever?"

"I was to have come out this season," said Gwendeline stiffly. "And now, my lord, if you would tell me how I may serve you? If my father owed you money, I must tell you that I can do nothing."

The earl raised his eyebrows. "You think I drove

halfway across Devonshire to dun a child?" He paused. "I've been precipitous, but I was surprised to find a beautiful young lady when I expected a wailing brat surrounded by troops of nurses and governesses." The corners of his mouth lifted as he watched the effect of these words. "You look a good deal like your mother, but I never saw Annabella blush."

To her chagrin, Gwendeline's color deepened further. She started to speak but was interrupted. "The same coloring," added the earl. "The pale blond hair, those aquamarine eyes. I daresay they'll inspire as many sonnets as hers did. The nose may be Roger's, however." He reached out and took her chin, turning her face to the side. "Yes, I think Roger's nose."

Gwendeline pulled away from him and rose to her feet, outraged. The man's casual arrogance was intolerable. She went to the corner of the room and put her hand on the bellpull. "I think perhaps you had better leave, sir," she said, and started to ring for Reeves.

The earl regarded her with bland surprise, though his gray eyes twinkled. "Such heat," he said, taking in the picture she presented with amused appreciation. Gwendeline's slender, erect figure was admirably set off by the pale wall, and anger had made her blue-green eyes sparkle. Though her gown was of country make and the wispy curls of her hair not precisely in the current mode, she was indisputably a very pretty girl indeed. "You've mistaken me," he drawled. "I'm the knight in shining armor, not the ogre. I have come to rescue the damsel in distress."

Gwendeline wished desperately to give him a setdown. She opened her mouth to speak, but Reeves chose that moment to enter with a tray holding a decanter of the good Madeira and some biscuits. He looked uneasy at finding Gwendeline holding the bell-pull and the earl standing in front of the sofa. Putting the tray on the table, he said, "Will there be something else, Miss Gwendeline?"

Before the girl could reply, the earl had strolled over and was pouring out a glass of wine. "Is this some of the Madeira Roger used to boast of?" he asked. "I must try it." He glanced toward the corner. "While I explain the purpose of my visit, of course." He raised his glass to Gwendeline, forcing her to come out of the corner and sit down, feeling foolish.

"That will be all, Reeves," she said, and the butler reluctantly left the room.

"Very good," Merryn remarked as the door closed. Gwendeline glared at him. "I mean the wine, naturally." He smiled again at the girl's set expression. "I do apologize. I should have explained myself at the outset, but as I said, I was surprised. And in any case, you've hardly given me the chance." Gwendeline began a hot retort, but he went on quickly. "I'm sorry that we've come to cuffs so soon, and I'm sure it's my fault entirely. Will you accept my sincere apologies and listen to my explanation?" He looked down at her with a mixture of amusement and what appeared to be genuine contrition.

A little mollified by his politeness, Gwendeline nodded.

"Thank you. Well then, when we heard in town that Gregory had succeeded in killing himself at last, and Annabella with him…" He paused. "I hope I haven't offended you again?"

Gwendeline looked at the floor, shaking her head. "No. I scarcely knew my parents. And I've heard enough talk of my father's wild habits in the last few weeks to believe your expression deserved."

"Scarcely knew them?"

"I saw them only when they came down for a few weeks each summer, with a house party. They never asked me to join it, even lately, when I was ready to come out. And they didn't seem to like Brooklands." Gwendeline didn't hear the wistfulness creep into her voice.

"Hmm. Perhaps your mother retained some remnants of sense after all. My respect for her increases." He continued before she could comment on this enigmatic statement. "At any rate, it was some time before word got about London that Roger and Annabella had a child. We heard about you at the same time that rumors began to circulate about the extent of Roger's debts, and the combination was appalling. One of the finest estates in England thrown to the winds in twenty years and a daughter left with nothing."

Gwendeline looked down, not knowing what to say to this.

"So, ah, several of us decided to do something about it. And as a consequence, I'm here to offer you one thousand pounds a year and a small house in London for your use. It's not what you should have had by right," he finished, looking around the delicate parlor, "but it is something."

Gwendeline simply stared at him for a long moment, then began to stutter. "A small... Some of us... One thousand." She stopped, knowing she sounded demented. "Are you mad, or am I?" she asked finally.

Lord Merryn smiled. "I hope neither of us is mad," he said. "I know this is a surprise, but I hope it's a pleasant one. I had thought to provide for an infant." He paused for a reply and when none came, continued. "It's a pleasant little house; it belonged to a great aunt of mine who died last year. Not in a particularly fashionable neighborhood." His expression was becoming progressively more meditative as he spoke, and he seemed to be thinking aloud. "You can't live there alone. I had thought there would be nurses and plenty of time to make arrangements. We can bring some of the servants from here, I suppose, but—"

"You actually intend to give me a house and an income," Gwendeline interrupted. "A girl you'd never met, had never even heard of until some weeks ago, if I'm to credit what you say?" The earl started to speak, but she held up a hand to forestall him. "A man appears at my door, a stranger to me, and offers me money and a house. I'm not addicted to novel reading, Lord Merryn, but even to me this seems unbelievable and highly suspicious."

He looked at her, the corners of his mouth twitching. "Do you think I'm making an improper proposal?" he asked. "I see that you do." To Gwendeline's chagrin, he began to laugh. "I came here to rescue a child, a little girl, and as far as I can see, that's exactly what I'm doing. You're older than I expected, yes, but a schoolgirl still, my dear Miss Gregory."

Gwendeline bridled. "I'm nearly nineteen and not at all a schoolgirl. I'm afraid I must refuse your kind offer, my lord, though I certainly acknowledge your goodness in making it. And now, I think there is nothing more to discuss." She rose haughtily from the sofa and looked down at him.

Unfortunately, the earl showed no signs of taking her cue. He simply looked vexed. "I suppose my mother was right, as usual. She said I'd make a mull of it and begged me to bring her along, for propriety's sake if nothing else. But I refused to listen." He frowned. "I daresay it's not too late to get her here. When do you leave Brooklands?"

Gwendeline, taken by surprise, answered. "Late this afternoon."

"So soon." He tapped his chin with one finger. "It would be difficult to return with my mother in less than a week. What are your immediate plans? Visiting somewhere?"

Things were going rather fast for Gwendeline. She glanced toward the desk where her list still lay and shook her head. "I have a little pocket money left. I thought of going to an inn near here and…and thinking what to do," she faltered.

"An inn? With all your luggage?"

"I won't have much really, only one trunk. I never had many clothes and…" She thought of her "jewels," one Christmas locket and a pearl ring she'd been told belonged to her grandmother. "Ellen, my maid, is staying with me for a while. Indeed, all of the older servants wished to do so, but I could not even feed them, of course, so…" To her horror, Gwendeline felt her lower lip begin to tremble, and she bit it convulsively.

"This is outrageous," said the Earl of Merryn. "You are coming to London with me immediately."

At this new instance of his arrogance, Gwendeline rallied. "Nonsense," she replied. "I shall do no such thing."

Two

THUS IT WAS THAT GWENDELINE GREGORY FOUND herself seated in a hired post chaise with Ellen, her maid, her trunk tied behind and the earl riding beside them, traveling up to London. Reeves, a groom, and a footman followed in another chaise, which was burdened with a great deal more luggage than Gwendeline had expected to possess. It was not the same afternoon, but three days later; however, Gwendeline thought resignedly, this was the only detail that had escaped Merryn's control. Leaning back in her corner of the carriage as Ellen dozed in the other, she was swept by conflicting emotions. The gratitude she should feel for her rescue was tempered by the offense she took at this high-handed takeover of her life.

In the days before their departure, conditions at Brooklands had changed radically and, Gwendeline had to admit, chiefly for the better. The earl had first gone into the village to see the estate agent and the representative of her father's creditors, who was down from London to supervise the sale of the property. Gwendeline had talked to these men several times since her father's death. The agent had been sympathetic but, so he said, helpless, and the creditor had been extremely unpleasant, first lecturing her on the evils of not paying one's bills and then leering at her in a very disconcerting way. Refusing to beg for objects she'd always considered her own, Gwendeline had finally given up trying to deal with either man.

But when the earl returned from his short visit, he informed her that she would be allowed to keep a supply of linen and other household items, as well as a few small pieces of furniture, which she might choose. To Gwendeline's astonished questions, he answered only that dealing with such persons required a firm hand, leaving her indignant at his implied criticism of her ability to cope. He proceeded to organize the servants she retained for the trip, hire conveyances, and generally oversee all arrangements. Gwendeline felt quite useless, even in the way much of the time, and whenever she questioned the expense, the earl replied only "nonsense."

Installed at the village inn, Lord Merryn had effortlessly overawed everyone he encountered, including, Gwendeline thought ruefully, her own servants. The cook was in ecstasy, Ellen called him "such a masterful gentleman," and even Reeves had been won over. Everything had begun to work smoothly when Merryn took over. Gwendeline felt sadly inadequate, very much swept up in a train of events beyond her control, and utterly relieved.

They clattered into London late in the afternoon, and Gwendeline stared out the coach window at streets crowded with other carriages and wagons, vendors hawking a startling array of goods, and what seemed to her thousands of pedestrians. The second chaise was sent on to her new house to leave the large luggage and give the servants a chance to survey it, while Gwendeline went to the house of the earl's mother, where she was to stay temporarily.

As they drove through the statelier streets of the West End, Gwendeline began to feel a bit nervous. She'd never traveled or visited before, and she felt more and more alarmed at the prospect of meeting the mother of her rescuer. When the chaise slowed to negotiate a corner, she leaned out the window and called to the earl, who was riding a little ahead. He obligingly dropped back beside her. "You're certain you told your mother I was coming?" she asked. "And she agreed, she didn't mind?"

"As I said, I sent word," he replied, "and she was quite pleased at the thought of entertaining a young visitor. In fact, if I know anything of my mother, she'll be making plans to bring you out." He smiled slightly. "I told her, you see, that you're quite lovely."

Blushing, Gwendeline drew her head back into the coach just as it stopped in front of an imposing graystone house.

Merryn handed her down from the carriage as one of the postboys knocked smartly on the polished front door. It was flung open almost immediately, and they walked up three steps into an elegant hall. "Is my mother in the drawing room, Allison?" the earl asked the towering butler who'd come out to greet them.

"No, my lord. She is in her, ah, study." Allison said this with a faint air of disapproval, leaving Gwendeline to wonder what there was in a study to disapprove.

The earl sighed. "Very well. This way, Gwendeline."

He had begun calling her by her Christian name on the second day of his visit to Brooklands, and repeated requests that he desist had had no effect. It made Gwendeline feel like a child, instead of the young lady she knew herself to be, and she was quite sure the earl knew this and did it on purpose.

They went upstairs and down a hallway, past a large drawing room beautifully appointed in fawn and pale green. The earl knocked on a closed door at the end of the passage; there was no answer, but he ignored this and went in, Gwendeline behind him.

"Hello, Mother," he said crisply. "We have arrived, as you see. Here is Gwendeline Gregory, come to stay with you."

The lady seated at the large and very cluttered desk in the corner of the room turned, and Gwendeline got her first look at the Countess of Merryn. She'd expected a large, overpowering woman, dressed in the latest mode and altogether magnificent, like her son. The countess was small, however, scarcely coming to Gwendeline's chin when she stood up, though Gwendeline was only slightly above medium height. Her dress was indeed well cut, but it was of lavender silk and very simple, long sleeved and high necked, fastened at the throat with a bit of lace and a cameo brooch. Lady Merryn's silver hair was also dressed simply, and she wore no cap and no other jewelry. Her eyes were the same cool gray as her son's, though her manner lacked his infuriating superiority.

Gwendeline had time to notice these things because the countess seemed quite vague at first as to why they'd come. "Alex, how nice to see you," she said, holding out her hand. "It's an age since we met. I've been so busy, you know, with the third volume that I've seen absolutely nobody for weeks." Gwendeline had a moment of panic, wondering whether the earl had really sent word of her visit, but then his mother turned to her. "And this is Gwendeline. She's perfect! Reared in the countryside, far from the nets of commerce and society. Have you read Rousseau, my dear?"

"B-beg pardon, ma'am?" stammered Gwendeline.

"But of course you have not." The countess's eyes took on a faraway look. "It would be a contradiction in terms for a child of nature to know Rousseau. She must *be*, while we less fortunate city dwellers read of her nature. Thus, they are antithesis, the theory and the creature. I must make a note." She bustled back to her desk and began writing furiously.

Wide-eyed, Gwendeline looked to the earl for help. If this was how people conversed in London, she would be lost. But Merryn merely raised his eyebrows and shrugged, offering her no aid.

The countess turned back to them. "A most interesting thought. I shall bring it up at the Literary Society meeting Thursday. But now, you must be exhausted from your journey, and I mustn't keep you standing. Let us go and sit down."

The servants were laying out the tea things when they reached the drawing room, and Gwendeline was glad to sink into a comfortable chair and accept the cup Lady Merryn poured for her.

"There," said the countess as she finished handing round the tea. "Just drink that, and then I'll show you to your room, my dear. You'll want to rest before dinner. Alex, you're dining with us, of course." She didn't wait for an answer, and Gwendeline was pleased to see the earl pulled into someone else's plans for a change. "I must apologize for my welcome, Gwendeline. We'll be so much together, may I call you Gwendeline?" Again, she went right on without waiting for permission. "I've been so involved in my latest novel, nearly finished now, that I've been forgetful. As soon as it's complete, I'll take the time to get you properly settled in London."

"Novel?" asked Gwendeline, again glancing at the unresponsive earl for guidance.

"Yes, didn't Alex tell you? Just like him, he's very selfish." She smiled engagingly at her son. "Never concerned with anything but his own interests."

The earl merely smiled wryly at this, and Gwendeline's respect for his mother increased.

"Chiefly, I write three-volume Gothic novels," the countess went on, "though I have tried other sorts. Medieval settings interest me most. Did you know, for example, why some consider it aristocratic to hold one's little finger out when eating?" She demonstrated, raising her teacup, her finger jutting out.

"No, ma'am," replied Gwendeline, hastily lowering her own cup. All of her fingers were tightly curled about the handle.

"It originated in medieval times." The countess was clearly ready to expound at length. "In noble houses, the salt and spices were kept in a bowl on the table, while people ate with knives and fingers. So inconvenient, I should think. The little finger was for dipping condiments, you see, so it was very impolite to use it in eating." She held up her hand again, triumphantly. "I learned that researching *Terror at Wellwyn Abbey*, my second book. One finds such wonderful facts in the oddest places. Have you ever visited the British Museum, my dear? Of course you haven't. I shall take you there."

She seemed ready to go on, but the earl interrupted her. "Fascinating, Mother. But perhaps Miss Gregory would like to retire to her room."

The countess looked surprised. "Have you finished your tea, dear? Come with me, then. We'll have many other opportunities to discuss literature, after all. I'm vastly eager to hear your views. You mustn't let me run on if you wish to make a point. I tell all my friends so. My tongue runs like a fiddlestick sometimes, but you mustn't let that silence you."

Gwendeline murmured a polite nothing as they climbed the stairs to the second floor. She was a little frightened at being left alone with this odd lady.

"Here we are, dear." The countess opened a door on the left. "This will be your room." The bedchamber was pleasant, carpeted in green, with a fire already burning in the fireplace and her trunk partly unpacked. The walls were papered in a floral pattern, and the hangings matched the rug. It looked very comfortable and very welcome at this moment. "This bell will bring your maid," the countess continued. "And you must tell Allison how you like to do things. Do you take chocolate in your room in the morning?" Gwendeline shook her head. "No? I find it so soothing. I often write late into the night—the atmosphere is so perfect then, quite chilling—and rarely come down in the mornings. Well, simply ask Allison for whatever you'd like. If you're an early riser, the house will be yours at that hour. And now I'll leave you to rest."

When the door closed behind her hostess, Gwendeline collapsed into a small armchair beside the window. Her head was whirling. She had never met anyone like Lady Merryn, and the idea that she was to stay with her for a lengthy period was quite daunting. How could she talk to a woman whose every second word was a mystery to her? And what a bird-witted creature Lady Merryn would think her when she discovered that she hated reading, even novels. Gwendeline thought of Brooklands and her uncomplicated life there. Her sudden longing for home momentarily blotted out all memory of how much she'd looked forward to coming to London for this very season. Brooklands now seemed a safe haven forever lost to her.

As she calmed down, however, clear-eyed common sense returned. Gwendeline's unconventional upbringing had left her with few illusions about her own importance, and even fewer expectations that her wishes would be put foremost. She was being silly, she scolded silently. Of course things seemed strange now. She was in a new place and with new people. No doubt all would be as familiar as her room at Brooklands within a very short time. And if she and the countess didn't get on, she remembered suddenly, she could go to her own house at any time.

With this comforting thought in her mind, Gwendeline rose and moved to the bed. She would just lie down for a moment and try to forget the bouncing of the chaise and the long, cold days on the road. Before long, Gwendeline's eyelids were drooping, and in a quarter of an hour she was sound asleep.

Three

When she awoke, Ellen was lighting the candles and drawing the curtains. "There you are, miss. I was just about to wake you. Time to dress for dinner."

Gwendeline rose from the bed feeling crumpled and untidy, as she always did after sleeping in the daytime. She stretched as Ellen began undoing the buttons at the back of her traveling dress.

"Your new house is very fine, Miss Gwendeline," Ellen said cheerfully. "I've just come from there. Mr. Reeves is proper set up, he is. The parlor maid is French, from Paris, France, and so is the cook. Chef, I should say. He's a man." She giggled. "And a fair strange little man at that. When I went to the kitchen for tea, he was carrying on something fierce because the cook boy had dropped his raspberry tart. All in French and mortal fast. Then, when he saw me, he just stopped dead and came to meet the new pay-teet mam-zel. That's what he called me, miss. And he kissed my hand." She giggled again. "Yvette, the parlor maid, didn't like that a bit, she didn't. They call the chef Alphonse."

Gwendeline took advantage of the momentary pause to steer Ellen's attention back to matters of dress. Soon her curls were newly arranged and she wore her black evening gown. As she surveyed herself critically in the mirror, she decided that black became her well enough, though tonight it made her look pale. She didn't care for the color, however, and wished she could put on her old pink evening frock. She sighed. She would have to buy more mourning clothes instead; she had only three black dresses.

Gwendeline started downstairs to dinner feeling less lost than when she'd first arrived in the house. Living in London would be stranger and perhaps more difficult than she'd thought. In the country, where she'd known just what to do, she'd felt much more grown-up. However, that life was gone forever, and she must make do with what she had. At this, she scolded herself again. Make do indeed; many girls would give a great deal to be staying in town with the Countess of Merryn as the season was about to begin. She smiled. Soon she would learn the way of things and be completely at ease in London.

When she reached the drawing room, she found the earl there alone. He bowed slightly as she entered, but said nothing. Gwendeline stopped beside him, in front of the fire. She wanted to ask him several questions about his mother, but it was difficult to find the proper words.

"You don't look as if your first impressions of London are favorable," said Merryn, looking down at her as she stared at the fire.

Gwendeline glanced up sharply, thinking he was

mocking her, but his expression was bland. "I must say, it's not just what I expected," she answered after a pause. "My conversation seems inadequate. Sometimes I didn't quite understand what your mother meant when she spoke to me, and I could *never* think of any reply."

The earl laughed. "You mustn't take my mother as typical of London, Gwendeline. At least, not of fashionable London and the *ton*. Mama fancies herself a literary light."

"Literary," said Gwendeline. "She must read a great deal. Her desk was covered with books. What was the name…Rousseau? Have you read that?" This last remark sounded slightly forlorn. "I'm afraid I'm not the least bookish. Your mother will find me quite stupid." The prospect of living with a literary lady, even temporarily, filled Gwendeline with dismay.

The earl laughed again. "Don't look so blue-deviled. My mother's literary 'fits' are worst while she's actually writing. Between books, she's a fairly normal member of polite society. And when she finds you're interested in other things, she won't plague you. At least, not often." But his expression was more hopeful than certain, and he turned the subject. "What sorts of things are you interested in, Gwendeline? I don't believe we've discussed that."

"You've never appeared unduly concerned with my interests, my lord, only in harrying me about in accordance with your own." Gwendeline paused and blinked. "Oh dear, that's unfair. I apologize. I really am most grateful for all the money you've spent to bring me here and the house and…and everything."

"You're much more amusing when you're berating me, Gwendeline. Your eyes flash so brilliantly."

"Oh," said Gwendeline. "You're insufferable, and I wish you would stop calling me Gwendeline. It is impossible to thank you. I—"

"Then cease trying. We were talking of your interests. Do you ride?" This question happily diverted them into an intense discussion of horses and hunting that lasted until the earl's mother entered the room.

"We'll have to see about getting you a mount," said the earl as they turned to greet her. "You'll want to ride in the park, I'm sure. Good evening, Mother, you're looking particularly dashing tonight."

Indeed, Lady Merryn's appearance in evening dress seemed to confirm what her son had said about her place in society. Her amber silk gown was cut in the latest mode, and her gray hair was dressed à la Meduse. She wore a set of magnificent emeralds and a paisley silk shawl with long trailing fringes. Gwendeline felt pale and countrified beside her. "Let's go directly down to dinner, shall we?" the older woman said. "We can make plans as we eat." With this, she took the earl's arm and led the way to the dining room.

The table was beautifully appointed, and the meal perfectly cooked and served, but Gwendeline later remembered little about the food. From the moment they sat down, her future was the topic, and she was seldom allowed to make any comment or offer any suggestion.

"Well," Lady Merryn began efficiently. "Of course, you'll want to get into society as soon as may be. Almack's, perhaps a presentation at court later on.

London will be very thin of company for a few weeks yet, but I daresay we could arrange a small private party to begin."

"Gwendeline is in mourning, of course, Mother," put in the earl.

"Oh lud," said the countess. "How shatter-brained I am! You must think me a monster, child. I haven't even mentioned your parents' sad accident."

"Not at all," said Gwendeline. "I was never close to my parents. Quite the opposite, in fact."

"Indeed," replied her ladyship. She looked thoughtful. "Well, I hadn't considered the question properly before, but I should think that's all for the best." She exchanged a significant look with her son, who nodded almost imperceptibly.

Gwendeline felt that she'd failed to catch some implication, but the countess quickly turned the talk back to her plans. "Do you consider that six months' mourning would be right, Gwendeline? I don't want you to feel pushed."

"It's difficult to feel grief for two people who merely brought me into the world, then ignored me," said Gwendeline. "I'll leave it to you to decide what is proper. I would be pleased to be done with all this black." She looked down at her dress with distaste.

The countess's eyes twinkled. "You are certainly honest, my dear. That is most refreshing. Well, then, I think that six months should be adequate. Do you agree, Alex?" The earl nodded. "And that will give you plenty of time to get settled," his mother continued. "And to get some clothes. We can begin tomorrow."

Gwendeline felt she must begin to assert herself before she was again swept up in someone else's schemes. "That's very kind of you," she said. "I'd be grateful for your help in choosing a few things suitable for London. But I don't wish to spend much money." She glanced at the earl. "And I hope to get my own house in order very soon so that I need not trespass on your hospitality." Lady Merryn seemed about to speak, but Gwendeline rushed on. "And I think one of my first duties should be to go and thank those people who have combined to help me."

"C-combined?" echoed the countess, looking mystified.

"I've told Miss Gregory that several of her father's friends gathered the means to aid her," interrupted St. Audley smoothly.

"Her father's friends?"

"Yes," he answered firmly. He turned to Gwendeline. "Unfortunately, most are out of town right now, but you'll no doubt have a chance to express your thanks later."

"I… All right," said Gwendeline. Lady Merryn's expression was odd, and Gwendeline was beginning to resent feeling out of her depth. "I suppose I can spend the time tidying up my new house," she said a bit defiantly. "May I go to see it tomorrow?"

"Certainly," the earl replied. "But if you wish to live there immediately, we must make some arrangements for a companion. You can't live in London alone."

"But there are the servants. Reeves is completely trustworthy, I assure you. We managed quite well at Brooklands."

"I'm sure you did. But even in the country, it was improper for a young lady to have no chaperone, and in the city it's impossible."

"But you are to stay with me," Lady Merryn broke in plaintively. "I thought it was all settled. I was quite looking forward to a very long visit. You mustn't leave immediately."

"You are very kind, my lady, but…"

"I won't hear of it," the countess continued. "This is utter nonsense. Why should you go and live in Green Street, quite out of the world, when you're perfectly comfortable here? Alex, I forbid it!"

"But you wouldn't wish to keep Miss Gregory here against her will, Mother," the earl replied. "Certainly if she wants to go to her own house, you will respect her wishes." There was a peculiar intensity to his words.

The countess frowned at him, then her face fell. To Gwendeline's horror, tears began to form in her hostess's eyes. "You're right, of course, Alex. It's just that I so looked forward to having some company." She turned to Gwendeline. "Since my husband died years ago, I have been rather lonely, you see, my dear. But I mustn't be selfish. I've accused Alex of it, and you'll begin to think he inherited the failing from me. Go to your house, of course, Gwendeline. I shall be quite all right." She sniffed quietly.

"Oh, I never meant… Your generous hospitality… I'm so sorry." Gwendeline was so intent on comforting Lady Merryn that she failed to see the gleam of malicious amusement in the earl's eyes. "Of course I will stay if you truly wish it. I was only worried about being a burden to you."

"No, no, Gwendeline," said her ladyship sadly. She sat up straighter in her chair. "You must not give in to my selfish whims. You must do as you like."

"But I *want* to stay," said Gwendeline desperately, feeling as if she had betrayed some trust. "I truly do."

"Well," began Lady Merryn, "if you're not just being kind." She brightened.

"Oh no, I mean it."

"Wonderful." She beamed at the girl happily. "That's settled. You'll stay with me indefinitely. Your house will remain in readiness for the time you decide to move. And tomorrow, I shall take you to Bond Street, and we can begin our shopping."

"All right," answered Gwendeline weakly.

"But now, my dear, you're looking completely fagged. Perhaps you'd prefer to go to bed early tonight, after your journey?"

Seizing this chance to escape, Gwendeline agreed. As she left the dining room, the earl directed a telling glance at his mother. She met it squarely. "Very neatly done," he said after the door had closed.

"I thought so," she replied complacently. "It was much like Melantha's speech in *Terror at Wellwyn Abbey*, wasn't it?"

"It was indeed, Mother, and I thank you. I had no idea how to persuade her, and I was afraid of setting her back up."

The countess smiled. "Gentle persuasion isn't one of your strong suits, Alex. You have a distressing tendency to command obedience. So like your father, and so very wrong in this case. I do wish you'd taken me to Devonshire with you."

Her son returned her smile ruefully. "As do I, believe me. But it's come out right in the end. She's settled here. Once you've taken her about a bit and society is accustomed to her existence, perhaps she can live in Green Street."

Lady Merryn looked doubtful. "A young girl all alone? No, utterly unsuitable. And such a sweet, innocent girl at that. I must keep her here. Particularly under the circumstances."

The earl shrugged. "Perhaps you're right. But she is a taking little thing, isn't she?"

"Extremely."

"I think a respectable match is the thing, if you can contrive it."

The countess considered. "Of course, that would be best. But with no fortune and the *on dits* still circulating about her parents, it will be a difficult thing to manage. It's a pity she resembles Annabella so closely."

"Her character seems quite unlike her mother's," offered Lord Merryn.

"So I hope, my dear, so I hope. One can never tell." As her son made a protesting gesture, she added, "Oh, I'm sure you're right, Alex. But a good match? I simply don't know."

"Well, you must do the best you can. It was only an idea." He rose. "And now, I must go, Mother."

The countess nodded vaguely, and he took his leave. Lady Merryn remained at the table for some minutes, a look of concentration sharpening her features. Finally, she too stood. "We shall see," she murmured, and she went back to her study, frowning.

Four

IN THE FOLLOWING WEEKS, GWENDELINE FORGOT THE uncertainty and fears of her first night in London. Lady Merryn took her to a dizzying series of shops, including the establishment of a modish Frenchwoman in Bond Street. This lady, enthusiastic over Gwendeline's blond good looks, sold them a gauzy ball gown which she insisted was "*précisément* the shade of mademoiselle's *ravissante* blue-green eyes." There was also a dress of sprigged muslin with puffed sleeves and ruffles at the hem, a fawn walking dress trimmed with dark green, and many others, as well as hats, gloves, slippers, and all of the other accessories necessary to a young lady about to make her bow in society. With irresistible zest, Lady Merryn threw herself into the task of equipping Gwendeline even to the extent of neglecting her novel. When Gwendeline worried over the expense, the countess waved her remarks aside with an airy, "Don't be a goose, Gwendeline, you must have clothes." And Gwendeline, breathless and dazzled, allowed herself to be persuaded.

But in the mornings, while Lady Merryn was still

abed, Gwendeline spent some time putting her new dwelling to rights. The house was small, narrow, and high, but she found it charming. The furnishings left by the earl's great-aunt were old, heavy pieces, and the curtains and carpets were somewhat worn, but they reminded her of Brooklands, which her parents had never bothered to furnish in a modern style, and she felt quite at home there.

She'd written to her old governess, Miss Brown, and asked if she could come to stay when she moved into the house. For some reason, Gwendeline kept Miss Brown's affirmative answer a secret. She told herself that she didn't wish to hurt Lady Merryn's feelings, but in fact, she couldn't banish the notion that more was going on than she understood, and she looked upon these private preparations as a defense against her ignorance and inexperience.

She met the new servants provided by the earl's agent when she first visited the house. Yvette, the maid, was merely pert and pretty, but Alphonse, her new chef, promised to enliven her household considerably, she thought. A small, dark man with snapping black eyes, he appeared to have strong opinions on every subject. When Gwendeline went down to meet him and see the kitchens, he followed on her heels throughout the tour, commenting on the newfangled kitchen stove, the size of the pantries, the worthlessness of the cook-boy and every other item at great length. His English was good, but highly accented, and Gwendeline had difficulty understanding him. She soon discovered that her French was no substitute, being rudimentary at best. However, when she sat down to a hurried tea in her drawing room, she discovered that Alphonse was a superb cook and should need little direction. His pastries were unparalleled in her experience. Indeed, she felt satisfied with all her staff, in spite of Reeves's dire mutterings about "foreigners."

On a sudden impulse, she invited Miss Brown to move in immediately, since she was eager to come. And this lady, who had been uncomfortably subsisting on the charity of her brother, arrived soon after. She was puzzled when Gwendeline asked her to manage the house for a while, until she could join her, but happy to oblige. Gwendeline was much comforted by the knowledge that Miss Brown, whose insistent common sense she'd often deplored in the past, was available to advise her.

The remaining months of her mourning passed quickly in all these activities. It seemed almost no time before Lady Merryn was planning the party she would give to introduce Gwendeline to society now that the season had begun. They were sitting in the breakfast room, lingering over their tea while the countess ticked off the names on her list. "I shall invite some of my literary friends, Gwendeline; I think you'll find them interesting." She'd given Gwendeline one of her novels and a volume of Rousseau to read, but Gwendeline hadn't managed to finish either. She had a distressing tendency to fall asleep over Rousseau, and Lady Merryn's novel made her restless and annoyed. The heroine persisted in screaming and fainting, alternately, until Gwendeline abandoned her in disgust. She'd pleaded stupidity and had mercifully been spared any further reading assignments, but she didn't relish the idea of trying to talk to the countess's "literary" friends at her first appearance in society. She could, however, see no way of avoiding it, and so she kept silent.

"But chiefly," continued her ladyship, moving her pen down the list and frowning, "we must have people who will help you enter *ton* circles. I'll get Sally Jersey to come; she'll give you vouchers for Almack's, I'm sure, and Lady Sefton as well, if she's back in town. Otherwise, I'm asking mothers who are bringing their daughters out this season and will be giving parties of their own. And, of course, some eligible gentlemen." She smiled at Gwendeline. "This list required a great deal of research, my dear. I'd grown out of touch with the younger generation. It was very like working on a new novel. In fact, I'm thinking of writing a contemporary story based on some of it."

"I'm very grateful for all you've done, ma'am," said Gwendeline. "I only hope I can justify your faith in my success."

"Nonsense, Gwendeline, naturally you will do so. You mustn't expect to take the *ton* by storm, of course, or become an accredited beauty all at once, but I have no fears for your success. When people have met you, there will be no more—" She stopped abruptly and turned back to her list, to Gwendeline's annoyance. "I wonder if I should try to get Lord Morley? I'll have to ask Alex to help me with some of his acquaintants."

"Is…is Lord Merryn to come, then?" asked Gwendeline. She'd seen little of the earl since her arrival. He'd escorted her to her new home and handed over the keys, but during these busy days of preparation he'd come to dinner only once. Rather to her surprise, Gwendeline had more than once caught herself wondering where he might be and how he spent his days.

The countess looked surprised. "But of course Alex will come to my evening party. How could we launch you else?"

"I wasn't sure that the earl would be, well, interested in such a gathering," replied Gwendeline. "He seems so much occupied with his own affairs. So busy. He always excuses himself from having dinner with us by saying he's engaged elsewhere."

The countess laughed. "My dear Gwendeline, Alex is absolutely deluged with invitations now that the season has started. He's quite the rage, you know. Indeed, he's so sought after that gossips have begun to label him 'The Unattainable.' Very silly and vulgar, of course, but he's such a good catch, you see, and he pays no attention to the scores of girls practically thrown at his head by ambitious mothers. Quite the wrong way to go about it, but how can they know that, poor things? In any case, he's indisputably a leader of the *ton*, an arbiter of taste. Alex need only show that he finds you charming and you will be *made*, my dear. So he must come, you see."

This recital did nothing to raise Gwendeline's opinion of the earl. No wonder he was arrogant, if this was the way he was treated. "Indeed?" she responded. "I wouldn't want to inconvenience him." The countess looked startled at her tone, and she hurried on. "What am I to wear?" The question of the earl was lost in a heated discussion of Gwendeline's new gowns and the variations of ensemble possible with each.

Alone in her bedchamber later in the day, Gwendeline thought over what the countess had told her. Why had such a sought-after gentleman, the type her father had called a real out-and-outer, taken an interest in her? Why had he been the one to come and fetch her, or the infant he said he'd expected? If he was a leader of the *ton*, and Gwendeline saw no reason to doubt his mother's description of his position, what was his interest in her? Friendship with her parents seemed the only possible explanation, but he never spoke to her of them or appeared eager to answer when she tried to do so. Quite the opposite, in fact.

This thought reminded Gwendeline of a series of odd remarks she'd caught since coming to town. Both Lady Merryn and her son had made references she didn't understand to her "situation." Gwendeline hadn't been aware that she possessed a situation in the sense that they used the word; seemingly, it was an awkward one. And she was becoming more and more interested in finding out exactly what it involved. She didn't relish the thought that the people surrounding her knew more of her circumstances than she, especially since the knowledge must be widespread. Gwendeline's chin came up. She was determined to find out the truth and not to flinch from it if it turned out to be unpleasant. Anything was better than this uncertainty.

But no opportunity presented itself in the following days, and thus, as Gwendeline stood beside Lady Merryn in the drawing room doorway three weeks later, ready to meet their guests, she felt rather nervous.

She thought she looked well in a dress of white sarsenet; her hair was newly cut and dressed in a cloud of curls called a Sappho by Lady Merryn's hairdresser. A silver ribbon was threaded through it, and she wore a new silver filigree bracelet, a gift from the countess for her debut, on her wrist. But as Allison called out the first names, and an elegant couple strolled languidly toward them, she wondered what these world-weary Londoners were thinking about her and what she would find to say to them.

An hour later, she was just as uncertain. The countess had introduced her to what seemed scores of people, and she had said "how do you do," and smiled a great many times. The guests and their names were jumbled together in her mind, and she knew she would never remember what to call anyone. She thought that they'd looked at her with sharp curiosity; indeed, sometimes she'd felt ready to sink under a particularly piercing glance. She longed to sit down for a moment away from the crowd and gather her thoughts.

"I think we can leave the door now, Gwendeline," said Lady Merryn. "I can greet latecomers inside, and we must give you a chance to become better acquainted with our guests. Come along." But as they were turning, the Earl of Merryn was announced, and they held back to greet him.

"Alex," cried his mother. "I'd nearly given you up. You promised you'd come early tonight."

The earl raised his eyebrows. "But, Mother, I am come early. I haven't arrived at an evening party before ten in years. Your guests will consider it a great compliment."

His tone annoyed Gwendeline. "Perhaps we should be grateful that you came at all."

"Indeed you should, Gwendeline," he replied. "I never attend come-outs. They are uniformly dead bores." She stifled a tart rejoinder as he went on. "You're looking delightful. You've done an excellent job of fitting her out, Mother."

Lady Merryn smiled complacently. "She does look well, doesn't she?"

"I chose my own clothes, sir," Gwendeline snapped. "I'm not a child." She faltered. "Of course, I'm very grateful for your help, Lady Merryn, I didn't mean…"

"Shall we go in?" said the earl, smiling. He offered each lady an arm. His mother accepted, smiling. Gwendeline hesitated but could see no way of avoiding entering the party on his arm. As usual, she was forced to fall in with his plans.

They paused just inside the drawing room doorway. The large space seemed completely filled with people. Chattering groups were crowded together, and their animated banter, the expert flirting of fans and focusing of quizzing glasses, and the sparkle of candlelight on jewels and fobs was overpowering. Gwendeline's anger faded to nervousness, and she suddenly felt glad to have the earl as an escort. Heads had turned to look at them, and she knew that the subject of many conversations must be herself, a daunting thought.

The countess stopped to speak to a friend, and Gwendeline continued into the room on Merryn's arm. A couple left the sofa against the near wall as they advanced, and the earl guided her toward it. "Shall we sit for a moment?" he asked, handing her to a seat. She sank gratefully onto the cushions. He sat beside her and smiled. "You look a trifle uneasy," he said. "You don't find your first London evening party altogether pleasant?"

"To be honest, it's more frightening than pleasant," said Gwendeline. "Your mother has been so kind and gone to such trouble for me, but I have no idea what to say to any of these people, and the thought that they have all come to see what I'm like is terrifying."

The earl laughed. "Many of them would be very pleased and flattered to hear you say so."

"Are they such horrid people," wondered Gwendeline, "that they enjoy frightening strangers?"

"They enjoy their power to do so, a great many of them." He looked over the crowd with some contempt. "However, you needn't fear the *ton*. It will find you charming."

"Because you tell it to, my lord?" asked Gwendeline, remembering what his mother had told her.

"Yes," replied the earl simply. "And there is no conceivable reason for you to look daggers at me because of it. I never asked anyone to care what I thought. Perhaps that's why they do so." He sat back and threw an arm along the sofa. "And now, tell me what you've been doing. You've clearly managed a great deal of shopping. Did you enjoy it?"

Swallowing her annoyance, Gwendeline nodded. "Oh yes. I have never had so many clothes. Or such beautiful ones. I used to think that Mrs. Creel, the seamstress in our neighborhood at Brooklands, was very skillful, but now I see that she was not at all up to snuff."

The earl raised his eyebrows, smiling. "Up to snuff?" he echoed.

Gwendeline flushed a little. "Oh dear, Miss Brown used to scold me about slang. She despaired of me."

"Miss Brown was your governess?"

"Yes. A very estimable lady."

Merryn nodded. "But a bit overmatched perhaps?" he suggested.

Gwendeline giggled. "Oh no, how can you say so!"

"I hardly know. Something in your tone, I think it was, made me doubt that you were a submissive pupil."

The girl smiled again. "Well, I was headstrong, I think, but she bore it well, and I have the greatest respect for her even now."

The earl bowed his head. "I'm certain she deserves it."

Gwendeline wrinkled her nose at him, but before she could reply he went on.

"So you have added to your wardrobe. Have you seen the park and the fashionable lounges?" And they proceeded to exchange a series of commonplace remarks about the sights of London. After nearly a quarter of an hour had passed, Lord Merryn rose. "We have now, I believe, suggested to the crowd that I find you captivating. Shall we go for some refreshment? You seem in need of a glass of lemonade."

One of Lord Merryn's most annoying traits, Gwendeline thought, as she rose to do his bidding, was that he was so often right. He escorted her into the back parlor, whose sliding doors had been opened to create more space, and procured lemonade for her and champagne for himself. They joined a group near the table—a young lady and several gentlemen, whose spirited conversation faltered at their approach.

"Good evening, Miss Everly," said the earl. "You're looking lovely, as ever."

The tall, dark young woman smiled satirically. "Thank you, my lord Merryn, you are too kind."

"Allow me to introduce my mother's guest," he replied. "Miss Gwendeline Gregory, Miss Lillian Everly, Lord Donwearing, Lord Wanley, uh, Mr. Horton, and Mr. Blane." He appeared surprised to see the last gentleman. "I had no idea you would attend this affair, Blane."

Mr. Blane bowed. "Indeed, I wouldn't have missed it. The opportunity to meet such a charming young lady must always be foremost with me." He smiled at Gwendeline, then frowned and looked at her more closely.

She smiled back at the group generally, looking at them with frank interest. Lillian Everly she thought quite the most beautiful girl she'd ever seen. Her shining black ringlets and brilliant complexion were wonderfully set off by a gown of vivid yellow. The bones of her face were exquisitely molded, her nose aquiline, and her eyes full of intelligence and sharp humor. Mr. Blane, the oldest of the gentlemen, she thought, was also very dark, tall, and slender and rather handsome in a saturnine way. His appearance was hawklike, his high cheekbones, thin lips, and prominent nose emphasized by piercing green eyes. Gwendeline found his gaze disconcerting, at once impudently appraising and mocking.

The three younger men were very different types.

Mr. Horton had nondescript brown hair and rather prominent eyes of the same color. His evening dress was not at all modish, and he looked out of place in this glittering crowd. Lord Wanley, large, blond, and blue-eyed, looked disheveled and upset. Instead of a neckcloth, he wore a spotted handkerchief negligently knotted at his collar. A sheaf of papers all written over and crossed protruded from the front of his coat, and he kept opening and closing his mouth as if he wished desperately to speak. Lord Donwearing looked the gentleman and nothing more. All of the group returned Gwendeline's gaze with interest.

"If you will excuse me," said the earl after making the introductions, "I must pay my respects to some of my mother's other guests. Will you stroll along with me, Blane?"

"Absolutely not. I shall stay to talk with Miss Gregory."

The earl bowed and walked away. He appeared dissatisfied to Gwendeline, but she felt abandoned. How could he leave her in a group of strangers who looked at her so expectantly, she wondered. He might at least have begun some conversation.

"You are new to London, Miss Gregory?" said Lillian Everly.

Gwendeline nodded.

"And how do you find it thus far?" the other went on. "Are you pleased with town life?"

"Oh yes, the city is wonderful," answered Gwendeline in a rush. "I've visited the Tower of London and the British Museum, and several other famous places, and Lady Merryn has taken me to Bond

Street. She's been most kind." Gwendeline faltered. Mr. Blane and Lord Donwearing had begun to smile. "I like it very much," she continued firmly, "although sometimes I find the bustle and hurry confusing. I grew up in the country, you see."

Miss Everly looked at her more kindly. "So did I. And I can assure you that everything will become less confusing very soon. In a few weeks, London will bore you, and parties will become commonplace." Her tone was both satirical and somehow self-deprecating.

"Do you think so?" answered Gwendeline, looking at her doubtfully. "I don't see how they could be precisely commonplace. Do you find them so?"

"Oh yes, frightfully flat," began Miss Everly languidly, then she paused. "Some of them at any rate," she finished with an odd expression. She changed the subject. "Do you ride, Miss Gregory?"

"Yes indeed," said Gwendeline. "Or, at least, I did at Brooklands. I haven't since I came to London."

"Splendid. We must ride together in the park very soon. It's difficult to find ladies who love riding as I do. I can lend you a mount if you haven't brought yours to town."

Gwendeline was about to agree enthusiastically, when Mr. Blane interrupted. She'd been conscious of his steady regard for some time, but now his eyes narrowed. "Brooklands," he said meditatively. "You *are* related to Roger Gregory then." He continued to survey her features. "You're the image of Annabella. It's amazing."

"I am their daughter, sir," Gwendeline replied, uncomfortable under his scrutiny.

"Indeed. And where had they hidden you all these years?" he said, smiling rather insolently, Gwendeline thought. "I was fairly well acquainted with your father and must deplore his selfishness in never introducing you to his friends."

"Unfortunately, I saw very little of my parents. And I never went into society with them," answered Gwendeline shortly. She was not enjoying this conversation.

"Ah. And how the deuce did Merryn come across you, I wonder?" Mr. Blane seemed lost in speculation.

"I would not say that he 'came across me' at all, Mr. Blane. A group of my father's friends very kindly aided me when my parents were killed."

"Such an unfortunate accident," put in Miss Everly. "I'm so sorry." Gwendeline thanked her quietly, as the other three young men added their sympathy.

"Group?" Mr. Blane began. "Just who—"

But Miss Everly didn't let him complete his question. "It's settled then that we ride together soon? I'll call on you." Gwendeline thanked her once more. She was afraid Mr. Blane would speak to her again, but Lord Wanley forestalled him.

"I *must* speak to you alone," he said to Lillian Everly. "I must." He spoke with a hissing intensity that made Gwendeline want to giggle. Miss Everly looked both embarrassed and annoyed, and Lord Donwearing grinned.

"As you see, my lord," Miss Everly replied, "I'm occupied at present. We'll have to talk another time."

"When?" he snapped back. "Only name the hour, the day."

"I b-beg pardon, but I…" Miss Everly faltered.

"I should like some lemonade," Gwendeline said in an effort to help the other girl as Miss Everly had aided her. "Shall we go and get some together?"

"Oh yes, I'm excessively thirsty," Lillian answered, taking Gwendeline's arm. And before Lord Wanley could do more than sputter, she'd led Gwendeline through the crowd and away. "Thank you," she said. "I can never think what to answer when Lord Wanley begins to persecute me. He is impossible to silence."

"Persecute you?" echoed Gwendeline.

"He thinks himself a poet, you see, and fancies he's in love with me. He's always requesting private interviews or trying to read aloud from Byron's works or some improper thing. He makes my mother so very angry."

"Do you like him?" asked Gwendeline.

"Not particularly. It's flattering, I suppose, that he wishes to compose poems to my eyes and so on. But he behaves in such an embarrassing manner that I never know where to look when he speaks to me. Here we are. Let's have some lemonade, and then I'll introduce you to my mother."

The rest of the evening was uneventful for Gwendeline. After talking awhile with Mrs. Everly, she was taken by Lady Merryn to meet a great many other people; faces and names blurred in her mind. Late in the evening, her hostess pulled her into a corner of the drawing room to be introduced to an odd-looking older gentleman. His hair was stiffly pomaded and stood almost straight up in a grizzled pompadour. His portliness was only accentuated by very tight yellow pantaloons and a bright blue coat, and when he bowed, there was an alarming creaking of corsets. Lady Merryn presented him in a hushed tone as "Mr. Woodley, the chairman of the literary society." She hissed in Gwendeline's ear, "He actually *knew* Walpole, my dear, and he is a dear friend of Scott. Visits him constantly."

Gwendeline had never heard of the former gentleman and had only the vaguest notion that Scott was a writer, so she responded to this information by saying simply, "How do you do, Mr. Woodley," and smiling sweetly.

Mr. Woodley beamed, possessing himself of one of her hands and pressing it to his florid waistcoat. "The young nymph!" he said dramatically, and rather too loudly for Gwendeline's taste, "the unspoiled child of nature." He transfixed Gwendeline with a gimlet eye, as the countess looked complacent.

Unable to think of a proper response, Gwendeline held her tongue and continued to smile. She tried unsuccessfully to disengage her hand.

"Lady Merryn tells me that you have been reading Rousseau," continued Mr. Woodley. "I should very much like to hear your views."

Gwendeline began to feel hunted. "Well, I didn't actually…that is, I read only a small part of the book. It was quite, uh, quite interesting."

"But tell me," said Mr. Woodley, thrusting his florid face very near hers and speaking with an embarrassing intensity, "did you feel *changed*?"

"Ch-changed?" echoed Gwendeline, looking sideways at Lady Merryn, who merely nodded. "I'm not sure I understand."

"Changed, altered," he said. "Did you feel your

whole personality undergoing a revolution as you read, your world transformed?" The last word was accompanied by an extravagant gesture. Several of the people near them turned to see what was going on.

"I felt much the same," answered Gwendeline. "I don't think I changed at all, really. I am rather stupid about books, you see, and some of the ideas confused me a bit…"

"Aha!" cried Mr. Woodley, and several more guests turned to stare. "I told you how it would be," he said to Lady Merryn. "The early orientation cannot be altered." The countess nodded as if impressed. "She will always remain a creature of nature," Mr. Woodley continued benignly. "Mere words could not quench the noble savage. I must tell Godwin of this tomorrow."

"You have met him at last, then?" exclaimed Lady Merryn. "You must take me there."

"I should be delighted, my dear lady," replied Mr. Woodley, bowing creakingly. "But I must consult them, of course. A very exclusive circle."

Gwendeline was bewildered. Mr. Woodley had seemed to say that she would never fit into London society, and their conversation certainly supported his view. She had no idea what he was talking about. Fortunately, before she was called upon to respond to his last remarks, some other guests came up to bid their hostess farewell. Soon, a great many people were leaving as the hour was by now very late.

By the time everyone had gone, Gwendeline was exhausted. She stood for a moment with Lady Merryn before they retired. The countess was pleased with the success of her party. "We've been promised vouchers for Almack's, Gwendeline. And I'm sure we'll receive all manner of invitations after tonight. And people will call." She cocked her head. "Did you meet some nice young people?"

"A young lady, Miss Everly, asked me to ride in the park," she answered. "I liked her very much."

"Ah, Julia Everly's daughter. That's splendid. Lillian is one of the reigning toasts of the *ton* this season. Though I'm sure you'll soon come up with her, my dear. What of the young men? Did you talk to some pleasant ones?"

Gwendeline sleepily tried to remember. "I can't recall anyone in particular," she said. "There was a Mr. Blane. I found him rather unpleasant, I must say."

"Mortimer Blane," said her ladyship slowly. "I'd forgotten he was to be here. He's certainly not always pleasant, though often amusing." She pondered. "You should avoid him, I think, Gwendeline."

"I shall." She remembered something else. "But he did say that he was a friend of my father's. Was he one of my benefactors? I should thank him, if so, no matter how unpleasant he may be."

"Oh, my dear, I think not," answered Lady Merryn quickly. "That is, I am almost certain... You must ask Alex just who..." She stopped. "Look at the time! We must get to bed." She turned and started up the stairs. "And only think, Gwendeline, I may get to meet Mr. Godwin and his circle! How I have longed to hear their discussions."

Gwendeline very much wished to continue and perhaps find out something concrete about her situation, but the countess gave her no opportunity. When she reached her bedroom, Gwendeline was too tired to do more than undress and fall into bed. Investigations would have to wait, at least until tomorrow.

Five

GWENDELINE DIDN'T TAKE THE TITLE OF REIGNING toast from Lillian Everly, but in the weeks that followed she received a creditable number of invitations and was present at many fashionable *ton* parties. She danced at Almack's, where the earl led her onto the floor on several occasions to confirm his high opinion of her. The patronesses were pleased to approve her and allow her to waltz, and some of the young gentlemen seemed flatteringly struck by her charms, and vied for the honor of partnering her. She went to Vauxhall Gardens to dance, eat wafer-thin slices of ham, and watch the fireworks display; she attended several plays and went riding in the park with Miss Everly more than once. She even began to feel that Lillian, as she had by now been asked to call the other girl, was becoming a friend. Gwendeline liked her very much and admired her assurance and quick wit. Lillian was her first friend of her own age.

Not everyone was as kind as Lillian, of course. One or two starched-up matrons snubbed her, and Mr. Blane continued to seek her out at every opportunity and try to engage her in conversation. She avoided him when she could; she didn't care for his manner. But sometimes she was forced to speak to him, and then the things he said made her painfully aware of her youth and ignorance.

Just the opposite was true with another new acquaintance. Mr. Horton, one of Lillian's court of admirers, sought her out when they attended the same gatherings, but he had even less "town bronze" than Gwendeline, and his awkwardness put her at ease. She also pitied him; he clearly felt much out of place in London and was unsure how to make himself interesting to the satirical Miss Everly. He seemed very grateful for Gwendeline's good-natured attention and often spent entire half hours pouring out his thoughts, hopes, and opinions to her. He was not at all shy or diffident at heart, and he showed some inclination to educate Gwendeline when he had plumbed the depths of her ignorance of literature and the classics.

Thus, on the eve of her first real ball in London, Gwendeline felt more at ease in society, if not yet completely at home, and much more knowledgeable about its workings. Though she would never be a belle, perhaps, she had an established place and was accepted. Altogether, she anticipated the evening with pleasurable excitement.

But as she donned her pale aquamarine ball gown that evening, half listening to Ellen's chatter about the antics of Alphonse, Gwendeline began to wonder what would become of her when the season was over. Lady Merryn, she had soon realized, expected that she would marry some eligible gentleman and thus solve the problem of her future. But Gwendeline had not yet met anyone she would think of marrying nor had she been the object of any eligible gentleman's marked attentions. Her father's disgrace and, even more, her penniless state would discourage almost any potential suitor. Probably she would end up retiring to her small house with Miss Brown and living a quiet life in the city.

"So he threw every last one of them out in the gutter," said Ellen.

"What?" Gwendeline was pulled from her thoughts by this remark.

"He threw them out of the house, miss," repeated Ellen. "Oh, if you could have seen him, waving his cleaver about and shouting at them in French. I couldn't understand a word." She pursed her lips. "And lucky for me, I say. Because some of it was French swearing or I'm a fool."

"Are you talking about Alphonse?" asked Gwendeline. "Whom did he throw out? Oh, it wasn't the chimney sweep, was it? I told him the chimneys must be cleaned."

"No, miss," answered Ellen, frowning. "It was the mice. You haven't heard a word I've said."

"Mice?"

Ellen sighed. "The mice what was eating foodstuffs in the pantry. Alphonse has been screaming and raging about them for days. La, miss, you should have heard him. 'The mice, they shall all be removed or I go! They must be executed. Vive la guillotine!'" She giggled. "He swore he would cut them into little pieces and get six cats to eat them. Finally, Mr. Reeves got some traps."

"Ah. And the mice were caught?"

"Aye. Seven of the little creatures. In a great cage. John, the footman you know, pulled the trap out of the pantry first thing this morning, and there they were. He held the trap up. You know how tall John is, miss. And Alphonse began to dance around him, waving his cleaver in one hand and a great knife in the other and yelling something fierce. I like to died laughing."

Gwendeline smiled. "But he didn't cut them up?"

"Him?" Ellen sniffed. "He couldn't hurt a fly. He's all talk. John took them outside, with Alphonse dancing after him every step. It was a sight."

"I'm sure it was. And I daresay they've all found their way back into the house by this time."

Ellen's eyes widened. "Do you think so, miss? I must tell Mr. Reeves. He'll set the trap again."

"No, no," said Gwendeline. "Don't start the whole crisis over again. Come, I must finish dressing. I'll be late."

Gwendeline clasped her silver bracelet on her wrist as Ellen put the finishing touches on her ringlets. Her thoughts strayed back to their original topic, and she sighed. Thinking of the future remained nearly as depressing as when she'd sat in her old room at Brooklands trying to decide what to do.

A tap at the door announced the entrance of Lady Merryn. "Gwendeline, only look! Two bouquets."

Gwendeline took the card from the bunch of pink roses. "Mr. Horton," she said with a smile. "Oh dear, poor man, pink. I can never carry pink with this gown. Isn't that just like him."

"Well, well, my dear, it's the thought, and so on,"

Lady Merryn put in. "This Mr. Horton must be fond of you. I don't believe I know much about him. Is he new to London?"

"He's from the country, I believe. His father is in the church, and Mr. Horton plans to follow him eventually. I don't know him well, really. I'm surprised he sent a bouquet."

Lady Merryn looked disappointed. "The church. A country vicar, I suppose, with hordes of children. They always have. Well, at least you have an admirer, Gwendeline, even if he is not…" She broke off. "I'm sure he's a very nice young man."

"Oh, he is." Gwendeline smiled. "Overwhelmingly nice. But really he's an admirer of Lillian's, not mine." She had an idea. "In fact, I wonder if Lillian suggested he send me flowers. It would be like her, and it seems most unlike him to have done so."

Lady Merryn's face fell further. "Well, what of the other bouquet? It's lovely."

It was. Delicate green leaves surrounded a few white rose buds and the whole was enclosed in a silver filigree holder that went well with Gwendeline's bracelet. She picked up the card. "The Earl of Merryn," she read with surprise.

The countess's disappointment was complete. "Alex," she said dully. "How thoughtful of him. They will go with your dress beautifully."

"You told him to send flowers, no doubt," Gwendeline said.

"No. He must have recalled that this is your first ball. Well, if you're ready, we may as well go, Gwendeline."

"B-but why should he send flowers to me? He rarely speaks to me; I sometimes think he hardly likes me."

The countess appeared distracted. "Nonsense, my dear. Don't be silly. You must bring your Mr. Horton to talk to me this evening."

Gwendeline said nothing as she followed Lady Merryn down the stairs, but she found she was very glad that Mr. Horton's pink roses had been so unsuitable to her costume. She held the white ones to her nose. It made her unaccountably happy to carry them instead.

The first ball of the season was at Lady Sefton's elegant town house, and when Gwendeline and the countess drove up, they had to join a long line of carriages waiting to deposit guests at the door. Linkboys with flaring torches ran here and there, and the scene radiated excitement and bustle. Gwendeline's mood lifted further, and she began to be impatient to get down.

When they entered the ballroom, it was nearly filled with ladies in glittering gowns and men in evening dress. Lady Sefton had hung garlands of flowers throughout, and the effect was dazzling. Gwendeline stood gazing for a moment, then moved toward the corner where she saw Lillian Everly standing. Lady Merryn saw her safely disposed, then went off to speak to some of her own friends.

"Isn't it lovely?" Gwendeline said to Lillian as she approached. "I've never seen such a room."

Lillian's answering smile held its customary touch of sarcasm, directed not at Gwendeline but at the world in general. "The flowers are very fine. And so are you. Your gown is lovely."

"Thank you," Gwendeline replied. She always felt

a bit pale and washed-out beside Lillian, whose vibrant coloring tonight was heightened by a dress of deep rose pink. The two girls were a study in contrasts. "How is Thistle's foot?" she continued. Thistle, Lillian's favorite horse, had injured her fetlock when the two girls were riding a few days before.

"Much better," answered Lillian. "My groom says she'll be quite recovered by next week. I'm so relieved."

"Oh, I am glad."

At this moment, they were approached by two young gentlemen soliciting their hands for the first dance. Lillian was already engaged, but Gwendeline accepted and was carried off to join the set forming farther down the room. There was little chance for any but the lightest conversation, since it was a country dance, and through the first three sets Gwendeline was kept busy watching her steps, managing her skirt and bouquet, and responding to the sallies of her partners. After the third set, however, she found herself standing alone beside one of the long windows which ran down the side of the ballroom. She was about to go searching for Lady Merryn when Mr. Horton came up to her and said good evening.

"I…I am late," he continued. "I meant to dance with you. That is, I still mean to. Er, what I am trying to say is, will you dance with me?" He had gotten a trifle red in the face, and he fell silent uncomfortably.

"Thank you," answered Gwendeline. "I'd like that." She smiled at him. "I must thank you also for the lovely bouquet you sent me. I'm terribly sorry I couldn't carry it with my dress."

"W–with your dress," Mr. Horton echoed, looking mystified.

"Your pink roses were lovely," she explained, "but my dress is the wrong color for pink, I'm afraid."

"Oh. Oh yes, I see," he replied. "Then you didn't just, that is, you would have, I mean." He paused, looking vexed with himself.

Gwendeline took pity on him once more. "I'm sure I'd have carried them had they matched my gown." She hoped, for some reason, that he would not ask whose flowers she was carrying.

His face cleared. "Would you? I'm so glad. You're a very sensitive and, and *kind* young lady, Miss Gregory. Not at all like most of the girls in London."

"There is the set forming," Gwendeline responded quickly. "We'd better join it, if we are to dance, don't you think?" And she led the way onto the floor without waiting for his reply.

Gwendeline managed to find them a place near Lillian Everly, who was dancing with Lord Wanley. She knew supper would be announced after this set and she hoped to go in with Lillian and her partner to avoid any more private conversation with Mr. Horton. Gwendeline was alarmed at his manner and wanted to give him no encouragement. As they danced, she saw Lord Merryn stroll into the ballroom, stopping here and there to speak to a friend. She was a little disappointed when she couldn't catch his eye, but he appeared quite uninterested in the dancers.

The four young people did go in to supper together, taking a table in the rear of the supper room. The gentlemen went off to fetch refreshments, leaving

Gwendeline and Lillian seated. Lillian, occupied with a torn ruffle on the hem of her dress, was annoyed.

"Lord Wanley dances like a bear," she said disgustedly. "I can do nothing with this. I must go upstairs after supper and pin it up." She abandoned her efforts to mend the flounce and straightened. "He was reciting his latest sonnet, to my eyes, when he made a misstep and tore it." She smiled crookedly. "The really maddening thing was that he didn't even notice. He went on with his poem, leaving me to manage a dragging ruffle and try to keep it out of others' way." She laughed. "He is the most provoking creature. What am I to do about him, Gwendeline?"

"Couldn't you simply refuse to dance with him?"

"With Lord Wanley? You must be all about in your head. The scene would be more embarrassing than dancing with him ever could be."

"Yes, I suppose it would." Gwendeline was preoccupied. "I also have a problem. Mr. Horton sent me a bouquet, and he has begun to talk very strangely to me."

Lillian was immensely amused. "Has he transferred his affections to you then? What a wonderful relief! Now if Lord Wanley would only become enamored of you, I would be saved." She looked at Gwendeline wickedly. "Perhaps I'll suggest it to him."

"You wouldn't!" began Gwendeline, horrified, then realized Lillian was roasting her. "But what shall I do about Mr. Horton?"

"And what shall I do about Lord Wanley?" echoed Lillian melodramatically. The two girls broke into laughter. "Oh, it's too absurd," said Lillian when she could speak again. "Was anyone ever so persecuted?"

"And who would dare to persecute so lovely a lady?" asked a voice behind them. "Tell me, and I shall call him out straightaway."

They turned to find Mortimer Blane bowing to them. He had left his own table, and he took one of the empty seats at theirs, unbidden. Gwendeline immediately began to feel uncomfortable. There was something about the man that made her uneasy. She could never decide just what. His eyes, Gwendeline decided as he sat down, so very brilliant and piercing, and his manner toward her were part of it. He always made her feel young and stupid and silly. And he looked at her with a speculative, sly impudence that was insulting without being tangible enough to warrant complaint.

Mr. Blane leaned back in his chair. "This is luxurious," he said smoothly. "Two lovely young ladies for tablemates. I inadvertently danced with Alicia Holloway and now am partnered with her for supper. She says no more than a stick."

"How comforting then," answered Lillian languidly, "that she is so very rich."

"Most comforting," Mr. Blane agreed affably. "I certainly wouldn't have danced with her else."

"Ah," replied Lillian. "Now we see where your interest in us poor females lies. We shall beware of you in future, sir."

"My interest in *you* ladies has nothing of the mercenary in it, I assure you," said Mr. Blane, with a telling look directed at Lillian.

"It just happens, then, that I am an heiress also," she replied daringly.

"It happens that you are adorable," he responded.

"As you find all heiresses, I have no doubt. We'll never trust him again, will we Gwendeline?"

"Oh, I don't…" Gwendeline broke off in confusion. She had no skill at this sort of conversation.

"If Miss Gregory would trust me," said Mr. Blane, "I'd be honored indeed." He smiled as Gwendeline blushed. "You look uncommonly like your mother in that gown, Miss Gregory. That blue-green. She used to wear it often." His voice took on a distant quality. "You are as lovely as she was. I remember her at a party several years ago in a gauze gown of that shade. She was ravishing!" He recollected himself. "As are you. Will you honor me with a dance later on?"

"I-I'm not certain I have one open. I must see," stammered Gwendeline.

"Of course." He stood as the two young gentlemen returned with plates of food. "I shall speak with you later. Ladies." He bowed and walked away.

Lillian directed a meaningful look at Gwendeline, but further conversation was impossible as Lord Wanley and Mr. Horton spread their spoils on the table, with complaints by the former about the appalling crush around the buffet. As she ate lobster patties and salad, Gwendeline pondered Mr. Blane's remarks about her mother. His tone had been very strange; it seemed to hold more than mere admiration.

Lord Wanley began to recite his sonnet once more. "Her eyes smite me like spears of dazzling light/ Her hair glows dark…"

"Spare my blushes, Lord Wanley," said Lillian, "if you please. Why not write a sonnet to Gwendeline?

I'm sure she's much more nymphlike than I." She glanced teasingly at Gwendeline.

"No one is more nymphlike, more perfect than you," responded Lord Wanley. "That is what I say in the sestet." He started to go on with the poem.

"No. I protest I will hear no more." Lillian stood. "Come, Gwendeline, let us retreat from this flattery. I must mend my gown." They left the table and walked upstairs to the bedroom set aside for this purpose. Several young ladies were repairing damage to their dresses. "I can never decide," said Lillian, as she began to pin up her flounce, "whether Lord Wanley is simply a dunce or only misguided by the current fashion for poetic indulgence. His poetry is certainly awful."

"Is it?" answered Gwendeline. "I confess I find it excessively silly, but I'm very stupid about literature."

"It's quite the worst poetry I've ever heard," said Lillian. "If he were a great poet, like Scott, one could tolerate his odd starts, but he is not, not in the least." Lillian shook out her skirt and eyed it critically in the mirror. "There. That should do, unless I'm forced to dance with Lord Wanley again." She smiled mischievously at Gwendeline. "Perhaps if he asks me I'll send him to dance with you."

"No, no." Gwendeline held up her hands in mock horror. "Isn't it enough that you urged him to write a poem about me? Have you no mercy? Besides, he's interested only in you. He was quite offended at the idea of writing about anyone else."

Lillian laughed. "Well, he's silly but harmless. Perhaps he'll get over this craze for sonnets." They started back to the ballroom; the musicians were beginning to strike up again after the supper interval. "I can't say the same for Mr. Blane, however," Lillian continued. "He's a strange man. Fascinating in a way, but harmless? I wonder."

"I don't like him at all," Gwendeline said firmly. "And I shan't dance with him, later."

Lillian glanced at her. "Indeed?" she said. "I'll be on the lookout. I should like to see someone refusing Mr. Blane. I imagine it's difficult; he's not an easy man to get round, I would say. I wonder if your mother found him so?"

"My mother? What do you mean?"

"Why only the obvious…" Lillian paused and looked at Gwendeline sideways. "Nothing, a meaningless remark. Here we are."

When they reentered the ballroom, the dancing had begun again, and Lillian was carried off by an eager partner to join the set. Gwendeline, not previously engaged for it, moved toward the side of the room where she saw Lady Merryn talking to a group of guests. Too late, she realized that it was a circle of her literary friends.

"His eyes burn, positively burn, when he discusses the rights of man or any of his own philosophical ideas," Mr. Woodley was saying. "It's almost frightening to see a man so possessed by thought." He looked around the group complacently. "A most wonderful thinker."

Lady Merryn noticed Gwendeline and leaned over to whisper, "He is telling us about Mr. William Godwin." Her eyes shone with excitement. "He has been to visit *again*, Gwendeline. He has talked with him at length. Think of it, the author of *Enquiry Concerning Political Justice* and *Caleb Williams!*"

"His wife, too," Mr. Woodley was continuing, "has a very creditable grasp of philosophy. She is composing a treatise on the rights and duties of women. A lovely creature."

"Indeed," said a sharp-eyed lady on the other side of Gwendeline. "She is an agitator for women's rights?"

"Oh, I think not, I think not," answered Woodley, smoothing his cravat. "A very gentle woman."

"Hmph," replied his questioner and flounced off.

"I should so like to meet her," exclaimed Lady Merryn. "Mr. Woodley, won't you take me there when you go next?"

"We shall see, my dear Lady Merryn. It's difficult to introduce a stranger on such short acquaintance, you see."

Gwendeline wandered away as Lady Merryn renewed her request with more vigor. She couldn't remember whether Mr. Godwin was the famous writer of Gothic novels, the newest poet, or another writer like Rousseau, though she did recall that he was very important in Lady Merryn's opinion.

Another set was forming, and Gwendeline was asked to join it. Several dances went by before she found herself standing in a group, chatting once more. She was rather tired and just thinking of finding Lady Merryn to mention the lateness of the hour when Mr. Blane came toward her. She watched his approach with a sinking heart.

"Miss Gregory," he said with a small bow. "May I have that dance now?"

"I'm sorry," replied Gwendeline quickly, "I'm very tired. I think I won't dance anymore."

"Splendid," answered Mr. Blane. "Let us go and sit down." He took her arm and guided her toward a vacant sofa against the wall.

Gwendeline pulled back. "Oh no, I was, I was just looking for Lady Merryn. I must go; it's so late."

"But you must allow me a few moments of conversation, Miss Gregory," protested Mr. Blane, retaining his grip on her arm. "We've had so little chance to get acquainted since you came to London. I feel ashamed to have neglected the daughter of old friends in this shabby way." He seated himself and pulled Gwendeline down beside him. "Ah, that's better. Now we can talk comfortably." He turned toward Gwendeline and surveyed her with hooded eyes. "Tell me your impressions of London, Miss Gregory, now that you are an established resident."

"I...I like it very much," faltered Gwendeline. "Everyone has been very kind."

"Particularly Lord Merryn, I should say."

"Yes. And his mother also."

"Ah yes, his mother. Are you happy staying with the countess? How long do you remain?"

"I'm not sure." Gwendeline felt no inclination to tell him about her own house.

"So like and yet so unlike," Mr. Blane mused. "It scarcely seems possible."

"B-beg pardon," said Gwendeline.

"Forgive me. But I cannot see you without thinking of your mother. Is it true that you never knew Annabella at all?"

"I rarely saw either of my parents. They were always busy elsewhere."

"Sad. Very sad. Your mother was one of the most spirited, delightful women I've ever met. You might have learned much from her."

"Perhaps, sir," Gwendeline said stiffly. "Many people seem to think it is better I didn't. And I must say I'm inclined to agree. My parents certainly didn't care about my happiness or my future. If it hadn't been for Lord Merryn and my father's other friends, I'd be destitute." She raised her chin.

"Ah yes, these unknown friends," Mr. Blane replied. "Do you know, I have made a few inquiries among your father's friends and acquaintances. None of them knows anything about a provision for you, though many would be delighted to make one, I'm sure. Strange, isn't it?"

Gwendeline felt cold. "Lord Merryn knows who they are. He has promised to take me to thank them all."

"Has he?" Mr. Blane sounded interested. "How charming for these mysterious benefactors. If only I'd known in time, I too might have had the pleasure of being thanked by you." His smile made Gwendeline even more uncomfortable. "Another odd thing. You know, it never seemed to me that Lord Merryn liked your father above half. Your mother now, that was another thing. But your father? They never appeared to get on at all."

"I'm sure…" Gwendeline stopped, not wishing to explain anything to this man or add to his alarmingly broad knowledge of her circumstances.

"It's very strange," Mr. Blane said reflectively. "Now what could Lord Merryn…"

"What of Lord Merryn?" said a lazy voice at Gwendeline's side. "I'm flattered to be the subject of your conversation." Gwendeline looked up to find the earl standing beside the sofa; she felt a great relief. "This is our dance, I believe, Miss Gregory," he said. "You haven't forgotten, surely?"

"Yes, I…I did," said Gwendeline, rising. "I mean no, of course not."

"Miss Gregory is tired," put in Mr. Blane. "She doesn't wish to dance again this evening."

"Indeed?" The earl raised his eyebrows. "But it's the last dance and a waltz. You promised it to me." He looked at Gwendeline.

"I feel much better after sitting down for a while," Gwendeline replied. "And I must keep my promise." She took Lord Merryn's proffered arm.

Mr. Blane stood. "I bow to necessity, but I am desolated. We must continue our delightful conversation some other time, Miss Gregory."

Lord Merryn looked at Gwendeline as they walked onto the floor.

"You've rescued me once again," she said a little breathlessly. "Thank you."

"You didn't enjoy your talk with Blane? Many women find him charming."

"Well, I don't. I find him extremely unpleasant. In fact, I would be happy never to see him again."

"Such heat." The earl smiled. "What has Mr. Blane done to earn your scorn?"

"I don't like the way he speaks to me or looks at

me. And he talks continually of my mother." She looked up at the earl. "Was he in love with her, Lord Merryn?"

For the first time in their acquaintance, the earl looked genuinely and completely startled. "What makes you ask me that?"

"He talks of her in such an odd tone. I really can't describe it. But it makes me believe that he felt something for her."

The earl was looking at her with a new expression that Gwendeline couldn't identify. "I really cannot tell you what Mr. Blane feels," he answered. "We are not well acquainted."

"That reminds me of something else he said," Gwendeline interjected. "He has asked my father's friends about the money provided for me, and none of them knows anything about it. You've never kept your promise to take me to thank them, Lord Merryn."

The earl smiled down at her as they whirled across the floor in the waltz. "Your tone is absolutely accusing. What is it you suspect me of? Stealing the money? I assure you I did not."

"No, of course not. But I can't seem to learn anything about the people who helped me, and Mr. Blane said that you and my father didn't, that is, were not good friends at all. I'm confused."

"Mr. Blane seems to have said a great deal. Whom do you prefer to believe, Gwendeline? Mortimer Blane or me?"

"You, of course," she answered. "But I should like to find out…"

"Then you will accept my word. There is nothing wrong or mysterious about your situation." He went on before Gwendeline could protest this highly unsatisfactory conclusion to the subject. "I hope you approve of the bouquet?"

"Oh, I forgot to thank you. It's lovely. And the holder matches the bracelet Lady Merryn gave me. It was so kind of you to send them. You shouldn't have taken the trouble."

Ignoring her last remark, the earl replied, "My mother tells me you also received flowers from a young admirer."

"Mr. Horton," nodded Gwendeline wryly. "I fear he's begun to think he admires me. It will pass perhaps. He was in love with Lillian Everly only last week."

Merryn laughed. "You're becoming jaded with the pleasures of the city, I see. A suitor leaves you yawning."

"Not at all," Gwendeline protested. "It is just that Mr. Horton is so, so…"

"I had the pleasure of talking with the young man," he agreed sardonically. "Mother inflicted him upon me. He is indeed."

"Oh, that is too bad of you," laughed Gwendeline. "He is very nice."

"An exemplary character," the earl said blandly. "You are to be congratulated. I'm sure he would make a model husband."

The thought of marrying Mr. Horton was so ridiculous that Gwendeline burst into laughter as the dance was ending. In her amusement, she forgot to question the earl further about Mr. Blane's puzzling remarks, and it wasn't until she was home and getting ready for bed that she remembered them. What had he meant by his insinuations about the earl and her parents? And what was Mr. Blane's own involvement with them? Gwendeline could think of no one she could ask these questions, save the earl himself. And he refused to tell her.

Six

GWENDELINE WOKE EARLY THE NEXT MORNING despite her late night, and she immediately resolved to go to her house for a visit with Miss Brown. She might well know something helpful about the tangle Gwendeline felt she was facing. Gwendeline jumped out of bed, rang for Ellen, and in less than an hour the two of them were walking along the streets of Mayfair. Few people were abroad at this early hour, but the sun shone brightly on freshly washed pavements and entryways, and the breeze was warm.

Miss Brown was already busy with the day's tasks when they arrived, as Gwendeline had known she would be. They greeted one another affectionately and ordered tea brought to the small drawing room. Gwendeline exclaimed over its appearance as she sat down. It was much more airy and welcoming than the last time she'd seen it.

"Well, we moved out some of that heavy furniture," said Miss Brown, "the pieces you said you didn't like. And we found these curtains in the attic, along with some of the smaller pieces. I can't understand why you're so surprised, Gwendeline. It was all done under your direction."

"Yes, but I didn't know just how it would look. It's amazingly improved, don't you think?"

Miss Brown looked around. "Yes, I do. The whole house is wonderfully changed, as you would know if you spent any time here." She shrugged. "Will you move in soon?"

Gwendeline looked down, frowning. "Perhaps. I'm confused lately, Brown. I've come to talk with you about it."

The older woman's fine eyebrows came together. She looked steadily at her former pupil. "I'll be happy to do anything I can, Gwendeline. What is the matter?"

"That's part of the problem. I hardly know. It involves my mother and father."

"I wondered if that would come," said Miss Brown. "What has been said to you?"

"Nothing specific, nothing I really understand. I had hoped that you'd tell me what you know about my parents' lives. Things that occurred when I was a child, perhaps, things I wasn't aware of or don't remember."

Miss Brown sat back, sighing. Though she was a tall, rangy woman, her graceful carriage and the immaculate neatness of her plain dresses and dark brown hair gave her a certain distinction. But now, this air was tinged with concern. "I'll try," she replied. "But I know very little, Gwendeline. I spent all my time with you in the country, as you know. However, since I left you a year ago, I have heard some talk about your parents. When people learn I was employed by them, they imagine I would be interested in gossip. And one of my school friends has just become governess to Lady Forester's children in Berkeley Square. She hears all the tattle-mongering."

"Oh, tell me what they say, please," said Gwendeline.

"I shall not repeat malicious stories," Brown answered disapprovingly. "But I have learned something of your parents' history. I can tell you that." She sat straighter. "They married very young, it seems, and most unwillingly. Your father especially, I've heard, was opposed to marriage at that time of his life. He was a very wild young man by all accounts, and his parents wished to see him settled. His father was ill, and by emphasizing that fact and using other pressures, they persuaded him at last. Your mother was just out, the darling of the *ton* in her first season—she was very beautiful, as you know, Gwendeline—and she, too, wished to wait before marrying. But all four parents felt the financial advantages were too important to put it off." She looked at Gwendeline. "As I think you know already, the lands that made up your mother's dowry were adjacent to the Brooklands estate."

Gwendeline nodded. This, at least, she'd been told.

"So they were married," Miss Brown continued. "It was the event of the season, I understand, a very elegant wedding. They went abroad, to Paris and Rome, on an extended trip, then came home to settle in London. You were born that first year." She paused, looking uncomfortable. "But the marriage was evidently, ah, not an entirely happy one, Gwendeline. Perhaps because they were forced into it. For whatever reason, the regard that married couples should have for one another did not develop between your mother and father. He returned to the activities and acquaintances of the past, and she gathered a circle of rather unsuitable friends about her. Like many couples today, their lives were almost separate."

"But they always came down to Brooklands together," said Gwendeline. "They can't have been always apart."

Miss Brown shook her head. "Of course not, Gwendeline, there were appearances to be maintained. And in the later years, those you remember best, your parents' two groups of friends were becoming one group. Your mother began to, ah, join in some of your father's pastimes."

"Perhaps they were becoming closer to one another after so many years," said Gwendeline hopefully.

Miss Brown seemed reluctant to continue. "I wish I could say that was so, Gwendeline," she went on finally. "But I believe the bond involved no more than your mother's developing interest in gambling. She started to accompany your father to the gaming table. And to go on her own account as well."

"Oh," answered Gwendeline. Her face fell. "I see."

"I tell you these things only because you ask me," Miss Brown said. "And because I think you should know them if you are to go about in London society. I would not hurt you for the world, Gwendeline."

"I'm sure of that. And you're right. It's important that I know something of my parents if I'm to get along in society. Do go on."

"There's little more to say. Things only got worse in the last years of your parents' lives, I understand.

I saw your mother once soon after I left you. She looked unhappy."

Gwendeline felt like crying. The story would have been sad in any circumstance, but to hear of so much unhappiness involving her own parents was doubly melancholy. She was silent for a few moments. "Did you ever meet a Mr. Blane or hear anyone speak of him?" she asked finally.

Miss Brown thought for a moment. "There was once some talk of a Mr. Blane among the servants, I believe." She looked doubtful.

"Yes, Brown," said Gwendeline. "He was a friend of my father's?"

"Well, he was mentioned more often in connection with your mother." Miss Brown was reluctant, but Gwendeline looked at her pleadingly. "You know how servants gossip, Gwendeline. Some said that there was a clandestine connection of some sort between your mother and Mr. Blane."

"Oh," said Gwendeline.

"I daresay it was nothing but backstairs imaginings. Doubtless entirely fabricated by a disgruntled footman." Miss Brown's gaze grew sharper. "Have you met the man?"

Gwendeline nodded. "And the way he talks of Mother... Well, he clearly admired her very much."

"I see." Miss Brown wore her stern governess look. "He doesn't sound like the sort of person you should associate with, Gwendeline."

"I don't wish to," she replied. "But he insists on talking to me at every opportunity. He makes me very uncomfortable."

"Has he been impertinent or insulted you?" asked Miss Brown indignantly.

"No, no, he is always polite. It is only his tone, his manner, that I don't like. I wish I needn't meet him at every *ton* party."

"It would be much more sensible to move in here and live quietly, seeing only a few good friends." She nodded impatiently in response to Gwendeline's gesture. "Yes, I know we've been over this before. Well, I think Lord Merryn should be told of this. I'm sure he could do something about Mr. Blane."

"No," exclaimed Gwendeline quickly. "I beg pardon," she went on as Miss Brown gave her a startled look, "but I'm also uncertain about Lord Merryn."

"Surely he hasn't behaved badly toward you," her old governess said. "He's so much the gentleman."

"No, of course not," answered Gwendeline. "He hardly notices my existence. But Mr. Blane said things that made me wonder at his behavior. He suggested that the earl was also more friendly with my mother than my father. In fact, he implied that he and my father were enemies." She looked at Miss Brown.

"I hardly consider this Mr. Blane a trustworthy source of information," she answered. "I never heard Lord Merryn mentioned at all around your parents' household. I cannot believe such assertions."

Gwendeline felt a vast sense of relief. She hadn't known until this moment how much Mr. Blane's accusations had upset her. "But if he was a friend of my father's?"

"He probably wouldn't have been a subject of servants' gossip," finished Miss Brown.

"Of course." Gwendeline sighed. "If he'd been an enemy, they would have talked of that. If they'd quarreled?"

"You've let this man's talk upset you, Gwendeline. That is too bad. Lord Merryn has been all kindness to you. Why should you suspect him of duplicity?"

"It is just that I can't find the others he says aided me with money and this house. He always evades my questions."

"Perhaps they wish to remain anonymous," offered Miss Brown.

"But why?" asked Gwendeline.

"In my experience, there are two types of philanthropists—those who wish to exert themselves as little as possible and to receive a great deal of credit, and those who do a great deal and tell no one. Perhaps your father's friends are all the latter type."

Gwendeline looked doubtful. "Perhaps. But it seems very unlikely. Especially considering my father's life and the sort of friends he must have had."

Miss Brown frowned. "When you put it that way, yes. But I think it could be true of Lord Merryn at least. He seems the sort of man who does not care to flaunt his good deeds."

"But why, then, was he made the agent of this group? You see how confusing it is, Brown? And one thing remains most puzzling."

"And what is that?"

"Why would he do this particular good deed?" Gwendeline looked at her. "If he wasn't close to my parents, why would he help me?"

Miss Brown was at a loss for a moment. "Simple kindness?" she said finally, but her tone was doubtful. "To help a fellow human being?"

Gwendeline shook her head. "A stranger, with no connection to him? No, Brown, there must be a better reason. I'm perfectly ready to accept the idea that the earl is a charitable man, but even he must have some motive. Having no idea what it is makes me uneasy. I don't distrust him as I do Mr. Blane, but I don't understand him either."

Miss Brown found nothing to say to this.

As they sat in silence, pondering the problem, Reeves entered the drawing room and stood before them. "Excuse me," he said, "but Alphonse wishes to see you, Miss Gwendeline."

"Alphonse?" asked Gwendeline, surprised. "What does he want?"

"I don't know," Reeves replied. "He refuses to tell me anything about it." The butler's expression was forbidding.

"Oh dear," said Miss Brown. "I wonder what is the matter now."

Gwendeline shrugged. "Very well. Ask him to step in here, Reeves."

Reeves's bearing stiffened further. "Yes, miss."

Gwendeline looked at Miss Brown. "Reeves is struggling not to tell me he knew this would happen, of course. Foreigners."

Miss Brown laughed. "Alphonse is a very excitable foreigner."

A few minutes later, Alphonse came into the room with his customary energy. He looked defiant as he stood before Gwendeline, his black eyes snapping and his small moustache bristling alarmingly.

"Yes Alphonse," she said. "What's wrong?"

"I wish to inform you that I depart *immediatement*," he answered dramatically. "I cannot work."

Both ladies sat up straighter. "But what's happened?" asked Gwendeline. "I thought you were happy here."

Alphonse gave a helpless shrug. "The house, it is good. I have nothing to say against it. But I cannot work with that dolt, that *imbecile* of a cookboy." His look expressed infinite contempt. "That Michael. He drive me crazy!" The little man struck his forehead with his palm.

Miss Brown glanced at Gwendeline with amused resignation. This was a recurrent problem. Whenever Michael made some mistake, Alphonse threatened to leave. Gwendeline had heard of such scenes, but she had never before had to cope with one herself.

"Oh, Alphonse," she said. "What has Michael done this time?"

"Well may you ask." Alphonse looked incredulous. "He has thrown away all the truffles. Ah, mademoiselle, he is a barbarian. He says he thinks them garbage." He made an extravagant gesture to convey his horror to his listeners. "Garbage, mademoiselle! It is too much; I cannot live with such ignorance. I, Alphonse Lorvalle, who have cooked for Brillat-Savarin. You know him, mademoiselle?"

Gwendeline shook her head helplessly.

"Ah. The greatest, the most subtle of palates. A genius, *en effet*. He has approved me, mademoiselle,

I swear it. Before we all have to flee from that *bête* Buonaparte. And now I should endure this Michael?" Alphonse looked outraged. "No," he finished. "It is not to be thought."

"Oh dear," said Gwendeline. "Well, let's go and talk to him. He must learn better than that." She rose and the three of them went downstairs to find Michael. After nearly half an hour of talk and negotiations, greatly aided by Miss Brown, Gwendeline pacified Alphonse and made Michael promise he would be more careful. She then made a thorough inspection of the house, before walking back to Lady Merryn's. As she went, her thoughts turned back to Miss Brown's story. She had found out a great deal, but she wished to know still more. Perhaps careful questioning would elicit some information from the countess, she thought. After all, she must know something of Gwendeline's parents and of her son's doings as well. Gwendeline quickened her pace, resolving to learn whatever she could from Lady Merryn that very day.

But when she arrived, she found the countess was entertaining part of her literary group, and there would be no opportunity for questions. Gwendeline was vexed and disappointed. Not only could she learn nothing now, but she would have to endure the conversation of Mr. Woodley and his ilk. She determined to avoid that if at all possible. As she was removing her bonnet in her bedroom, one of the maids knocked. "Lady Merryn's compliments," she said as she came in, "and she says would you join the luncheon party as soon as may be."

"Thank her for me please, Mary, but say that I am tired and have a slight headache. I beg to be excused from luncheon."

Mary's eyes widened. "Oooh, but miss, there's all sorts of important ladies and gentlemen come to lunch. My lady is half-distracted."

"Even so," replied Gwendeline firmly. "Please tell her what I said."

Mary went out, but in a few minutes there was another knock and Lady Merryn entered Gwendeline's room. "Gwendeline! You can't miss luncheon. Mr. Woodley is here to tell us more about the Godwins, and Lady Penton is just back from abroad. She has brought mounds of French novels"—she paused—"which you, er, would not like, I imagine. But this is one of the most important literary gatherings since you arrived in town. You can't miss it."

Gwendeline repeated her plea of tiredness and headache.

"Well, you'll make yourself ill if you insist on rising at dawn the day after a ball and going out. Where have you been at this hour, by the by? When I came to find you, the servants told me you are often out early."

Gwendeline braced herself for reproaches. "I like to get a little air in the mornings, Lady Merryn. Sometimes I stop to check on my house, to make sure the servants are getting on all right."

"Do you indeed?" asked the countess. She looked at Gwendeline worriedly. "Well, I am sure they manage perfectly well. You mustn't worry over that house."

Gwendeline said nothing.

"If you really don't want to come down…" Lady

Merryn looked at her doubtfully, but Gwendeline shook her head. "It's a pity to miss such an opportunity, Gwendeline. You don't hear such talk at *ton* parties." She brightened. "Though they are giving me a wealth of material for my new novel. I've definitely decided to write a society novel; did I tell you? A sort of *roman à clef* full of well-known persons, disguised of course. That sort of thing is excessively popular now, you know."

Gwendeline murmured something noncommital.

"I hope to start writing next week, and I know I shall receive a great deal of invaluable advice today. Perhaps you'll be able to help me as well, my dear. You've met all the young people." She smiled brightly. "I must go down. You rest, Gwendeline. I'll have a tray sent up. You mustn't be fatigued for the musical party this evening." She hurried from the room.

Gwendeline sat down in her armchair and put her chin on her hand. She *was* tired, she found, and dispirited. She didn't wish to go to another party this evening. She sat for a while staring out the window, then she shook herself. You are ungrateful, she thought, you don't wish this and you don't understand that. You're becoming a bore. She rose and rang for Ellen. "I shall go riding," she said, "to clear the cobwebs out of my brain."

Within a short time, Gwendeline had changed into her dark blue riding habit, eaten a light luncheon from the tray, and gone down to the stables. She found her horse saddled and ready. The young groom who would accompany her held the bridle. Gwendeline took it and stroked the nose of the lovely little roan mare that Lord Merryn had sent over for her use some weeks ago. "Hello, Firefly," she said to the horse. "You're glad to get out, too, aren't you?"

They rode to the park and through its gates. The day was still sunny, and there were a number of coaches and riders already there. Gwendeline turned into a nearly empty track and set her horse to trot. Coming to the end, she reined in and turned onto the broader, more traveled path that intersected it, the groom keeping just behind her. She hadn't gone far when she heard someone call her name. It was Lord Merryn, mounted on a magnificent black, rapidly coming abreast of her.

"Shall we ride together?" he asked, as he reined in beside her. "It's a fine day for it."

Gwendeline nodded her agreement, and they went on together. Lord Merryn seemed in good spirits.

"I'm glad to see that you're getting some use out of your horse," he said. "I thought she would suit you. Do you like her?"

"Oh yes," answered Gwendeline, patting Firefly's neck. "We've taken many rides together, but I'm usually out rather earlier."

"Ah. You ride very well, Miss Gregory."

Gwendeline flushed with pleasure at this compliment. "Thank you. Riding in Hyde Park is very dull, however, don't you think? How I long for more space and a fast gallop." She laughed up at him guiltily. "You'll think I'm ungrateful, but riding at Brooklands there were miles of fields."

"I agree with you completely. Riding in the city is very flat," replied the earl. "Perhaps we should get up a party to go riding in the country?"

"I'd like that very much. And I know Lillian Everly would be delighted also."

"Then it shall be done," said the earl, smiling at Gwendeline with no trace of the sardonic gleam that she disliked. "If only because it is the one thing I have seen you express real enthusiasm for since you came to London."

"That's not true," cried Gwendeline. "I like everything excessively, and I'm very grateful for all…" She paused as she encountered the earl's teasing glance. "Oh, you're roasting me again."

"I was," he said. "But it is true that you haven't shown such eagerness many times. Seeing you at gatherings lately, I almost concluded that you disliked London." His eyes grew teasing again. "Or that you had become as blasé as some of the other young ladies."

Gwendeline didn't rise to his bait this time. "I'm not blasé. But I admit that I often feel restless or, or not quite happy, or… I can't really explain the feeling. There are so many things I can't understand. I've been thinking more and more lately of retiring to my—to the house you have kindly lent me, and giving up parties entirely."

Though he looked a bit amused, the earl responded to her tone. "You're free to do so if you wish. But I see no need for you to cease attending parties. My mother would be happy to accompany you until we found a suitable companion."

"Oh, I have Miss Brown," said Gwendeline before she thought. Then she flushed with annoyance and embarrassment. She'd been so enjoying the ride and the easy conversation that she'd forgotten to mind her tongue.

"Miss Brown?" asked Merryn, watching her confusion with a mixture of perplexity and amusement.

"Yes. I, uh, you see, when I was readying the house." Gwendeline paused. She took a deep breath and continued more coherently. "I told you of Miss Brown, my governess for many years. When I knew about the house, I wrote to her and asked her to come. She kindly consented, and she has been living there for some weeks." Gwendeline glanced apprehensively toward the earl. "She's very respectable. I'm sure there could be no better chaperone for me."

Lord Merryn was smiling at her. "I've underestimated you, I fear, Gwendeline. There are devious twists to your character that I never imagined. Does my mother know of the existence of this Miss Brown, pray?"

Gwendeline shook her head. "Are you angry?"

He laughed. "Why should I be angry? I'm much relieved to find that you're capable of managing such things. Shall I be allowed to meet Miss Brown?"

His tone was so encouraging that Gwendeline risked teasing him a little. "To make sure she's suitable?" she asked slyly.

The earl held up a hand. "Merely to make the acquaintance of an estimable lady. She must be quite extraordinary to have been your governess for years."

"Well, I'll ask her," answered Gwendeline, laughing. "But she's very strict. I'm not sure she would receive you alone. I may have to accompany you." The earl's response was a laugh so hearty and genuine that Gwendeline was surprised. She'd never seen him so unguarded.

She returned from her ride much more cheerful and ready for another foray into London society. It was nearly time to change, as dinner would be early tonight, and she ran lightly up the stairs to her room to dress. There was no sign of Lady Merryn.

When Gwendeline descended to the drawing room, wearing her new evening dress of pale blue trimmed with knots of dark blue ribbon, there was still no sign of the countess. She sat down to wait for her, a bit puzzled, since it lacked only a few minutes to dinnertime. But Lady Merryn had not appeared when Allison came in to announce dinner. Gwendeline asked him if her ladyship had gone out.

"I don't believe so, Miss Gwendeline," he answered. "She left no word if she did. I shall inquire." Gwendeline sat down again, uncertain whether she should worry. Lady Merryn had never been absent without leaving a message for her.

Very soon, Allison returned; he looked resigned. "Her ladyship's maid informs me that Lady Merryn went up to her study after luncheon," he told Gwendeline. "She has not come out or rung since then."

"I see," said Gwendeline. "Perhaps she's very busy. I'll go up and see if she wants to have dinner sent up to her."

Allison's resignation deepened. "Yes, miss. I will inform the kitchen," he said as Gwendeline left the room.

She walked down the corridor and knocked softly at the door of Lady Merryn's study. There was no answer, but she opened the door slightly and saw the countess seated at her desk. The desktop was covered with papers, as was the floor around her chair. There were several open volumes before her, and Lady Merryn was writing furiously. She had a spot of ink on her sleeve.

"Excuse me," said Gwendeline quietly. "Shall I have some dinner sent up to you, Lady Merryn?"

For a moment, she seemed not to have heard. Then, the countess ended a sentence with a flourish and put down her pen. "Two chapters," she said to Gwendeline triumphantly. "Finished! I've written thirty pages without stopping once. The ideas discussed at luncheon fired my imagination, and I resolved to begin my new novel at once. I think it will be my best so far."

"That's wonderful," replied Gwendeline. "I'm very glad."

"Thank you, my dear. Did you want me? I think I'll go on working since it's going so well. We can talk at dinner."

"I came to see whether dinner should be sent up to you," Gwendeline answered.

"Good heavens," Lady Merryn exclaimed. She suddenly seemed to notice Gwendeline's evening dress. "Is it dinnertime already? And we are to go out this evening!" She got up hurriedly, knocking a book off the desk. "I must dress immediately. Ring for Mary, would you, my dear."

Gwendeline went to the bell. "We needn't go out if you'd rather write," she said. "I don't want to keep you from it."

"Nonsense, my dear, I'll be gathering material the whole evening. A much more intriguing way of doing research. I'll be down instantly." She hurried off to her bedroom.

Gwendeline returned to the drawing room and informed Allison that dinner should be put back half an hour. He took the news well, but Gwendeline heard him tell the footman as he crossed the hall that the cook "would be fair enraged."

They were a little late for the musical evening. The entertainment had started when they arrived, and they were forced to find seats near the back of the room, behind most of the other guests. Gwendeline could see little besides the backs of the people in front of her, so she gave herself up to listening until the interval.

When refreshment was offered, Gwendeline had a chance to survey the crowd. Looking from group to group as they stood chatting, she saw many acquaintances. Lillian was present, talking to her hostess near the piano. And Gwendeline saw Lord Wanley, Mr. Horton, and Mr. Woodley, among others. But she couldn't find Lord Merryn, look as she would. She'd hoped to see him there and was disappointed at his absence.

"If only I could believe you were searching this crush for me," said a voice close to her ear. Gwendeline jumped, startled. "Pardon me," said Mr. Blane. "I didn't mean to frighten you."

"Not at all," said Gwendeline coldly.

"I need not ask how you are this evening," Blane went on smoothly. "Your looks tell me that you are well."

"Thank you," she replied. "I was just going to speak to Lillian Everly. If you'll excuse me." And she moved to cross the room.

Blane stopped her with a hand on her arm. "I almost feel that you're trying to avoid me, Miss Gregory. I'm hurt."

Gwendeline shook off his hand. "I have something important to say to Miss Everly. That is all, sir."

Mr. Blane looked at her speculatively. His eyes held both amusement and a hardness Gwendeline found unsettling. "Then you must allow me to escort you," he said, offering his arm.

Gwendeline took it, seeing no alternative. Together, they crossed the room to Lillian.

Mr. Blane bowed, "I'll leave you then to make your important communication to Miss Everly," he said to Gwendeline. "I hope we will have an opportunity to talk later." With a malicious glance, he turned and walked away.

Gwendeline turned to find Lillian looking at her. "Shall we take a turn about the room," she said, seeing Gwendeline's confusion. "If you will excuse us?" This was addressed to their hostess and the two young men she'd been talking to. Lillian linked arms with Gwendeline and guided her toward the more open space by a bow window. "Did you wish to tell me something?" she asked.

"No, no," said Gwendeline miserably. "I merely wished to get away from Mr. Blane. It was very unkind of him to repeat my excuse before everyone."

Lillian's perplexity disappeared, but she looked concerned still. "Was he rude to you?"

"Not at all, he is always excessively polite. But I don't like him, and I wished to avoid private conversation with him." She felt both foolish and upset.

"I see," said Lillian. "It's a difficult situation. He's known to have been such a, er, friend of your parents."

"Yes, indeed," said Gwendeline bitterly. "I have heard what a good friend he was." She stopped in confusion lest Lillian ask her to explain.

"Have you?" responded the other girl, looking at her closely. She seemed reassured by what she saw. "That's good."

Gwendeline looked back at her, and Lillian nodded. "I've heard a few things myself," she added. "My mother has a very liberal view about what I should be told. She usually answers the questions I put to her. It's an extraordinary help."

"I should think it would be indeed," said Gwendeline feelingly. "I wish I had such a mother."

"She's wonderful," agreed Lillian. "And I think you're right to try to avoid Mr. Blane. I'll help you if I can."

"Thank you," Gwendeline said. "He's very persistent."

The hostess began to reorganize her guests for another session of music, and the conversation was interrupted. The two girls sat together; however, just as the musicians struck up, they were joined by Mr. Horton and Lord Wanley with much embarrassing clattering of gilt chairs and dislodgement of their neighbors. Gwendeline merely looked at the floor, but Lillian said, "Shh," as the gentlemen dropped into their chairs and seemed about to speak. The music drowned their objections.

Gwendeline was able to avoid Mr. Blane for the rest of the evening, staying close to the group of young people. Lord Merryn never appeared, and she found herself tiring early. Finally, she pulled Lady Merryn away from a spirited investigation of the latest *on dits*—splendid material for her book she protested— and they left the party. Gwendeline felt only relief to be home again.

Seven

THE NEXT MORNING, GWENDELINE SOUGHT OUT LADY Merryn as soon as she came downstairs, determined to put several questions to her. She waited until Allison had served the countess's breakfast, then she leaned across the table toward her and said commandingly, "Lady Merryn."

The older woman looked up from the paper she was scribbling on, surprised. "Yes, dear?"

"I want to have a serious talk with you. It's important."

"Really?" She put aside her papers. "You have my full attention then, Gwendeline." She looked at her expectantly.

Gwendeline took a deep breath. When it came to the point, she was uncertain exactly where to begin. "Well," she said, "since I came to London, I've heard a great deal of talk." She paused.

The countess nodded wisely. "One does in town, dear. Most of it utter nonsense, of course. Has someone said something rude to you?"

"No, not rude, but I have heard disturbing things

about my parents and—and others." Gwendeline found she could not bring herself to mention the earl outright.

Lady Merryn nodded again. "I daresay. I'm afraid I must tell you, Gwendeline, that your parents have been the subject of a good deal of gossip. They were a heedless couple, care-for-nobodies as the young men say, and they sometimes set people's backs up with their behavior."

It was Gwendeline's turn to nod. "I've heard that. But frankly, I'm less concerned about my parents' reputation than about my own situation. It may sound callous to you, but they never cared about me, so I don't particularly care what people may say about them."

"Understandable," agreed Lady Merryn. "Though unfortunately gossip sometimes carries over. Has something specific happened to upset you, Gwendeline?"

"No, but it would be a great help to me if I understood more. The thing that concerns me most is the income I've been given. I've never been comfortable spending it, and now I feel it even more. I must learn who my benefactors are, Lady Merryn. Will you help me?"

The countess appeared confused. "Well, but Gwendeline, surely you should discuss this with Alex?"

"I've tried, but he fobbed me off." She looked steadily at Lady Merryn, making it clear that she wouldn't be evaded again.

The countess dithered. "Yes, but my dear, I really have no notion... Alex has not taken me into his confidence... really, I can't..." She trailed off.

"I understand that you don't know precisely who

joined to help me," replied Gwendeline. "But you must have some idea of who my father's friends were. Who would have been likely to aid me?"

The older woman looked hunted. "Your father's friends! Oh, my dear. An extremely ramshackle set."

Gwendeline gazed at her. "The only friend of my father that I have so far met is Mr. Blane. He knows nothing of any income for me. I ask you, Lady Merryn, what am I to think? I begin to fear that there are no benefactors except Lord Merryn, and you must see that I couldn't accept support from an unmarried man in no way related to me. It would be quite improper."

Lady Merryn seemed much struck by this point. "Oh, quite," she said quickly. "Only think of the scandal it would raise! But Gwendeline, you can't think that Alex would put you in the embarrassing position of living on his bounty." She looked very worried, then her face brightened. "Besides, it's not just Alex. I'm helping you too, you know, so all is well."

Gwendeline was momentarily silenced by this telling point. It was true that a scandal was unlikely while she lived under the protection of the earl's mother, even if it turned out that he was supporting her. But even granting that, she didn't wish to be beholden to Lord Merryn. She struggled for a moment to think why. It was a humiliating position, she decided, and not one she wished to occupy where he was involved. She looked up at the countess again. "What you say is true," she admitted, "but I was told that a group of people helped me, and I insist upon thanking them. If the earl won't take me to them, I must find them myself. Please tell me who my father's particular friends were." And she directed an uncompromising stare at the older woman.

"Oh dear," said Lady Merryn again. "I don't know what I should do. I can't think." She seemed to consider a number of possibilities, then her expression lightened. "There was Sir Humphrey Owsley. He was forever in your parents' house, Gwendeline. He is not likely to… That is, you might speak to him, if you meet him."

"Will you not introduce me, ma'am?"

"I? Oh, I am scarcely acquainted with him myself. I'm not certain I could…"

"Very well," answered Gwendeline impatiently. "And who else?"

Lady Merryn shook her head regretfully. "Dear me, I can't think. You know, I never was well acquainted with your mother's set, my dear. I can't for the life of me think of any others."

Gwendeline sighed and returned the countess's innocent gaze rather angrily, but try as she would, she could get no more names from her. She had to content herself with the one. She resolved not to wait for a chance meeting but to seek out Sir Humphrey herself, no matter what that might involve. She started to ask Lady Merryn for his address, then hesitated. The countess would certainly try to stop her if she knew what she planned. Excusing herself, Gwendeline left the breakfast room, leaving a worried and rather relieved Lady Merryn staring anxiously after her.

Gwendeline found out the address by asking Allison to get it for her, and since she was sure that Lady

Merryn would tell her son of their conversation at the first opportunity, she set out to call on Sir Humphrey the very next morning. By nine she was smartly attired in a dove gray walking dress, fastened at the sleeve and up to the demure neckline with tiny amber buttons. As Ellen did her hair and got out the dainty high-crowned bonnet which completed this dashing toilette, Gwendeline said, "I'll need you to accompany me this morning, Ellen."

"Yes, miss," responded the maid, "but I thought you told Mr. Reeves you wouldn't be by the house today."

"No, I am not going to the house. We're going to make a call."

Ellen looked gratified. "Well, that's fine, Miss Gwendeline. I declare we haven't gone calling together above once or twice since we came to London. Is her ladyship busy?"

"She will not have left her bedchamber as yet. Come, are you ready?"

"Just give me one minute to fetch my hat, miss." And Ellen fairly ran out of the room and up the stairs.

Gwendeline went down to the front hall to wait. She stood before the door pulling on her gloves when she heard a sound that made her freeze in dismay. Lady Merryn's voice was issuing from the library just opposite. On this morning of all mornings she had chosen to break with her custom and come downstairs early. Gwendeline looked up the stairs anxiously, but there was no sign of Ellen. She shrank back beside the hall table; there was no place to conceal herself, and Lady Merryn seemed to be approaching. The girl sighed in annoyance. Now she would be forced to explain where she was going. Or to lie, she thought guiltily. She had so hoped to leave the house unobserved.

Just as Ellen appeared and began to descend the stairs, when Gwendeline dared hope she could get away after all, the door to the library opened and Lady Merryn emerged. She saw Gwendeline immediately, as indeed she could not help but do, and wished her a cheerful good morning. She observed her walking dress with some surprise. "Are you going out so early, Gwendeline?" she asked. "Why, it can't be much past nine. Have you breakfasted? Where are you going?"

Gwendeline smiled nervously and twisted her remaining glove between her fingers. "Only walking, ma'am," she replied. "It's such a fine day, I thought I would get some air."

"Is it?" answered Lady Merryn vaguely. "I haven't had a moment to observe. Only fancy, Gwendeline, Mary threw out ten pages of my manuscript. Can you credit it? I searched for quite two hours last night, but they're gone. And the worst of it is, I can't remember precisely what they contained. I know it was very important, vital to the plot in fact, but I can't quite recall... And ten pages! It will take me all morning to make it up. It is all very well to say that I left them crumpled on the floor; I daresay I may have, though I distinctly remember putting the pages in my drawer as I went up to bed the night before. However, when I got them out last night, it was the laundry list, you know, so I suppose... But that's beside the point. I have told all the servants never to disturb the papers around my desk. You would think Mary would have better sense than to throw them out, wouldn't you?"

"Yes ma'am," replied Gwendeline, as Lady Merryn interrupted her flow of talk to look at her. The countess seemed to have forgotten their conversation of the previous day.

"Of course," she continued. "And so I rose very early today, almost at the crack of dawn, my dear, to inquire. I thought to catch the servants before the dustbin was emptied. But I was too late. They take it away by six, Gwendeline! Can you imagine? What dreadful lives the dustmen must live." Lady Merryn shook her head. "And so, now I must try to recall the story and rewrite it all." She sighed heavily as she set her foot on the first stair. "It is excessively annoying."

"I am sorry," said Gwendeline. "I hope it's not too difficult."

"Yes, so do I, my dear," replied the countess doubtfully. She seemed to recall herself. "So you're going walking? What odd habits you have, to be sure. Are you certain you wish to go out so very early? No one will be abroad at this hour. And have you eaten?"

"Yes ma'am. I had tea and toast with a boiled egg over an hour ago."

Lady Merryn seemed to shudder. "How you can eat a meal so early I do not understand. I can face no more than a cup of chocolate. Well, but your maid is to accompany you?" She looked around and saw Ellen. "Oh yes. Don't tire yourself out, my dear." And with this admonition, she continued up the stairs.

Gwendeline breathed a sigh of relief and turned to go out. She'd been saved explanations after all. Silently, she thanked Mary for her misguided diligence.

It was indeed a lovely spring morning. The air was a

little sharp, but the sun shone brightly, and the breeze carried a hint of growing things even here in the city. Gwendeline walked briskly along the pavement to the busier thoroughfare at the end of the row. "We must get a hack," she said to Ellen. "It is a little distance."

"Yes, miss." Ellen was frowning. "We do be going for a walk then?"

Gwendeline flushed slightly. "Well, yes, after we make our call, we'll walk a bit." She saw a hack passing by and signaled the jarvey, who pulled up beside them. "Come along."

Ellen joined her in the carriage without demur, but as it started up, she asked, "Who are you visiting, Miss Gwendeline? Not Miss Lillian, I guess."

"No. Someone else," replied the girl shortly. She had no wish to argue with her maid, as she surely would be forced to do if Ellen knew they were bound for a gentleman's residence.

But the other girl was not to be fobbed off so easily. She observed her young mistress narrowly for a time, then said, "You're up to some mischief, I'll be bound, Miss Gwendeline. One as knows you well can tell it, though her ladyship had no notion."

"I don't know what you mean," responded Gwendeline, trying to sound haughty and aloof.

Ellen sniffed. "Don't you now? Well, you needn't tell me anything about it, but I know what I know." And Ellen folded her arms and subsided into silence.

Gwendeline was thinking nervously of what she would say when she arrived at Sir Humphrey's house. She knew that it wasn't proper to call at a gentleman's home, particularly when she hadn't even been introduced to the man, but in her impatience and eagerness to solve the mystery of her rescue she didn't care. When she'd stated her business, surely Sir Humphrey would see the necessity of her flouting of convention. But even as she comforted herself with this assurance, she doubted it.

Too soon, the hack pulled up before Sir Humphrey's impressive town house. The girls climbed down, and Gwendeline paid off the driver. She'd never handled such details herself, and she felt a bit clumsy doing so. The fare the man requested seemed absurdly high to her, but she didn't dare dispute it. She'd heard cabdrivers arguing with one another or with their patrons in the street, and she had a strong sense of their pugnaciousness.

Finally, all was concluded, and they stood on the top step before the massive oaken door. Resolutely, Gwendeline reached up and plied the brass knocker. It wouldn't do to hang back now.

After a moment, the door was opened by a tall footman in scarlet livery. Though his countenance was rigidly impassive, an eyelid flickered when he saw who had knocked and when Gwendeline asked to see his master. He stood back, however, and admitted them to the hall. "If you will wait one moment?" he said, gesturing politely to a pair of gilt chairs by the wall.

Gwendeline led the way to them and sat down. The footman disappeared. Ellen gazed at the shining parquet floors, the marble walls, the curving staircase which seemed to extend to the upper regions without supports, and the magnificent crystal chandelier. "La, miss," she said finally. "What a fine house this is. Even finer than her ladyship's, and I did think her house the most elegant thing in the world when we arrived. But why did you go and ask for a gentleman, Miss Gwendeline?"

Gwendeline swallowed. "Because I have come to call on a gentleman," she replied brusquely.

Ellen gasped. "But miss," she began. She got out no more than that, however, before the footman returned, bringing with him the haughtiest and most high-nosed butler Gwendeline had ever seen. Instinctively, both girls rose.

"Good day, Miss, ah, Gregory," said this awesome individual. He surveyed Gwendeline with a practiced eye, but as he did so, something of his disapproval and aplomb seemed to leave him. The tiniest of frowns showed on his wooden visage. "I regret to tell you, miss, that Sir Humphrey has not yet descended from his bedchamber. Can I be of assistance to you, perhaps?"

"Oh dear," said Gwendeline. "Has he not? How stupid of me not to think of that. What shall I do now?"

"Perhaps, if I might suggest," answered the butler. "If you were to return later in the day, say about twelve, you might catch Sir Humphrey before he left the house." It was a measure of the favorable impression Gwendeline had created that the man unbent enough to tell her this.

"Twelve?" echoed Gwendeline. "Oh, I don't see how…"

"Nor do I, Miss Gwendeline," put in Ellen, upon whom the patent disapproval of the two servants had worked strongly. "I don't see at all. But what I do see is that this is what comes of calling on gentlemen and such carryings-on. I say we should go on home and forget all about it."

The butler's expression softened noticeably at this, and as Gwendeline came near to wringing her hands, he said, "If it is important, miss, I might just inform Sir Humphrey that you have called. I cannot guarantee that he will see you, as he never receives guests in the morning, but I will take it upon myself to ask, if you wish."

Gwendeline looked up at him gratefully. "Oh, would you?" She felt a great relief. She had been odiously uncomfortable since she entered this house, and she knew that if she gave up now, she would never return. Having screwed up her courage once, and having found the task more unpleasant than she'd expected, she longed to carry through. If Sir Humphrey wouldn't see her now, she would never find out if he'd helped her, and she didn't know whom else to ask.

The butler bowed. "If you would care to wait in the library?" He opened a door on the left and ushered her into a book-lined room. "I shall be a moment." And shutting the door again, he left her alone.

Gwendeline didn't sit down. Rather, she paced the room, heedless of the rich carpeting, fine paintings, and comfortable furniture. She was wondering what she would do if Sir Humphrey refused to receive her. But in a few minutes, the butler returned to tell her that he would be down directly. He smiled benevolently and added, "No need to take on if he is a little mifty, miss. He's always so in the morning." And with these daunting words, he left Gwendeline alone once more.

Sir Humphrey's idea of "directly" seemed more

flexible than his guest's, for it was quite half an hour before the library door opened again and he walked in. Gwendeline never knew what his butler had told him about her, but judging from the apprehensive expression on his face when he entered, it must have been a round tale. She could say nothing to dispel his mistake at first, however; she was struck speechless by the unusual appearance of her host.

Sir Humphrey Owsley was the fattest man Gwendeline had ever seen. His multiple chins seemed to merge with hardly a break into his enormous paunch, his arms were as large as her legs, and his legs were like tree stumps. Even his fingers were fat; the rings he wore were imbedded in and nearly hidden by overlapping skin. The tight pantaloons and cutaway coat of current fashions did nothing for this figure. In fact, these articles of dress, particularly the bright yellow pantaloons he affected, showed alarming signs of strain at the seams. And Sir Humphrey's exaggerated shirt points and elaborate neckcloth looked as if they pressed too tightly on his chins. His eyes seemed to bulge with the pressure, and all in all, he looked most like a turkey cock ready for roasting.

As Gwendeline stared at him, wide-eyed, he surveyed her through the quizzing glass that hung round his neck. He seemed both appreciative and uneasy as he took in her blond curls and neat figure. Under this scrutiny, she recovered herself enough to drop a small curtsy and say, "Good day, Sir Humphrey. It's very good of you to see me so early."

At this, the man harrumphed. "Not at all, not at all," he said. His voice was low and gravelly. "Only too happy, charming young lady, glad to…" His disjointed remarks gradually trailed off.

"Yes, but your butler told me that you never receive guests so early. I apologize for calling at an unreasonable hour. But I wanted to speak to you on business of some urgency, you see, and I haven't met you at any of the parties I've attended."

"Ah. Just so. Business." Sir Humphrey appeared more mystified by Gwendeline's explanation. His jowls quivered. "Don't get about much anymore," he offered. "See m'friends here or at the club, you know. Not as active as I once was." He patted his large stomach.

"Oh, I daresay that explains it."

He goggled at her, then frowned. "Here. Let us sit down. What am I thinking of? Would you care for some refreshment? Perhaps, what, tea?"

"No, no. You're very kind, but I can't stay long."

"Ah." Sir Humphrey seemed at a loss.

She shifted in her chair. "I must explain why I've come. Or perhaps you've guessed?" She looked at her host hopefully, wondering if he might ease this awkward moment. It was difficult, she found, to look at a stranger and ask him if he was supporting her.

But this request only made Sir Humphrey's eyes bulge further. "Guessed?" He gulped. He gazed at her. "Afraid not." He seemed to come to a decision. "In fact, I'm dam…dashed if I can recall where we met, Miss, uh. Was it at Vauxhall? Or one of the Opera masquerades? You must pardon me; memory's not what it was, you know."

"Oh, we haven't met before," responded Gwendeline in surprise. "Did I not say so? I'm sorry."

A great weight seemed to lift from Sir Humphrey's mind. "Haven't met," he echoed. "Ah. Well, then." His expression lightened. "Then what, may I ask, are you doing here, young lady? It's not at all the thing to come calling on gentlemen you've never met, you know. Or even on gentlemen you have," he added.

Gwendeline flushed. "I know. You will think me quite brass-faced, I fear. But I couldn't think what else to do. I so wanted to ask you about…about my father, you see."

Sir Humphrey's eyes started alarmingly once again; his color rose to purple, and all his apprehensions seemed to return. "Your father?" he managed. "What would I know about your father? Nothing to do with it, I assure you."

Gwendeline stared at him. "But they told me you were a friend of my father's, indeed a close friend. Is it not true then?"

He sat back again, looking more perplexed than fearful now. "Can't tell you that until I know who you are, can I? Who the devil is your father?"

"Why, Roger Gregory, sir," answered Gwendeline in astonishment. "Didn't the butler tell you my name?"

"Roger? Well, bless my soul. Are you Roger and Annabella's girl? Of course, now that I look at you, you're the image of Annabella. I'll be…" He slapped his massive thigh and laughed. "That fool Gilling said some name or other, but I didn't catch it. We've been talking at cross purposes, my dear. Good joke on me, what?"

Gwendeline didn't understand the joke, but she was relieved to be recognized. "Yes," she replied. "So you were a friend of my parents?"

"Absolutely. Spent many a pleasant evening at the house. Annabella gave the most splendid parties."

"Did she, sir? I wish I might have attended them."

Sir Humphrey coughed. "Ah, well, as to that. Not sure you would have liked them, you know. Not just, that is… Well, and so you've come to call on an old friend of your parents'. Very kind. I should have come to see you. Would have, but I don't go out much, as I told you. Too much effort, hauling myself about. And so, you've come to London?"

"Yes," said Gwendeline. She looked at him eagerly. "Thanks to my kind benefactors."

He nodded knowingly. "Benefactors. Well, that's good then. Heard that Roger was all to pieces when he was killed. Sad accident. Accept my sincere sympathy, my dear. Terrible thing."

"Thank you. Indeed, it is only due to the help of friends of my father that I can live now. I'm so very grateful to them; I wish to thank them all."

Sir Humphrey frowned at her. "Friends? Ah yes, heard something. Who was it said…?"

"Yes," Gwendeline went on eagerly. "It was the kindest thing imaginable. Only think, a group of my parents' friends combined to help me after they died. I have a little house of my own in London and an income. But it's vexing; I can't discover who is behind it all. I so wish to express my gratitude properly, but until I know the names of the people involved… I thought perhaps you could help me, since you were a friend. Do you know of this scheme, Sir Humphrey? Were you even in it, perhaps?"

Sir Humphrey was muttering to himself. "Splendid

idea. Can't think why I wasn't… What? What's that, my dear? Yes, a bang-up idea. I approve wholeheartedly. Give my mite gladly, too. Ain't as if I'd feel it."

Gwendeline jumped to her feet. "Then you did help me." Overcome by her feelings of gratitude and relief, she leaned over and hugged her massive companion. "Oh, I'm so grateful to you. You cannot know. If it weren't for you and the others, I'd be quite destitute. Thank you, thank you."

She stood back, smiling brilliantly. Her elation came as much from relief as from gratitude. Sir Humphrey dithered a moment, recovering from his surprise and straightening his neckcloth, then he looked up at her radiant face doubtfully. "Well, but my dear girl, there is no need…"

"Oh, you mustn't be modest. You saved my life. Or the next thing to it. Please accept my earnest thanks."

Sir Humphrey couldn't meet her sparkling gaze. "Well, well." He sighed and muttered again. "Would have, of course. Glad to. Can't think why…" He frowned. "Who told you of my interest in this thing?" he asked finally.

"Oh, no one told me," answered Gwendeline. "Lord Merryn would say nothing; I was quite out of charity with him over it. Did you wish it kept a secret? Oh, do not say so. I had to thank you."

"Just so. Merryn, you say? Hmmm."

"He didn't betray you, no. It was his mother who told me that you were a close friend of my parents, and I drew my own conclusions."

"Ah."

"And so, I do thank you over and over. I'm sorry

if you didn't wish it, but I couldn't be easy, you see, until I'd done so. Tell me, do you know the names of any of the others?"

"Others?"

"Yes, the others who helped me."

"Oh. No, no, I'm afraid not."

Gwendeline's face fell. "Perhaps, though, you can direct me to other of my parents' close friends. Then I can call upon them as I did you."

Sir Humphrey's eyes bulged again. "Good God," he exclaimed. "That is, no, no, I shouldn't do that if I were you. People, ah, dislike being thanked, you know. Dashed embarrassing. Better to let it be. Nice of you to wish it, but better not."

"You're so kind," said Gwendeline, her eyes filling with tears. "All of you."

"No, I say, no," replied her companion, aghast at this sign of feminine vapors. "Nothing, you know. Nothing at all."

"It's not nothing to *me*," answered Gwendeline emphatically.

"Yes, well, glad it all came out right." Sir Humphrey began to pull himself laboriously out of the armchair. "Don't wish to be impolite, but engagements, you know. Haven't breakfasted."

"Of course. How heedless of me to keep you." She made as if to assist him in rising, but he waved her off and slowly got to his feet. "I'll go," she continued, offering him her hand, "but I'm so happy we had this talk."

He took her hand in his giant paw and gallantly kissed it. "My pleasure," he murmured politely.

"I do hope we meet again soon."

"Ah, well, as to that. Can't say, you know."

"Perhaps you can come to dinner one night and tell me about my parents. I know so little about them."

This suggestion seemed to make Sir Humphrey uneasy again. He muttered something indistinct.

"So. Goodbye, then."

"Goodbye, my dear." He escorted her to the door and left her in the hands of his butler, who was hovering in the hall awaiting the outcome of this interesting visit. When she was gone, Sir Humphrey frowned. "Merryn," he said to himself. "Strange. Have to speak to the fellow."

Gwendeline, riding along in another hackney coach, had no regrets or feeling of puzzlement. She was convinced that she had partly solved the mystery of her income, and she was very pleased with herself. Lord Merryn was not her only benefactor, as she had begun to fear, but only the agent and spokesman for men who were reluctant to appear in the matter. She need no longer worry about her ambiguous situation. Though it still held some undeniable awkwardness, it was not as bad as she'd feared. More important, Lord Merryn had told her the truth. As she climbed happily down from the hack and entered Lady Merryn's town house, she was more at ease than she'd been for some weeks. She even thought that her father couldn't have been quite as black as many painted him if he'd had such truly loyal and generous friends.

Eight

THINGS WERE MUCH CHANGED AT LADY MERRYN'S house when she devoted herself to novel writing. The smooth routine disappeared; the countess had to be reminded of mealtimes and social engagements, then ready herself in a flurry. She began to resent callers, and several people asked Gwendeline if they'd offended her in some way. Allison's resigned, disapproving expression grew more and more pronounced, while Gwendeline heard tales from Ellen of the near hysterical state of the kitchen. They went out less and less. At first, Lady Merryn continued to "gather material," but as her writing progressed she became engrossed in it. The book was going slower, and she struggled with its intricacies for most of the day. In a few weeks, they were attending only those gatherings that Gwendeline recalled to her mind, and they were not many.

Gwendeline found she much preferred this style of life. Going out once or, at most, twice in the week made the outings much more special and enjoyable. And she still saw Lillian and her particular friends during morning calls or rides in the park. She occasionally met Lord Merryn there, and he usually joined her party for some distance, chatting in that pleasant, easy fashion which had marked their first ride together. With her worries relieved, Gwendeline felt happier than she had at any time since she came to London.

She was sitting with Lillian Everly in the drawing room one morning, looking over the fashion plates in the latest number of *The Ladies' Home Companion*, when Allison entered to announce another caller. "I think that the trim is hideous," Lillian was saying as she bent over a page of willowy ladies in evening dress. "And we should look positive frights in this shade of yellow, Gwendeline, both of us. A color that suits neither of our complexions must be dreadful."

"Mr. Horton is here," said Allison sonorously.

"Oh no," cried Gwendeline, looking up. She had been too engrossed by a cerise silk ball gown with demitrain and flounced sleeves to note the butler's entrance. "Tell him that Lady Merryn is occupied and cannot see anyone," she said quickly.

"I've already done so, Miss Gwendeline," replied Allison. "But he has asked particularly to see you."

"Me," echoed Gwendeline, "oh dear." She looked at Lillian. "He's come to see me again."

Lillian was laughing. "I see that he has. There can be no doubt of it, you have an official suitor. I wonder, when he will come to the point?"

"I shall say I have the headache."

"You said that the last time he called. You'll hurt his feelings."

"It's all very tiresome," said Gwendeline with a

sigh. "He's a very nice young man, but I don't wish to encourage him."

"Then you should let him in but behave very coldly," Lillian answered. "Respond to his conversation with monosyllables." She gave Gwendeline a mischievous smile.

"Yes, it's easy for you to laugh and give good advice," responded Gwendeline with a rueful expression. "He's jilted you. But you know perfectly well that it's impossible to behave coldly to Mr. Horton. If one tries to speak in monosyllables, soon there is no conversation at all. He simply becomes redder and redder and looks pleading, until you feel so guilty that you say something kind."

"Oh yes, I know." Lillian laughed again. "You're too kind altogether, Gwendeline. I suppose you'll have to accept him in the end."

Gwendeline wrinkled her nose. "If you were truly my friend, you'd try to win him back. He was so lost among your train of admirers that he never bothered you." Both girls laughed at this.

Allison cleared his throat. "What shall I tell the young gentleman?" he inquired from the doorway.

Gwendeline straightened guiltily. "I suppose we must let him in?" she said to Lillian, who nodded. "You may ask him to come up, Allison." They closed the fashion book and adjusted their expressions. Mr. Horton, entering the drawing room some moments later, found two very sober and correct young ladies.

He bowed. "Good morning Miss Gregory, Miss Everly," he said.

"Good morning," answered Lillian distantly.

"Will you sit down?" added Gwendeline coolly.

"Thank you," he replied, looking daunted. "You are well, I trust?" The remark seemed directed equally at both ladies, and they nodded. There was a short silence. "It…it is a fine day," Mr. Horton finally blurted. He was beginning to turn red, especially about the ears.

"A trifle cool, I fancy," said Lillian, looking out the window.

"It will rain later, I should think," added Gwendeline. But the sight of Mr. Horton's discomfort was weakening her.

"I was sorry not to meet you at Lady Woolton's evening party last night," Mr. Horton said to Gwendeline. "I had looked forward, that is, I wanted, er, I had hoped to see you there," he finished lamely.

"Lady Merryn has been so busy," replied Gwendeline. "We don't go out so often." Unable to bear his miserable expression, she added, "She's writing a book, you know."

"Is she indeed?" responded Mr. Horton, eagerly grasping this conversational opening. "I know how that can be. My father often shuts himself up for weeks when he's writing."

Gwendeline looked at Lillian. "Does your father write also?" Lillian obediently asked. "How interesting. What sort of books does he write? Not novels?" The corners of her mouth twitched.

The suggestion appeared to shock Mr. Horton. "No, of course not," he replied. "He has published several volumes of sermons and a book on religious philosophy." He looked at them defiantly. "He's a very learned man."

Gwendeline was contrite. "I'm sure he must be. I have a great admiration for those who can do such things. I'm so stupid about books."

Mr. Horton leaned forward, putting his hands on his knees. "Do you truly admire them?" he asked earnestly. "I'm sure you wouldn't be stupid at all, with proper guidance; you would love books, I'm sure."

Gwendeline was taken aback. Lillian was perilously near outright laughter. "You're too kind," Gwendeline replied. "I assure you I dislike reading excessively."

"But that is only because of your training. I know it could be changed. If you would permit me to lend you some volumes I have here in London, I'm sure you would see what I mean."

"I hardly have time for reading." There was a choking sound from Lillian. Giving her a sharp look, Gwendeline continued more firmly. "And Lady Merryn lent me several books; she has many literary friends. So you see, my reading is well supervised."

"What books has…" began Mr. Horton, but he was interrupted by the entrance of Allison.

"Excuse me, Miss Gwendeline," said the butler, "but there's a footman from Miss Everly's house below. He's come to fetch her. Evidently, she is needed at home."

"Why, what could be the matter?" said Lillian, rising. "I told Mother I was staying for luncheon."

"He didn't say, Miss Everly," Allison replied.

Lillian looked perplexed. "I suppose I must go, Gwendeline."

"Shall I go with you?"

"I'm sure it's only some domestic crisis and

Mother wants moral support." She smiled. "Good day, Mr. Horton. I shall see you tomorrow I hope, Gwendeline." And with this, she left the room.

Gwendeline remained standing, concerned about her friend. "I'm afraid you must excuse me now, Mr. Horton."

"I'll go very soon," he answered. "But I'd like some private conversation with you first, if you will permit me." In response to Gwendeline's nervous look, he added, "It's so difficult to find an opportunity to speak to you alone."

"Oh, but I…"

"Please," interrupted Mr. Horton. His prominent brown eyes pleaded with her. He presented such a sad appearance, with his drab, outmoded garments and nervous manner, that Gwendeline was filled with compassion. She sat down again reluctantly. "Thank you."

There was a pause; Gwendeline looked at him. "It's very difficult to begin," he finally said. "I…I am not particularly good at pretty speeches. I wish to ask you, Miss Gregory"—he paused again—"if…if you would consider becoming my wife." Gwendeline stared at him. He hurried on. "We haven't been acquainted long, I know. But your kindness and gentleness have so impressed me in this short time that I have come to love you very much and to wish to spend my life with you."

Gwendeline found her voice. "I'm honored and flattered by your offer, Mr. Horton, but…"

He held up a hand. "Please. Before you answer, I'd like to tell you something of my circumstances, which are not well known in London. I come from the north, from York. My father is a bishop there, and very well thought of. I shall be ordained next spring and take over a very adequate living that is being held for me." He paused nervously. "I think you'd like living there; it is in the country."

Gwendeline stopped him. "I'm afraid I must refuse. You can find a much more suitable wife than I."

"I don't believe it," he cried. "I wish to marry you."

"I'm sorry," Gwendeline said unhappily.

He took her hand. "Perhaps I've gone too fast. You feel you hardly know me. If I waited and asked you again after our acquaintance has improved?"

Gwendeline shook her head. "I won't change my mind. We shouldn't suit. Please, Mr. Horton." She pulled her hand away. "I would not say so if I didn't mean it. I don't wish to hurt you, but I cannot marry you."

Mr. Horton seemed about to press his argument further, but he was forestalled by a voice from the doorway. "I beg your pardon," said the Earl of Merryn. "I appear to have intruded." Mr. Horton turned scarlet and rose to his feet. Gwendeline stood also.

"Excuse me," said Mr. Horton in a strangled voice, and he fled from the room.

Gwendeline sank back on the sofa; she was on the verge of tears. The earl sat down opposite. "I congratulate you," he said affably. "Your first proposal of the season."

"Oh, how can you? It was quite horrible. There is no kind way to tell someone you don't wish to marry him. I hated it!"

"I see that you did. But it's all over now. There's no need to be upset."

Gwendeline was incredulous. "No need? When I shall see him at every party I attend for the rest of the season? What shall I say to him, what shall I do?"

"You forget that no one will know what passed between you save yourselves," the earl replied soothingly. "You will be polite to each other, and I'm sure Mr. Horton will have the good sense and manners not to put himself constantly in your way."

"Do you think so?"

"I think he is a sensible young man," he replied.

"I hope you're right. How glad I am that you called at just this moment," she added feelingly. "I was never so pleased to see anyone."

"Once again I play the rescuer," he answered lightly. Gwendeline smiled at him. "Though I begin to realize," he continued, "that you don't really trust me in that role. It's a pity I must be always filling it."

Gwendeline stared at him. "What do you mean?"

"I had a very surprising conversation with Sir Humphrey Owsley at my club yesterday. He sought me out. Unheard of for the laziest man in London. All present were amazed."

Gwendeline flushed. "Oh," she said.

Lord Merryn cocked an eyebrow. "Is that all you have to say?"

His tone made her angry. "What should I say? You know very well that I've been eager to thank my benefactors, yet you've refused to take me to any of them. So, I found one myself. You might have told me that they asked you not to reveal their names. In fact, I can't think why you didn't."

The earl was watching her, bemused. "You're an

extremely resourceful girl. There's certainly nothing of the shy, simpering, retiring miss about you. You continually surprise me. I apologize for not telling you more. I didn't see that your will was so strong."

Gwendeline was a bit startled.

"Or perhaps I should say your resolve," he added smoothly, "to acknowledge your 'benefactors' as you call them."

"As anyone would, I think. Will you take me to see the others?"

Lord Merryn looked regretful. "Alas, I cannot. It is indeed as you surmised. The group is not eager to have its individual members known. Sir Humphrey was quite out of charity with me, in fact." He smiled wryly. "So instead of taking you to meet them, I must rather ask you not to search further. It's what they wish, you see. I've conveyed your sincere thanks to all concerned, you know."

Gwendeline frowned. "Well, but it's excessively annoying. Why must they be so secretive?"

Lord Merryn took a breath. "Some, like Sir Humphrey, don't wish to exert themselves in any way. He never hesitates to spend money but will not lift a finger for anyone but himself." He smiled again. "And sometimes not even then. Others live out of town, even abroad. I beg you to be content with your one discovery, Gwendeline, and let the matter rest."

Gwendeline looked at the floor, frowning. "Very well," she said finally. "I cannot see that there is much else I can do. You will tell me nothing; Lady Merryn flatly refuses to name my father's friends. Even Sir

Humphrey wouldn't help me. It is hardly something I can ask strangers."

The earl seemed relieved. "Good."

Silence fell. Gwendeline was lost in thought, and Lord Merryn was watching her. A few minutes passed before Gwendeline looked up, started, and recovered herself. "Your…your mother is upstairs in her study, if you wish to see her," she told him.

"She's writing again? I wondered why you were alone here at the mercy of stray suitors." He smiled at her, trying to recapture the light note of their earlier conversation. "I must scold her; she's sadly absentminded when she's working on one of her 'Gothics.' But actually, I called to see *you* this morning."

"Me?" Gwendeline asked, surprised and pleased.

"Yes, I'm arranging the expedition we spoke of making. To ride in the country. You haven't forgotten?"

"Oh, no," Gwendeline replied eagerly. "But I thought that you…that is…"

"You had thought that *I* had," finished the earl, grinning wickedly. "I see you have a very low opinion of my manners. I must do something about that."

"When?" she asked.

He laughed. "Friday week. I called to ask you whom you wish to invite."

"I?" answered Gwendeline.

"Or perhaps I should say whom you wish me to invite," he amended. "The party is planned for you, after all."

"But I cannot choose your guests," she protested.

"Nonsense," he replied. "I don't know your

friends. You must help me make the list. Only imagine, I would have asked Mr. Horton."

"Oh dear." She thought quickly. "Lillian would like to come, I know. Let me see."

They decided on Lillian Everly and the Misses Greene, two sisters Gwendeline sometimes rode with. Lady Merryn would be lured from her book to serve as chaperone, riding in a coach rather than on horseback, and two of her friends would be asked to accompany her in it. But when it came to the gentlemen, Gwendeline was at a standstill. "Sophy Greene is engaged, but I've forgotten his name," she said plaintively. "We must ask him."

"I shall inquire," said the earl, smiling. "What of her sister?"

"I don't know." Gwendeline frowned in concentration. "She's only just out this year. I've seen her dance with one of her cousins. Oh, who is it? Sir Randall Jacobs, I believe his name is. Do you know him?"

He nodded, still smiling. "Is there someone Miss Everly would like to meet?"

"*Not* Lord Wanley," Gwendeline said.

Lord Merryn laughed. "I'll make a note of that. Perhaps I should choose the other gentlemen?"

"Oh yes. That would be best."

"Good," he replied, rising. "I must go and speak to Mother about our arrangements."

Gwendeline rose and held out her hand. "I look forward to it so much," she said. "I know we'll have a splendid time."

"Indeed," he said. "Are you perfectly recovered

now?" Gwendeline nodded. "I'll leave you, then." He bowed and turned away. "I remain at your disposal if you require rescuing from any other ardent suitors," he said over his shoulder. Gwendeline swept him a mock curtsy and he laughed.

When he'd gone, Gwendeline sat down and stared thoughtfully out the window. The morning had been very eventful, and she felt in need of a respite. As if in response to this thought, Lillian Everly entered the room suddenly. "Lillian," she cried. "I didn't think to see you again this morning."

"My mother twisted her ankle running down the stairs to scold the cook," Lillian answered. "I arrived to find her in bed, surrounded by several maids, the doctor, and four of her friends. She was absolutely livid when she heard that the servants had called me and my father home in a panic." She shrugged. "She sent me directly back here. So I am thrown on your hands once again."

"I'm so glad to see you," Gwendeline replied. "Mr. Horton made me an offer!"

"Just after I left you?" Gwendeline nodded. "Good heavens!" Lillian stared. "I never thought he would bring himself to it."

"It was horrible," Gwendeline said. "It's so hard to tell a man that you don't care for him."

Lillian nodded. "Poor Mr. Horton."

"And he explained his prospects to me. His father is a bishop, Lillian. He lives in York."

"Really?" responded the other girl, interested. "We'll have to quietly inform society of that fact, Gwendeline. He'll be more sought after then."

Gwendeline grimaced. "Yes, I know," Lillian said, "but it may make him happier and help him find a wife, if that's what he wishes. Do we know anyone suitable, I wonder?" She pondered. "What about Alicia?"

"Lillian!"

"Well, she likes to read."

"Do you take nothing seriously?" asked Gwendeline.

"I take many things seriously," Lillian replied, "but proposals of marriage are not among them. Come, Gwendeline, these things happen every day. It is not a matter of life and death."

"They do not happen to *me* every day," Gwendeline said.

"I beg pardon. You must think me shockingly callous. But I'm sure you and Mr. Horton will both be completely recovered by tomorrow. Truly, Gwendeline, it's not a tragedy."

"I suppose you're right," answered Gwendeline. "I've never received an offer of marriage before."

"Lord Wanley offers for me every few weeks," Lillian said with a laugh. "He would be greatly discomfited if I accepted."

Gwendeline's eyes grew wide. "But he must wish to marry you very much."

"Nonsense. He wishes to find himself in interesting emotional situations. The last thing he really wants is a wife."

Gwendeline looked at her, mystified. "It seems extremely odd. I shall never understand such behavior. If Lord Merryn hadn't come at just the right moment, I don't know what I would have done."

"Lord Merryn?" repeated Lillian.

"Yes, he arrived as I was refusing Mr. Horton. It was very embarrassing, of course, but it made Mr. Horton excuse himself."

"I should think so." Lillian seemed preoccupied. "You've been seeing more of Lord Merryn lately, haven't you?"

Gwendeline looked down. "Not really. We've met riding, and I see him at parties."

"Has he mentioned that his brother has returned to town?"

"His brother?" Gwendeline was surprised. "No, I didn't know he had a brother."

"Yes, he has one younger brother, Andrew. He's in the army, a major I believe." Lillian looked out the window as she spoke.

"Indeed?" responded Gwendeline. "He never mentioned him. Nor has his mother. I wonder why?"

"Major St. Audley has been out of the country for some months," Lillian told her. "I understand that he was on a diplomatic mission of some delicacy in Russia."

"Is he a friend of yours?"

"No," answered Lillian quickly, "that is, we're acquainted and we used to meet at parties when he was in town."

"I'll ask Lord Merryn to invite him on our outing. I'd like to meet him."

"Outing?" Lillian asked.

"Oh, you know nothing of it. The earl is getting up a party to go riding in the country. We can have a good gallop at last. You'll receive an invitation tomorrow, I think. I'll tell him you're acquainted with his brother."

"Please don't," Lillian interjected. "That is, he knows already, of course. I...I would not wish to seem to be dictating who shall come," she finished weakly, as Gwendeline looked at her in surprise.

"Do you dislike Major St. Audley?" she asked. "Would you prefer not to see him?"

"No, it's not..." Lillian appeared confused. "You must do as you please. Don't ask him on my account."

Gwendeline agreed, puzzled, and went on to tell her friend about the proposed expedition and who else was to attend. Lillian's responses were subdued at first, but she agreed that it sounded like great fun. They talked of nothing else until Allison called them to luncheon.

When they entered the dining room, they were surprised to find Lord and Lady Merryn ahead of them. The earl had coaxed his mother from her work, and he was staying to lunch. It turned out to be a delightful party, punctuated with a great deal of laughter. Gwendeline enjoyed herself immensely. As it broke up, she managed to catch the earl for a moment. "I've told Lillian about our plan," she said to him. "She's very ready to attend. She mentioned that you have a brother just back in town."

"Did she?" said the earl. "Actually Andrew is to return on Thursday."

"I'd like to meet him. Do you think he would join us next week?"

"I can certainly ask him," he replied. "Did Miss Everly request it?"

"Oh no," she answered airily. "She merely mentioned his name. I didn't even know you had a brother," she added accusingly.

"I beg pardon," he said. "I freely confess that I do."

"You must not be so secretive, for you see that I find out all these things in time. It's no good trying to hide them."

The earl looked at her sharply, but seemed satisfied with what he saw. "I am warned," he replied. "I'll be more circumspect in future. And I'll try to convince Andrew to join us next week." He took his hat and greatcoat from Allison and stepped back to the door of the dining room, where Lillian and Lady Merryn still sat talking. "Goodbye, Mother, Miss Everly," he said. He turned to leave. "Goodbye, Gwendeline. I'll let you know how our guest list shapes itself." He went out, and Gwendeline returned to the dining room, her mind busy with several new ideas.

Nine

NOTHING INTERVENED TO POSTPONE THE PROPOSED expedition, and on the appointed day the party met early at an inn near Richmond Park, on the outskirts of the city. All the invitations had been accepted, and the group consisted of Gwendeline and Lillian, the Greene sisters, Mr. Gorham, the elder sister's fiancé, Sir Randall Jacobs, and the earl and his brother. Lady Merryn and her friends sat comfortably in her barouche, ready to look on and gossip. Surveying the party, Gwendeline felt that they made a very creditable appearance. The Greene sisters both wore becoming pale blue habits, and though neither was more than passably pretty, this dress set off their fresh complexions, blue eyes, and brown hair. Lillian looked beautiful in a cherry-red riding dress topped by a rakish hat with curling ostrich feather. Gwendeline wore her dark blue habit, in which she always felt well-dressed and modish.

The gentlemen also looked well in buckskin breeches and gleaming top boots. Mr. Gorham's Hessians had white tops and silver tassels that matched the large silver buttons of his green riding coat. Gwendeline thought him rather dandified and not very handsome. His light brown hair was thin and his eyes rather close together, but he was a cheerful, friendly young man. Sir Randall, a solid, muscular gentleman, looked much more at home in the saddle than Gwendeline had ever seen him look in a ballroom—her opinion of him rose. But her keenest glances were directed at Andrew St. Audley, to whom she had been introduced only that morning. The major resembled his brother in coloring with auburn hair and cool gray eyes. But he was an inch shorter and slightly stockier than the earl. From her short observation, Gwendeline thought him more relaxed and open than his brother. As they readied themselves for the ride, he stood chatting easily with Sophy and Adele Greene, making them laugh at his stories of mishaps that had overtaken him as he traveled to Russia.

By eleven, they were well under way, the riders in front and Lady Merryn's carriage following. They took the road at first, then turned into a lane lined with high hedges. The day was fine, and the bright sun counteracted the effects of a sharp breeze from the north. As she rode beside Lillian, Gwendeline felt her spirits rise effervescently. "What a glorious day," she said buoyantly. Lillian agreed, but she seemed subdued. They rode on in silence until Adele Greene joined them.

"Oh la," bubbled Adele. "I'm so excited, I can hardly keep my seat. I must thank Lord Merryn once again for asking me. I could scarcely credit it, you know, when we received the invitation. The Earl of

Merryn! Why, he's the greatest catch in London. I can't tell you how many girls have set their caps at him. So handsome!" Adele sighed dramatically. "And so rich!" she giggled, looking at the earl's back as he rode ahead of them. "I was never so surprised in my life when I saw the card."

Gwendeline found this speech both surprising and unpleasant. When she'd ridden with the sisters before, talk had been chiefly of Sophy's approaching marriage.

"I'll ride up and speak to him," Adele continued. "Shall I? I hadn't the faintest notion he even knew who I was, but I mean to take every advantage of the opportunity." She smiled at them as she straightened her lace cravat. Spurring her horse, she rode up to join the earl and his brother in the first rank of riders.

Gwendeline looked at Lillian. "What happened to her?" she asked. "I've never seen her act so."

Lillian smiled. "You've never seen a great deal of her."

Gwendeline made a face. "Sophy is so sensible. I wonder how sisters came to be so different?"

"Perhaps Adele is jealous of the attention Sophy has received since her engagement," Lillian suggested. "But many girls have lost their heads over Lord Merryn. They call him The Unattainable, you know."

"Whatever that may mean."

"It means that every eligible female in the *ton* has been thrown at his head for years, and he's offered for none of them. That, along with his appearance and position, have given rise to that nickname."

"It's extremely silly," said Gwendeline, annoyed. "And who would wish to marry anyone who behaves like that?" She watched Adele simper and smile.

"They haven't all behaved so," Lillian said. "Girls of all kinds have tried and failed to captivate him. That's why there was such a furor in the *ton* when it first heard of you."

"Me?" echoed Gwendeline, puzzled.

"Yes, when the earl brought you to his mother's house, the gossips predicted that he'd made a choice at last."

"Nonsense." Gwendeline flushed. "He meant nothing of the kind."

"And all acknowledge that now. The gossip has ceased; you needn't worry."

For some reason, Gwendeline didn't feel unalloyed relief at this news.

"But Lord Merryn is a figure of fascination for many young ladies," Lillian added. "Don't be too hard on Adele."

"The whole subject is ridiculous," Gwendeline replied. "Come, let's see if we can have our gallop now." She spurred her horse, and Lillian followed. They found they were approaching a series of open fields and were soon flying across the countryside, the rest of the party in pursuit.

Gwendeline bent over Firefly's neck, her hair and habit streaming in the wind. Her annoyance dissolved as she galloped across the open ground with Lillian beside her. The earl and his brother came up to them and passed, the other four remaining somewhat behind.

When they finally reined in, Gwendeline was out of breath. "Oh, I haven't had such fun since I left Brooklands." Her cheeks were glowing and her eyes sparkled.

"I'm glad," said the earl, looking at her appreciatively.

"Indeed, this was a capital idea, Alex," said his brother. "It's wonderful to get out of the city for a while."

"Isn't it?" replied Gwendeline. "I miss the country so much. I used to ride like this every day."

"We must see that you get the chance more often then," said Major St. Audley, "if only because galloping becomes you so."

Gwendeline blushed. "Thank you." She turned to Lillian. "Isn't it splendid?"

"Yes," she answered. "Quite wonderful. It's a fine day." In spite of the gallop, she didn't seem in her best spirits.

"It seems to do everyone good," said the major. Lillian bowed but said nothing. "I'm pleased to find you well," he continued. "I've been away from London so long, I thought to hear news of your marriage, or at least engagement, 'ere now."

Lillian raised her eyes to his face, then hurriedly looked down again. "Oh no," she replied quickly. "I have no plans..." She was interrupted, to the evident annoyance of the major, by the noisy approach of the other four riders.

They rode on through the morning, taking occasional gallops across the fields and chatting happily. The party worked its way gradually toward an inn where the earl had arranged for luncheon. Lady Merryn's coach had proceeded directly there by the roads, and they found the countess comfortably settled under a spreading oak. The young ladies exclaimed over the crisp white cloths and vases of daisies and daffodils on each of the three tables.

One of the chambermaids took them upstairs and aided in brushing the dust from their habits and combing out tangled curls. Adele Greene was in raptures over the scene below. "Flowers and eating out of doors. It is quite pastoral. I declare I've never had such fun in my life! I shall try to sit at Lord Merryn's table. He flirted with me quite outrageously this morning. Did you see?" Giving her skirts a hurried final shake, she went downstairs.

The others followed more slowly. "Adele is a bit overexcited," said Sophy Greene as they descended. "She has been out very little, you know, and that chiefly with my mother." Lillian and Gwendeline murmured polite rejoinders.

They found Lady Merryn and her friends already seated at one table. Adele was talking with the gentlemen as they waited. "Miss Gregory, if you would sit here," said Lord Merryn. He handed her to a seat.

"And I shall sit here," cried Adele before he could go on. She seated herself opposite Gwendeline.

The earl looked slightly vexed, but he said nothing. "Miss Everly and Miss Greene?" He handed them to seats at the remaining table. "And perhaps Mr. Gorham will join you? And…" He paused and looked at the others.

"And I," said his brother, sitting down.

"Very good," continued the earl. "I believe that leaves us at this table, Sir Randall."

They were served with cold meat, bread and butter, and a wonderful selection of fresh fruits. There was also lemonade, tea, and ale for the gentlemen. For a while, relative silence reigned; everyone was hungry after the morning's riding.

Even luncheon, however, did not quiet Adele, who kept up a ceaseless flow of chatter. Gwendeline became more and more annoyed. The earl appeared unmoved, and Sir Randall seemed to enjoy Adele's remarks, even though they were chiefly addressed to Lord Merryn. When she had finished eating, Gwendeline could endure it no longer. She rose abruptly. "I shall take a stroll," she said. The gentlemen stood. "I shan't go far, please don't trouble yourselves."

"I'll join you," said Lord Merryn. He took her arm and led her away, out of the inn yard and down the lane.

"Well, I'm sorry I invited her," Gwendeline said abruptly when they were out of earshot. "She was never like this before."

The earl smiled, not pretending to misunderstand. "Miss Greene is very young," he said. "One must make allowances."

"She's only a year younger than I," answered Gwendeline. "And she says such awful things."

"Awful?" asked the earl, surprised. "I should have said inane rather."

She laughed a little and colored, not wanting to repeat Adele's remarks about him. "Awfully inane," she suggested. "But let's not talk of her."

"I hope you're enjoying yourself otherwise."

"Oh yes," said Gwendeline. "I'll be sorry to return to London."

"I thought we might go back by a different route," answered the earl. "Past the ruins of an old abbey. My mother is eager to see it."

"Certainly, if you think it will please her," she said. "I'm not excessively interested in ruins."

Lord Merryn smiled down at her. "You're interested in riding and nothing else, I believe."

"That's not true," Gwendeline protested. "What a poor creature I should be if I cared only for riding. I'm interested in a great many things."

"Tell me of them," he urged her.

"I'm interested in my friends and in their concerns. I hope to see them happy and do what I can to make them so."

"Yes, I believe you do." He looked into her eyes for a moment. "What else?"

Gwendeline felt rather nervous; her interests suddenly seemed pitifully few. "I used to draw a good deal. At Brooklands."

"So. An artist?"

"Not really. But I enjoy sketching and painting. Miss Brown always encouraged me."

"You must show me some of your pictures," the earl said.

"Oh, it is not… You would find that very dull, I'm sure."

"I wouldn't," he replied. The look in his eyes made Gwendeline's heart beat faster. "Nothing about you is the least bit dull, Gwendeline."

To her intense frustration they were interrupted by a shout ahead of them. Turning, they saw Lillian and Major St. Audley walking at a little distance.

"We slipped away to join you," said the major, looking over his shoulder in mock alarm. "Where can we conceal ourselves?" The two girls laughed at his hunted expression, and the earl smiled. "Laugh if you like," the major went on, "but they'll be after us momentarily. Miss Adele has clearly set her cap at you, Alex."

"Don't be silly, Andrew. Shall we walk back together?"

Lillian and the major fell in behind them. They seemed to have renewed their old acquaintance over luncheon and chatted easily of mutual friends and parties they'd both attended.

"You haven't kept your promise, you know," said Lord Merryn after a bit. "I'm disappointed in you."

"What promise?" said Gwendeline.

"To take me to meet your Miss Brown. You're not going back on your word?"

Gwendeline laughed. "No, indeed. We'll go whenever you like."

"Tuesday next," he replied promptly.

"All right," she agreed. "I'll warn Brown that you're coming."

"Will she approve of me, do you think? I've developed quite a fear of her rigorous judgment."

"We can only wait and see. You must be on your best behavior."

"Naturally," he answered, and they laughed together.

"There you are," a voice broke in. "We thought you quite lost and were coming to find you." Adele and the rest of the young people were approaching, and all returned together to find Lady Merryn and her friends readying themselves for departure.

"Alex," called the countess when she saw them. "We must start back to town if we're to be in time to change for dinner."

The earl agreed and went to order their horses. He made no mention of the ruined abbey, Gwendeline noticed.

As they were preparing to mount, a post-chaise-and-four swept into the inn yard and jerked to a stop. "Fresh horses immediately," called an imperious voice from within. "And some refreshment for the lady." The voice sounded vaguely familiar to Gwendeline, but she was surprised when Mr. Blane leaped out of the chaise. For a moment, she had the unpleasant thought that he'd followed them and meant to join the party, but it was immediately clear that this was not the case. Mr. Blane was obviously astonished, and most displeased, to see them. He glared for a moment, then recollected himself and bowed. "I must see about a fresh team." Blane gave the chaise one sharp glance and strode into the inn. His driver, a seedy-looking individual in a frieze overcoat, laughed harshly and spat.

Lord Merryn's party was mounted by this time. The Greene sisters turned their horses toward the gate and were about to start off when the door of the chaise was flung open suddenly and a young girl jumped out. "Oh, help me, help me, please!" she cried, running to the nearest rider, Adele Greene. "Please help me get away from here." The girl was dressed as a chamber-maid and very pretty. Her black ringlets were disheveled and her face flushed. She looked very frightened.

"Abandoned creature," replied Adele, pulling her skirt away from the girl's clutching hands. "Let go of me."

The girl began to sob and fell to her knees, still holding Adele's skirt. Adele tugged at it. "Let go I said.

You'll tear it. Will someone please get this creature away from me?" She looked at the earl.

"Indeed I will," cried Gwendeline, jumping from her horse. She ran to the weeping girl and knelt beside her. "Here. I will help you. Please don't cry. It will be all right." She patted the girl's back, and her sobs diminished. "There," said Gwendeline, when she stopped crying. "Now, tell me your name and what's wrong." The girl looked at her warily. "I will help you. I promise."

The earl had dismounted by this time, leaving the others still frozen in surprise, though his brother was watching the inn door. "Yes, speak up. We'll help you if we can."

His voice seemed to frighten her further, but Gwendeline patted her hand, and this appeared to give her courage. "My...my name is Rosie Grimes. I'm in service with Lady Dorn. He...he..." She stopped and looked nervously toward the inn. "He took me away when I was going to buy some ribbon for my lady. Pulled me into that carriage, right in the street. I seen him once or twice at her ladyship's, but I never spoke to him or nothing. I didn't!" Her tears seemed about to start again. "I'm a good girl, miss. And he tried to kiss me and maul me about..."

"That will do," interrupted the earl. "We understand. Gwendeline, you'd better go on ahead. I'll handle this."

"Yes indeed," put in Adele above them. "Can you imagine? I feel quite faint." She swayed in her saddle, but her face showed only avid curiosity.

"What will you do?" Gwendeline asked Lord Merryn. "We must help this poor girl."

At this moment, Mr. Blane came out of the inn and, seeing them, strode over. "You little slut," he hissed at Rosie. "What have you been saying?"

"She says that you kidnapped her," retorted Gwendeline.

"Oh, that's what she's saying now, is it? She came willingly enough *before* she got her money."

"It's a lie," cried Rosie. "I never took no money and wouldn't. I'm a good girl, I am." She began to cry again.

"Gwendeline, I really believe you should go," said the earl. "I'll see this taken care of. The girl will be all right."

Gwendeline looked uncertain, but Rosie grabbed her hand. "Don't leave me with them," she said tearfully. "Gentlemen don't care what happens to the likes of me."

"I'll help you," Gwendeline promised. She looked around. "Only I don't know just…" Her gaze lit on Lady Merryn's carriage.

"Couldn't Rosie ride back in your mother's carriage?" she asked the earl. "We could take her back to Lady Dorn's." One of the ladies in the countess's carriage objected shrilly and insisted they leave at once.

"Gwendeline," Merryn began, but he was interrupted.

"A touching sight," sneered Mr. Blane. "Like calls to like. Your mother was mistress to half of London; it's no wonder you feel a bond with a slut like this."

"Hold your tongue, damn you," said Lord Merryn through his teeth.

"Of course, you come to her defense," replied Blane. "You had her mother, as did I. And I suppose you mean to put her in Annabella's place, milksop that she is." He said no more because Lord Merryn knocked him down with one strategically placed blow. Adele began to scream. Major St. Audley dismounted and went to put his hand on his brother's shoulder. The earl shook himself. "Yes, I'm all right," he said. "Sir Randall, perhaps you could aid Miss Greene." Sir Randall jumped like a man waking from a dream and hurried to comfort Adele. "Mr. Gorham," the earl continued, "I would be much in your debt if you and Sir Randall would escort the ladies home. My brother I will detain, if I may." With a jerk of his head he directed Andrew to the inn. Mr. Gorham bowed his agreement, his pale blue eyes bulging nervously.

"No!" said Lady Merryn and Gwendeline simultaneously.

"I wish to stay and help," began Gwendeline.

"Alex, I shall take that poor creature to town," said his mother.

"I shan't have her in the carriage," said one of Lady Merryn's companions. "She can walk."

"Nonsense, Helen, she's exhausted," snapped Lady Merryn. "And it's *my* carriage."

"She can ride with me," said Gwendeline. "I am sure Firefly can carry us both."

"Ladies, please," the earl said. "Trust me to arrange things."

His brother returned, and the two men exchanged nods. "We've hired a conveyance for Miss Grimes, and if you, Mother, are willing to accompany her, that will be all to the good. If the rest of you ladies will now return to London, all shall be made right. Allow me to help you mount, Miss Gregory." Reluctantly, Gwendeline let herself be assisted into the saddle. She looked down at Lord Merryn, but the things she had heard moments ago kept her silent.

Lady Merryn stepped down from her carriage and took charge of Rosie. The rest of the ladies started back to London under the escort of Mr. Gorham and Sir Randall. Gwendeline rode next to Lillian. Looking back, she saw Lord Merryn standing over Mr. Blane. She heard the latter's hideous accusations again and felt her world tumbling about her ears.

Back in the inn yard, the earl handed his mother and Rosie into the inn's vehicle as Mr. Blane was reviving. It drove off as he rose to his feet, looking murderous. "This isn't the first time you've crossed me," Blane hissed. "First Annabella, now this stupid servant girl. I should kill you, Merryn."

"You're welcome to try."

"Here, with your brother behind you to finish me?" jeered Blane. Major St. Audley clenched his fists but remained silent. "I'm not so stupid. Or perhaps you think I'll call you out?" A sneer made his dark face ugly. "Forcing you to flee the country isn't worth dying for. But I'll repay you. Perhaps with our pretty Gwendeline, eh? She's not quite the innocent she seems, I wager. Not with the mother she had. I daresay you have plans for her."

A vein stood out on Merryn's forehead. Otherwise, there was no visible reaction to these words.

"And I've already put a spoke in those plans," Blane added with an ugly laugh. "She'll not likely follow her mother of her own will."

"I have only this to say to you," replied the earl evenly. "Stay away from me and my friends, for the next time you annoy any of them, I'll see that you pay." He turned on his heel and went to his horse. The major followed, keeping one eye on Blane as he went. They mounted and rode off, leaving Mr. Blane standing in the inn yard, a bruise forming on his jaw. Swiftly, they caught up to the inn's carriage, then slowed to escort it back to town.

Farther ahead, Gwendeline found the ride home endless. Her mind was in turmoil, and Adele Greene's laments over her shocked sensibilities were no help. Thoughts of her mother, of the earl, of Mr. Blane, and of what she was to do now revolved in her brain. It was as if a nightmare had become real, and she wanted nothing so much as to fling herself down on her own bed and cry. Lillian reached over and pressed her hand sympathetically, but nothing could comfort Gwendeline now.

They reached London at last, and Gwendeline ran up the stairs of Lady Merryn's house to her room. She sat on her bed, covering her mouth with her hand, trembling. Then she jumped up and pulled a bandbox from the wardrobe. She stuffed some of her things into it and started out the door. The long skirt of her habit tripped her, and she looped it up impatiently. She had to get away from this house, from the man who had been her mother's lover. She ran back down the stairs, out the front door, and through the streets, heedless of the stares of passersby, heading for Miss Brown and sanctuary.

Ten

WHEN SHE WOKE THE NEXT MORNING, GWENDELINE was bewildered. The dawn light fell across a coverlet of gray silk and struck a wall papered in gray with pink roses. The furniture and pale pink curtains were unfamiliar, and she felt a moment of panic. Then memory returned, and she realized that this was "her" room in her own house. With that realization came the events of the previous day. Again, she heard Mr. Blane say that her mother had been the earl's mistress, and again she realized that here was a reason for his aid to her. But more important, even worse, she acknowledged that she loved him. The feeling had been growing outside her conscious knowledge, and this crisis had revealed it. And the realization that followed this one shocked her most; she didn't care about his relationship to her mother. She wanted him to love her regardless of the past. This was what had driven her here and what made her now leap from her bed and dress hurriedly to go in search of Miss Brown.

The older lady was also up early, drinking tea in the

breakfast room. She looked up with a worried frown when Gwendeline came rushing in.

Gwendeline allowed her no time to speak but blurted, "Brown, how much money have we?"

"What?"

"How much money, in the household account? I know money was put there, how much is left?"

"About five hundred pounds," Miss Brown answered automatically. "Gwendeline, please tell me what's wrong."

"So much," said Gwendeline. "That should do. I'm leaving London, Brown."

"What? But where are you going? Why?"

"I've learned some very unpleasant things, which make it necessary for me to go away. I must leave immediately." Gwendeline paused for breath. "I'd like you to come with me, if you will."

"I must have some explanation first, Gwendeline," the older woman replied. "What exactly is going on?"

"I won't repeat it," she said. "I'm very unhappy, and I will go alone, if I must."

"Of course, I will go with you, but…" Miss Brown began.

"Good. We must leave immediately."

"But where are we going? How do we travel?" asked her old governess.

Gwendeline sat down abruptly opposite her. "Where shall I go?" she said to herself. "Oh, what shall I do?"

Three hours later, Gwendeline had poured out her story to Miss Brown, and though Miss Brown felt they should wait for explanations, she finally gave in to

Gwendeline's frantic denials. She'd suggested a small seaside town she knew in the south. The inn there was run by friends of hers. This settled, Miss Brown was sent out to withdraw the money from the household account and purchase tickets on the stage. Gwendeline informed the servants that she was going on a visit of indefinite length. Miss Brown returned, packed her things, and they departed by ten o'clock.

The journey was long and tiring, and Gwendeline remembered little of it later. As the distance from London increased, her tension lessened, though she was more miserable than ever. She still believed she'd done the right thing, but the future looked empty and bleak as she rested her aching head in the corner of the coach.

They reached Penwyn on the third day, very late. Gwendeline scarcely knew how she got up to a cozy bedroom and into bed. She could hear the sea from her window, and as she fell asleep, she thought that the murmur sounded melancholy.

Staring at the waves some days later, the same thought was in her mind. She sat at a writing desk before the window of the neat little parlor set aside for their use, a book open in her hands. Today, the water was gray and lashed with rain and wind.

She looked down at her book. It was a French grammar. Gwendeline had decided that Miss Brown should tutor her in all the subjects she'd neglected as a schoolgirl and thus prepare her to make her own living. But the harder she tried to master them, the more facts seemed to elude her. As now, she found herself spending more time gazing out the window than learning. She sighed, closed the book, and went to stand in front of the fire.

Gwendeline caught herself thinking of Lord Merryn. She recalled the way his eyes lit when he was amused and the smile he showed only to his friends. Secretly she'd begun to think that Miss Brown had been right to suggest they wait for explanations. She wanted to make excuses for the earl, and excuses for herself to return to him. But what reasons were there? What could Lord Merryn say to her after Mr. Blane's accusations, and worse still, what could she say to him? All society must know by now what had happened. There would be sneers and laughter wherever she went, whatever she did. No. She straightened; she couldn't go back. She turned to the desk and sat down again, opening the grammar. I'll make myself learn it, she thought fiercely, setting her jaw.

Miss Brown came in. She'd gone out walking earlier in the morning. "A fire," she said. "Just the thing. The rain came on so suddenly that it caught me before I had half finished my walk. I was wet through and had to change." She took the armchair in front of the fire.

"I'm sorry," Gwendeline replied listlessly.

Miss Brown looked at her. "And guess what I found when I stopped to shelter in the circulating library? All of Lady Merryn's books!" She paused, but Gwendeline turned away toward the window. "I nearly brought you *Terror at Wellwyn Abbey* to read, but I couldn't through the rain."

Gwendeline burst into tears.

Miss Brown rose and went to her. "Gwendeline, my dear, I'm so sorry. You're too sensitive; I meant only to amuse you." She knelt and put her arms around her.

Through her tears, Gwendeline said, "I-it's no u-use, Brown. I l-love him. I sh-shall never be h-happy again."

"You love Lord Merryn?" Miss Brown asked gently. Gwendeline nodded and began to cry harder, her head on Miss Brown's shoulder. Her old governess patted her back, saying over and over again, "There. It will all come right," but her expression was sad.

When Gwendeline had cried herself out, she felt exhausted but oddly relieved, though there was still nothing to be done as far as she could see. "So I have resolved, Brown, that I'll study very hard," she said. "I'll force myself every day. Then, by the time our money is gone, I'll be ready to find a position and support myself." Miss Brown said nothing. "I could teach very young children, couldn't I?"

Miss Brown seemed abstracted. "I'm sure you could."

"I'll start immediately," Gwendeline said. "I'll study all day very, very hard. You'll see, Brown. I know you don't think I can do it, but I will."

Miss Brown nodded. "I believe I'll write some letters then, Gwendeline."

"You can quiz me at tea."

Gwendeline's resolution lasted longer this time, and for several days she studied conscientiously. But the length of her reading periods shortened. She spent more and more time outdoors, and got into the habit of carrying an easel and sketching materials with her, drawing and painting for hours. Her room at the inn gradually filled with studies of the sea and cliffs about Penwyn and of the countryside near the inn. She even tried a sketch of Miss Brown, but her skills didn't run to portraiture.

She'd set up her painting things on the beach one day when she met one of their neighbors. "It's really quite good, you know," said a voice behind her. "You've caught the waves, and that's difficult."

Startled, Gwendeline turned. Standing behind her, surveying her canvas critically, was a small man of about fifty. His hair was white, unkempt and bushy, and his coat was of a loose baggy cut that Gwendeline found odd. But his blue eyes twinkled.

"If I could suggest," he continued, "just a touch of the green, here," he moved closer and pointed at her painting, "and even a bit of red there. It sounds strange, I know, red in the sea, but it would be a marked improvement." He appeared completely engrossed in the question of color as he surveyed the painting with narrowed eyes, but he slowly realized that Gwendeline was staring at him. "Oh, I beg your pardon, young lady, but I noticed your drawing as I passed, and I was much taken with it. You have some real talent." He tapped the top of the canvas. "I had to stop and comment."

"I...I see," said Gwendeline, still mystified.

"I'm an artist myself, you see," the man explained, as if that made all obvious. "Live up there." He pointed to a house perched on the edge of the cliffs north of them. "This part of the country is just right for a painter. The sea, you know, and the rocks."

"They are very beautiful."

"Beautiful, yes, and a sight more interesting than Lady This, or the Countess of That. I can't abide portraits. Used to do 'em, you know. Painted a dashed gallery of such rubbish. But I've given it up. The sea, now, there's a subject for a painter. The Greeks knew that, young lady, the sea." He smiled down at her and seemed to recollect himself. "Oh, my name is Ames, Carleton Ames." He looked at her. "You've heard of me perhaps?" Gwendeline shook her head. "Ah, well, some pieces in the Royal Academy, you know. Nothing too important. Keep the best ones myself." He winked. "Say, you must come to tea. I'll show you my pictures, and you can criticize them. Turn about, you know. My wife will be happy to see a new face. Are you visiting near here, Miss, Miss?"

"Gregory," replied Gwendeline mechanically.

"Miss Gregory. Are you staying hereabouts?"

"At the inn." Gwendeline felt a bit dazed by this flow of talk.

"Ah, with your parents, perhaps?"

"No, with Miss Brown, my old governess."

"Well, splendid, bring her along. Four sharp, mind. I'll tell my wife." He started off down the beach, swinging an ivory cane.

"But I—" Gwendeline stammered.

Mr. Ames waved cheerily. "Four sharp," he repeated and walked on.

"I had no chance to refuse," Gwendeline said when she told Miss Brown of the encounter. "He hardly gave me time to say anything. What an odd creature! Shall we send a note round with our regrets?"

"Why not go?" Miss Brown replied. "You say he was a gentleman?"

"Oh yes, though a strange one," answered Gwendeline.

"It might prove interesting. I've never met an artist." Miss Brown looked at Gwendeline. "And it would be good for you to go out. You've been moping about far too much."

"Perhaps I have. Very well, then, we'll go."

Accordingly, at half past three, they set out to walk across to Mr. Ames's house. Miss Brown had asked her friends, the Wilsons, who ran the inn, about him, and they assured her he was perfectly respectable, though considered odd by many of his neighbors.

The walk up the cliffs took more than twenty minutes, for the path was narrow and steep, and they had to go slowly. The clock in the church tower below was striking four when Miss Brown knocked on the door of the small white cottage and was greeted by Mr. Ames himself. "Hello, hello," he cried. "Miss, uh, Gregory, yes. Delighted to see you. Come in." He ushered them into a narrow hall.

"This is Miss Brown," said Gwendeline.

"Delighted," said Mr. Ames. He guided them through an archway and into the parlor. The chief features of this chamber were walls covered with pictures, and the view, a breathtaking vista of ocean and sky. "My wife," said Mr. Ames. "Here is Miss Gregory, my dear, whom I mentioned, and her friend Miss Brown."

"Good afternoon," said the small, fluffy white-haired lady seated behind the teapot. "I'm so pleased you could come."

Gwendeline hardly knew where to look first. The

paintings attracted immediate attention, but there were so many of them that she could attend to none. And Mrs. Ames, too, drew the eye. In general appearance she was like her husband—small, with a great deal of white hair and twinkling blue eyes—but her costume was decidedly original. It seemed to consist wholly of pale blue ruffles. Gwendeline couldn't see how they all held together, and each flounce appeared to move gently of its own accord.

"Please sit down," said Mrs. Ames. "Here on the sofa, so you can look out the window. It's a charming view, is it not?"

"Spectacular," answered Miss Brown, as they seated themselves.

Mr. Ames beamed. "Thought so myself when I chose this spot for a house years ago. I do a lot of painting right here, as you see." He made a sweeping gesture with his arm, and Gwendeline saw that several of the pictures were studies of the view.

"Will you have some tea?" asked Mrs. Ames. "I have some fresh seed cake as well. Very good." There was a bustle as everyone was served. "My husband tells me you have quite a talent for drawing," the lady went on then. "He waxed eloquent on the subject."

"Oh," said Gwendeline. "He's too kind."

"Not at all," put in Mr. Ames. "Never flatter anyone about talent. You need training, of course, to make anything of it, but it's definitely there."

"Miss Brown taught me a great deal about drawing," Gwendeline answered. "In fact, everything."

"She did well," the man replied. "Do you paint also, ma'am?"

"No," said Miss Brown. "I'm one of those who know the principles but cannot execute. I am a better teacher than doer."

"A very good teacher, I warrant," said Mrs. Ames. "There are few who can say so."

Miss Brown smiled. "I daresay your husband would be a much better one when it comes to art, Mrs. Ames. But I thank you nonetheless."

"Oh, Carleton doesn't care to teach. They wanted him in London once, to give lectures. But he refused. He cares only for his own painting."

"Now, now, my dear," her husband put in. He turned to their visitors. "She had some crackbrained notion of setting up in London and racketing about the *ton*. Her mother's cousin to a duke or some such nonsense, and all her family urged her on. Ridiculous. How am I to paint in London, with people constantly calling or inviting us out and a pack of wastrel students dogging me to lecture?" He smiled at his wife. "And don't I take you up to London every year, my dear, and let you racket about to your heart's content?"

"Yes, yes, Carleton. I wasn't complaining," said his wife. "I also prefer the country. I was simply demonstrating your dislike of teaching."

"Well, I don't know," he replied meditatively. "I shouldn't mind giving a talented student a few hints. We might work together here and there on the beach of an afternoon, if you like, Miss Gregory."

"Oh, I thank you very much, but..." Gwendeline began.

"Nothing formal, mind," he interrupted. "No schedules and all that nonsense. But I shouldn't mind giving you a pointer when you go wrong." He smoothed his flowing jacket complacently. "Glad to be of help."

"I think that's a splendid idea," put in Miss Brown. "A great opportunity for you, Gwendeline."

"And you can both come to tea afterwards," added Mrs. Ames. "We'll make a party of it." Clearly, the idea appealed to her.

"Well," Gwendeline faltered. "I suppose…"

"Good," said Mr. Ames. "And when you go up to London, I'll give you a list of pictures to view."

"Oh, I shan't be going to London," blurted Gwendeline.

"Really?" Mrs. Ames shook her head. "But you must have one season at least. It would be a great shame for a young girl as lovely as you to miss that."

Gwendeline shook her head.

"You really must speak to your parents," continued Mrs. Ames. "A season in London is simply essential."

Gwendeline shrugged, and a short silence fell.

"Well, if you've finished your tea," said Mr. Ames, "I'll show you my pictures."

Gwendeline rose with relief. "I'd like that very much," she said.

"And I," added Miss Brown, also rising.

"Capital. We'll start right here, and then I'll take you up to my studio. Here, you see, are most of my landscapes."

The rest of the afternoon was spent looking at pictures. Mr. Ames was an enthusiastic showman, and Gwendeline and Miss Brown agreed as they walked home that he was also a fine artist as well. They felt they'd made an interesting new acquaintance. Too, Gwendeline realized that she'd hardly thought of the past all afternoon. She resolved to try the art lessons Mr. Ames had offered.

Eleven

IN THE WEEKS THAT FOLLOWED, GWENDELINE MET with Mr. Ames often, and as she became more and more interested in what he had to teach, her spirits did rise. She gained skill rapidly, pleasing both Mr. Ames and herself. They met on the beach or in the countryside when it was fine, and at his home when it wasn't, and Mrs. Ames provided tea after all their sessions. The four of them, for Miss Brown joined them for tea, became good friends, and Miss Brown sometimes visited Mrs. Ames while Gwendeline painted.

Thus, the days passed more easily for Gwendeline, and she began to feel more or less happy again. Her life took on a quiet rhythm, and she even progressed a little in her studies with Miss Brown. She felt that a great deal of time had passed since the events in London; she seemed to herself much older, though it had only been a few weeks.

One rather cold, damp morning, Gwendeline and Miss Brown sat again in their parlor before a good fire. Gwendeline studied Italian at the desk, feeling remarkably content to do so, and Miss Brown read the letters she'd received in the morning post. There were several of these, and she'd been engrossed in them for some time. As she perused the last, she exclaimed, "Good heavens," causing Gwendeline to look up.

"Some news in your letter?"

Miss Brown refolded the page. "Yes, that is…a startling bit of gossip. "

"What is it?"

Miss Brown put the letter in her pocket. "Oh, nothing. I don't wish to talk of it."

"Of course," replied Gwendeline. She turned back to her book, a little hurt.

Miss Brown stared into the fire, frowning. She got up and moved restlessly to the window. "What a dreary morning. I would so like a walk, but I suppose it's too wet."

Gwendeline looked up. "I should think so. It looks as if it will rain again."

"Yes." Miss Brown turned back to the sofa. "How tiresome." She stood in front of the fire, looked through the books lying on the mantelpiece, then went back to the window.

Gwendeline was surprised. Brown never fidgeted, but here she was pacing the room. "What was in that letter? I wish you would let me help."

"There is nothing you can do," Miss Brown answered rather sharply. "I shall go out. The rain will keep off, I think." And she quickly left the room.

Mystified Gwendeline turned back to her studies, resolving to be very kind and thoughtful with Brown that evening.

Miss Brown did not return for some hours, and

Gwendeline had just begun to worry when she swept in. The rain had not held off, and she was soaked. She paused for a moment in the parlor. "I must go and change," she said, "but I have something to show you. It's fascinating!" She swept out, leaving Gwendeline even more puzzled over her uncharacteristic mood.

When she returned, in dry clothing but still rather disheveled, she was carrying three thin books bound in red Morocco. She placed them on the sofa beside her as she sat down. "Look," she said. "I stopped in the library to shelter again, and as the rain didn't stop, I began to look for something to read. Lady Merryn's new novel arrived a few days ago from London, so I glanced through it to amuse myself." She paused, and Gwendeline looked at her with some distress. Why should Miss Brown bring up the past again, just as she was beginning to be free of it? "Gwendeline, you *must* read it," the older woman continued. "It's not at all like her other books. Not a Gothic at all, in fact. It is…"

"I don't wish to read it," Gwendeline interrupted. "I don't wish to think of Lady Merryn, or of London, or…" She stopped, for she was near tears.

"I know your feelings on the subject," Miss Brown replied. "But I think there may be something important in this novel. Gwendeline, almost every character I came across is perfectly recognizable."

"All the more reason not to read it!" Gwendeline answered. "If Lady Merryn has used the events of that awful day." She paused miserably. "Oh, now I can never go back."

"But Gwendeline, there may be some information in the story to make things right between you and the

St. Audleys. The countess is close to her son; she may know some facts that vindicate him." Gwendeline frowned. "And look here," continued the other, "look at the dedication." She opened the first volume and handed it to Gwendeline.

"*Betrayal of Love*," Gwendeline read, "a story of modern society." She looked farther down the page. "To a young lady whose hasty flight from London all regret; may she soon return." She closed the book. "I don't care, Brown. It is too painful to think of."

Miss Brown frowned at her. "You're being silly, Gwendeline. I know that you want to return to London and your friends. Perhaps if you found out more…"

"No!" Gwendeline exclaimed. "Every time I've discovered something new, it's been more horrible." She turned to the window, blinking back her tears. "Oh, Brown, why did you bring all this up again? I thought I hardly cared anymore; I find I was wrong."

"That is exactly why," answered the other woman. "I could see that you weren't really regaining your former spirits." She paused, then added, "The letter I received this morning was from London, from my friend who is employed by Lady Forester. She'd heard of Lady Merryn's new novel, actually. It seems to be causing quite a stir in the *ton*. She said that your sudden departure caused a good deal of talk, though that has died by now. It seems that the actual events of that afternoon ride are not widely known. At least, they weren't a subject of gossip." She paused again. "But her most suprising news was word of the Earl of Merryn's engagement."

"What?" exclaimed Gwendeline.

"Incredible as it seems to me, it appears that Lord Merryn is engaged to Miss Adele Greene. My friend enclosed the announcement from the *Morning Post.*"

Gwendeline wondered for a moment whether she would faint. Then she realized dismally that she wouldn't. She felt frozen.

"Adele was there that afternoon," said Miss Brown. "And she was upset. But if there is some explanation that has satisfied her and her parents, then perhaps it would ease your mind as well. Miss Greene wouldn't knowingly marry a libertine."

Gwendeline smiled sourly. "Wouldn't she? Not even a rich libertine?"

"Please, Gwendeline, read the book. It may vindicate him." She held the three volumes out to the girl.

Gwendeline took them automatically. "What does it matter now?" she asked dully. Miss Brown started to speak. "All right, I'll try."

Gwendeline made little progress at first with her reading. She'd agreed to meet with Mr. Ames for a lesson. She and Miss Brown were invited to luncheon afterwards, a sort of celebration since the Ameses were leaving for their annual stay in London the next day.

Accordingly, she readied her drawing materials and walked up to the Ames house at the appointed time. She found the couple in high spirits, preparing for their journey. "Three trunks!" she heard Mr. Ames exclaiming in the drawing room as the servant let her in, "three trunks for a stay of four weeks? It's incredible."

"Now, Carleton," Mrs. Ames's voice replied. "You wouldn't wish me to look dowdy and countrified when we visit our friends. And I must have

some vacant space for the clothes I shall have made."
She glanced up from an illustrated fashion paper as
Gwendeline came into the room. "Oh, good morning, my dear. Have you seen this latest issue? They say
mauve is à la mode this season."

Mr. Ames struck his forehead. "Mauve!" he
exclaimed. "What a pack of nonsense! These idiots
always hit on the dullest, least becoming colors and
call them all the crack. And hundreds of bird-witted
females will deck themselves in mauve, I suppose."
He shook his head at Gwendeline. "Frightful," he
finished. "I am not sure I can face it."

Mrs. Ames smiled blithely. "Well, perhaps you're
right, Carleton," she said. "I shan't have mauve. But this
purple..." She bent over the illustration with interest.

"Trash," said Mr. Ames, indicating the paper.
"Nothing but trash. Come up to the studio, Gwendeline."

Gwendeline loved Mr. Ames's studio. It was a
high, airy room filling the former attic of the cottage.
Nearly half the roof had been replaced by a skylight,
and sunshine and a sweeping panorama of sky and
sea extended down the length of the chamber. The
opposite side was filled with paintings, blank canvases,
and drawing supplies.

"Now," said Mr. Ames, removing his coat and
pulling on a smock. "Let's continue our work on
light. You've improved immensely, but you still need
practice. And catching the light in different settings is
the hardest thing a painter does." He smiled at her. "A
good painter, I should say. A poor one does nothing
of the kind."

They began on a fresh canvas, Gwendeline trying

various effects, and Mr. Ames directing her. But she was preoccupied, and Mr. Ames soon became impatient with her errors.

Finally, he took the brush himself. "No. You see it is thus." He made a few quick strokes, changing her daubs of blue and yellow into shafts of sun striking water. "There. That was simple really, Gwendeline. You aren't trying."

"I'm a little tired. I didn't sleep well."

"A girl of your age? Ridiculous!" exclaimed Mr. Ames. "Well, it's no use trying to concentrate when you're tired." He put down the brush. "Perhaps we should go down and sit with Mrs. Ames until luncheon?"

Gwendeline nodded. "I'm sorry to be so stupid."

"Well, well, no harm. But you should practice that effect when I'm gone. Then we can continue with something else."

Gwendeline nodded again, saying nothing, and they began to tidy up their tools.

In the parlor, they found that Miss Brown had arrived. She and Mrs. Ames were chatting about the people, plays, and shops the latter planned to visit in London. "And she will drag me with her to most of them," Mr. Ames said to Miss Brown. "I'll be the most bored man in town. You don't ask what I wish to do and see."

"Only because I haven't yet had the opportunity," answered Miss Brown, smiling. "I should very much like to know."

"Well, I shall see what they've hung in the Academy since last year. Nothing much, I expect. And I look forward to visiting with a *few* friends." He frowned comically at his wife. "I have some close acquaintances among the 'artistic' set."

"Do you know Lady Merryn?" Gwendeline interjected.

"Merryn?" said Ames. "No, I don't believe I do." He frowned. "Stay. Isn't she the countess who writes Gothic novels?"

Gwendeline nodded.

"Hah!" he replied. "Don't know her and wouldn't. There is nothing so stupid as these noble ladies who dabble in the arts. Either a pack of harpies or completely dotty. Can't abide 'em."

"Carleton!" put in his wife, "perhaps you're speaking of one of Miss Gregory's friends."

"You don't read such stuff, Gwendeline?" Mr. Ames looked horrified. "You mustn't waste your time with novels. I am certain Miss Brown agrees with me." At this moment, the servant came in to announce luncheon, and they all went into the dining room. Conversation became more general, and Gwendeline relaxed. It seemed doubtful that the Ameses would meet any of her friends in town. She had thought to find some excuse to ask them not to mention her name, but she abandoned the idea, thinking perhaps it was unnecessary.

Gwendeline and Miss Brown returned to the inn at midafternoon, having bid the Ameses farewell. Gwendeline realized that she would miss them very much. She'd become accustomed to her lessons and excursions to their cottage, and she was fond of the couple. She was thinking of them with regret as she settled herself in the parlor to work at her studies, and this seemed to keep her from concentrating. Repeatedly, she found herself staring blankly at the sea instead of at her book. After a while, she realized that what was bothering her was not the Ameses' departure, but Lord Merryn's engagement. The more she thought of it, the less she understood how it could have happened. Adele! The earl had not even *liked* her. She remembered Lady Merryn's novel. She went up to her bedroom and returned with the first volume. Reclining on the sofa before the fire, she started to read.

When Miss Brown entered the parlor at teatime, she found Gwendeline deep in the book. It took her a little time, in fact, to attract the girl's attention. Finally, however, she tore herself away. "Brown," she cried. "I think it's about my mother! You're right. Some of the characters are perfectly recognizable. The heroine is a beautiful young girl who becomes the toast of London but is forced to marry before the end of her first season. Lady Merryn has changed the names, of course, but in appearance she's very like my mother and her husband like my father. The countess is in it also and her husband. The earl is a very young man at the beginning, only sixteen. It's excessively interesting."

"Really?"

"Yes, and oh, she's put in Mr. Blane as well. I am sure it is he, though she's made him a young Italian adventurer, Montaldo Blanco."

Miss Brown burst out laughing. "Montaldo," she gasped. "An Italian villain. She couldn't wholly give up her Gothics, could she?"

Gwendeline smiled. "Everyone will know him. Mr. Blane must be very angry, because he is not at all nice in this story, I must tell you. Not a gentleman in manners or birth." The two women laughed together. "But Brown, why has she written about my mother?"

"Perhaps she wished to explain something and could reach you in no other way," suggested Miss Brown. Gwendeline looked thoughtful. "Of course," the other woman went on, "the story makes an exciting novel." Miss Brown smiled. "Lady Merryn must have realized it would create a sensation. I hope she's enjoying being a nine-day wonder."

"Do you suppose she'll tell about my mother and Mr. Blane and—and the earl?" Gwendeline asked.

Miss Brown shrugged. "You'll have to read on and see."

Gwendeline rose. "I'm going to my room. Will you ask them to send my dinner up on a tray, Brown? I cannot bear to be interrupted."

Gwendeline finished Lady Merryn's novel very late the following day, too late in fact to tell Miss Brown of its outcome. As she undressed and got into bed, she pondered what she'd learned. Her mother's story, if this was truly that, was a sad one. Unhappy and reviled in her marriage, Annabella Gregory had turned to parties, gambling, and admirers for solace. She'd been giddy, foolish, and increasingly reckless as time went by. But according to the book at least, not until about four years before her death had she done anything really bad. It was then that Mr. Blane—or Montaldo Blanco, as Lady Merryn called him—had captivated her with his wit and seeming kindness.

But once he'd lured her into an illicit relationship, he began to lead her deeper into play for high stakes and other imprudences.

Gwendeline leaned back against her pillows. The last volume of the novel had been quite upsetting. Her mother had evidently seen, after a time, the true baseness of Blane's character. But when she tried to break away from him, he threatened her with exposure, vowing he'd spread word of her debts and connection with him through London society. By blackmail, he forced her to remain with him.

It was then, according to Lady Merryn, that the earl entered the story. As an adolescent, he'd followed Annabella Gregory about, fancying himself in love with her, but she'd treated him kindly and sent him on his way. Now, as a man of thirty, he offered to help. She accepted his offer with gratitude, and they became close friends, nothing more, as they worked together to pay her debts and find some escape from Blane. They'd continued until her death, never finally succeeding because she refused to let him simply pay her creditors and Blane resisted all their efforts to be rid of him. He struck back at the earl by spreading rumors of a liaison between them. Once Annabella was dead, the earl thought his dealings with Blane at an end.

Gwendeline stared at the walls of her room, feeling an immense relief at this explanation of the earl's behavior. That he would act to rescue the child of his friend was natural. Perhaps he had even organized the group who rescued her. But along with relief, she felt despair. Why hadn't she waited to hear the truth? Could she ever return to the city? How could she face them all, especially the earl whom she hadn't trusted after all his kindness to her? Then she remembered. She wouldn't have to face Lord Merryn. He was engaged to Adele Greene, perhaps soon to be married. He wouldn't be concerned with her. She'd made a mull of her life just as her parents had, she thought. Perhaps she was their daughter in spirit as well as body.

Twelve

GWENDELINE EXPRESSED THESE BITTER SENTIMENTS
to Miss Brown the next morning, after she'd told her
the story of the novel. "So you see, I've been stupid
and imprudent about everything, Brown," she finished. "But I'm justly punished for it. I have lost all
chance of happiness in life through my foolishness.
Perhaps that should give me some satisfaction. It
does not, however."

Miss Brown patted her hand. "You acted from the
right motives, and you were very hurt and upset. It's
difficult to think clearly at such times."

"I could have listened to you. You gave just the
right advice. You knew what was best to do, but I
insisted on my own way, like a spoiled child."

"Well, Gwendeline, don't talk as if all were lost.
You can put things right, return to London and see
your friends again."

"Return?" echoed Gwendeline incredulously.
"How can I return after the way I have acted? How
could I face anyone? What would I say?"

"You might apologize for your abrupt departure

and mistrust," answered Miss Brown. "I think you've gained the necessary maturity to do that at least."

Gwendeline stared at the floor. A strange reluctance to return to London, the thing she'd most desired for weeks, came over her. "Let us wait a few days and think it over."

Miss Brown looked at her. "If you wish. But I thought you'd be eager to return."

"I'm a coward, it appears. When I think of walking into a London drawing room, with all the people I knew awaiting me there, I feel utterly unnerved."

"The season is nearly over. People will be going away."

"Oh, Brown, a few days will make no difference. Lord Merryn is engaged, perhaps even married by now. I can't change that, and the rest isn't terribly important."

"But perhaps... This engagement, I cannot believe in it. I think there must be some mistake."

"The earl is not the kind of man who puts a mistaken announcement of his engagement in the *Morning Post*," answered Gwendeline. "Today is Tuesday; let us go on Monday next."

Miss Brown sighed. "Very well, Gwendeline. I'll ask Mr. Wilson about hiring a chaise."

"I'll write Reeves to prepare the house," she replied. "And, and perhaps I'll also write Lillian Everly."

"A splendid idea. She'll be happy to hear that you're all right and can tell you how things really stand."

Gwendeline smiled thinly. "You're too optimistic. But I'll write the letters."

Gwendeline sent her letters off in the early post. In the afternoon, she took a long walk alone. Her future, she told herself, was actually much brighter. She could return to her house in London and give up the idea of earning a living. She could see friends again and go out. Though she could never feel proud of her parents and their lives, perhaps, she at least knew the truth now and need no longer fear the unknown. As she turned back to the inn, however, she acknowledged that none of this convinced her that she would ever be happy again.

The week passed. Miss Brown bustled about making arrangements for their journey, cleaning and packing clothing. Gwendeline sometimes helped her, but more often she spent the days outside. By Saturday, however, she was beginning to wish she hadn't put the trip off so long. She wasn't eager to get to London, but she now wished to get it over. Late in the afternoon, she started out for her usual walk. The sky was threatening, and Miss Brown tried to dissuade her, but she insisted on going out. "I must get some air, Brown," she told the older woman. "I shan't stay out long, and the storm will hold off till this evening, I think."

"At least take a cloak, Gwendeline, in case it begins sooner," replied Miss Brown. She'd given up trying to shake Gwendeline out of her lethargy. She left that for London.

Gwendeline agreed and fetched a cloak. She started out along the road but soon turned into a lane. She walked for some time in the fields nearby and found she was glad of the extra clothing. The wind was freshening and it was clear that a storm would break later in the day. Because of this, she headed back to the inn sooner than usual. In her hurry, she took a wrong turning in the high-hedged lanes and had to retrace her steps for a good distance once she realized she was lost. Thus, the early darkness of the storm was beginning to descend when she reached the road again, and the first large drops of rain had spotted its surface.

In her haste, she took no notice of the post chaise standing farther down the road. She turned away from it and strode toward the inn and shelter. Its windows shone warmly through the gathering dusk, and she thought eagerly of the warm fire within and a cup of tea. But before she had covered half the distance to the building, she heard running footsteps behind her. The rising wind had muffled them until they were very close, and because of this Gwendeline had no time to turn and see who approached before a piece of dark cloth descended over her head, blinding her. Her wrists were seized in an iron grip, and someone clutched her waist and began to force her back along the road.

Gwendeline struggled and tried to scream. The cloth stifled her cries, but she found she could hinder her attacker's movements, if not break his hold. She kicked wildly and managed to stop their progress down the road. Then she heard a hoarse voice call, "Here. Help me with this wildcat." Another set of footsteps approached, Gwendeline felt a sharp blow on her head, and she knew no more.

When she awoke, Gwendeline was alone, lying across the rear seat of an unmoving post chaise. Her wrists were bound behind her, and a scarf tied across her mouth; her head ached where she had been hit. Though she was frightened, she was also angry. She managed to pull herself into a sitting position in the coach. Her feet hadn't been tied, but someone had taken her cloak. Heavy rain beat against the windows of the chaise, and the night was pitch black. Gwendeline peered out the window nearest her, trying to see where she was, but the rain and darkness obscured everything. She was just about to try to jump from the coach when the door opened and a man got in. He sat down across from her and threw off his streaming cloak.

"So you're awake at last," said Mr. Blane. Gwendeline glared at him. He reached for her, and Gwendeline shrank back into the corner of the vehicle. "I mean only to remove your gag," he said, smiling unpleasantly. "You see I do not repeat the mistake of leaving a reluctant lady free to ask help of some officious passerby." He untied the knot in the scarf and pulled it free, caressing Gwendeline's neck with cold fingers as he did so. Gwendeline shuddered.

"There," he said. "Now we can be comfortable." The chaise started moving, and Mr. Blane cocked his head. "Ah, the fresh horses. We paused at a small inn to change the team," he told the girl. "I'd have preferred to stay the night there with you, but I feared we might be interrupted so close to Penwyn. I plan to give you my full attention later." He smiled again.

"Where are you taking me?" asked Gwendeline, her voice trembling with anger and fright.

"It happens I have a house about halfway back to London. We're going there for a short stay. Not so elegant as the town houses you've frequented, perhaps, but it will be quite cozy. Then, we might go on to Paris, if you like. I haven't really decided."

"I won't go anywhere with you," Gwendeline hissed. "I demand you let me out of this carriage immediately!"

"In the rain?" said Mr. Blane with mock surprise. "Without your cloak, which I must apologize for having left behind on the road?" His voice hardened. "No, my dear, we're going to travel together for some time. At least until your whining irritates me too much. Then I'll let you go. Perhaps I'll return you to Lord Merryn. Do you think he, or I should say he and his charming intended, will welcome you then?" He grinned. "I fancy not."

"You are despicable," said Gwendeline, turning away from him. "I'll get away from you somehow."

"Yes?" answered Blane politely. "I think not. However, it is cheering to find that you have a bit of your mother's fiery spirit after all. Perhaps you'll be more sport than I dared hope."

"My mother!" said Gwendeline. "You dare to mention her to me? But then, it's all of a piece, your behavior to both of us."

"Ah. I see my dear Lady Merryn's abominable scribblings have reached even you. And I can see that you believe the whole rigamarole. Alas." He shrugged. "But I admit it adds a certain piquancy to this little adventure. I think you'll like Paris; your mother did." He reached out and flicked her cheek with his finger; Gwendeline twisted out of reach. "At any rate, it is of no consequence, because London is decidedly tiresome lately. Society is so gullible that most believe the harpy's story. I feel the need of a change."

"If it's all a rigamarole, as you say, why not stand

up in London and deny it. Someone would believe you, I daresay."

"You should not try sarcasm, Gwendeline," he replied. "You are really not skillful. I do not choose to do anything so dull. I prefer to travel for a time and return to town when the story is forgotten. As it will be. And now I shall try to sleep. You should also. We'll be driving through the night and well into tomorrow. Lovemaking in a chaise is deucedly awkward, but I promise you better quarters tomorrow. You'll want to be rested." He grinned at her horrified look, then wrapped himself in a fur rug and reclined in the corner of the chaise. In a short time, he had dozed off.

Gwendeline didn't fall asleep. Her arms and head ached, and she was very frightened. By the time the sky began to lighten, she was nearly desperate. She had struggled frantically with the ropes that bound her wrists but succeeded only in chafing her arms. Mr. Blane had wakened briefly at every stop through the night, and she knew he would soon rise for the day. She was ready to throw herself from the moving coach, if only she could escape detection. But the ropes held fast, and with her arms bound, she couldn't open the door.

Blane woke soon after, but he was rather morose until they stopped once more for a fresh team and he got out of the chaise to wash and have breakfast. He retied the scarf before leaving, saying, "I do apologize for this indignity, my dear, but as I said, I've learned my lesson about talkative ladies." When he was gone, Gwendeline tried repeatedly to reach the door handles and force the chaise door open. If she could manage only to fall out on the ground, she thought, surely her condition would attract some help. But she had no success, and all too soon Mr. Blane returned and they were moving again.

He removed her gag and offered her some tea from a flask and some bread and butter. She refused at first, then realized that weakness from hunger was the last thing she wished to feel now. He untied her hands to let her eat; it was an immense relief to have them unbound, though her muscles were cramped and stiff.

"We're on the last stage before reaching my house," Blane said. "So these regrettable measures are surely no longer necessary." He handed her her breakfast. "There you are. Isn't this cozy?"

"How did you find me?" asked Gwendeline abruptly. She had done a good deal of thinking during the long night.

"Now, that is a fascinating coincidence," he answered. "I was attending one of the dullest of evening parties in the history of the *ton* when I suddenly heard your name mentioned in a group behind me. The insufferable Mr. Woodley was telling one of his interminable anecdotes. It seems he had been to visit a well-known artist…"

"Mr. Ames," Gwendeline burst out. "Oh, no."

"Precisely." Blane smiled at her. "And Mr. Ames had mentioned a delightful new pupil he had met with in the country. It was no great matter to find out where he lived. Art lessons! I should never have thought it of you. Is this Ames very romantic and charming?"

Gwendeline ignored this. She was thinking furiously. "Then everyone probably knows," she said to herself.

"Yes, I imagine you're right," he replied. "Exactly why our journey has been so hurried, my dear. I had no wish to be interfered with again." His eyes narrowed and his expression was frightening as he looked at Gwendeline. "Do not expect it. No one knows of this house of mine or where I've gone. You will not be found until I wish it." Gwendeline shrank away, and he laughed unpleasantly. "And after all, my dear, you've already spent a night alone with me. In society's eyes you're ruined. Why not give up this obstinacy and let us enjoy ourselves?" He moved as if to take Gwendeline in his arms, and she drew as far from him as possible in the coach. She clutched the opposite door handle and prepared to throw herself out.

Mr. Blane grasped her wrist. "No, no. You mustn't do yourself harm. Perhaps you're right. It will be more comfortable to wait until we reach the house. Sit back and relax." He exerted an irresistible pressure on her wrist and forced Gwendeline back onto the seat. "There we are."

There was no further conversation for some time, and soon Mr. Blane began looking out the window expectantly. Not long after, the chaise turned off the road into a lane, and a few miles farther on, they turned once again, entering a hedge-lined drive. Almost immediately, they pulled up before a low stone house. The building was surrounded by a high wall, its yard and garden very small. Ivy covered it, giving it a dark and forbidding appearance, and it was not in the best of repair.

Mr. Blane got out and turned to offer a hand to Gwendeline. She shrank back. "You may as well step down," he said. "I'll certainly drag you out if you don't."

Furious but helpless, Gwendeline stepped down. Mr. Blane was looking about the yard with annoyance. The house looked deserted; the shutters were up and the front door firmly shut.

"Where is that cursed woman?" he muttered. He strode over to the door and began to knock sharply with his stick, but this brought no results. "Go round to the back," he said to the burly individual on the box. "See if the door is open there."

"And 'oo'll 'old these 'orses?" he replied sullenly.

"Leave them," snapped Mr. Blane. "They're tired, not likely to bolt."

Grumbling, the driver climbed down and disappeared around the corner of the house. Soon, they heard noises within. There was a crash of crockery and a yell. Then the driver opened the front door. "She's in the kitchen," he said, pointing back down the hall with his thumb. "Shot the cat, she 'as." And with this enigmatic phrase, he returned to his seat on the chaise.

"Damn!" Blane exclaimed. He grasped Gwendeline's arm above the elbow and hustled her down the passage. At its end was the kitchen. It was indescribably filthy; dirty pots and crockery littered every flat surface, and dust had accumulated on many of them on top of dried food. In the middle of the room was a large kitchen table, and a woman was slumped over this, her head pillowed on her arms. Several empty gin bottles stood in front of her.

Releasing Gwendeline, Blane strode over and took hold of the woman's hair. Pulling her head up, he slapped her sharply several times, but this produced no visible effect. He looked about the room and finally discovered a pitcher of water among the pots. Lifting her head again, he dashed it in her face.

This raised some incoherent sputtering, but the woman didn't really wake. Gwendeline didn't know whether she was glad or sorry for this. The woman seemed unlikely to help her. Her bright yellow silk dress was encrusted with all manner of unidentifiable substances. Her frizzled hair was red with streaks of gray, and her face was seamed with wrinkles and plastered with rouge.

With an oath, Mr. Blane gave up his attempts to revive her. He seemed at a loss for a moment, then he grabbed Gwendeline's arm again and dragged her out through the hall and up the narrow cramped staircase. Gwendeline tried to fight him, fearing she knew what he intended, but he shook her impatiently saying, "Come along; you don't think I shall attempt lovemaking in this filth." When they reached the upstairs hall, Blane shoved her into a room off it, slammed the door, and locked it. Gwendeline heard the key turn. The sound of his footsteps retreated back down the stairs.

Her first thought was escape. The small, rather shabby bedchamber had no carpet, and the coverlet on the bed and the curtains were dirty and worn. But the windows were what interested her. She rushed to the two small apertures in the far wall, but they were tiny—mere ventilators set below the eaves. There was no possibility of squeezing through. Bitterly disappointed, Gwendeline turned away. She tried the door for form's sake, but as expected, it was securely locked. There was no other avenue of escape in the room. Besides the bed, there was a small round table holding a candlestick and a straight chair. Gwendeline collapsed in the chair. She was trapped.

A short while later, she heard the post chaise drive away, then there was nothing but silence. Gwendeline sat trembling with tension and fright for some time. But when there was no sound, her sleepless night began to catch up with her. She fought drowsiness and succeeded for a while. But finally her head sank onto her crossed arms on the table, and she slept.

Thirteen

GWENDELINE WAKENED WITH A START TO THE SOUND of pounding and a rasping voice calling, "'Ere, who locked this door?" She was furious with herself for sleeping and leaped up immediately. The room was unchanged; it appeared no one had entered, and she wondered where Mr. Blane had gone. She crossed to the door as the pounding continued, undecided whether to answer or stay quiet. Finally, she called, "I cannot open the door; I'm locked in." Silence fell and lasted so long that Gwendeline became frightened.

"It's the young 'oman," the voice said at last and chuckled. "Bless me, I forgot." Footsteps retreated, then returned after a few minutes. The key turned in the lock, and the door opened to reveal the woman from the kitchen swaying in the doorway. Gwendeline backed away a few steps.

The woman looked her over. "A pretty one," she said. "But then they're generally pretty. What a fine dress that is. Hello, dearie. My name is Calkins, Mrs. Calkins. Welcome to ye." She grinned, revealing several gaps among her teeth.

"Oh please," said Gwendeline. "Won't you help me? I must get away from here. If you will only let me leave the house, you need do no more."

"Say," answered Mrs. Calkins, frowning, "you talk like a regular toff. Where did he find you, then?"

Gwendeline threw back her head. "My name is Gwendeline Gregory. I am the daughter of Baron Gregory of Brooklands." She tried to sound confident and impressive. "And Mr. Blane has kidnapped me, a very serious crime. If you do not wish to be implicated also, you'll help me to escape."

The effect of this speech was not what Gwendeline had hoped. Mrs. Calkins looked frightened, indeed, but she simply exclaimed. "Lordy, a baron!" and slammed the door, locking it again. Gwendeline heard her return to the kitchen, and the clink of glass followed soon after.

Gwendeline thought of calling to Mrs. Calkins, but she had no money to offer her, and the promise of payment in the future didn't seem likely to lure her. If only there was some way of getting out of the house, she thought desperately, she could hide and make her way to some refuge after dark. The sound of carriage wheels entering the yard came to her ears. Blane, returning! Gwendeline grasped the brass candlestick on the table and moved over behind the door.

At first, nothing happened. There was pounding on the front door, and Mrs. Calkins's footsteps going to it. Then Gwendeline heard loud angry voices and the clattering of pots in the kitchen. This was followed by silence, then a quieter conversation. Gwendeline strained her ears, but she could catch none of the words. Finally, a man's footsteps ascended the stairs. Gwendeline took a deep breath and tightened her hold on the candlestick. She felt as if she could kill Mr. Blane and feel no guilt.

The key turned in the lock, and the door began to open. Gathering all her courage, Gwendeline rushed from behind it and struck the man whose hand was on the knob a sharp blow on the head. He fell heavily to the floor. "My dear Gwendeline," said the Earl of Merryn from the hall, "if you've killed Andrew, what are we to tell my mother?"

With a cry, Gwendeline sank to her knees, for she had indeed struck Major St. Audley rather than Blane. "Oh God, what have I done!" she said and burst into frantic tears.

The earl bent to place a hand on her shoulder. "It's all right. You didn't hit him nearly hard enough to kill him. It was a poorly timed joke. Forgive me, Gwendeline."

But her tears had been building for nearly twenty-four hours, and she couldn't stop them. Lord Merryn put his other hand on her hair, and they remained thus for a moment. Then his face twisted and he pulled her to her feet. "Gwendeline, Gwendeline," he repeated and pulled her into his arms.

She could think of nothing but how safe it felt to be pressed to his chest. She cried even harder as he stroked her hair and murmured comforting phrases. After a while, her sobs began to subside. She sniffed and looked up at him. "I am s-sorry," she stammered. "I've been so frightened."

He nodded, showing no signs of letting her go. "I know. I only wish we might have reached you sooner.

When I thought of you in the hands of that scoundrel, I was nearly beside myself. Thank God you are all right. He didn't hurt you?"

Gwendeline shook her head, looking down. His arms tightened around her. "Thank God for that."

There was so much feeling in his voice that she involuntarily looked up at him again, and the expression she saw in his eyes then made her heart beat fast. "Oh, Gwendeline," he said again. "What a fool I've been." Before she could ask what he meant, there was a low groan from the floor.

"Major St. Audley," cried Gwendeline. The earl released her, and she fell to her knees. "I'm so sorry. Please forgive me. I hope I didn't hurt you terribly."

"No, no," said the major from the floor. "Only stunned me for a moment. My head is much too hard to be cracked by a blow like that. And very plucky it was. I'll be perfectly fine directly."

The earl bent to help his brother up and seated him on the bed. He checked his head and pronounced it unwounded. Gwendeline found that her knees were trembling and she sat down on the chair. Watching the earl minister to his brother, she could think of nothing but the feel of his arms around her. But when he turned and smiled tenderly at her, she remembered that he was engaged to Adele Greene, and a cold lump spread from her stomach. How could he have held her that way and looked at her so when he was to marry someone else? She'd been mistaken. He'd been comforting her, being merely kind, and she'd misunderstood because of her love for him. She must be more careful to mask her feelings in future.

Lord Merryn helped his brother to his feet, and Gwendeline rose also. "I fear we must ask you to travel a little farther, Gwendeline," said the earl. "I think it would be best for you to leave before Blane returns."

All thoughts of love left her mind in an instant. "Yes," she said. "Oh, we must get away. There is a woman in the kitchen. You must have seen her?"

"We did," replied Lord Merryn grimly. "She won't trouble you further."

"Did…did you kill her?" asked Gwendeline, for the earl's eyes were chilling.

This drew a laugh from the major. "We did not," he said, "but you seem more worried about her welfare than about mine." Ruefully, he rubbed a large lump forming on his head.

"No, no, I'm so sorry I hit you."

"Let us save recriminations for the journey," interrupted the earl. "Shall we go down?"

There was a post-chaise in the yard, along with several riding horses and a group of men. The major escorted Gwendeline to the chaise and handed her in, while the earl went to speak to one of the group. "What's happening?" Gwendeline asked Major St. Audley.

"We brought constables," he answered. "Mr. Blane will be arrested." He walked over to confer with his brother, and soon, they returned together.

"One of us will come with you, Gwendeline," said the earl. "What do you think, Andrew? Do you feel well enough to stay and manage this business?"

"Of course," replied the major. "What do you think I am made of, spun glass?"

Lord Merryn laughed. "Well, then I will take

Gwendeline to the inn." He started to climb into the chaise, smiling at Gwendeline. The look tore her heart, and before she thought, she said, "Alone, my lord? In a closed carriage? Whatever will Adele say when she finds out?"

Her tone drew a surprised look from Major St. Audley, but Gwendeline's gaze was focused painfully on the earl. Would he deny the engagement? But he merely raised his eyebrows, then smiled sardonically. "What indeed?" he replied. "A telling point, Gwendeline. Andrew, perhaps you should ride beside Miss Gregory's carriage. That should be unexceptionable, should it not?" He looked at Gwendeline. "As a free man I suppose he may ride beside you?"

The major looked from one to the other of them, but neither noticed him. Dismayed at the effect of her impulsive remark, and deeply ashamed for having made it, Gwendeline could only nod and pull her head back into the chaise. The earl strode away.

The major shrugged. "Very well. I shall accompany you to a respectable inn out on the main road not far from here. We sent a messenger to your friend Miss Brown last night, and we hope she may be arriving there soon. In any case, I shall stay to escort you both to London." He walked over to his horse and mounted. "Goodbye, Alex," he called. "We'll meet in London." The earl turned to bow distantly to Gwendeline, then resumed his conversation with the head constable.

Gwendeline wished she might speak to him again, but the chaise began to move, and they rode out of the yard and away. She had no chance even to thank him.

By the time they reached the inn, her fright and exhaustion had caught up with her, and she was near collapse. Miss Brown had not yet arrived, but Gwendeline was taken up to a comfortable bed-chamber and brought hot water. She undressed and washed, pulling on a nightgown borrowed from the landlady's daughter. Gwendeline got into bed and was instantly asleep.

She didn't wake until the morning sun came through the curtains and fell across her bed. Then she sat up, stretched, and luxuriated in her relief. It was like waking after a long nightmare. The sunshine and cheerful room roused a deep gratitude in her, and she felt more glad to be alive than she had for months. Jumping out of bed, she found that a trunk containing her things had been brought in. She put on a fresh gown, wondering if she would ever be able to bear the one crumpled in the corner again. It would always remind her of Blane.

Downstairs, she found that Miss Brown had arrived and was sitting at breakfast with Andrew St. Audley. Seeing her, the older woman rose and came to hug her. "Oh, Gwendeline," she exclaimed. "Thank God you're all right. I was frantic with worry."

Gwendeline smiled at her. "I am all right," she said. "I feel splendid." She eyed the breakfast table. "But hungry," she added. The others laughed.

"That is easily remedied," replied the major. Soon, she was seated and eating hungrily. "If you ladies will excuse me for a moment," the major went on, "I want to check on my horse. He's very particular about his food." When he'd left them together, Gwendeline poured out the whole story of her abduction. Miss Brown was horrified, outraged, and astounded. She could hardly believe in such villainy. "So he is arrested, and I am glad," finished Gwendeline. "I don't care if they hang him."

"Gwendeline!"

"Well, he deserves it, almost. But let's not talk of him. How did the earl and the major find me? Do you know?"

Miss Brown nodded. "It seems Mr. Woodley is acquainted with Mr. Ames." Gwendeline nodded. "And the former told Lady Merryn of Ames's new pupil and where you were. Then, Lillian Everly received your letter, and everyone looked forward to your arrival. But the earl had seen Blane talking to Mr. Woodley at some length, by no means a usual occurrence I gather, and he became concerned. He went to call on Blane the next morning and found he had gone out of town mysteriously. Lord Merryn made some inquiries. He evidently had some knowledge of that house from the past." Miss Brown paused, but Gwendeline nodded again. "And thus, he arranged your rescue."

"And very dashing it was, don't you think?" put in the major, who returned to the room at that moment. "Of course, I cut a rather poor figure, floored by the damsel in distress, but otherwise it was highly romantic."

"Yes," agreed Gwendeline. "And I'm so very grateful to you. Is Lord Merryn… Does he go straight back to London?"

"Yes," he answered. "He wished to make certain Blane's arrest is handled properly. I've never seen him so angry." There was a short silence, then he continued. "I came back to discuss our plans," he said. "The landlady wishes to know whether we'll be staying long." He grinned. "She's in quite a flurry. I take it this inn is not much frequented by 'gentry and such.'"

Miss Brown smiled. "Perhaps I should speak to her. You'll wish to rest a few days, Gwendeline?"

"No, I want to get to London as soon as possible."

"Bravo!" said Major St. Audley. "That's the spirit."

"Are you sure?" asked Miss Brown doubtfully. "After what you've been through…"

"Really," said Gwendeline, "I'm perfectly recovered. Can we leave today?"

Major St. Audley laughed and jumped up. "I'll inquire," he said, and went out.

They were on their way by noon and expected to reach London the following evening. The major rode with the two ladies in the chaise for part of the journey, keeping them in high spirits with his flow of stories and anecdotes. Gwendeline decided he was a thoroughly likable young man, though not as exciting as his brother. It appeared that he had seen a good deal of Lillian Everly since that first afternoon. "How is Lillian?" Gwendeline asked him. "I've missed her very much."

"And she you," he answered. "She was overjoyed when your letter arrived. I've seldom seen her so happy as when she showed it to me."

"Oh, did she show it to you?"

"Yes, well, that is, I'd called, you know, and she naturally wished my family to have the news."

"You've spent a lot of time with Lillian this season?"

"Not so much," he floundered. "That is, some,

but…" He paused. "Dash it, Miss Gregory. I've been in love with Lillian Everly for more than a year. I wanted to ask her to marry me last season, but her parents gave me to understand that it would not be allowed. Nothing against me or my family, but they're looking higher than a younger son with a commission in the army. Can't blame them; Lillian has a large fortune. So I never spoke to her. I took that assignment abroad, thinking to forget. It was no use, of course." He stopped and seemed to recollect himself. "I shouldn't have said any of that. I apologize and hope you will keep my confidence. I have been driven nearly mad in these last weeks, seeing Miss Everly almost every day and not telling her how I feel."

"But you should tell her," said Gwendeline. "Surely her parents couldn't refuse if you truly love one another."

Major St. Audley smiled thinly. "No? But I won't ask her to defy her parents. They're right. I have nothing to offer her. It would be her money, and society would call me a fortune hunter." His mouth hardened. "And I have no assurance that Lillian cares for me. Sometimes I think…but I don't know."

Gwendeline kept her views on Lillian's feelings to herself. "Well, you'll never know unless you tell her how you feel," she said. "I think you're foolish to delay."

"Gwendeline," put in Miss Brown.

"It's all right," said the major. "I daresay you're right, but I must do as I think best."

"It's what your brother did, after all, isn't it?" Gwendeline continued daringly. "When he found he cared for someone, he told her immediately and became engaged." She waited for his reply with muscles tense.

He made a face. "Oh, Alex," he replied. "I find that situation incredible. And so does my mother. That girl is…" He pressed his lips together. "I shouldn't say anything about it. In any case, it has no bearing on my position. No sane parent would refuse Alex permission to marry his daughter. I'm not so eligible." He was silent after that. When they next stopped to change horses, he mounted his own and rode behind them.

Gwendeline received a brief scolding for her part in the conversation, but that didn't keep her from resolving to find out Lillian's opinion of the major. If she cared for him, Gwendeline was determined to find some way of uniting them. Her own happiness was ruined, but Lillian's shouldn't be.

They slept that night on the road and continued early the next morning. The day passed slowly, and all of them grew tired. Finally, late in the evening, they reached London. The major escorted them to Gwendeline's house. They bid him farewell with gratitude, and he promised to call the next day.

Inside, they found a gala welcome. Reeves was jovial; Ellen was crying noisily in her joy. And Alphonse came up from the kitchen to caper hilariously about the hall. In addition, they found flowers everywhere, and notes from Lady Merryn and Lillian. The first insisted they come to dinner the following day. Lillian expressed her gladness at their return and promised to call at the first opportunity.

Gwendeline fell into an armchair in the drawing room, touched and very happy. It was good to be back, she thought, and at this moment, she had to believe that everything would work out for the best.

Fourteen

THE CALLERS BEGAN AS EARLY AS POSSIBLE THE NEXT morning. Most simply left cards, as Gwendeline had told Reeves she was not in save to a few close friends. There was much to be done to the house, her wardrobe, and her state of mind before she faced curious acquaintances. Lillian Everly was the first visitor to be admitted; Miss Brown had disappeared belowstairs hours ago and was supervising a thorough cleaning.

"Gwendeline!" cried Lillian when she entered the room, giving Reeves no time to announce her. Gwendeline rose to meet her hug. "Oh, it's so good to see you again. How unkind you were to go off without a word!"

Gwendeline hung her head. "No one could scold me as much as I have myself. If only I'd stayed for some explanation of that day's events."

Lillian nodded. "We were all so worried about you. No one had any idea where you could have gone. Lord Merryn made all sorts of inquiries but could find out nothing."

"Did he? We went to a place Miss Brown knows, a

lovely little seaside town." She proceeded to tell Lillian the full story of her flight and residence in Penwyn.

"So Lady Merryn's book really made you return? She'll be so pleased!" Lillian smiled mischievously. "If she can be any more pleased. She's created a sensation, you know, and society is positively lionizing her."

Gwendeline laughed. "Well, I'm certainly grateful to her for writing it, though it's a very sad story, of course." She didn't mention the role of Lord Merryn's engagement in her return. "We're to dine there this evening. I expect we'll hear all about it. And I must thank her for portraying Mr. Blane in his true colors." This came out rather fiercely.

Lillian agreed. "He's gone out of town, Gwendeline. So you needn't fear to see him. He'll never really be accepted in polite society again, I should say."

Gwendeline looked at her, astonished. "But, then, you don't know?"

"Know what?" asked Lillian.

"I...I somehow thought that you'd been told of Major St. Audley's journey and its purpose."

Lillian flushed. "Major St. Audley? Has he left London again? He didn't tell me." She looked rather vexed.

Gwendeline hesitated. Should the story of her abduction be kept from everyone? The St. Audleys had evidently thought so. But when she looked into Lillian's puzzled eyes, she felt that she must tell her. And so, she related the whole history of her kidnapping and rescue.

Lillian was shocked and astounded. "Oh, Gwendeline," she said, taking the other girl's hand, "how glad I am that you're safe. What a horrible experience!"

"I need not tell you that this isn't to be repeated. Much as Mr. Blane deserves public exposure, I don't wish it known."

"Of course," said Lillian. "I'm sure that no one will hear of it. Lord Merryn somehow managed to keep the events of our ride that afternoon completely secret, and even fewer people know of this."

"He has recently become engaged, I understand," said Gwendeline with studied unconcern.

Lillian frowned. "Did you see the notice? It seems so, but it has puzzled many people. Adele doesn't seem the sort of girl he would choose." Lillian smiled and shrugged. "But one often thinks that of one's acquaintances. It's certainly true that they're engaged. Adele has become intolerably conceited."

"Ah," answered Gwendeline. She'd hoped for some better answer.

"I've nearly decided to remain single," Lillian went on. "When I see how unhappy so many married people are, it quite discourages me."

Diverted from her own problems, Gwendeline studied her friend carefully. "Oh, Lillian," she said. "Among all your suitors you'll surely find one who will make you happy."

Lillian grimaced. "My mother believes me to have done so. The Duke of Craigbourne has been particular in his attentions of late, and Mother has hopes he may offer for me."

"And are you fond of him?" asked Gwendeline.

"What has that to do with marriage? He's very rich and has rank and position. If he's rather fat and twenty years older than I, what concern of mine is that?"

Lillian seemed close to tears suddenly. "I don't know what I'll do if he comes to the point."

"You must refuse him, of course," answered Gwendeline indignantly. "He sounds completely unsuitable."

Lillian laughed, though her eyes were damp. "Oh, Gwendeline, I'm so glad you're back. Perhaps with you here, I could even summon the courage to do so."

"Of course you will," Gwendeline replied. "He must be perfectly horrid."

"No," admitted the other girl. "He's not horrid. He's a kind and jolly man. I fancy I could like him if I didn't have to consider marrying him." She sighed. "My parents, particularly my mother, have been so good to me and given me so much that other young girls are denied. I don't think I could bear to disobey and disappoint them in this matter." She paused, looking sad. "And it's not as if I've been asked by someone I love."

Gwendeline spoke carefully. "Major St. Audley talked of you on our journey. It seems you've seen quite a bit of each other this season." She plunged recklessly on in spite of Lillian's blush and averted head. "He's a charming man."

"The major is quite charming," answered Lillian tonelessly. "But he hardly enters into a discussion of marriage. He's completely uninterested in the subject and the state."

"Indeed?" asked Gwendeline. "What makes you say that?"

Lillian was looking out the window. "Oh, a group of us were talking of marriage, joking you know, at a ball some weeks ago. Major St. Audley stated very positively that he did not expect to marry for a long time, if ever." Her expression hardened. "Obviously, he cares for no one but himself."

"Perhaps he wishes to make his fortune before he marries." She tried to speak lightly and yet seriously, but Lillian didn't appear to understand.

"In the army?" she replied scornfully. "No, his chief interest is his own pleasure. Let's talk of something else. Lord Wanley has also published a book, you know."

Gwendeline allowed the conversation to be diverted. "Has he? Poetry, of course?"

Lillian nodded, smiling. "Very poor poetry. And very embarrassing. He used all those awful things about me. Everyone is most amused."

Gwendeline laughed. "Poor Lillian. You remain the nymph."

The other girl made a wry face. "It's excessively silly. But at least he's been kept so busy that he stopped offering for me quite so often. He paid for publication himself, and the printer is encouraging him to do another. They say his mother is furious. Oh, and Gwendeline, I nearly forgot. An old friend of yours has undergone a complete change of character."

"Who?" asked Gwendeline.

Lillian's eyes twinkled. "Mr. Horton. He's become one of the leading lights of the dandy set. He looks absurd, but then, all of them do."

"What happened to him, I wonder?"

"He began receiving much more notice after I discreetly made his financial circumstances known, but I can't say what led him to change. He is paying marked attentions to Alicia Holloway. An interesting announcement is expected momentarily."

Gwendeline dissolved into laughter. "Oh, it's good to be back. I haven't laughed so since I left London."

Lillian smiled at her. "I hope that will keep you here with us. It's been very flat without you." She squeezed Gwendeline's hand, then rose. "I must go. I promised to meet my mother in Bond Street. She wishes me to have a new gown for the Duchess of Craigbourne's ball. It closes the season, and will be very brilliant."

When Lillian had gone, Gwendeline sat by her drawing room window, pensive. She believed Lillian had shown signs of feeling for Major St. Audley. Something must be done, she thought.

Gwendeline spent the rest of the day on household chores, seeing no other callers. As she was going upstairs to dress for dinner, she met Miss Brown coming down. "I'm still not certain I should accompany you to Lady Merryn's this evening," her former governess said. "She invited me to be polite but…"

"Nonsense," interrupted Gwendeline. "Of course you'll come. You'll be obliged to go everywhere with me now that I've set up in my own house, Brown. You cannot escape and may as well get used to it."

Miss Brown smiled. "I'm sure you can find other chaperones, but I'll come this once if you wish it. I admit I'm rather curious to meet a real novelist."

Gwendeline took pains with her appearance that evening. Not only was it her first venture into society since her return, but she expected to see Lord Merryn as well. She wished to thank him, but chiefly she wished to find out more about his engagement. To gather the courage to do that, she needed to look her best. She put on a pale green gown trimmed with French braid and threaded a green ribbon through her curls. She'd purchased the dress just before her abrupt departure and had never worn it.

She met Miss Brown in the hall and together they descended to the coach waiting to take them to the countess's house. Miss Brown looked well in a lavender silk gown with lace at the throat and seemed pleased when Gwendeline complimented her on it. They arrived a few minutes early. Gwendeline hoped to have an opportunity to greet Lady Merryn and talk with her before any other guests arrived. They found the countess and her younger son in the drawing room, and Lady Merryn rushed up to Gwendeline and hugged her. "Oh, my dear," she cried, "you cannot know how glad I am to have you back! Andrew has told me something of the horrors you endured. Why didn't you stay here with me?" She paused as if struck by some idea. "What a novel it would make," she finished.

"Mother," began the major warningly.

"Of course, I should never write such a book, but the story is very exciting."

"Only in a novel, I assure you, Lady Merryn. To live through it was not at all romantic."

"Of course not, you poor darling," agreed the countess. "You must have been terrified."

"Not too terrified to hit me a sharp crack with a candlestick," put in Major St. Audley.

Lady Merryn nodded approvingly. "Very courageous of her, too," she said. "I hope I should have done just the same in her situation."

"I beg your pardon, Mother," protested her son. "But I hope you would not."

"You know what I mean, Andrew. Don't be a ninny." The major held up his hands in mock defense.

Lillian entered then, followed by a footman with a note for Lady Merryn. She read it as the others greeted the new arrival. "Oh dear," said the countess. "This is dreadful news."

"What is it?" asked the major quickly.

"It's from Alex," the countess went on. "He says…" She paused, glancing uncertainly at Lillian Everly.

"I've told Lillian everything," Gwendeline put in.

Lady Merryn nodded. "Alex says that Blane has gotten away across the Channel. They waited for him at that dreadful house, but he never returned. Someone must have warned him. They set off to take him too late, he reached the coast and went on to France." She looked up from the note. "Alex will not be able to dine tonight," she added anticlimactically.

Gwendeline was disappointed to hear that she wouldn't see Lord Merryn, perhaps more disappointed than by the news of Blane's escape. Lady Merryn rose and rang the bell. The butler appeared in the doorway. "Tell the cook to serve dinner, Allison," the countess said, and he bowed and disappeared.

Their mood lifted a little over dinner. The major took the head of the table and made a great many jokes about his luck in dining alone with so many lovely ladies. Everyone but Lillian seemed amused by his chatter, though Gwendeline couldn't summon any real high spirits.

Lady Merryn talked enthusiastically of her novel. It

had been read by all society, and everyone was talking of it. "I'd already begun a society novel, as you know, Gwendeline. But when you left I wished to do something. I knew many of the true particulars of your mother's life, since I had joined Alex occasionally in helping her, so I determined to write it all without telling anyone. I hoped the novel might reach you when letters were impossible." The countess looked smug. "My books circulate very widely, you know. With a small amount of alteration, my early chapters were made to fit, then it was just a matter of finishing. Very easy and a great deal of fun." She looked thoughtful. "In fact, I may switch to that sort of novel entirely." She smiled at the company. "At any rate, I succeeded in bringing Gwendeline back to London and eased everyone's minds. I'm very pleased with myself."

"As we have noticed, Mother," answered the major.

"Well, I'm very grateful," said Gwendeline. "You repaired my foolish mistake, for which I sincerely apologize to all. I was so relieved when I read your book, though the story was sad."

Lady Merryn nodded. "Yes, poor Annabella was never very happy after she married. It was most unfortunate. She was such a lively, beautiful girl." This remark sobered the group once again, and soon after, Gwendeline and Miss Brown took their leave. They were home by ten and in bed early. Gwendeline lay awake for a while, thinking of her mother, the whereabouts of Mr. Blane, the earl, and other things. She felt that a great deal of resolution would be required of her if things were to be set right. As she fell asleep, she determined to have it.

Invitations began to arrive the next day. Gwendeline had returned just in time for the final whirl of parties that would close the season, and she found herself with a choice of several outings for most evenings during the next three weeks. Brown was overwhelmed by the number of gilt-edged cards that came in the post each day. "But Gwendeline," she protested, "We won't have a night at home. I simply can't accompany you to all of these." She indicated the pile of cards.

"Oh yes you can, Brown. And you must have some evening dresses. Shall we go shopping today? I would like a new gown for the Duchess of Craigbourne's ball."

"You mustn't buy clothing for me," replied Miss Brown.

"Nonsense," said Gwendeline. "Of course I shall. I can't have my chaperone looking less splendid than the others, especially when she is so much nicer."

"You should go with Lady Merryn. She knows how to manage these affairs."

"No, Brown, I don't want to be chaperoned by Lady Merryn. I don't want to depend on the family now that Lord Merryn is engaged."

Gwendeline eventually won this argument, and they went out shopping later that day. They ordered several gowns suitable for an older woman in society, and Gwendeline ordered an exquisite ball gown of white crepe embroidered with tiny blue flowers and green leaves. Seed pearls formed the center of each flower, and the dress had tiny puffed sleeves and a narrow blue sash. Gwendeline fell in love with the pattern as soon as she saw it.

They returned home for tea laden with parcels

and tired out. They were engaged to attend a musical evening after an early dinner, and thus had to go up to change almost immediately. A celebrated singer was to perform for a "select" group which, Gwendeline thought, meant everyone in the *ton* who could be got to come and hear her.

As they walked up the staircase to their hostess later that evening, she could hear the buzz of conversation from the crowded room beyond. She felt a little nervous at the thought of facing so many curious questioners. They entered the room without mishap, however, and for some time Gwendeline was kept busy explaining her long absence from town in the middle of the season. She'd already decided to say that she had been exhausted from the rigors of constant socializing and in need of a rest. Many inquisitive ladies appeared to find this explanation incredible; they seemed to believe that the embarrassment attendant on publication of Lady Merryn's book had routed her. Gwendeline allowed this story, seeing in it a plausible excuse and a way of discouraging further questions. But she firmly denied any estrangement between herself and the countess. She'd moved, she insisted, only because the time set for her visit was over. The gossips had to be satisfied; they got no other tale from Gwendeline and Miss Brown.

The chief attraction of the evening, Madame Carrini, was delayed, and the hostess fluttered about looking harassed. Gwendeline waved to Lady Merryn, who had come in and been immediately surrounded by a large group of admirers. She was about to make her way across the room to Lillian, similarly encompassed, when she heard a man's voice behind her say "Good evening, Miss Gregory. I hope you are well."

Gwendeline turned to find a stranger confronting her. He was an unprepossessing young man, slight and brown-haired, but this lack was offset by the magnificence of his attire. His bottle-green coat was hugely padded at the shoulders and nipped in to a wasp waist; its silver buttons were the size of sovereigns, and its tails nearly swept the floor. Skin-tight yellow pantaloons were buckled under his insteps, and his shirt-points were so stiff and high that it was clearly impossible for him to move his head. An awesomely intricate neckcloth and a waistcoat of startling brilliance, heavily encumbered with chains and fobs, completed the costume. "I beg your pardon," Gwendeline said.

"I inquired after your health," the stranger simpered. "You've been out of town this age."

As he spoke, Gwendeline suddenly recognized him. It was Mr. Horton, utterly transformed. "I'm well, thank you," she replied. "I hope you are also enjoying your customary good health."

"Tolerable good," he said, flicking an imaginary speck of dust from the sleeve of his coat. "I've been fagged to death by constant demands that I attend this rout or that dinner party. I declare I haven't spent an evening at home in weeks. So many of the hostesses insist they cannot do without me."

Gwendeline murmured something. "You must miss your evening reading."

Mr. Horton sighed. "Prodigiously. So fatiguing, you know. I often long for a quiet dinner alone and my books. Ah, you must excuse me." He gestured toward the far corner of the room, making sure Gwendeline saw the young lady signaling him to approach. "The heart calls." He laid his hand dramatically on his breast. "And I must obey."

"Of course," Gwendeline replied, trying to control her twitching lips. "Don't let me keep you." Mr. Horton turned and minced away, and Gwendeline allowed herself to smile.

"Your erstwhile suitor has changed a good deal," said Lord Merryn, joining her. Gwendeline jumped, and her heart began to beat very fast. She turned to him, looking up into his face. The earl looked magnificent. His coat and pantaloons were black, and this color accentuated the auburn of his hair and lightness of his gray eyes. There were touches of silver in his white silk waistcoat, and his cravat was a miracle of deceptive simplicity. He had no need of padding or ornaments to look splendid. "Yes," she replied. "I hardly knew him at first."

Returning her smile, he said, "Mr. Horton has blossomed in these past weeks. And found someone most willing to hear his addresses, I believe, as I told you he would." He nodded toward the corner where Horton and Alicia Holloway were deep in conversation.

"He made sure to let me see." She took a deep breath. "Several things have changed since I've been in London. I haven't yet properly congratulated you on your new state. We saw the notice in the *Morning Post* while still in Penwyn." Gwendeline paused, then went on daringly. "Miss Brown was much surprised. We—she had no notion you were planning such a step."

"Didn't she? Alas, one doesn't plan such events, does one? They seem to order themselves."

Gwendeline looked down. "I suppose so."

Lord Merryn watched her for a moment, amusement, admiration, and something else, more elusive, in his expression. When Gwendeline looked up again, he said, "Since Miss Brown is so concerned about me, you must fulfill your promise at last and make us known to each other."

"That's right. You haven't met. It seems so strange." She looked around the room. "There she is, sitting by the wall. Oh dear, she's not talking with anyone." They started across the room. "Miss Brown dislikes playing duenna and going into society."

"Does she?" replied the earl. "Well, I'm sure my mother would be happy to fill that position."

"No," Gwendeline said. "I prefer... That is, it's good for Brown." They approached this lady, who stood. "Lord Merryn, Miss Brown," Gwendeline continued.

"How do you do," said Lord Merryn. "I've tried to make your acquaintance for some time."

"How do you do," answered Miss Brown. "I'm happy to meet the man who has been so kind to Gwendeline and, indirectly, to me."

The earl bowed. "Gwendeline tells me that you're not fond of gatherings like this."

Miss Brown directed a sharp look at her charge. "It's true I prefer more quiet pursuits. I was never good at idle talk."

"Few worthy people are," replied the earl. "I dislike it myself." He smiled. "But you'll find the skill easy to acquire, I'm sure."

"Perhaps," said Miss Brown, doubtfully.

Gracefully, the earl turned the subject. "I understand that you both made an exalted acquaintance during your absence. Indeed, Gwendeline, we've been much impressed at his praise of your artistic abilities. You…"

"Here you are," a voice broke in. "I've been looking everywhere." Adele Greene stopped beside Lord Merryn and took his arm. "You must come meet my aunt. She's in London for a short time and eager to make your acquaintance."

The earl raised his eyebrows. "I'll be along in a moment. As you see, I'm talking with Miss Gregory and her friend, Miss Brown."

"Yes. How do you do, Miss Gregory. I'm pleased to see you back in London." Adele did not sound pleased. "You must come, Alex. My aunt is very particular about these matters." The earl's jaw tightened.

"I was just going to speak to Lillian Everly," said Gwendeline. "Shall we go?" she asked Miss Brown, who nodded.

"I hope we can talk at greater length on some other occasion, Miss Brown," said Merryn. "I'm pleased to have met you at last."

"Thank you," said Miss Brown. She nodded to Adele, who ignored her, and went with Gwendeline across the room.

"How tiresome," they heard Adele remark as they walked away. "Do come along now."

As they joined the group around Lillian, Miss Brown expressed shock at Adele's poor manners. For her part, Gwendeline was surprised by the sight of Lord Merryn being ordered about in such a way. Could he love Adele, she wondered. She had found

herself close to hating Adele Greene during the last
few minutes. What was to be done?

"You seem very far away tonight," Lillian said to her.

"I am thoughtful, I suppose," Gwendeline replied.

"Talking with Lord Merryn and Adele is enough to
make anyone think. About never marrying, I should
say. Do you know, they say there is betting at the clubs
on how long it will last. And everyone has his own
explanation of how it came about. Adele's appearance,
family, and fortune are all passable; indeed, her fortune
is excellent. But they are not such as to attract The
Unattainable. Speculation is rampant."

Gwendeline shrugged miserably, and Lillian's eyes
narrowed. A new idea appeared to strike her, and
she surveyed Gwendeline. "Even if Lord Merryn
has simply decided it's time he married, why choose
Adele? No one can credit it."

Gwendeline was saved from replying by the belated
arrival of Madame Carrini amid voluble Italian apologies
and crowds of retainers. Conversation was lost in the
flurry to set up the music stand and get the guests seated.

Gwendeline hardly heard the music when it finally
began. Her mind was busy and her emotions uncertain. When there was a pause in the entertainment, she
found Miss Brown and left early. She'd had enough
excitement, she thought, for one evening.

Fifteen

LATE THE NEXT MORNING, AS GWENDELINE SAT IN HER drawing room mending some lace, she regretted accepting so many invitations for the coming weeks. Her enjoyment of the party last night had been quite spoilt by Adele Greene, and she had no doubt that would continue to be the case. What was needed, she thought, was a plan of action. She must do something. She looked out the window for several long minutes; no thought came to her. What could she possibly do?

Reeves entered the room. "Miss Adele Greene," the butler announced.

Gwendeline looked up in astonishment. It really was Adele. She stood before Gwendeline, looking very smart in a gold walking dress lavishly trimmed with yellow ribbons. "I can't stay long," she said, seating herself on the edge of one of the armchairs. "I'm on my way to Bond Street for a fitting." She lifted her chin. "My wedding clothes, you know."

Gwendeline merely nodded.

Adele appeared nervous, and this made Gwendeline feel more relaxed. "I wished to speak with you alone," her visitor said, "about Lord Merryn." Adele opened her reticule and took out a crumpled sheet of paper. "I received this in this morning's post," she said, smoothing it. "It isn't signed." She didn't offer the page to Gwendeline. "Of course, one should pay no attention to such things, but I couldn't help wondering, and I decided finally to ask whether it's true." She stopped, and there was a short silence.

"I have no idea what you're talking about," said Gwendeline. "Do you intend to show me this letter?"

"No! I mean, perhaps. I'm not sure."

Gwendeline frowned at her.

"It says that Lord Merryn is supporting you," Adele said. "That he gave you this house and an income to live on."

Gwendeline was at first taken aback, then a little angry. This was none of Adele's business. Or, if she was to marry him, perhaps it was. "A group of my father's friends provided for me, Lord Merryn was among them."

"That's what the letter said you would answer," Adele cried. "That's exactly what it says, that you would try to fob me off with such a story." She crumpled the paper into her bag again. "So it is true then. But I've come to tell you that you can't interfere with my engagement." She glared at Gwendeline. "I don't understand your position with Lord Merryn, and I don't care to, but there is nothing you can do." She sounded very certain. "It's settled; I shall be Countess of Merryn. It won't be broken off."

Gwendeline rose from her seat on the sofa. "I cannot conceive why you came to tell me this. But I think you should go now." She started to ring for Reeves.

"He speaks of you to others," Adele replied almost wildly. "He was nearly distracted when you ran away. He has given you a house. Why are you no longer with his mother? Did she find you out?" At Gwendeline's outraged look, she jumped up, clutching her reticule. "It doesn't matter. That's what I came to say. I shall marry him. You can't spoil things. It's settled."

Gwendeline rang for Reeves. Though she was trembling, she kept herself under control. "Reeves," she said when the butler entered, "Miss Greene is just going."

Adele had recovered her composure. She bowed slightly to Gwendeline. "I'm very certain of what I've said," she added and swept from the room.

When she was gone, Gwendeline sank back and took several deep breaths. Her hands trembled. What had Adele meant by saying that the earl "could not break it off"? Lord Merryn was a thorough gentleman, of course, and would not willingly do such a thing to a lady, but "could not"?

And who had sent Adele the letter? Gwendeline's frown deepened. She had realized by now that most people assumed Lady Merryn was the source of her income, and she'd been content to have it so, for it was the easier and more proper explanation. Would Adele now spread her version of the story? The fact that Gwendeline had moved from Lady Merryn's house might lend credence to it. She flushed scarlet suddenly. Even the thought of living on the bounty of a man she secretly loved made Gwendeline ready to sink.

She thought of Sir Humphrey. Should she go to him again and ask that he allow the truth to be published? But she doubted that he would agree. Abruptly, she realized that Sir Humphrey had never said outright that he was helping her. Gwendeline went cold. In fact, he'd seemed rather befuddled. At the time, she had put his behavior down to surprise and diffidence about revealing his charity, but what if that was wrong? Gwendeline wrung her hands. She could go to him again to make sure, but Lord Merryn had spoken to him long since. What had he said?

Gwendeline sat back on the sofa. It came to her that Adele wasn't likely to spread this rumor, since it involved her fiancé and might cause a scandal about him. She took a further breath. Nothing had really changed then.

But the small doubt that had begun to grow would not be silenced. Gwendeline got up and began to pace. If Lord Merryn was supporting her and she found out, she'd be forced to leave London and this house and find some other means of living. And she would also be obliged to cut all connection with the earl, for he would have put her in such a compromising position that the only recourse would be a complete break. She didn't think she could bear that.

The train of thought had taken only a moment, and Gwendeline's decision came as quickly. She would do nothing overt. But for herself, she must know the truth. And if it turned out that the earl was indeed her sole supporter… She paused here and looked wide-eyed at the wall. Well, she would decide what to do about that when the time came.

In the meantime, she told herself firmly, she must draw even farther away from the St. Audleys. She mustn't depend so heavily on them or see them so often. It would be good for her to deal with her own problems instead.

Just as Gwendeline came to this decision, Miss Brown hurried into the drawing room. She stopped near the doorway, looking perplexed. "Reeves told me that Miss Greene had called. I came as quickly as I could, thinking you might want my help in the conversation. Has she gone so soon?"

Gwendeline nodded. "Her visit was short, if not pleasant."

"Was she rude to you? I wonder why she visited here?"

Gwendeline described the events of a few minutes past to the older woman. "I hardly knew what to say to her. Who would write such a letter?"

Miss Brown shook her head. She appeared both shocked and puzzled. "Some malicious person who has unearthed half-truths and wishes to stir up trouble, I suppose. Shockingly vulgar and hurtful. And Miss Greene's actions were impertinent, though I can see why the letter worried her. How fortunate that you know its falsehood already and can shrug off such base insinuations."

"Yes," agreed Gwendeline uneasily. She almost told Miss Brown of her new doubts, but something stopped her. "Anonymous letters are beneath notice. Even I know that."

"Yes, but it must be quite horrid to receive one."

"I suppose so. But if she's so certain that the engagement cannot be broken off, why should she attend to it?"

Miss Brown shrugged. "I have no idea. How any young lady could speak of her engagement in such a fashion I do not know."

"Her remarks about Lord Merryn were most curious."

Miss Brown shook her head. "Just don't allow yourself to, well, to hope too much, Gwendeline."

Gwendeline looked at her, then nodded.

They were sitting in silence when Reeves returned to the room, wearing his most stiffly disapproving look. Gwendeline prepared herself for some further unpleasantness. "Alphonse insists on speaking to you," he said.

"Oh dear, has Michael been careless again? Or the greengrocer?"

"No miss, there have been no untoward events in the kitchen since your return."

"I see. Well, ask Alphonse to come up."

Reeves went out, and a few minutes later the chef hurried into the room. He appeared even more excited than usual as he stood before them. "Good morning, Alphonse," said Gwendeline. "You wished to speak with me?"

"Yes, mademoiselle. I have something of the most important to say. It is the, the affair of the heart, you comprehend." Alphonse clutched his chest dramatically.

Gwendeline looked at Miss Brown. "But why discuss that with me?" she asked the little man. "Do you have some problem?"

"Oh no, mademoiselle, no problem," he replied. "I only wish to ask your permission to marry Miss Ellen."

Gwendeline looked again at Miss Brown for enlightenment, but this lady was also taken aback, it seemed. "You want my permission to marry Ellen, my maid?" Gwendeline said finally.

"Yes, mademoiselle." Alphonse waved his arms about. "She is the most beautiful, *charmante* young lady I have ever known. I am *bouleversé*."

"What did Ellen say when you asked her?"

"Oh, I have not asked her yet," replied Alphonse. "I hope that you will do it. Everything must be *comme il faut*, you understand."

"I?" Gwendeline gazed at her chef, bemused. "But isn't that up to you?"

"Ah, mademoiselle," said Alphonse sadly. "I am so very shy, you see." The two ladies exchanged incredulous glances. "I cannot do it, *en fait*."

"But Alphonse," began Gwendeline.

"Oh, mademoiselle," he broke in, clasping his hands before him, "she would attend to you. She would consider. Me, she laughs." He shrugged elaborately. "I do not comprehend these *Anglaises*."

"Well, I suppose I could speak to Ellen," Gwendeline said doubtfully.

Alphonse grabbed one of her hands and kissed it. "Oh, thank you, Miss Gwendeline. I will be so grateful. You will see. I will…I will cook for you the masterpieces."

"Don't get too excited, Alphonse. I'll tell Ellen what you've said. I can make no guarantee of her response."

"No, but if you ask her, mademoiselle, she will listen. I know it." Alphonse clasped his hands together in joy.

"All right, Alphonse, you may go. Ask Reeves to send Ellen in."

The small man stopped in midstride. "I cannot." He shrugged. "She is out."

"Is she? Well, I'll speak to her later then."

"Oh, thank you, mademoiselle, thank you." Bowing and smiling, Alphonse left the room.

Gwendeline turned to Miss Brown with raised eyebrows. "What do you think of that?"

"I had no idea romance was afoot, I must admit," she replied.

Gwendeline nodded. "I wonder if Ellen knows anything about it? I wager she doesn't."

Miss Brown agreed. "I'd like to see her face when you tell her."

"Why did I agree to do so? But it will have to be later."

Gwendeline was invited to Lady Merryn's that afternoon for a chat and tea. The countess was eager for a talk, and even Gwendeline's resolve to see less of the St. Audleys couldn't stand against her pleas.

She found Lady Merryn in her study, busily writing at her desk, surrounded as usual by piles of papers. But she looked up immediately when Gwendeline entered and greeted her affectionately. "I'm answering letters," she said. "Many people have written me about the novel, you know. No one ever did about the others. And, Gwendeline, you would be astonished at the number who are convinced that it is about them alone! I'm quite determined to write only modern novels after this. But how good it is to see you. Come into the drawing room for a chat."

Smiling, Gwendeline followed her down the hall. "Now," continued Lady Merryn when they were seated, "you must tell me all about your stay in the country. I understand you've become quite an artist. If only you'd told me you were interested in painting, I could have invited some artists to meet you. Mr. Woodley is acquainted with several prominent painters."

"I'm hardly an artist," replied Gwendeline. "I've done some drawing, and then I chanced to meet Mr. Ames."

"Carleton Ames!" broke in Lady Merryn. "One of the foremost painters in England. Oh, Gwendeline, will you introduce me? I should so like to meet him."

"Of course," answered Gwendeline, a little embarrassed by this appeal. Then she remembered Mr. Ames's remarks about Lady Merryn's books. "That is, if he remains in town. He meant to stay only a short time, I believe."

"Oh, he's still here," said the countess eagerly. "Mr. Woodley says he's at The Crillon. Will he call on you soon?"

"I'm not sure," faltered Gwendeline. "He doesn't know I came to town."

Lady Merryn looked worried. "Dear me. We must tell him."

"I'll send a note. Perhaps you can both come to tea."

"That would be splendid," answered Lady Merryn.

"Now you must tell me all about your adventures," continued the countess, settling back on the sofa. "I want to know everything."

Gwendeline retold the story of her stay in Penwyn, frequently interrupted by questions. Lady Merryn was thrilled by her narrow escape and speculated on Mr. Blane's current whereabouts. "You must be very careful, my dear. He may return to England and try again."

Gwendeline shook her head. "I don't think he's so foolish," she said. "Or so interested in me. I believe he kidnapped me for revenge on Lord Merryn."

"Alex?" exclaimed Lady Merryn. "Well, he was certainly clever there. Alex was— That is, what a horrid man! But you're quite all right again, thank heavens. That's the important thing."

Gwendeline nodded. She was intrigued by the remark Lady Merryn had cut off. Hoping to elicit more information, she said, "You've had some changes in your family since I left you. I must offer my felicitations."

"What?" replied the countess.

Gwendeline blushed. "Lord Merryn is engaged."

"Oh yes, of course. So kind of you." Lady Merryn rose and went to ring the bell. "It is nearly teatime already!"

And this was all the response Gwendeline could get. The rest of her visit was taken up by talk of Lady Merryn's books, both the recent one and a new project she'd just started. Gwendeline had no further chance to discuss Lord Merryn, and she returned home no wiser.

Though she would have preferred a quiet evening alone with her thoughts, Gwendeline had promised to attend a theater party that night, organized by Lord Wanley. Lillian Everly had begged Gwendeline to come, since she thought the party a scheme of Lord Wanley's mother. The formidable Lady Wanley was determined to marry off her son and wean him from poetry to the management of their deteriorating estates, and Lillian very much feared that she was the chosen bride. Thus, she wanted Gwendeline's support through the evening.

Gwendeline wasn't in the mood for a noisy theater. Altogether, she wasn't looking forward to a "splendidly instructive"—Lord Wanley's words—evening of *Macbeth*. She was, she had to admit guiltily, not fond of Shakespeare.

And she'd nearly forgotten her promise to speak with Ellen. The maid was chattering happily as she combed out Gwendeline's hair, and Gwendeline found it awkward to broach the matter of Alphonse's proposal. At last, she hardened her resolve and interrupted. "Ellen, there is something about which I wish to discuss with you."

"Yes, miss?" said Ellen. "If it's the scorched ruffle, I'm sorry. I just looked away for one minute and there it was. But I can mend it and…"

"No, it's not that. It's about Alphonse." Gwendeline watched the girl's face for some reaction.

Ellen seemed only surprised. "Alphonse, miss?"

"Yes." And she told her of the chef's request that morning.

Ellen seemed stunned. She said nothing for several moments. Then she found her voice. "Me, marry Alphonse? Why, the man must be daft. He never said nothing to me." She looked at Gwendeline incredulously.

"He asked me to inform you of his offer."

"But why, miss? Begging your pardon, but I think it should be between him and me."

"I agree completely, Ellen, and I tried to tell him so. But he insisted he was too shy to approach you."

Ellen goggled. "Shy! Him?" She shook her head. "He's gone daft. I'll go down directly and give him a piece of my mind."

"Yes, well, I suppose you know best what to do."

Ellen put her hands on her hips. "I do. You mustn't worry yourself. The idea! Going to you without a word to me first. I'll teach him." She finished Gwendeline's hair with such vigor that it brought tears to her eyes more than once. When Gwendeline was dressed, Ellen left the room with grim purpose in her eyes, and Gwendeline felt somewhat sorry for Alphonse. As she went down the stairs, she wondered what news there would be from the kitchens when she returned.

Lady Wanley's carriage arrived in good time, and Gwendeline joined Lillian and her hostess in it. The gentlemen were apparently to meet them at the theater. This was Gwendeline's first encounter with Lady Wanley, and she felt rather intimidated by this very large woman, whose sharp, cold blue eyes and prominent nose seemed to pin one to the side of her carriage when she talked. Lady Wanley wore a dress of heavy turquoise brocade and a turban of the same material. The latter was adorned with several nodding ostrich plumes whose hypnotic motion held Gwendeline's eye as they rode. Their conversation on the short journey consisted chiefly of questions directed at each of the girls in turn by their hostess. Lillian's answers were somewhat more spirited than Gwendeline's soft replies, but both girls arrived at the theater very subdued.

They found their box occupied only by a reedy young man with pale blond hair and a stammer. His extreme youth and the cut of his jacket proclaimed his status, and the girls hardly needed to be told that he was a young cousin of Lord Wanley's and still at college. Mr. Devlin appeared cowed by the presence of his aunt and two fashionable young ladies, and after responding nervously to a barrage of questions about his family, he subsided into a corner of the box and said little else for the rest of the evening. Gwendeline felt rather sorry for him, especially after Lillian took advantage of an unobserved moment to whisper, "She's made very sure that Lord Wanley will have no competition, hasn't she?"

Lady Wanley preferred to arrive early at the theater, and so they were nearly alone in the auditorium for a while. But soon the house began to fill. There was no sign of Lord Wanley, and his mother was looking more and more put out. Watching her, Gwendeline was profoundly glad that it was not she who was late.

"What did Eliot say to you?" Lady Wanley snapped at Mr. Devlin for the third time, as she surveyed the audience with a gimlet eye.

"H-he a-assured me," the young man replied hurriedly, "th-that he would a-arrive in g-good time. H-he h-had an appointment w-with his p-publishers."

Lady Wanley snorted, as she had with each previous mention of this engagement. "His publishers!" she repeated indignantly. "Those bloodsuckers he pays to bring out the hogwash he scribbles, you mean. He'll ruin us with publishers." She caught herself after this more extended response to her nephew's answer. "Only a figure of speech, of course. Eliot's preoccupation with poetry has me quite distracted. I wish that you would speak to him, my dear." This last was addressed to Lillian.

"I?" she responded.

"Yes, if you would only discourage this poetry silliness. I'm sure Eliot would listen to you."

"I fear you're mistaken, Lady Wanley. You overestimate my influence," Lillian answered. A gentlemen in the pit bowed to the young ladies in the box, and Lillian nodded to him, as she had to several others who had saluted them.

Lady Wanley looked sharply down, fixing this presumptuous sprig with a deadly stare as he chatted all unknowing with a group of friends.

"Young pup," she muttered. "All the young men look such fools today. This ridiculous cropped hair and not a ruffle or a bit of lace about them. When I was a girl, no man would have ventured out of his dressing room without hair powder and a satin coat. And much more handsome they were, too." She sniffed. The play was about to begin, and Lady Wanley scanned the crowd once more. "Where is Eliot?" she repeated.

Lord Wanley did not appear before the curtain rose, and Gwendeline sat through the first portion of the play very conscious of his mother's anger. She thought her remarkably like one of the three witches in the opening scene, and the girl was even less able to enjoy the drama than she'd expected. Lady Wanley seemed completely uninterested in *Macbeth*. She fidgeted in her chair and muttered as she drew her lorgnette back and forth between her hands. When the curtain descended at the first interval, she sent Mr. Devlin out to look for her son, with curt instructions not to return without him. A silence fell in the box after his departure, and Gwendeline felt even more uncomfortable.

The one remark about the play that Lillian ventured was met with a discouraging monosyllable, and she too subsided, with a humorous look at Gwendeline.

Both girls were relieved when visitors began to arrive. Several young men braved Lady Wanley's patent disapproval and sat down to talk for a moment to the Beauty. Lillian was soon surrounded, and Gwendeline joined the light chatter gratefully. A few minutes later, an older man appeared. He was rather portly and his brown hair was thinning on top, but his expression was kind and unassuming. Even Lady Wanley was impressed when Lillian introduced him as the Duke of Craigbourne.

He sat for a few minutes in the chair Mr. Devlin had vacated and talked amiably with Lillian and Lady Wanley. Gwendeline, prepared to dislike him, found herself rather taken with his easy manner and open countenance. She agreed with Lillian's view that he was the sort of man one could like very much if one didn't have to consider marrying him.

The next visitor drove the duke from Gwendeline's mind, however; Lord Merryn entered the box and greeted her. As he took the remaining empty chair, he asked Gwendeline, "Are you enjoying the play?" His quizzical expression as much as said that he knew she couldn't be, with such a play and in such company.

Gwendeline remembered that they'd once discussed Shakespeare and her sad dislike of his plays. She smiled at him sheepishly. "Very much," she replied, feeling Lady Wanley's eyes on her back.

The earl leaned forward a bit. "She's not listening, you know," he said quietly. "She's occupied with her distinguished guest."

Gwendeline laughed, then quickly composed her features again. "Don't set me off, please. I'm terrified of saying something stupid and earning her displeasure."

He grinned appreciatively. "However do you come to be in her box?"

"Lillian asked me to come. She wanted support."

"Ah," he nodded. "Sensible of her but not pleasant for you." He glanced over at Lillian. "Craigbourne is surprisingly particular in his attentions. I wonder if he's decided to settle at last."

"I fear so," answered Gwendeline. "I don't know what to do."

The earl raised his eyebrows in surprise. "Do?" he echoed.

"Yes," said Gwendeline very softly. "Lillian's parents wish her to marry him and she does not…" Gwendeline stopped and flushed deeply. "I shouldn't have said anything. Oh, my wretched tongue."

Lord Merryn smiled. "I shan't repeat it. But do you seriously tell me that Miss Everly doesn't wish to be a duchess?" He looked a bit skeptical.

"Not at all," Gwendeline answered.

The earl looked very thoughtful, but before Gwendeline could ask him why, two events occurred simultaneously. The duke rose to take his leave, and Lord Wanley arrived at last, his cousin at his elbow. Lady Wanley was patently torn. She wished to be all politeness to the duke, but an irresistible urge to scold her errant son was obvious in her reddening cheeks and swelling breast. She struggled with herself, her grip on her ivory lorgnette tightening alarmingly, but finally she contented herself with one withering look at Lord Wanley before she turned back to His Grace.

Gwendeline couldn't help giggling as Lord Wanley turned and began to chatter nervously with them. He looked very apprehensive. People were beginning to return to their seats, and Lord Merryn took his leave. As soon as the box was empty of visitors, Lady Wanley drew herself up and said, "Well, Eliot, what have you to say for yourself? You've insulted me and these young ladies with your heedless manners. What excuse do you offer?" She eyed him wrathfully. "And do not talk any nonsense about publishers to *me*, pray."

Lord Wanley muttered a nervous apology for his tardiness, but this by no means satisfied his mother. She launched into a furious catalogue of his faults that was only staunched by the beginning of the next act and the indignant stares of their neighbors. But though she was finally forced to contain herself, her expression declared that she was not defeated by this temporary setback.

When the curtain fell again, Lord Wanley devoted himself to Lillian, talking so continuously that he left his mother no opening to begin berating him. Gwendeline watched with some amusement, and after an abortive attempt to converse with Mr. Devlin, sat back in her chair to appreciate the scene. Lillian chatted amiably, occasionally glancing toward Gwendeline with twinkling eyes. Lord Wanley leaned toward her, and Lady Wanley sat behind them, arms folded, glowering. Gwendeline maintained her composure only with difficulty.

The entire interval passed in this manner. Lord Wanley wisely avoided the subject of his new book and poetry in general and turned the talk to Shakespeare, about whom he was surprisingly learned. He even managed to pry a few remarks on this subject from Mr. Devlin who, it appeared, was studying literature at Oxford. Gwendeline found herself interested in his explanation of beliefs in witchcraft in Shakespeare's time. She'd never been so impressed by Lord Wanley; it seemed he had read *all* of Shakespeare.

The last act passed swiftly and soon the ladies were again in their hostess's coach, driving home. Lady Wanley was in no mood for civilities, however, for her son had escaped to his club, pleading lack of room in the carriage—a point Lady Wanley couldn't honestly dispute. They rode in stony silence, Lady Wanley's anger a palpable presence. She made no effort to be polite to her guests, and the girls didn't dare speak, though Lillian choked back a laugh several times. When Gwendeline climbed down at her house, Lillian squeezed her hand, promising to call the following day. Gwendeline went straight up to her room. Miss Brown had already gone to bed, but she found that she wasn't particularly sleepy, and she sat down on her bed to think. She wondered if Lord Merryn knew about Adele's visit. Somehow, she doubted it. She very much wished to talk it over with someone. Perhaps she would tell Lillian after all.

This made her think of another problem. What to do about Lillian's situation? The duke was amiable, but Lillian mustn't be forced to marry him. And what of Major St. Audley? She would ask them both to tea, she decided. Her expression lightened further. She would have a tea party to which she could also invite Lady Merryn and Mr. Ames. Thus, she could introduce Lady Merryn but not force Mr. Ames to talk only with her. Gwendeline's spirits rose. She could ask Lord Merryn to repay him for the riding party and allow him to see the changes in the house. Gwendeline remembered her renewed doubts about her situation. She had vowed to see less of the earl, and now she thought to ask him to her house. This was certainly not following through on her resolve.

She put her chin in her hand and stared at her reflection in the mirror above the dressing table. What to do? How to lay her doubts to rest without wrecking everything? She considered the problem for some minutes but did not find a solution.

Gwendeline looked again in the mirror. A strained, rather pale face looked back. "So many goals," she said aloud, "and not a practical plan in your head. It is ludicrous." A wan smile came to the face in the mirror. Gwendeline shook her head at it. "You're a hopeless conspirator," she finished. She rose, shrugged, and began to undress. I shall give a party, she thought. I don't care. And I shall invite the St. Audleys. Defiantly, she made a list of tasks in her mind. Tomorrow, she'd speak to Alphonse about food; Reeves would know about the silver. Gwendeline fell asleep still ticking off details and forgot even to wonder what Ellen had said to Alphonse.

Sixteen

LILLIAN CALLED EARLY THE NEXT DAY, BUT Gwendeline had been up for some time. The house was in a minor uproar. The previous evening, Ellen had, as she put it, "given Alphonse what for" in the presence of several of the other servants, then flounced off in a huff. Alphonse, his pride grievously wounded, first threw a tantrum in the kitchen, then proceeded to drown his sorrows in the cooking sherry. John, the footman, and Yvette had alternated as interested spectators or sympathetic confidants, as circumstances warranted. Reeves, though he kept aloof and maintained his dignity, relieved his outraged sensibilities by scolding any servant who came within his reach.

The first Gwendeline knew of these developments was when she sat down to breakfast and found the toast burned, the tea tepid and weak, and the eggs watery. When she leaned back in her chair and looked disgustedly at these unappetizing failures, someone cleared his throat behind her. She turned to discover Reeves hovering by the breakfast-room door. She looked at him inquiringly.

"Yes, miss, I am sorry," he said. "I fear the eggs are a trifle underdone."

"Nothing is properly done, Reeves," Gwendeline replied. "What's happened to Alphonse? Has Ellen killed him?"

Reeves permitted his expression to show strain. "No, miss. But Alphonse is, er, indisposed this morning. I prevailed upon Yvette to do the cooking temporarily."

Gwendeline sighed and rose from the table. "How indisposed, Reeves? Does he refuse to work? Or is he really ill?"

"I believe his state is usually known as 'sleeping it off' among those conversant with such matters," answered Miss Brown, who had just appeared in the doorway of the breakfast room. Gwendeline turned to her, surprised, and Miss Brown nodded. "He appears to have drunk everything alcoholic in the kitchens."

"Do you wish me to dismiss him, Miss Gwendeline?" asked Reeves hopefully.

"No, no. Of course not," she said. "I'll take care of this, Reeves. You may go."

"Very well," Reeves replied stiffly. He left the room.

Gwendeline looked at Miss Brown. "What do you suggest?"

"Alphonse is upset because Ellen scolded him before everyone. We must smooth that over somehow. I suggest we talk to each of the servants in turn and try to do so."

Gwendeline agreed, and they spoke first to John, then to Yvette. Though the former was inclined to take Ellen's side and the latter was a strong partisan of Alphonse, the two ladies finally got them to agree not to mention the matter again. Ellen was a more complicated problem, but after long and earnest discussion, she promised to apologize publicly to Alphonse, declining the honor of marrying him with more tact than before.

Thus, when Alphonse finally appeared in the kitchen once more, this scenario was followed, and he was at least partially placated. It seemed that things were back to normal for a time. Only then could Gwendeline mention her plans for a tea party. Miss Brown was agreeable when consulted, and Alphonse seemed quite his usual self as he described the cakes he would concoct. Gwendeline wrote out a little stack of invitation cards, requesting the presence of her close friends for Tuesday week at tea. Just before Lillian came in, she sent the footman out to deliver them, saving Lillian's to give herself.

Lillian smiled. "So you're beginning to entertain, are you?" She settled herself comfortably on the sofa. "You are so lucky, Gwendeline. To have your own house and to be able to give parties here for your friends sounds heavenly."

"You wouldn't say so if you'd been here two hours ago." And she told Lillian of the current domestic upheaval. Lillian was hugely entertained; she loved to hear the exploits of Alphonse. "I am lucky, I know," Gwendeline continued. "However, my situation is the result of my parents' deaths and all that followed. Few people would wish to make such an exchange."

"I'm not so sure," replied Lillian, putting her chin on her hand.

"What?"

Lillian shook her head. "Oh, of course I wouldn't, but sometimes I envy you so, Gwendeline."

"You envy *me*," said Gwendeline, surprised.

"Yes," said Lillian. "You have no worries about your future. You can stay here in this house forever if you like. And you have your own income under your control. I only wish I could be in your position."

"No worries!" Gwendeline thought of the various doubts and uncertainties that plagued her. "You are the toast of the *ton*; you're beautiful, rich, and the most sought-after girl in London. I'm sure you'll be happy once you find someone you love and marry."

"What a list of attributes! I should be grateful indeed. By an accident of birth, I'm not ill-looking. I possess a fortune I cannot touch. And I'm to marry in order to be happy. Luck indeed!" And to Gwendeline's dismay, she burst into tears.

"Lillian!" Gwendeline went to sit beside her friend on the sofa and put an arm around her. "What's the matter?"

Lillian tried to control her tears. "I'm sorry. I'm not myself this morning." Gradually, her sobs subsided; she wiped her eyes. "What a fool I am," she continued when she could speak. She sounded annoyed.

"What's wrong?" asked Gwendeline. "What can I do?"

"There's nothing to be done. I spoke with my mother this morning about our evening at the theater. She wished to know whom I had seen, and when she heard that the duke had come by our box, she was so glad." Lillian's shoulders drooped. "I ventured to suggest that I didn't wish to marry the duke, that I didn't really love him, and she was very upset."

"Oh dear," sighed Gwendeline. "Did she scold you?"

"No, no," Lillian replied. "That would have been bearable. She just looked sad; she nearly wept, Gwendeline! And she spoke of everything she and my father have tried to do for me, how they've given me more latitude than many young ladies are ever allowed. She ended by saying that they only wished for my happiness and talking of the necessity for material security and respect in a marriage." Lillian was close to tears again. "Gwendeline, she made me feel so foolish and ungrateful."

Gwendeline patted her hand. "I can understand that. But you mustn't marry because of a sense of obligation, Lillian. It would be a dreadful mistake."

Lillian shrugged. "I'm not sure of that. The duke is very kind and gentlemanly. I suppose I'd be happy with him, in a mild way. And pleasing my parents so much would also make me happy."

Gwendeline was torn between a desire to stop Lillian's seeming capitulation and her promise to keep Major St. Audley's confidence. "Lillian, you mustn't say that," she said finally. "You mustn't just give up."

"Gwendeline, you are the only one who doesn't tell me to take my chance to become a duchess and forget such silly scruples." She sighed again. "I'm not so sure anymore that the others aren't right."

"Don't do something that you will regret all your life," cried Gwendeline.

Lillian laughed. "Well, he hasn't asked me yet, has he? Perhaps he won't, and my problems will be solved. At any rate, you can see now why I envy you."

Gwendeline looked at her worriedly. "Lillian," she began.

But the other girl interrupted. "Enough maundering. Let's hear some of your woes instead." She smiled at Gwendeline with an attempt at gaiety.

"But I wish to tell you…"

"No," Lillian broke in, "nothing more about me. I won't hear it. Tell me more about Alphonse and his tantrum."

"You are impossible."

"I?" replied Lillian, with mock astonishment. "You can say this to me after spending an evening with Lady Wanley?"

Gwendeline laughed. "I was so frightened the entire evening that I would do something to earn her displeasure."

"Poor Lord Wanley! I never felt such sympathy for him before. I begin to admire his persistent interest in poetry. I'm not sure I could sustain it in the face of Lady Wanley's extreme displeasure."

"I couldn't, I know. Think of the rows! I was also surprised to find how much Lord Wanley knows about Shakespeare."

"There's more to the man than I ever realized." Lillian looked very wise. "They say it is only in adversity that true character is revealed."

Gwendeline giggled. "Only think what a mother-in-law she would be."

Lillian fell back on the sofa in horror. "Don't mention it, I beg you. It's one of my recurring nightmares. My father tells me they have a huge moldering castle in Ireland, and I dream of being trapped there with the two of them—he reading poetry all day and she lecturing us both on our sins."

This ridiculous picture sent Gwendeline into peals of laughter. "And Mr. Devlin," she gasped. "Don't forget him. I daresay he would come to live with you."

"Indeed," cried Lillian. "Mr. Devlin sitting in a corner of the castle in silent gloom for years at a time." They collapsed in laughter.

Both girls felt better after this. The air seemed to have cleared, and their mood lightened. Reeves brought in some tea, and they chatted easily over it.

"And so, you have no problems," Lillian said lightly some time later. "You are free as the air."

"I never pretended to be without worries," she answered. "No one can say that, I think. In fact, just yesterday I had a strange and rather unpleasant encounter with Adele Greene."

"She's been insufferable since her exalted engagement. I'm not surprised."

"This was rather more than rudeness," said Gwendeline, and she related the happenings of the previous morning.

Lillian was silent for several moments when Gwendeline had finished. She looked very thoughtful. Finally, she said, "I don't wish to pry, Gwendeline, and you must stop me if you feel I'm doing so." She hesitated. "But are you…do you care for Lord Merryn?"

Gwendeline looked away. "Why do you ask?"

"Please don't take it amiss. It's just that I've noticed something in your tone when you speak of him."

Gwendeline gazed at the floor, trying to decide whether to tell Lillian the truth. "I do care for him," she said at last. "Very much."

Lillian nodded sympathetically.

"Does everyone know it then?" continued Gwendeline miserably. "Oh, I thought I had hidden my feelings so well."

"No one else can have noticed. We've been so much together and have become, I think, close friends." Lillian squeezed Gwendeline's hand. "You needn't worry about gossip."

Gwendeline returned the squeeze gratefully. "But perhaps Adele has observed something," she said. "She may have come because of that."

"She's not especially sensitive to the feelings of others. I'm sure it was that horrid letter. Who can have sent it?"

Gwendeline shrugged.

"How people can twist the truth. It's horrid. And for her to say that Lord Merryn *cannot* break off this engagement. Strange. If one could only ask him about it."

"You wouldn't!" exclaimed Gwendeline.

"No, no, it's clearly impossible," said Lillian. "I only wish one could. So many things could be cleared up easily if one could only ask the people involved."

Gwendeline remained silent. Things did not seem so simple to her, but she hesitated to tell Lillian of her new worry. Lillian believed Lord Merryn's story of a group of benefactors and thought Gwendeline's income wholly secure. Just as Gwendeline feared to tell Miss Brown the truth, so she kept it from her other friend.

"But we must do something about Adele," Lillian continued. "She's clearly wrong for him in any case."

"There is no acceptable way of…"

"Nonsense," said Lillian. "I'm sure I shall think of something. I'm determined that you will be happy."

Gwendeline smiled; this remark was so similar to one she'd made to herself about Lillian. "Perhaps we'll both be happy," she replied. "Who knows what will happen?"

"That's the spirit. We won't give up. You've given me courage, Gwendeline. I'm determined we will win out. Let's plot something."

Gwendeline laughed. "What?"

"Something mildly wicked. Think!"

"I'm no good at plotting. I'll leave it to you."

Lillian looked disgusted. "Who is the faint heart now? Well, I'll think of something. Wait and see." For the rest of her visit Lillian outlined more and more outrageous schemes for putting things right. Gwendeline had never laughed so much. But as she was leaving, Lillian was serious for a moment. "I meant what I said," she told Gwendeline, "in spite of my joking. I'll think of something."

"I hope you do," answered Gwendeline, "something reasonable."

Lillian grinned at her and took her leave.

Gwendeline worried a little about what Lillian might do through luncheon and an afternoon linen-sorting session with Miss Brown. She was so wrapped up in her thoughts that she several times failed to hear Miss Brown's count of their supplies. The fourth time Miss Brown became a bit annoyed as she repeated "Gwendeline, five large tablecloths."

"What?" asked Gwendeline, starting guiltily.

Miss Brown put her hands on her hips. "Gwendeline,

I can easily get Ellen or one of the other servants to help me with this. There's no reason for you to stay to write the list when you're preoccupied with other things."

"No," answered Gwendeline. "I want to help, and to know just how much of everything we have. Five napkins, you said?"

"No, I did not. I said five large tablecloths. If I had said five napkins, we'd be woefully short."

Gwendeline looked at her list and wrote "five large tablecloths" at the bottom. "There," she said. "I have it. I'll pay attention now, Brown, I promise."

At this moment, Reeves entered the linen room, effectively filling the remaining space. "A Mr. and Mrs. Ames have called, Miss Gwendeline," he said. "Shall I tell them you're not in?"

"Mr. and Mrs. Ames!" exclaimed both ladies.

"No indeed, Reeves, tell them we'll be down directly," said Gwendeline. "And take some refreshment to the drawing room." They hurried to their respective bedrooms to tidy up.

The two ladies were soon downstairs exchanging cordial greetings with the older couple. "But my dear," said Mrs. Ames, "why didn't you tell us you were coming to London? When did you arrive? We had no idea. And we've met several people who know you. It is all very mysterious."

"I came to Penwyn from London actually. But I didn't want to think of... That is, I wanted to get away from town and the season for a rest."

"Yes, but why not even mention all that?" replied Mrs. Ames wonderingly. "Even when we were preparing to come to town."

"I must apologize for what looks like deception. But I was rather upset and…" Gwendeline looked to Miss Brown for help.

"Of course," Mr. Ames put in. "No wish to rake over all the parties and such when you're exhausted. Tire yourself all over again! Don't even want to think of 'em. Perfectly understandable to *me*, I'm nearly fagged myself after only two weeks in town." He grinned at Gwendeline. "I've been dragged from one end of Mayfair to the other since I arrived. Hardly had a moment to myself." He shook his head.

Gwendeline laughed. "I hope you will come to tea?"

"We shall be delighted," answered Mrs. Ames. "Carleton is exaggerating to roast me, as usual. He'd be very disappointed if we never went out in town." She leaned forward a bit in her chair. "Tell me, my dear, is it really true that this novel everyone is talking of concerns your family?"

Gwendeline blushed a little as she nodded.

Mrs. Ames was highly gratified. "How romantic!" she exclaimed. "To have a novel written about one's own parents. My parents were frightfully dull."

"Trash," snorted Mr. Ames. "These women have no business being published and spreading their tales about. Half of it untrue and the rest imaginary; I call it an inexcusable invasion of privacy. You should take them to court, Gwendeline. Ruins the minds of half the country besides."

"Oh, Carleton," said his wife. "You're just jealous of all the attention the novelists receive. You'd be very pleased if your paintings created such a sensation."

"Nonsense," he responded indignantly. "I've no

desire to be admired by those without knowledge or taste!"

"Lady Merryn is a good friend of mine," said Gwendeline. "She is really quite talented. She's also coming to tea next week."

"Splendid!" answered Mrs. Ames. "I shall look forward to meeting her."

Gwendeline waited nervously for Mr. Ames's reaction. He was glowering at her. "Lady Merryn admires your work so much, Mr. Ames," she added. "She begged me to introduce her, and I couldn't refuse. If you like, I can also ask some particular friend of yours. Someone for you to talk to. Perhaps Mr. Woodley?"

"Woodley! That leech! Trying to worm his way into the company of really talented men where he's never wanted. Wouldn't be in the same house with him."

"I'm sorry," said Gwendeline. "I thought he was a friend of yours. He always speaks as if…"

"Speaks!" interrupted Mr. Ames. "I daresay he speaks as if we were brothers. He lives on his talk. Blustering man-milliner."

"We shall certainly *not* invite him then," said Miss Brown. "But I must agree with Gwendeline; Lady Merryn is a charming woman and not at all like Mr. Woodley."

"Of course she's not," said Mrs. Ames. "And we'll be delighted to meet her here." She went on before her husband could speak again. "Tell me, Gwendeline, have you seen any paintings since you returned to London?" Her expression was serious, but her eyes twinkled.

"No. I haven't had time."

"Time!" exclaimed Mr. Ames. "What other

nonsense have you had time for, I wonder? Novel reading, I suppose."

"You're right," put in Gwendeline to keep the conversation from turning back to Lady Merryn. "I'd certainly like to see some paintings. I must arrange to go."

"I'll take you," said Mr. Ames. "You won't know which to admire."

"That would be most kind of you. I know I would learn a great deal."

Mr. Ames looked at her sidelong. "You're all very clever, aren't you? Think you've maneuvered me. Got me on my favorite subject and so on." He smiled at all the ladies. "Well, I don't mind, but just don't think you're getting away with anything." Gwendeline and Miss Brown returned his smile a bit sheepishly; his wife merely looked complacent.

Their conversation turned to more general topics. Mrs. Ames described some of the grand entertainments she'd attended, and they discovered a few mutual acquaintances. Mr. Ames had a new store of anecdotes about his fellow artists. He amused Gwendeline by thoroughly deflating Mr. Woodley's pretensions to friendship with several famous men, and Gwendeline thought with guilty amusement of his continually deferred promises to introduce Lady Merryn to these personages. It turned out to be a delightful afternoon, and the four of them vowed to meet again before Gwendeline's tea, if it could be managed.

Gwendeline arranged to view pictures with Mr. Ames the next day. He had quite a list of things she must see, and she planned to devote the whole afternoon to them. Unfortunately, both she and Mrs. Ames had dinner engagements for that evening, so they couldn't go on to dinner.

The Ameses took their leave, and Gwendeline and Miss Brown sat back in their chairs. "It turned out well," said Gwendeline. "I was afraid they'd be angry with me."

"They're too kind to have been really angry. But they were puzzled, no doubt. However, all is well now. Mr. Ames is such a charming man."

Gwendeline smiled. "I look forward to our expedition."

"You'll see a great many pictures," replied the older woman with some amusement. "I hope you'll be attentive and learn something."

"I'll have no choice."

They laughed together and went back to their work. It took rather longer than they expected, so that they had a hurried tea and went directly up to dress for dinner. They were invited to the Everlys' for the evening, and Lillian had asked Gwendeline to come early to meet some friends of hers visiting from the country.

The evening went well, though Gwendeline felt a little ill at ease with Lillian's parents at first. She was conscious of all that she'd heard of their plans for their daughter and of Lillian's worries. But they were kind and charming, and she soon felt comfortable. Their guests were also compatible people, and the party was pleasant. They had some music after dinner; Lillian sang and played, as did the two daughters of their visitors. This was followed by a cheerfully noisy game of loo. Gwendeline returned home in good spirits, tired but content.

Reeves let them in, and Gwendeline started directly up to her bedchamber. She paused on the stairs, however, when the butler addressed her.

"I beg your pardon, Miss Gwendeline," he said, "but two letters were delivered by hand while you were out. I thought you would wish to have them as soon as possible." He held out two envelopes to her.

"Thank you, Reeves," she said as she took them. She continued up to her room, saying an affectionate good night to Miss Brown as they separated.

She didn't open the letters immediately but undressed and made ready for bed. When she was settled, propped up against the pillows in her nightgown, she took them up again. If either required an answer, she thought, it would just have to wait until morning.

The first envelope contained a note from Lord Merryn. Gwendeline's heart beat faster when she saw the signature and read his request to call tomorrow to speak with her. For some minutes, she lay back against her pillows wondering what he wanted to say and thinking of him dreamily. Finally, she reached for the other letter and pulled the single sheet of paper from the envelope. The note, printed in rough block letters and unsigned, said, "You will be found out. You cannot escape."

Gwendeline got out of bed and threw it into the fire. She watched it burn, then climbed back under the covers, trembling. Who would send her such a vile thing? She remembered the letter Adele Greene had brought with her, and her shock began to develop into real fear. Was the same person the author of both notes? Who could be waging this anonymous campaign against her? And why?

Seventeen

WHEN SHE WOKE, LATE IN THE MORNING, GWENDELINE realized that she should have kept the letter instead of burning it. Yet it must have been the work of some malicious prankster and nothing more. She would ignore it.

She dressed carefully, remembering that Lord Merryn was to call, and had Ellen pay special attention to her hair, brushing the pale blond curls until they shone, and arranging them à la Tite. She chatted with Ellen, who'd been subdued for the past several days, trying to find out how things were going belowstairs. But Ellen would say almost nothing, which was most unusual for her.

When she finally stood before the mirror, she was pleased with her appearance. She had chosen a gown of white sprigged muslin with long sleeves and a high ruffled neckline. A flounce circled the hem, and a row of tiny blue buttons closed the back and cuffs. She went downstairs with a feeling of anticipation. She still had no idea what Lord Merryn wished to discuss, but she was eager to see him.

Miss Brown was in the breakfast room, though she had long since finished her meal. She was writing letters when Gwendeline entered, and paused only to smile a greeting and her approval of Gwendeline's dress. Gwendeline hurried through breakfast, and indeed she'd hardly finished when she heard the bell and Reeves entered to tell her Lord Merryn was in the drawing room. Miss Brown looked up, surprised, and Gwendeline said, "He wrote me yesterday and said he would call. I don't know what he wishes to discuss."

Miss Brown put down her pen. "Shall I remain here? Does he wish to speak to you alone?"

"He didn't say so. You may come if you like."

"I should much prefer to finish my letters, as you know very well. You go on. If you want me, I'll be here."

Gwendeline nodded and left the room. She paused for a moment outside the drawing room doorway, then walked in. The earl rose from the sofa at her entrance. "Good morning, Lord Merryn," she said. "I received your note late last night and thus had no time to reply."

"Good morning," he replied. "I hope my call doesn't then come at an inconvenient time?"

"Oh no," answered Gwendeline, taking the armchair. "Please sit down."

The earl did so. "How wonderfully polite we are!"

Gwendeline laughed. "Yes indeed."

"And I must say now that you are looking lovely this morning."

"Thank you, my lord," replied Gwendeline demurely. "You are too kind."

"Oh no," said the earl. His expression turned

serious. "I've come to discuss a rather delicate matter," he said. "I'm not certain how to begin, in fact."

"Oh?" said Gwendeline. "What's wrong?"

"Nothing is precisely wrong," he went on, "but a very odd conversation I had with Adele last evening left me puzzled, and I hoped you could enlighten me."

"I?" Gwendeline wondered whether Adele had told Lord Merryn of her visit and its purpose. She couldn't believe that she had.

"Yes. You have no idea to what I am referring?"

"I'm not sure," said Gwendeline. "You must explain."

"Very well," he answered. "The first thing Adele said to me when we met last night at Almack's was 'I suppose you have already heard all about my visit to Miss Gregory.' I replied that I knew nothing of any visit, whereupon Adele refused to say any more about the subject and even became angry when I pressed her to explain." Lord Merryn raised his eyebrows. "Can you throw any light on the topic?"

"You put me in a difficult position, Lord Merryn," answered Gwendeline. "Surely I shouldn't discuss a matter your fiancée doesn't wish pursued." Gwendeline had no intention of telling the earl what Adele had said to her.

"My… Don't be a goose, Gwendeline. Has Adele said anything to upset you? That's really all I wish to know. Don't go all missish on me now."

Gwendeline lifted her chin and looked directly into his eyes. "No," she answered mendaciously, "not at all."

The earl surveyed Gwendeline skeptically. Finally, he sighed. "I don't think you're being entirely honest with me," he said. "But I suppose I can expect no more." He looked resigned, and Gwendeline nearly blurted out the truth. "Only promise me, Gwendeline, that you won't run away again if anything should happen to upset you. I couldn't stand it. Ask for an explanation first, please." He leaned forward and took her hand. "Will you promise me that?" he continued, gazing into her eyes.

Gwendeline could hardly speak through the beating of her heart. "I'll never be so foolish again."

"Good." He squeezed her hand and released it. There was a short silence. It was all well and good to speak of explanations, Gwendeline thought, but one couldn't ask a man why he'd become engaged to a girl who seemed entirely wrong for him. Not when all she wanted was to throw herself into his arms. The answer might be more than she could bear.

"I understand you're beginning to entertain," said the earl.

"Yes." And so they were doomed to chitchat. "You received my invitation? I hope you will come."

"Certainly. Is it true that you are to have Carleton Ames to meet my mother?"

"I've asked them both."

Lord Merryn smiled. "It's very kind of you. Mama has wished to meet a well-known artist or writer for years and has never managed it. She will be in ecstasies."

"I hope so. She's been so kind to me. I'd like to do something to repay her."

"You have repaid her tenfold," he answered. "You've fulfilled her dearest wish."

Gwendeline smiled. "Well, I'm glad. Do you

know, I believe Mr. Woodley is something of a fraud. Mr. Ames says he is not a friend of his at all. In fact, he said that Mr. Woodley doesn't really know any of the celebrated people he claims as friends."

"Of course he doesn't. He is a crashing bore. But your influence with Mr. Ames must be large if you could make him agree to such a party. I've heard that he dislikes both society and novelists of all sorts. You've scored quite a coup."

"Oh, now you're bamming me," Gwendeline answered. "I shan't listen."

"In that case, I'd better take my leave." Lord Merryn rose.

Gwendeline realized this was an ideal opportunity to ask the earl about her income. She didn't wish to, but she felt she must. "Could you stay a moment more?" she asked him.

He raised his eyebrows. "Of course." He sat down again. "Do you wish to tell me what Adele said, after all?"

Gwendeline shook her head. "You will think me foolish, I suppose, but I have been worried once again about my situation."

Lord Merryn looked at her.

Gazing at the elegant, handsome figure next to her, Gwendeline's heart nearly failed her, but she made herself say, "Yes. My income, you know, and this house."

"I thought we'd settled that long since. What has occurred to upset you?"

Gwendeline was staring down at her folded hands. "I've heard some things, and, and thinking over my conversation with Sir Humphrey, I realized that he didn't…" She broke off and looked up into St. Audley's gray eyes. "Lord Merryn, is there truly a group of my father's friends helping me? Or are you the only one involved? I can't dismiss the idea that you are, and it worries me considerably. You must see how improper it would be, that is…" Her eyes dropped. "I've been very uneasy."

"I can see that you have," he replied. "What would satisfy you? Shall we visit Sir Humphrey together and ask him to confirm his role in your rescue? Would that make you easy?"

Gwendeline gazed at him with painful intensity. "Would he?"

"He would," answered Lord Merryn positively. "I will take you there whenever you like." He chuckled. "Though the old man will hate to be bothered, of course."

"No, no, that isn't necessary." Gwendeline sighed as a wave of relief washed over her.

"Is it so good to find that you don't owe your rescue wholly to me?"

"Yes," replied the girl fiercely.

"Ah. Well, I'm glad to have set your mind at rest." He rose rather stiffly. "And now, if there's nothing else?" Gwendeline shook her head, and he bowed. "Goodbye."

"Goodbye. And thank you." When he was gone, Gwendeline leaned back and felt again the luxury of her relief. Why did she persist in doubting him? She thought over their visit. He certainly talked of Adele in an odd way for a man who was engaged to her.

She suddenly remembered the anonymous letter,

and in the same instant wondered if Adele might have sent it. Her own letter might have inspired a sort of tit for tat, a mean-spirited prank. Who else could it be? Gwendeline dismissed the matter from her mind and went to look for Miss Brown.

The rest of the day passed uneventfully, and they spent a now-rare quiet evening at home, having can-celled plans to go to the theater.

Gwendeline rose early the next morning and held a long conference with Alphonse on the subject of tea cakes. With some difficulty she persuaded him to forego the elaborate many-layered, cream-covered confections he had in mind in favor of some simpler sweets. As they talked, it seemed to her that he had regained his former spirits. Greatly encouraged, she began to hope that the latest domestic crisis was really over at last.

Gwendeline had promised Mr. Ames to be ready promptly at one for their picture viewing expedition, and he arrived as the hour was striking. Gwendeline was amazed and a bit dismayed to find that he had made extended arrangements for the afternoon, including viewings of several paintings in private houses. It was to be a thorough lesson.

They said goodbye to Miss Brown and entered the open carriage Mr. Ames had rented in town; he'd carefully plotted the best route to take in order to reach all stops and return most expeditiously. He was in high spirits and looked jollier than ever, with his halo of white hair blown by the breeze and his eyes twinkling. "A capital day," he said to Gwendeline when they were settled in their seats and under way. "You're going to enjoy this, I promise."

"I am sure I shall," replied Gwendeline.

And somewhat to her surprise, she did. Mr. Ames spent some time with each picture they saw, explaining the effects it achieved, the brush strokes, the color use, and the individual techniques of the artists. Gwendeline's part in the afternoon's conversation consisted chiefly of murmurs of agreement, but she thoroughly enjoyed his explanations. His discourses were fascinating, and the paintings they saw were beautiful. She particularly liked a series of aquatint lithographs they looked at in a private home. Mr. William Daniel had formed the idea of cataloguing English harbors and seacoast towns in a "Voyage around Great Britain," and since the responses of "those noblemen and gentlemen who wish to become subscribers" had been very favorable, he was now doing so. Mr. Ames pointed out the fine detail in the works so far completed and praised the concept. He, too, was most interested in landscapes.

Gwendeline's head was whirling by the time they'd finished only half their tour, and Mr. Ames was beginning to realize that his plan for the day had been too ambitious. They both agreed that a cup of tea would be welcome and stopped in a tea shop near Bond Street.

As they sipped, Mr. Ames continued his talk of the surprising way in which completely alien colors could be used effectively to convey a scene. "Blue in the trees, say, or purple in a stone." He cocked an eye at Gwendeline. "But we talked of this the first time I saw your painting, didn't we?"

"Did we?" answered Gwendeline. "I've forgotten."

"Red in the ocean it was. I'm certain of it." He

grinned. "I may forget a name or a face, but never a painting. Did you put it in?" Gwendeline looked a bit puzzled, so he continued. "The red, you know, did you put it in your painting?"

"Oh," said Gwendeline. "I must have." She remembered that she'd done no such thing but had dismissed Mr. Ames as something of a busybody. "I'll have to look for that canvas."

The twinkle in Mr. Ames's eyes grew more pronounced. "Indeed," he answered, "I should like to see how the red came out." When Gwendeline, unable to frame a truthful yet tactful reply, grew obviously uncomfortable, Mr. Ames burst out laughing. "What a goose you are. Of course you didn't put in the red. No decent artist lets someone else dictate his strokes." He drew out his handkerchief to wipe his eyes. "Your face," he went on between great bursts of laughter, "you looked so guilty, like a little girl caught stealing jam, you know."

Gwendeline smiled. "I only meant to be polite," she replied, as Mr. Ames's laughter began to subside.

"Oh, ah." He wiped his eyes one last time, put his handkerchief back in his pocket, ran a hand through his untamable hair, and sat back, hands folded over his stomach. "Polite!" he said with contempt. His expression grew more serious. "Never be polite about art, Gwendeline. Or indeed about anything really important. You have to say what you think when it matters, when a thing means something to you." He stared at Gwendeline. "Do you understand me?"

"Yes," said Gwendeline. "But it's not always

possible to say what one means. There are times when politeness is very necessary."

"No." Mr. Ames looked at her from beneath his bushy eyebrows and opened his mouth to say something further, but at that moment a voice behind Gwendeline said, "Miss Gregory." She turned to find Major St. Audley standing there.

"Hello," she answered, surprised. "I should never have expected to find you here, Major." She smiled at his obvious discomfort in the tea shop.

He looked around the room. "Nor will you ever again," he said with a grimace, "but I promised to meet my mother here this afternoon. Some nonsense about parcels." He grinned. "I think she just wants one of her sons dancing attendance, and she knows there's no hope of getting Alex."

Gwendeline laughed, but she grew a little uneasy, hearing that Lady Merryn was expected. "I'm sure she'd rather have you," she said.

"Much the better man for a tea shop and shopping expedition?" he asked her wryly. He made a face and bowed mockingly. "Thank you very much."

As she laughed at this sally, Gwendeline glanced across the table. "Mr. Ames, allow me to introduce Major St. Audley. Major, Mr. Carleton Ames."

The two gentlemen said how do you do; Major St. Audley bowed. "So, I take it you haven't seen my mother?" he went on.

"No," answered Gwendeline. "Oh, is that her carriage coming down the street?"

The major peered out the window. "I believe you're right. I think I'll try to outflank her." He grinned as he said his farewells. "Perhaps I can keep her from dragging me in here for tea," he said over his shoulder as he left.

Gwendeline watched him walk out the door and over to the carriage. After some conversation, the major climbed into it, and they drove away. Gwendeline breathed a sigh of relief. She'd been afraid Lady Merryn would come in to join them and upset Mr. Ames. When she turned back to this gentleman, he was eyeing her. "Major St. Audley is a son of Lady Merryn's," she said.

"Ah, a friend of yours then?" he replied, still surveying her.

"Yes, that is, an acquaintance." Gwendeline took another sip of her tea. She hoped Mr. Ames wouldn't take up the subject of lady novelists.

"This reminds me of something I wished to speak to you about. My wife insists that I do so, in fact, and I must say that for once I agree."

"What is it?" asked Gwendeline, puzzled, as he paused.

Mr. Ames appeared uneasy. "Rather difficult to begin," he said. "The thing is, we were wondering, my wife and I, whether you're in trouble of any kind."

Gwendeline frowned at him.

"What I mean is, not trying to pry or any such thing, but we've been worried about you. All that nonsense about your family in that foolish book. And your never mentioning London when we were in the country. I got to thinking perhaps there was something amiss."

"It's very kind of you to be concerned, but I assure you that I'm fine. There's nothing wrong."

Mr. Ames looked dissatisfied and more uncomfortable. "What you would say to put me off, of course. The thing I mean to say is, no need to explain anything to me, but if I can help in any way…" He paused, coughed, and went on a bit gruffly. "Have a bit of money, you know. You're welcome to whatever you need."

Gwendeline was surprised and touched by this offer. "Thank you, Mr. Ames," she said. "I don't know what to say to you, except that everything is all right with me now." Mr. Ames started to speak again, but Gwendeline forestalled him. "I was rather upset and uncertain when I first came to Penwyn, I admit. I had run away from London without waiting for explanations of some rumors that worried me. I was very foolish. But since then, I've found out the truth and all is well." She smiled.

Mr. Ames appeared partly satisfied, but still a little nervous. "The thing is," he brought out finally, "m'wife received some letters from home. Something about a disappearance or some such nonsense. All a hum, I'm sure, or twisted about by some tattling gabblemonger, but she's been fidgeting." He became more emphatic in response to Gwendeline's distressed expression. "None of our business; I told her so. Told her it wouldn't do for us to intrude ourselves where we weren't wanted or needed. But she made me promise I'd try to help." He paused, looking embarrassed.

Gwendeline's dismay at hearing that someone in London knew of her abduction lessened. "I'd prefer to say nothing about this story," she told Mr. Ames. "But I can honestly assure you that the trouble has been remedied."

Mr. Ames was relieved. "That's good then. Must apologize, but I promised I would ask, you know."

Gwendeline nodded. "It was very kind of you to be concerned."

"Wish I could have helped," he replied. "Never had any children, you know, but... Ah, well, I'm very glad you've come about all right and tight." His expression lightened. "My wife had some ridiculous idea that you'd tried to elope with a young man and were prevented by his family. Then, when you spoke to that youngster, well, I began to jump to conclusions." He laughed ruefully. "You'll think us a pair of old fools. M'wife wished to help in the romance and give you a dowry or some such silliness. Daresay you don't need anything of the kind." He looked a little hopeful.

"No indeed," replied Gwendeline.

His face fell. "That's what I told her. Ridiculous idea."

"You are the kindest people I've ever met, and I only hope I can repay you someday for your offer," said Gwendeline. "I'm deeply touched by what you have tried to do."

Mr. Ames coughed. "Ah, well," he said. "No need for that. Just keep us in mind if you need anything, you know."

"Thank you," she answered.

"Well, if you've finished your tea," said Mr. Ames heartily then, "we must get on. A great many pictures still to see today." He rose from his chair.

They continued their tour, though they didn't see everything Mr. Ames had planned to view. Gwendeline returned home just in time to change for her dinner party, tired but warmed by the Ameses's gesture of friendship and eager to reciprocate in some way. When she told Miss Brown, she too was touched, saying that this confirmed her high opinion of the Ameses.

Throughout the very dull evening, Gwendeline thought periodically of them and of what she might do to show her appreciation. By the time she was ready for bed later on, she was rather annoyed that she could think of nothing, but she vowed she would not give up.

Eighteen

THE FOLLOWING EVENING GWENDELINE AND MISS Brown were to go to Almack's, the first large public gathering they'd attended in some time, and Gwendeline readied herself with care. Her dress was one she'd worn before, a sea-green crepe, but she looked well in it, she knew, and tonight she added a filmy wrap of real lace.

As she dressed, she once again encouraged Ellen to talk, and she soon had the girl chattering as constantly as ever. This further sign that things were returning to normal in her household was a relief. Moreover, it seemed that Ellen was striking up a friendship with Yvette, a gratifying development. The two had always maintained a certain distance, which had led to some quarreling and discord. But now it seemed that this was past. Yvette had expressed her sympathy with Ellen's position and won her over. As she went downstairs that evening, Gwendeline felt rather complacent about the way she'd managed during this difficult period.

The two ladies arrived on the steps of Almack's by

nine thirty, well before its doors would be closed to latecomers. They chanced to encounter Lillian Everly and her mother as they were going in, and since the girls hadn't seen each other for an entire day, they were soon deep in conversation. Miss Brown chatted amiably with Mrs. Everly, and the two of them found chairs together; they had become friends since Gwendeline's return to London.

Gwendeline told Lillian all about her tour of English paintings. The latter was a little envious. "To be escorted on a picture viewing expedition by one of our foremost living artists! Really, Gwendeline, that's a bit ostentatious, is it not? Splendid luck you have, that's all I can say. Things fall into your lap."

Gwendeline retorted in the same facetious spirit. "Someone born both beautiful and rich shouldn't belittle luck, my dear Lillian." She grinned at her friend, and they laughed together.

"Well, I really am envious," Lillian went on. "I spent the day most drearily. First, endless fittings for my new ball gown. Mother is never satisfied with it because I'm to wear it to the duchess's ball; she wishes me to look perfect. And then"—Lillian paused dramatically, giving Gwendeline a mock tragic glance—"in the afternoon, who do you think called on us?"

"The queen?" answered Gwendeline.

"No, goose, and you've quite spoiled the effect of my revelation. The Duchess of Craigbourne herself called."

This information sobered Gwendeline. "Really, Lillian? What did she want?"

"Just to look me over, my mother believes," Lillian replied. Her gaiety had begun to sound slightly false.

"She thinks it a very good sign, for the duke is much influenced by his mother's opinion."

"Ugh," said Gwendeline. "Just like poor Lord Wanley. I suppose the duchess is even worse than his mother. How horrid!"

Lillian considered. "No," she said. "If I'm honest, I must say that the duchess is nothing like Lady Wanley." She turned to look at Gwendeline. "She's a very formidable woman, but she has a kind of dignity and true politeness that Lady Wanley will never approach." Lillian shrugged, smiling ruefully. "I admit I rather admired her. I hope to be half so composed one day."

"Lillian, you're not changing your mind about marrying the duke because of his mother?"

"No, indeed. It's just more proof that they're a charming family and I am a fool to reject such a chance."

"That is what your mother says, I suppose," answered Gwendeline.

Lillian nodded. "And you know as well as I that she's right, Gwendeline. Such matches are very rare. I would have everything. Rank, wealth, social position, and a pleasant, considerate husband and mother-in-law. When she talked of how she would be moving to the dowager's residence as soon as the duke married, for she does not believe that young couples should be burdened with family, I was ready to sink."

At that moment both girls were solicited for the first dance and conversation became impossible. Gwendeline danced the first few sets with some of her usual partners, young men whom she liked and could chat with easily. She tried several times to speak with Lillian, but could find no opportunity for private

conversation. The set preceding supper was just forming when she saw Lillian solicited by the Duke of
Craigbourne, and Gwendeline realized with chagrin
that the duke would take her in to supper. She was
just wondering whether she could somehow separate
them when a voice beside her said, "They make a
fine couple, don't they?" It was Major St. Audley, and
his tone was bitter. "They have all the prerequisites.
He has great wealth and position; she has beauty,
elegance, and enough money to tempt him. It's a
perfect match."

"Oh, I'm nearly out of patience with the two of
you. Why must you be so foolish?"

The major looked rather surprised. "What would
you have me do? I can't compete with the likes of
Craigbourne."

"Of course you can," insisted Gwendeline. "If you are
truly in love. Lillian cares more for love than position."

"You seem very sure of that, but I'm not. She would
be the foolish one, to take me over Craigbourne.
And I'm not even certain she cares for me at all, you
know." He turned back to Gwendeline suddenly.
"Unless... Has she said something to you?"

Gwendeline shook her head, and the major's face
fell. "But I have a feeling," Gwendeline said, "that she
is not indifferent to you."

He brightened for a moment then looked down
again. "A feeling," he said. "You're imagining things
because you wish to help me." He put up a hand to
forestall her answer. "And that is very kind. I'm grateful. But it's no use." The music was beginning. "I
came over to ask you to dance, in any case. Shall we

join the set?" He held out his hand, and Gwendeline took it, though she felt like shaking him. He and Lillian would never overcome the obstacles in the path of love if they remained so obdurate. For a moment she felt like giving up and leaving them to their fates.

But as she danced, she reconsidered. It wasn't Lillian's fault entirely that she was acting foolishly. She had no idea that the major loved her. And he believed that he was being noble, sacrificing himself for his love. Gwendeline wouldn't give up yet. As the dance ended, she tried to ensure that they stopped near Lillian and the duke. The major was reluctant, but Gwendeline maneuvered him close enough so that they had to speak. As the two of them approached from one side, Gwendeline was rather annoyed to see Lord Merryn and Adele coming from the other. All four converged on Lillian and the duke at the same time.

Adele Greene appeared upset. "We're so late," she told anyone who would listen. "Alex delayed so long that we barely got in before the doors were closed, and now I have hardly danced and it's already time for supper. It's all exceedingly stupid."

Lord Merryn appeared blandly unaffected by this speech. As the party began to drift in to supper together, Major St. Audley looked little short of miserable; Adele was petulant, Lillian withdrawn, and Gwendeline was anxious. Only the duke and Lord Merryn, who remained his usual imperturbable self, seemed at ease. The latter moved to smooth things over. "Adele," he said, "I don't believe you've met the duke."

The change in Adele's expression was immediate and complete. Suddenly, she was smiling brilliantly.

"Why, no," she replied, turning toward Craigbourne. "I haven't had that honor." Lord Merryn performed the introductions with a mocking smile. Gwendeline caught his eye for a moment, and he raised his eyebrows sardonically, as if inviting her to join in his enjoyment of the scene. Gwendeline looked away, not knowing how to respond to this seeming mockery of his betrothed.

When they seated themselves at a table in the supper room, Gwendeline found herself between the major and Lord Merryn. It seemed to her that the earl had purposely placed Adele next to the duke, and she knew that she had hurried the major into the seat next to Lillian. Conversation was strained at first, as they tried to talk in one large group. But gradually, Adele began to monopolize the duke's attention, excluding Lillian, and the major perforce engaged her in conversation. This left Gwendeline and Lord Merryn to talk to each other, though Gwendeline's attention was diverted by the other conversations around the table.

Adele was acting surprisingly meek. She was listening with rapturous interest to the duke's description of his country house, really a rambling palace, in the north. Gwendeline could tell from the way he talked that he loved it dearly. Indeed, she heard him say that he always hated to leave it and come to London. Adele agreed fervently with this sentiment, as with all the duke's opinions, and Gwendeline smiled. She'd more than once heard Adele express complete distaste for country living.

Gwendeline sat back and sighed. Actually, she thought, Lillian is probably right; she could be more or less happy married to the duke and living in such a place much of the time. Lillian really loved the country. Perhaps Gwendeline was wrong to try to interfere in other people's lives. She made a wry face; she certainly hadn't done so well with her own.

"If you're going to make faces as we sit here," said Lord Merryn, "I shall talk to you. I have no objection to a little quiet. But you will have everyone in the room believing that I have done something very odd if you persist in grimacing."

Gwendeline smiled. "I'm sorry," she said. "I was thinking. I haven't been a very amusing dinner companion."

"I do not require always to be amused," he replied. "What were you thinking, to give rise to such an expression?"

"I was wondering whether it is better not to interfere in other people's lives," she answered slowly.

The earl looked genuinely startled. "Whatever made you think of that?"

Gwendeline looked up quickly and gave an embarrassed shrug. "It was simply idle speculation."

"You don't think that one should interfere for the good of all concerned?"

"How is one to judge what is for the good of everyone?" replied Gwendeline. She put her chin in her hand. "I've tried to do so on more than one occasion and have sometimes acted on my decisions, but I began to wonder just now whether I was right to do so. In my own life, I've made mistakes, so how can I presume to judge for others?"

"I think it's often easier to see the right path for another than for oneself."

Gwendeline brightened a little. "That seems true," she said. "Perhaps you're right."

Lord Merryn started to answer her, but at that moment Adele, seeing that he'd become engrossed in conversation with Gwendeline, claimed his attention. She laughingly appealed to him to confirm some story she was telling the duke, and Lord Merryn was pulled away.

Gwendeline, left to herself, turned her attention to the major and Lillian. Immediately, she felt better. The reserve she'd noticed in Major St. Audley when they first sat down had disappeared. He and Lillian were talking animatedly but comfortably like old and dear friends. When Gwendeline saw the eyes of each, she was sure she'd done the right thing in throwing them together and certain that they were in love. There was no mistaking their expressions.

Gwendeline sat back in her seat, her supper plate forgotten. How unfortunate it was that the major had no income of his own that would allow him to marry Lillian. A thought struck Gwendeline. Lord Merryn was said to be very rich. Wouldn't he give his brother a generous income if he knew his plight? Even as she asked herself this question, Gwendeline was sure he would. A man who would go to such lengths to help her, the daughter of a friend but almost a stranger to him really, would surely share his wealth with his own brother. She turned back to Lord Merryn, the request on her lips, but he was still talking with Adele and the duke.

Gwendeline realized that this was hardly the moment to bring up such a subject. The major or Lillian might have heard her! She must wait for the proper opportunity. Perhaps Major St. Audley was too proud to ask his brother for money, but she wouldn't hesitate to do so to ensure Lillian's happiness.

The earl turned back to Gwendeline. "Are you too warm?" he asked. "You look quite flushed." He smiled. "Or perhaps Andrew has said something improper?" His brother didn't hear this remark; he was too deeply occupied with Lillian.

Gwendeline smiled. "Oh no, perhaps I am a little warm."

"I wish I could offer to take you for a stroll, but I fear we could only walk about the ballroom, and it isn't much cooler there," he answered.

"No, but I should very much like some private conversation with you. On a matter of some importance."

"Indeed." He raised his eyebrows. "In that case, we should take a turn about the room. I go out of town tomorrow and won't return for several days. I have some business to see to in the country."

"I see," replied Gwendeline. "Could we talk now?" She looked about the room uncertainly.

"This appears to be important."

"I think it is." Gwendeline half rose from her seat. But at that moment two things occurred. The music started up again in the ballroom, causing a beginning exodus of diners, and Adele once more claimed the earl's attention. Gwendeline had already promised the first dance after supper, and as Lord Merryn tried to escape Adele, the young man came to claim her so that they might join a set of his friends. Everything seemed to conspire against any private talk with the earl.

As she made her way back to the ballroom,

Gwendeline noticed that Adele and the duke, and Lillian and the major, were following to join the dancers. This was something, at least. She went through the movements of the quadrille impatiently, eager to get away to talk to Lord Merryn.

But for the rest of the evening, she could find no opportunity to do so. Either she was occupied, dancing or chatting, or he was engaged, and when he attempted to ask her to dance, she had already promised the set to someone else. Gwendeline felt very frustrated. Only as she and Miss Brown were leaving was she able to speak to him alone for a moment. He came up to say good night when Adele was occupied in bidding the duke farewell. "I'm sorry we've had no chance to talk," he told Gwendeline. "It's always difficult in such surroundings. Can this matter wait a little while?"

Gwendeline nodded. "I suppose so. You're going out of town tomorrow?"

"Very early."

"You will return for my party?" she exclaimed.

He smiled. "That would bring me back if nothing else did," he replied. "Though I may not return until that very day." At this point Adele called to him that their carriage was ready, and a look of annoyance crossed his face. "I must go. But I will call as soon as I'm able." He bowed and walked away.

Gwendeline went home dissatisfied but resigned. She comforted herself by imagining how happy Lillian and Major St. Audley would be when her plan succeeded. She was tired and eager to get to bed, but as she started up the stairs, Reeves once again handed her a note that had been delivered by hand. Gwendeline took it gingerly, staring at it for some moments before she continued up to her chamber. She laid the envelope on her dressing table, and while she made ready for bed, she glanced at it repeatedly. She began to feel as though it was a snake or some other venomous creature lying there waiting to strike. Finally, she picked it up. "I am *not* afraid to open it," she said fiercely to her image in the mirror. "It's probably nothing." She ripped open the envelope and pulled out the contents. Then, she fell back in her chair. It was exactly like the last—the uneven black printing and the threatening message. Gwendeline dropped it on her dressing table.

This time she would keep the note and show it to Miss Brown, she decided. She should have done so in the first place. Having decided this, she felt better, and after a time, was able to sleep.

In the morning, Gwendeline sought out Miss Brown as soon as she returned from her early errands, showed her the note, and explained its history, as well as her connection of it with the one sent to Adele Greene. When she'd finished, Miss Brown said nothing for a while, but she looked very serious as she stared at the note. Finally, she tapped it with her finger and said, "I believe Lord Merryn should be told of this immediately. Two such letters, and the one sent to Adele, are not to be taken lightly. We must ask for help in this matter. It calls for investigation. Lord Merryn will agree with me, I'm sure. We should send a note round to his house immediately."

"He has gone out of town," Gwendeline replied. "He won't be back for several days. He mentioned it last night at Almack's."

Miss Brown frowned. "Well, I suppose it will do no harm to wait that long." She looked steadily at Gwendeline. "I doubt there is any real threat to you. Persons who write such letters generally do nothing further, I've heard. But it will be wise to be careful, and we shall ask Lord Merryn to look into it as soon as possible." She folded up the note. "I shall keep this," she finished.

"But who can be sending these dreadful things, Brown?"

"Most likely an unpleasant individual has lighted on your name and is playing a wicked prank."

"But what of Adele's letter? The writer of that knew something of me and my circumstances."

Miss Brown frowned. "I'm not convinced all the letters came from one person," she answered. "But as I said, we would do well to be careful."

Reeves entered the breakfast room. "Lady Merryn has called," he announced.

Gwendeline and Miss Brown looked up in surprise. It was not yet nine, well before the countess's usual hour of rising. Lady Merryn followed Reeves into the room, and she spoke breathlessly before they could greet her. "I had to come immediately," she said. "I know it's terribly early, but I was sure you would be up and I have just had such news! Alex has been attacked by highwaymen!"

"What!" exclaimed both of her listeners.

Lady Merryn appeared very satisfied with the reaction she'd provoked. She sat down at the breakfast table and helped herself to the remains of the tea in the pot. "I rushed out so early, I had no time for breakfast," she said, reaching for a muffin.

"But what's happened?" cried Gwendeline. "Is Lord Merryn hurt?"

The countess looked a little surprised at the intensity of this outburst, then turned contrite. "No, no, Alex is perfectly all right. I'm sorry for being so dramatic in my announcement. I've upset you."

"You've certainly made us eager to hear your story, at any rate," replied Miss Brown, mildly censorious.

"Of course." Lady Merryn abandoned her breakfast and sat back. "Well, Alex started out of town at first light this morning. Perhaps you knew he was going to look over some properties in the country?" At their nods, she continued. "He'd hardly passed the city limits when his carriage was set upon by two highwaymen, with pistols." Lady Merryn's eyes glowed. "Imagine, real highwaymen!"

Gwendeline shuddered. "I'm trying my best not to do so," she said. "You're sure he's not hurt?"

"No, no, he's all right. His groom, however, received a ball in the shoulder."

"What?" cried Gwendeline. "Someone was shot?"

"Hitchins," answered the countess, looking slightly perplexed, "the groom. The two villains demanded money, and Alex gave them his purse. Very cowhearted of him."

"Rather, very sensible," put in Miss Brown.

"Well, in any case, they weren't satisfied with that, which is excessively odd because Alex had nearly a hundred pounds with him. They demanded that everyone descend from the carriage. Alex had his valet with him as well, you know." She stopped and took a sip of tea. Gwendeline, wild with impatience, felt like shaking her, but she knew it would do no good. Finally, Lady Merryn went on. "Well, at that request Hitchins became angry. He's been with Alex since he was a child, you know, and he is quite attached to him. He tried to draw his pistol. Alex always insists on carrying guns when traveling. It makes me very uneasy. One of the highwaymen saw his movement and shot him through the arm. Only a flesh wound, whether by intent or from poor shooting, I do not know." Lady Merryn waved her hand airily. "The robbers' attention being diverted by this incident, Alex and his valet managed to reach their weapons. The valet actually fired, I believe, but he missed his aim. He is, in any case, a shockingly poor shot." She put her chin in her hand. "A pity. I should have liked to interview a real highwayman."

"What happened then?" asked Gwendeline anxiously.

"Oh." Lady Merryn started. "The ruffians were scared off. They fled, and Alex brought Hitchins to me because of his wound. He is properly poulticed and bandaged now. The foolish man wished to continue on, but he's much too weak."

"You mean Lord Merryn resumed his journey?" asked Gwendeline.

"Oh, yes," answered the countess. "He is gone again."

"Why? How could he start out again after being attacked in that way?"

Lady Merryn looked surprised. "He had business waiting. You wouldn't expect him to remain cowering in London?"

"Yes, I would," insisted Gwendeline. "At least until

those men are caught. How could he go back out on the road when they're lurking there?"

"Oh, I think highwaymen rarely attack one twice," replied the countess. "Why should they indeed, once they have taken your money?"

Gwendeline was speechless with frustration at Lady Merryn's careless attitude.

"I'm sure he'll be all right," continued the latter soothingly. "Alex is well able to take care of himself. Has been since he was a boy."

"If he thought it right to go on, I am sure he had good reason," said Miss Brown.

Unable to contain herself any longer, Gwendeline jumped up and ran from the room.

"Well." Lady Merryn seemed surprised. "Everything is all right now, after all."

Miss Brown only nodded.

The countess rose. "I must go. I wanted to tell you the news and reassure you. I feared you might hear gossip later in the day. These sorts of things get so distorted when they circulate about town, you know."

"That was very kind of you," answered Miss Brown. "I know Gwendeline appreciates it also. I will see you out."

When she had said goodbye to Lady Merryn, Miss Brown went in search of Gwendeline. She found her in the drawing room, sitting in one of the armchairs staring at the wall. The girl looked up when she entered. "I'm sorry, Brown. I simply couldn't endure it any longer. How could she be so calm? To call such a horrible thing romantic!"

"She knew her son was safe and the groom taken

care of," replied Miss Brown mildly. "For her, the whole incident was past, while for you, it was fresh and new."

"And just after we were talking of those horrid letters. It was too much." A thought struck her suddenly. "You do not think the two could be connected?"

"The letters and the highwaymen?"

Gwendeline nodded.

"What possible connection could there be?" asked Miss Brown.

"I...I don't know. They are both dreadful..." Gwendeline trailed off uncertainly.

"They are," Miss Brown agreed. "And that is all they have in common."

"You're right." Gwendeline sighed. "But I find life a bit too eventful these days. At Brooklands a broken plate was the greatest tragedy."

"In that, I must agree," replied Miss Brown. "Let us hope all of the excitement is over now."

Nineteen

FOR SOME DAYS THEREAFTER, IT SEEMED THAT MISS Brown's wish would be granted. No untoward events marred their peace, and the only excitement was preparing for Gwendeline's approaching tea. As it grew closer to the day, that topic came to occupy the attention of most members of the household. And on the day before it was finally to occur, when Lillian called to see her, Gwendeline was busy with preparations still. "Lillian!" cried Gwendeline when the other girl followed Reeves into the drawing room that morning. "I'm so glad to see you. I can hardly keep still. And Alphonse will not listen to me about the muffins."

"Muffins?"

"He says the Englishman's excuse for a muffin is inedible and will sit in the stomachs of my guests like a cannonball. He refuses even to attempt to make any muffins," finished Gwendeline with a wail.

Lillian burst out laughing. Gwendeline looked at her with indignation at first, then gradually began to smile. Finally she, too, laughed. "Well, it is annoying," she said when their laughter had subsided. "I so wish my tea to be perfect, and some little detail is always going wrong. First, a hole is found in the best table-cloth, then the silver polish is mysteriously missing just when Reeves is preparing to do the silver, and now there will be no muffins. I'll never give another party as long as I live."

"I'm sure it will be splendid," answered Lillian. "You sound just as my mother always does before entertaining. But all the problems will resolve themselves before tomorrow; they always do."

"You needn't worry. You're only a guest," Gwendeline retorted. "No one will blame you if there are no muffins." But she couldn't help smiling at her own remark.

"Why not simply buy some muffins?" suggested Lillian, "and smuggle them in to tea without Alphonse's knowledge?"

Gwendeline brightened. "What a wonderful idea!"

"But, of course, if they aren't eaten, you'll be forced to finish them before the trays are taken back to the kitchen." Her eyes twinkled. Gwendeline's fondness for muffins was a recurring joke between them.

"I shall simply have to endure the hardship. One must make sacrifices for the sake of one's guests. But you are resourceful! You've solved my final problem."

"Then you can cease pacing and sit down," Lillian said. "You've been prowling about the room since I arrived."

Gwendeline did so, looking a little sheepish. "I know you think me a goose, but I've never given any sort of party before."

"It will go perfectly, I know. Did your preparations keep you from Almack's last night?"

"Yes," answered Gwendeline. "The hole in the cloth. Was the evening very gay?"

"Oh, it was much as usual. Adele Greene made a nuisance of herself. I begin to wish I weren't acquainted with her at all."

"What now?"

"She attached herself to me almost from the beginning of the evening. When I was talking with the duke soon after I arrived, she joined us and wouldn't take herself off. The duke was finally forced to ask her to dance."

"Does he dislike her also?"

"He has not said so," Lillian replied. "He's much too polite. But he is a sensible man; he must be repelled by her simpering airs."

"As is Lord Merryn?" asked Gwendeline skeptically.

"Oh." Lillian waved a hand. "That is a mystery which will be cleared up very soon, I'm sure."

Her tone made Gwendeline suspicious. "Have you hatched some scheme?"

Lillian's eyes were wide and innocent. "I?" she replied. "I'm sure I don't know what you mean."

"What have you done? Oh, Lillian, please tell me."

Lillian continued to declare that she'd done nothing, though her tone told Gwendeline otherwise. But she would reveal no details of her plan and finally rose to leave when Gwendeline's questions grew too insistent.

"You may believe what you choose," she told Gwendeline as she went out, "but you know I shall do what I can to ensure your happiness." And with these enigmatic words, she was gone.

Gwendeline sat back in her chair with a sigh. She did not at all like the feeling that someone else was trying to order her future. At this thought, she smiled. "It's only what I deserve, after all," she said aloud, "for what else have I been doing to Lillian?" With a rueful smile and a shrug, she resolved to try to accept whatever Lillian was planning with good grace. Perhaps then Lillian would do the same for her scheme.

The day passed in a bustle of household chores, and the following morning was even busier, but by four that afternoon Gwendeline was sitting in her drawing room ready to welcome her guests.

She looked around with some satisfaction. The room was filled with fresh flowers, and the table in the corner looked splendid. Miss Brown had mended the cloth exquisitely; it was impossible to tell where the hole had been. The silver was shining, and Alphonse's cakes were a triumph. Miss Brown came in just then with a large plate of muffins and set it beside the silver teapot. She smiled at Gwendeline, who giggled. The stratagems involved in getting that innocent-looking plate to its present place had been tortuous. Miss Brown placed a cloth over it and came over to sit beside Gwendeline, sighing as she leaned back. "Alphonse has no notion," she said, "but I was obliged to ask Yvette to steal a plate for me from the kitchen. I hope he won't miss it. And I hope the muffins will stay warm."

"Well, even if he should, it's too late. We have the muffins now. He can't rush in and take them from the table."

"No?" Miss Brown smiled ruefully. "You underestimate him."

"Oh, but he would not!"

"No, I don't think he would quite dare. But if he should learn of our ruse, you may be sure we'll hear from him."

Gwendeline tossed her head; her mind turned to more important questions. "Where is everyone? Do you think they have all decided not to come?"

"Do not, I pray you Gwendeline, begin to upset yourself. It is only just four thirty, and no one arrives exactly at the time set. You know that."

"Yes," said Gwendeline. "It's just that I have been preparing and anticipating so long I want it to begin and be over."

"Go downstairs and see that the tea is being prepared."

"Oh, I don't want to." Gwendeline stood and pirouetted before the drawing room mirror. "Do I look all right, Brown?"

Miss Brown surveyed the slender blond figure with fond approval. Gwendeline was wearing a pale green muslin gown sprigged with tiny flowers in the most-delicate possible shade of apricot. Her ribbons matched these blooms; her eyes sparkled and her bright curls shone. "You look very well."

As Gwendeline turned from the mirror, Reeves brought in Lillian and Lady Merryn. The countess settled herself on the sofa, insisting that the others sit elsewhere. "I shall keep this seat for Mr. Ames," she said, patting the place beside her. "I mean to have a good talk with him."

Gwendeline smiled a little nervously at this, but Miss Brown calmly took one of the armchairs opposite the sofa and began to chat with Lady Merryn about her recent activities.

Lillian, meanwhile, was looking over the tea table. She lifted the cloth on the muffin plate with exaggerated care. "I see you succeeded in procuring muffins," she said softly.

Gwendeline turned with a smile. "Yes, but at such a cost! The footman was sworn to secrecy very early this morning and sent in search of them. He had a great deal of trouble finding proper muffins, too. When he finally returned, we were in despair; they were cold, and we couldn't imagine how we were to warm them, with Alphonse busy in the kitchen. Miss Brown was forced to heat them over her bedroom fire after getting Yvette, the maid, to steal the necessary tools from under Alphonse's very nose."

"If he finds out," Lillian said through her giggles, "you may tell him that I especially requested muffins, forcing you to get them at the last minute."

"I shall," replied Gwendeline. "In fact, I'd already planned to do so."

"I hope he won't take his revenge by ruining everything I eat in your house in future." Lillian looked around the room. "Everything looks lovely, Gwendeline. You've done a splendid job."

"Do you think so?" asked Gwendeline. "Truly?"

"I do. And it is well that it does. You've devoted all your time for days to this occasion. I missed you sadly in the park yesterday afternoon."

Gwendeline sighed. "Was the riding good? I was sorry to miss it."

"Wonderful. And I also saw some interesting sights."

Lillian raised her eyebrows and looked teasingly at the other girl. "You've become such a domestic creature, I daresay you aren't interested in frivolous gossip?"

"Tell me," cried Gwendeline commandingly.

Lillian laughed. "Very well. I saw Adele Greene out riding with the Duke of Craigbourne in his new curricle."

"Really? I thought they were hardly acquainted."

"They are rapidly becoming close friends," Lillian continued. "Adele is seeing to that. But it is a great relief to me; it solves the mystery of Adele's sudden cultivation of my company."

"Why?" Gwendeline frowned.

"She wished to know the duke," explained Lillian. "So she hung about me knowing that I was acquainted with him and would be bound to speak with him. When he approached me, she seized her chance to entrap him. I'm surprised I didn't perceive her intent earlier. The only thing that puzzles me now is how the duke can tolerate her company with such apparent equanimity."

"You sound almost jealous, Lillian."

Lillian paused and looked meditatively at the wall. "I do, don't I?" she said after a moment. "It's most curious. I suppose I am a very selfish creature underneath. I don't want the duke's attentions, but when he distinguishes someone else, I'm unreasonably annoyed." She grimaced. "It's hard to lose such an eminent suitor."

Gwendeline looked at her sharply. "But Adele is already engaged. She's no danger to you. She wouldn't give up Lord Merryn for the duke. Would she?"

Lillian seemed to recall herself then. "Oh dear,

I've let my imagination and my wretched tongue go too far again. I forgot your interest in this; I'm sorry. Adele wishes to be seen with titled persons and men of fashion. I hope I haven't upset you with my silly talk?"

"Of course not," replied Gwendeline. "I was merely surprised." But when she turned away to speak to Lady Merryn, Gwendeline realized that she had for a moment entertained a real hope. She was bitterly disappointed.

Her other guests began to arrive soon after this. Major St. Audley came in looking very pleased with himself, bearing a huge bouquet of yellow roses, which he presented with a flourish to Gwendeline. "For your table," he said grinning, "tea roses."

Gwendeline laughed and took the offering from him. The bouquet was so large it nearly overwhelmed her. "Thank you very much," she said from behind the flowers. "They're lovely." She peered around at him. "There are so many."

"I wished to commemorate your first tea party properly," he answered. "Perhaps I was a bit overenthusiastic. Shall I take them?" But Reeves reappeared at that moment with a vase and rescued Gwendeline from the flowers.

The major walked over to greet the other ladies as Gwendeline and Reeves settled the bouquet in the vase. They had only just finished when the Ameses arrived, and the effect of their entrance was immediate and impressive. Most of the people in the room reacted visibly to Mrs. Ames's costume, a flowing purple tea gown with a mass of fluttering draperies. Lady Merryn's attention focused on Mr. Ames. To Gwendeline's relief, she didn't pounce on him directly, but she appeared poised to do so, and Gwendeline hurried over to the doorway to welcome them.

"Do come in and sit down," said Gwendeline. "I should like to introduce my friends." When Gwendeline turned, Lady Merryn's gimlet eye was fixed firmly upon her, and she could do nothing but take the Ameses over to the countess. "Lady Merryn," she said with some trepidation, "I should like you to meet Mr. and Mrs. Ames." Lillian and the major strolled over from the opposite side of the room where they'd been talking, and Gwendeline made the whole party known to one another at once.

"I'm so pleased to make your acquaintance," said Lady Merryn as soon as the formalities were completed. "Won't you sit here?" She patted the sofa beside her and fixed Mr. Ames with a piercing glance. He was forced to take the seat, but he looked reproachfully at Gwendeline as he did so. Gwendeline made a helpless gesture.

Miss Brown and Mrs. Ames seated themselves in chairs nearby, and Lillian and the major returned to their talk. As Gwendeline surveyed her guests, she saw them all suitably occupied. Only Lord Merryn remained absent. Gwendeline wondered whether he'd been detained in the country and would not come after all. Surely he would have sent word? But it was time to call for tea; she was uncertain whether to wait or go on without him.

The problem was solved for her when Lord Merryn entered the room. Gwendeline told Reeves to begin serving as she went over to greet the earl.

"I'm sorry to be late," Lord Merryn told her as

Reeves went out. "I see you've waited for me. My delayed start from town kept me away until just a little while ago."

"I hope your return journey was less eventful than your departure?"

The earl sighed. "Of course Mother has told everyone in London of that stupid mishap. I suppose I'll have to talk of highwaymen for the next month."

"I beg your pardon," answered Gwendeline a bit stiffly. "I didn't mean to bring up a forbidden subject."

"No subject is forbidden you, Gwendeline," the earl answered. "I was simply anticipating a great deal of boredom."

The servants brought in tea before Gwendeline could reply, and for some time she was busy filling cups and offering them, along with the muffins and cakes. She noticed with amused resignation that Alphonse had sent in one of his whipped cream-covered French constructions with the tea despite her prohibition.

Finally, everyone was served, and Gwendeline relaxed a little and looked around the room. Her guests appeared content. Mr. Ames had escaped from Lady Merryn and was now more happily chatting with Lillian. The countess was involved with Mrs. Ames and Miss Brown in the corner, and the earl and his brother were engaged in what seemed a serious discussion across the room. Everyone was well supplied with refreshment, and no one was left alone. The party was a success.

Gwendeline started across the floor but was stopped by a call from Mr. Ames. Shaking his finger at her, he said, "I'm quite put out with you. You unfeelingly left me talking with that lady novelist for half an hour. It's only because you also invited this charming young woman that I forgive you." He gestured toward Lillian.

"Lady Merryn is really quite charming," replied Gwendeline. "Was your conversation not pleasant?"

"Hmph," said Mr. Ames. "Actually, the lady knows a good deal about art. Quite surprised me, you know. And she refrained from talking about her novels."

"Lady Merryn mentioned that she particularly likes Mr. Ames's seascapes," put in Lillian. "She prefers them to his other work, that is." She smiled at Gwendeline.

"Yes," said the artist with rising enthusiasm. "Fancy a lady novelist knowing even that much about painting. Her reasons were all wrong, of course, but still she had the taste to prefer my new things to that early trash. I was impressed. I shall forgive you this time. And now, you may run along and I shall continue my talk with your charming friend."

Gwendeline smiled and dropped him a small curtsy. "Yes, sir," she said. "I'll hope to talk with you later, then." She continued across the room and stopped near Lord Merryn and his brother. They didn't notice her at first, they were so deep in conversation.

"Have they found no trace?" the major was saying. "That's outrageous. You might have been killed, Alex."

"They were indeed rather unusual highwaymen," replied the earl. "Any footpad, one would think, would have been more than satisfied with £150 from a private coach. Why they didn't take to their heels immediately is a mystery." Turning his head, he caught sight of Gwendeline standing behind him. "Ah, Gwendeline. Your tea is excellent."

"Do you think they were not real highwaymen?" answered Gwendeline, ignoring the commonplace.

Lord Merryn raised his eyebrows. "They were real enough to shoot my groom. I would never question their reality."

"You know that's not what I meant," replied Gwendeline impatiently. "You said they were unusual. Do you believe there was something strange or mysterious about them?"

"I believe," he replied, "that they were unusually greedy."

"Oh, you don't wish to tell me what you think. I can see that. But I wish you might. With all these horrid things happening lately, I'm nearly frantic."

Both men looked surprised. "What other horrid things have occurred?" asked the earl.

"I think Gwendeline must be referring to these," Miss Brown said. Seeing Gwendeline in earnest conversation with the St. Audleys, she'd moved to join them. And now she held out the note Gwendeline had received.

The earl took it, frowning, and read the message. His brother looked over his shoulder to see the contents. When he'd finished, Lord Merryn glanced up sharply. "You said 'these.' Are there more of them, then?"

"One other," said Gwendeline. "I burned it before I thought. I was upset."

"I should think you might be!" put in the major. "Beastly thing."

Lord Merryn folded the note again and put it in his pocket. "I shall look into this," he said, with a grim expression on his face.

"Thank you," said Miss Brown. "We hoped you would do so."

"You'll tell us what you discover?" asked Gwendeline.

He nodded. "This was the matter you wished to speak to me about, no doubt. I should have delayed my journey. I'm sorry you've worried longer than necessary."

"Oh, it wasn't that," Gwendeline answered automatically. Lord Merryn looked at her. "That is, I did wish to tell you. But there was something else." She glanced nervously at the major. "Perhaps you can remain after my guests have gone." The earl bowed, and Gwendeline walked away quickly. She was embarrassed to have made such a bold public request. If it weren't a case of Lillian's future, she told herself, she would forget the whole matter.

Gwendeline chatted for a time with each of her guests. Mrs. Ames catalogued for her all the dresses she had purchased in London, and Gwendeline had to admit they made an interesting and unusual list. Lady Merryn told her of some new letters she'd received from readers of her book. The thrill of recognized authorship had not worn thin. She also told her how much she had enjoyed meeting Mr. Ames. The latter lectured Gwendeline on all the paintings they'd missed seeing and her duty to view them as soon as possible. Gwendeline began to feel that the party was growing long; it was less pleasant, it seemed, to be a hostess than a guest. But once the Ameses had taken their leave, the others didn't linger. She was glad to see the major join Lillian and his mother in Lady Merryn's carriage. Miss Brown saw them out and did not return to the drawing room, leaving Gwendeline alone with Lord Merryn. He looked at her, and she moved nervously to the sofa. Now that her long-awaited opportunity was here, she found it difficult to begin. "Shall we sit down?" she asked.

The earl obligingly seated himself opposite her and Gwendeline searched for words. "You did wish to speak to me?" asked the earl after a long pause.

"Yes," said Gwendeline quickly. "I'm having some trouble beginning, however. The matter is rather delicate, and you will say perhaps that I have no right to bring it up."

"I hope there is nothing we cannot discuss freely," answered Lord Merryn.

Gwendeline did not feel particularly reassured by this remark. "Well, it is about…about your brother."

Lord Merryn's serious expression turned to astonishment. "Andrew?"

"Yes," Gwendeline hurried on. "We've become better acquainted in these past weeks since I returned to town, you know. Indeed, we had a great deal of conversation on the journey back. He told me something of himself." Gwendeline faltered; the earl's expression was not encouraging.

"Go on," he said when she paused. "He told you something you wish to discuss with me?"

"Y-yes." Gwendeline looked worriedly at the earl. "That is, he knows nothing of our conversation, of course. I'm sure he would be very angry, but I wish to help him and…"

The earl's face had resumed its usual impassive look. He nodded when she paused again. "Yes?"

"Well." Gwendeline could see no help for it; she plunged directly on. "Major St. Audley has had some thought of marrying, I believe, but he could not do so because he has no money." She drew a deep breath and waited anxiously, hoping Lord Merryn would see her point. This request, which had seemed an easy enough thing when she conceived it, was turning out to be uncomfortable and embarrassing.

The earl was looking at her with perplexity and amazement. "What?" he said.

Gwendeline was forced to go on. "And I thought... That is, I felt that if you knew this, you would want to give him an income, so that he could ask...so that he could marry."

Lord Merryn was frowning. "Andrew has said nothing of this to me."

"Of course he wouldn't," Gwendeline answered eagerly. "He would never ask you for money. He's far too proud."

The earl's expression had become almost grim. "You seem very conversant with his character."

"As I told you, we've become better acquainted lately." Gwendeline tried to rouse some spark of sympathy in her listener. She was beginning to fear she'd misjudged his generosity. "He's very kind and jolly. I should so like to see him happy."

The earl looked down and gazed thoughtfully at the carpet for a moment, then he raised his head, his expression unreadable. "As should I, of course. But my dear Gwendeline, this entire conversation is off the mark. My brother is completely provided for and knows it very well."

"What?"

"Indeed. With only two of us to think of and ample resources, my father made careful provision for Andrew. My brother has had a very generous allowance throughout his school and military life, and it is provided that when he marries this will be increased by several times. He will have a very good income by any standards. This was all laid out at the reading of the will." He paused and looked at Gwendeline with something very like reproach in his eyes. "Could you think I would have taken everything and left Andrew to shift for himself?"

"No," faltered Gwendeline. "I only... I'm sure the major has forgotten or doesn't understand about this provision of your father's will. He believes he hasn't the income to marry."

The earl looked steadily at her for a few moments, then frowned. "He was only ten when my father died." He concentrated briefly, but recovered himself almost at once. "I'll review the will with him," he said to Gwendeline. "Will that be satisfactory?"

"Oh yes, of course," answered Gwendeline. "I knew you, who have been so kind to me, could never be ungenerous."

The earl's answering smile was slightly askew. "Kinder than you know perhaps." He rose before Gwendeline could frame a reply to this puzzling remark. "Your problem is solved then?"

"Yes," said Gwendeline. "I'm so glad."

Lord Merryn looked down at her. "I too am glad, then," he replied. He bowed slightly. "And now I must go."

Gwendeline saw him out, then returned to the drawing room, almost skipping, so buoyant was her mood. She'd secured the happiness of her dearest friend, she was sure. Her only wish now was for someone to tell of this wonderful event. How could she wait for the major to hear the news and offer for Lillian? She wished it to happen immediately. She jumped from her chair and paced about the room. She was to ride with Lillian tomorrow afternoon; perhaps there would be news then. She hurried from the room to find Miss Brown.

Twenty

When Gwendeline met Lillian the next day for their ride, she scanned her face eagerly for some sign that the major had made an offer, but Lillian looked much as usual. There was no particular excitement in her expression; indeed, she seemed unusually subdued. As they started down a path, her conversation was of commonplace things. Gwendeline sighed. It seemed that nothing had happened yet. After a while, they sank into the companionable silence of old friends, and rode for some time without speaking. They'd reached a rather deserted stretch of parkland—their grooms had fallen behind and were talking together—when Lillian spoke again. Her tone was uncertain. "Gwendeline, have you had any, well, any rather strange conversations with Lord Merryn lately?" she asked hesitantly.

Gwendeline looked up sharply. Could Lord Merryn have told Lillian about her request to him? She felt the blood rush to her face. "Strange?" she replied. "What do you mean?"

"I don't really know," said Lillian. Her eyes

remained on the ground. "But has he said anything to you or done anything unusual lately?"

"Unusual?" Gwendeline was mystified.

"Unusual," repeated Lillian, sounding rather impatient. "Out of the ordinary, atypical." She stopped suddenly and put a hand to her forehead. "Oh, Gwendeline, I'm very much afraid I've done something gooseish."

Gwendeline's puzzlement was only deepened by these remarks. "Whatever are you talking about?"

Lillian turned to look at her finally, and her eyes showed real concern. "I've been arrogant and foolish and tried to interfere in your affairs, Gwendeline. I only deserve to fail, but you should not suffer for my meddling." She appeared to be near tears.

"Lillian, tell me what you've done."

Lillian straightened a bit in her saddle. "Yes, I must tell you. I hope you can forgive me, Gwendeline. I never meant to… Well, that is beside the point." She brushed back a lock of black hair that had escaped from her hat. "You know I wished to help you extricate Lord Merryn from this ridiculous engagement?" She looked nervously at Gwendeline.

"Oh, Lillian," said the latter. "I begged you to do nothing."

Lillian nodded miserably. "I know. I wish I'd listened to you, but I thought I had a plan that could not harm anyone."

"Tell me."

"After I learned of your feelings, I thought for a long time. Finally, I hit on the idea of making Lord Merryn jealous." She glanced at Gwendeline, who was frowning, and went hurriedly on. "I began to drop hints when I talked to him about your many admirers and..."

"But I have no admirers," Gwendeline broke in. "Whom did you name?"

"No one," replied Lillian. "I never used names. I was not completely idiotic. And you do *so* have admirers."

"A few acquaintances who partner me at dances I have, I admit," Gwendeline said, "but somehow I doubt that you told Lord Merryn that."

Lillian hung her head. "I tried to be very careful, but I seem to have given him an entirely false impression."

"Oh, Lillian."

"Well, I never meant to suggest to him that you were about to marry," she protested.

"What!"

Lillian hurried on. "I only meant to show him that you were sought after. I thought that if he believed others were interested in you, he might give up this stupid engagement with Adele and seek to fix his interest with you before it was too late."

"What exactly did you say to him?" asked Gwendeline grimly.

"Only vague hints, I promise you. I said nothing specific." Lillian paused and sighed. "But when I met him in Bond Street this morning, I realized I'd made an utter hash of things and I had to confess it all to you."

"You met Lord Merryn?" Gwendeline frowned. "Did he say something about me?"

Lillian looked out over the shrubbery next to the path. "He was quite strange. I've never seen him so... so... Well, I don't know what to call it. He was very abrupt, almost impolite, which is not like him at all. But he was also almost, almost grim. That's the only word I can think of to describe it. Perhaps he was thinking of something else entirely as we spoke. I don't know. But his mood was peculiar."

"But what did he say?" Gwendeline was bouncing in her saddle with impatience.

"Well, we exchanged commonplaces at first, and I was just telling him that I was to ride with you today when he turned away very brusquely, saying he must go. I was taken aback. Then, as he was leaving, he said, 'I believe we will hear some interesting news about Gwendeline very soon—possibly an announcement in the *Morning Post*.' I asked him what news, and he looked at me very closely. He said, 'You've heard nothing of a wedding?' When I shook my head in astonishment, he appeared very annoyed with himself and strode away." Lillian shook her head again now. "The whole scene was very unlike him. You're not planning to be married, are you, Gwendeline?"

"No, of course not," Gwendeline replied, "but perhaps you've made Lord Merryn believe I am. Oh, how I wish you hadn't spoken to him about me!"

Lillian hung her head. "Can you ever forgive me?"

"Of course I forgive you. But what am I to do now? I can't go to Lord Merryn and tell him that I'm not getting married."

"You could hint perhaps," began Lillian, but she quailed under Gwendeline's stern look. "No, no, you're right. Hinting has not been very useful. You must simply wait. Eventually, he'll see that you're not preparing to marry and realize his mistake."

Gwendeline looked thoughtful. "You know, Lillian, I have just realized how foolish we're being."

"What do you mean?"

"Whatever Lord Merryn may think about me, he's still engaged to Adele. Nothing has really changed. You haven't done anything so terrible."

Lillian looked at her dejectedly. "I suppose you're right. I wanted so much to change everything, and I have succeeded only in upsetting everyone."

"Please don't try anything else. It is hopeless."

"Alas," Lillian agreed, "I promise to tend to my own affairs exclusively henceforth."

They reached the end of the wooded path and turned onto a busy avenue of the park. It was full of carriages and riders, and they amused themselves by watching the crowds and commenting on the behavior of those they knew. They saw Mr. Horton some distance away, mounted on a hack and escorting Alicia Holloway's carriage. Lillian had several things to say about his horse, which she characterized as a slug. And Gwendeline caught an unexpected glimpse of Sir Humphrey Owsley, traveling in state in the opposite direction in a modish open carriage. His great bulk nearly filled the vehicle, and he was wrapped in so many fur rugs and blankets, despite the warmth of the day, that he looked immense. Gwendeline waved vigorously. It took a moment for her to catch his eye, but when he saw her, he bowed graciously and moved a hand slightly in response. "Let's go and speak to Sir Humphrey," said Gwendeline eagerly. This sight of her benefactor buoyed her spirits.

Lillian turned, curious. "Sir Humphrey?"

"Yes, Sir Humphrey Owsley. The man in the carriage there." Gwendeline pointed.

"Do you mean to tell me that you're acquainted with him?"

"Yes. Haven't you met him? I'll introduce you."

Lillian shook her head. "I never get your limits," she said, smiling. "First, Carleton Ames and now this. How do you manage it?"

"I don't know what you mean," replied Gwendeline.

"Do you not? Well, it happens that Sir Humphrey Owsley is something of a legendary character in London. No one knows him. Or, that is, very few do. He is extremely particular about whom he admits to his circle, and he is quite the richest man in town. Richer than Golden Ball, they say. Now wherever can you have met him? I understand he almost never goes out now."

Gwendeline was digesting this information with some surprise. Had she known more about her benefactor, she thought, she would never have been able to nerve herself up to visit him uninvited. "He was a friend of my parents," she told Lillian.

"Oh. Well, that explains it then. By all means, let us catch up with him. I'd love to meet this mythical personage." They turned their horses and were about to follow Sir Humphrey's carriage, when someone hailed them from the grassy border of the lane. Riding over, they discovered Adele Greene. Somewhat to their surprise, she urged them to dismount and walk a little with her, as she was out for a stroll with only her maid for company. Gwendeline grew cold as she wondered if Lord Merryn had said something to Adele about her recent activities.

However, no conversation could have been more ordinary as they began to walk across the lawn. Lillian and Gwendeline looped the skirts of their riding habits over their arms, but Adele took no notice of any inconvenience she might have caused them. She chattered on about her wedding clothes, the parties she'd attended recently, and the beauty of the park, leaving the other girls little to do but murmur polite affirmatives. Finally, they reached a bench and sat down at Adele's request. Gwendeline was wondering how soon they could excuse themselves and continue their ride.

"There," said Adele when they were seated, "now we are all cozy and private and can have a comfortable talk."

Lillian raised her eyebrows but said nothing.

"I've been so very busy lately," continued Adele, gesturing helplessly. "I've scarcely had time to see any old friends. I'm so glad we happened to meet today."

Lillian directed a sidewise glance of astonishment at Gwendeline. Neither girl knew how to reply to this remark, but Adele gave them no chance in any case.

"I've missed feminine companionship," Adele said. "My sister is married now, and I never realized that becoming engaged would cut me off so from my former pursuits." After this statement, she paused as if for a reply.

"It is indeed unfortunate," answered Lillian after a short silence. When Adele looked away, Lillian shrugged slightly and shook her head wonderingly at Gwendeline.

"There are so many things I've wished to discuss with someone who could truly understand," Adele went on. Her remarks seemed directed only to Lillian; she hardly glanced at Gwendeline. "I've felt the need of a friend more than once." Though she paused again, there was no reply to this sally, and after a moment, she continued. "You must know what I mean, Lillian. You are about to become engaged yourself. You must have felt the burdens of that new state."

"I?" said Lillian. "I have no plans of that nature." Gwendeline wondered wildly if Lord Merryn had confided her efforts and his brother's feelings to Adele.

Adele raised her eyebrows. "Really? You're not simply being modest about your great good fortune? I have heard that, or I mean, I thought that you'd come to an understanding with the Duke of Craigbourne."

Lillian sat back on the bench as Gwendeline breathed a sigh of relief. Lillian's eyes began to twinkle. "Ah," she said. "I know what you're referring to now."

Adele waited in vain for her to expand on this noncommittal statement. "It is true then?" she asked finally. "I must wish you happy."

Lillian looked tempted. For a moment, Gwendeline feared she would say something imprudent. But her reply was unexceptionable. "No, Adele, you've been taken in by rumors."

"Then he hasn't offered for you?" Adele leaned forward. Her eyes glittered, then she seemed to recall herself. "I'm so concerned that you should be as happy as I, Lillian."

"You're too kind," replied Lillian. "I do not hope for such bliss."

Adele didn't appear to hear her. "Oh dear," she said, rising. "I've just remembered I promised to accompany my mother on a shopping expedition. I'll see you at the duchess's ball tomorrow, I'm sure. Goodbye." She hurried away.

Lillian burst out laughing. "Adele's audacity is always a step ahead of my expectations."

"She seems rather sneaky to me," said Gwendeline.

"Of course she is," replied Lillian. "That's what makes her so amusing. Truly good people are never so entertaining. I wonder what she's plotting?"

"She's so interested in the duke. One would almost think she has set her cap at him."

"Oh, I believe she has. There's no question about that."

"But she's already engaged. She cannot…"

"I wouldn't be too quick to say what Adele cannot do. She's put me in the wrong more than once on that score."

"What shall we do?" Gwendeline asked.

"Do? There's nothing to be done except watch events take their course. I've learned my lesson about interference."

They remounted and continued their ride in silence. Gwendeline felt that she ought to be more pleased with the turn things were taking, but the uncertainty was almost worse than resignation. They came to the end of the avenue and were about to turn toward home when they saw Major St. Audley riding toward them. He was moving fast, and many heads turned to watch his headlong progress.

He pulled up sharply next to them with a rather breathless good day. His usual lighthearted good humor seemed to have deserted him.

"Where are you off to in such a hurry?" asked Gwendeline with a smile. "Weren't you one of those who told me that it wasn't at all the thing to ride faster than a sedate trot in the park?"

"I saw you from quite a distance," explained the major. "I hurried to speak to you before you'd gone."

"That was good of you," Gwendeline replied. A silence fell. The major seemed to have nothing to say in spite of his efforts to join them.

"It's a fine day," Lillian said finally.

"Yes," answered Gwendeline. She looked at the major. "We've had a splendid ride. The air is wonderful."

The major did not seem to hear her. He was frowning in the general direction of a nursery governess and her two charges at the side of the path. The girl was beginning to exhibit some signs of annoyance at his steady regard, though in reality he didn't see her at all. "I stopped at your house," St. Audley said abruptly. "They told me you were here. I wonder if I might call again later today." The governess gathered her children about her and walked indignantly away over the lawn.

"Why, of course," Gwendeline answered. She was puzzled and afraid that the major had heard something of her interference in his affairs. Intrigue was apparently a very tiring pastime; she had to worry about what everyone was thinking. "You're welcome at any time," she added.

The major's head jerked. "No, I… That is, I meant to address Miss Everly."

Now Lillian was surprised and a little flustered. "You're welcome in my parents' house also," she said awkwardly. "Come to tea, if you like."

The major shook his head. "I should like to speak to you privately, if I may. Perhaps tomorrow morning?"

"I'm sorry. We'll be out all morning, and perhaps all day. My aunt has come to stay for the end of the season, and we are to spend the day shopping."

The major's face fell. "I see."

"You might call later in the week," Lillian's voice expressed her puzzlement at his behavior, and it held the slightest of tremors as well.

"No," he answered. "That is, yes, of course. You must excuse me. I have a great deal on my mind." And with no further explanations, he turned and rode away.

Lillian glanced at Gwendeline with raised eyebrows. "Whatever do you suppose has come over him?"

Gwendeline shook her head, but her spirits had risen. She took the major's behavior as a sure sign that he had spoken to his brother and was planning to offer for Lillian now that he knew his true circumstances. She could barely contain herself. It was unfortunate, she thought, that no time had been set for the meeting, but the event was sure to be very soon. Perhaps she could arrange something.

Her mood was so buoyant that Lillian commented on it. Gwendeline could say only that she felt happy after their ride, a lame excuse which left Lillian eying her curiously. But Gwendeline didn't care. She reached home just before tea and ran gaily upstairs to change into a gown of white muslin. She was brushing her hair and humming when she noticed a square envelope propped up on her dressing table. Abruptly, she sobered, and she reached for the letter.

Her fears were confirmed when she tore the

envelope open. Written in the same rough characters as before were the words, "Your time is up. Beware." Gwendeline rose with an exclamation and rang for Ellen. When the girl hurried in, surprised to find her mistress home without her knowledge, Gwendeline held up the envelope.

"La, I had no idea you'd come in, Miss Gwendeline," Ellen exclaimed. "Why didn't you ring sooner? I was just down in the kitchen. You won't ever guess what's happened!"

"Never mind that, Ellen," replied Gwendeline. "I wish to know who delivered this note."

Ellen peered at it. "Note? I'm sure I don't know, miss. I never brought it in here. But I must tell you…"

"All right. I shall ask Reeves." Gwendeline strode out of her room and down the stairs, leaving Ellen gaping.

But Reeves also denied all knowledge of the note, and when they'd questioned all the servants, none would admit to placing it in her room. Gwendeline grew cold as the inquiry proceeded. How had the writer of these horrid documents gained access to her bedchamber?

By the time Miss Brown returned home from a shopping expedition, the house was in an uproar. The older woman listened calmly to Gwendeline's story and read the note. She looked worried as they sent the note to Lord Merryn, enclosing with it an explanatory letter.

As Gwendeline sat in the drawing room that evening, trying to do some sewing, she couldn't help feeling that some ominous progression of events had caught her up. Where would it end? And how?

She looked up when Miss Brown came in. "I've

found out nothing further about the note," the older woman said. "Except I may have discovered approximately when it was placed in your bedchamber, along with some news that will interest you."

"What is it?" asked Gwendeline.

"Well, while we were out this afternoon, all the servants were gathered in the kitchen for quite some time, it seems."

"Is there some new problem?"

"Not at all. It was a celebration. It seems that Alphonse and Yvette *and* John and Ellen have announced their engagements. There was a party for most of the afternoon. An intruder could have taken advantage of that fact."

"How did all this come about?"

"Evidently, John and Yvette gradually turned from sympathetic listeners to eager participants in the romantic complications. And now it appears that you'll be losing nearly all your servants within the month. John and Ellen talk of returning to the country and Alphonse and Yvette of leaving for France now that the war is over."

"It needed only this," said Gwendeline.

Twenty-one

As she dressed for the Duchess of Craigbourne's ball the following evening, Gwendeline congratulated Ellen, and the girl looked very happy as she fluttered about putting the finishing touches on her hair. As Gwendeline stood to survey herself in the mirror, she almost envied her maid, who'd been able to refuse the suitor she didn't want and accept the man she loved so openly.

Gwendeline wore the ball gown she'd purchased especially for this event; the tiny blue flowers sprinkling the white background and the pearls at their centers caught the light as she moved. She picked up her fan and reticule from the dressing table and went downstairs to meet Miss Brown, who had no doubt been ready for some time. There were no flowers tonight; no one had sent any. Gwendeline smiled a bit sadly as she thought of the two bouquets she'd received for her very first ball. It seemed so long ago now.

Miss Brown was in the drawing room, looking stately in a dress of dark blue crepe trimmed in Mechlin lace. They reached the duchess's huge town house in good time, only to join a long line of vehicles waiting to set down passengers at her door. By the time they entered the ballroom, it was nearly filled with a glittering crowd; the *ton* had sought to outdo itself on this final night of the season. The dancing was about to begin, and Gwendeline was soon solicited for the first set. She'd seen none of her friends so far, and as she danced she looked for them. Finally, she spotted Lillian, dancing far across the room, but there was no sign of any of the St. Audleys, not even the countess. Nor did she see the Ameses, whose visit to London this ball was to crown and close. The crowd was so large, however, that she wasn't surprised.

The first few sets passed in this manner; Gwendeline danced and chatted with her escorts, but had no conversation with anyone else. She longed to talk to Lillian, but she had no opportunity. During a pause, she went to look for Miss Brown. She'd just glimpsed her, sitting with some of the other chaperones across the ballroom, when a voice behind her said with great formality, "Good evening, Miss Gregory."

Gwendeline turned to face an extraordinary figure. His knee breeches were of bright blue satin, and his coat was yellow with seal buttons the size of sovereigns. The latter garment was extravagantly padded at the shoulders, tapering to a wasp waist, and his shirt points were so high that he could not turn his head at all. But it was his waistcoat that transfixed Gwendeline. She'd never seen such an elaborate brocade or so many fobs and seals. It was with great difficulty that she tore her eyes from it and raised them to the man's face, recognizing **Mr. Horton**. "How do you do," she said to her former suitor.

"Very well," he answered solemnly. He pulled an enameled snuffbox from his waistcoat pocket and delicately took a pinch of the mixture, dusting his face and coat with a scented handkerchief. He looked at her again with an expression he appeared to think was elegantly bored. "Quite a dreadful squeeze, is it not?" he drawled. "One can scarcely breathe." He fanned himself languidly with the handkerchief. He seemed even more affected than when they had last talked.

"It is crowded," Gwendeline agreed. There was a pause, and she began to feel uncomfortable. Why had the man approached her? "I hope you've been well," she said finally. "It has been some time since last we met."

"Oh, tolerable well. I've been frightfully busy, of course, with all the preparations."

"Preparations?" asked Gwendeline politely, feeling it was expected of her.

"You can't have missed the notice? In the *Morning Post*?" Mr. Horton looked shocked at the thought. "I should think you would have heard in any case." He looked at Gwendeline suspiciously, as if he would accuse her of hiding her knowledge. She shook her head.

"My engagement, of course," he continued then. He put a hand over his waistcoat front. "I have won the woman of my heart. Alicia and I are to be married next month."

"Oh," replied Gwendeline. "That is indeed good news. I wish you every happiness."

Mr. Horton put on a superior smile. "That is very magnanimous. These things are inevitable, you know."

This time Gwendeline's smile escaped her. "They are indeed. I'm sure everything has worked out for the best."

Mr. Horton agreed enthusiastically, and with this small encouragement, launched into a long and very boring account of his bride's sterling qualities, their wedding plans, and his overwhelming felicity. The next set began, but he showed no sign of asking her to join it. She endured him for some time, feeling that she owed Mr. Horton some consideration, but finally she was looking desperately round for some escape.

None of her acquaintances was near, and since the dancing was in progress, none was likely to approach. She broke into Mr. Horton's description of the splendid barouche Alicia's father was having built for her, saying, "Isn't that Alicia now? She's looking for you, I believe."

Mr. Horton turned quickly. "Where? No, no, that is someone else entirely. Alicia has gone to dance with her cousin. She will be occupied this half hour." And he resumed his discourse.

After several more minutes, Gwendeline could bear it no longer. "You must excuse me," she said. "Miss Brown is summoning me." She turned quickly and walked down the room, leaving Mr. Horton openmouthed.

Near the corner of the ballroom, Gwendeline came to an archway, and feeling Mr. Horton's eyes still on her, she ducked through it, crossed the hallway beyond, and went into the room across the corridor. She breathed a sigh of relief when she found it deserted.

She looked around the room curiously. It appeared to have been added to the ballroom wing of the house at some later date, for it jutted out at right angles to the bulk of the building. The space was large, and it was set up as a conservatory, with walls of frosted glass and large plants set in pots across the floor. Gwendeline strolled over to a group of small palms to the left of the door. Several of them in blue ceramic pots formed a kind of alcove screened from the rest of the dimly lit room. To her delight, she found a bench in this recess, and she sat down, pleased with the completeness of her escape. She breathed the scents of growing things and relaxed, leaning against the wall. It was very pleasant to rest for a moment in this place that seemed so far from the ballroom across the hall.

Gwendeline heard the music end; the sound of talking swelled as the dancers joined the rest of the crowd. She felt some reluctance to join them, but she was just about to rise and do so when two people entered the conservatory and stopped near her hidden seat.

"I must talk to you privately," said the man to his companion.

"Oh, my lord," she answered.

Gwendeline sat up sharply. She recognized them. It was the duke and Adele Greene! She started to rise to make them aware of her presence, but before she could do so, the duke spoke again.

"I have tried to hide my feelings," he said. "But it's no good. I must tell you. I cannot deny my regard for you any longer."

Gwendeline hesitated, blushing. It would be terribly embarrassing for all of them if she walked out now.

"I…I don't know what to say," Adele replied, in a soft, quiet voice Gwendeline had never heard her use. "I am overwhelmed."

The duke shifted uneasily from foot to foot. "I know you must think me dishonorable. You're promised to another, even though he, he… But I must say nothing of that. I vowed over and over that I would never speak of this, but tonight, as we danced, I could dissemble no longer. I have lowered myself irretrievably in your good opinion, I know."

"Oh, no," murmured Adele. "Nothing could do that. I have the highest regard for you. Indeed, lately, I have thought perhaps I'd made a mistake, settled my future with too little thought." She trailed off with a girlish hesitation.

The duke took her hand. "Do you mean, can I hope that you mean there's some chance for me? Adele! I ask nothing more from life than to make you my duchess. Can it be possible?"

Adele looked down shyly. "Indeed, my lord duke, that would make me very happy also."

"And Lord Merryn?" he asked with some anxiety.

"Oh, it is very distressing to be sure. But our engagement was a mistake from the start, I see that now. I was dazzled by him. He never really cared for me, I fear."

"That is what I've come to think," replied the duke eagerly. "I wouldn't say so before, but he has never treated you with the consideration you deserve. He is not a good match for someone so…so sensitive and delicate as you."

Adele sighed and looked soulful. "Alas, I fear you're right. I must tell him all is ended."

"Poor man." The duke patted her hand. "I'll go with you. I'll stand by you. And afterward we will go to tell my mother of our own engagement."

"Oh, my lord," breathed Adele. They left the room together.

Gwendeline stared across the room, stunned. She could hardly believe what she had heard, despite Adele's revelations yesterday. She almost felt she should run after them and try to tell the duke that Adele was a scheming creature, but she wasn't quite so idiotic. And in any case, he seemed to have fallen in love with Adele.

Gwendeline leaned back against the wall. Lord Merryn would now be free, she thought, filled with elation and hope and uncertainty. She sat for some minutes, her mind whirling, and was just ready to rise when another couple entered the room.

Gwendeline put a hand to her forehead. Was she to witness the trysts of every pair of lovers at the ball? Resolving to forestall such an event, she stepped forward and parted the palm fronds. The couple walked past her hiding place, farther into the room and away from the door. Seeing their backs, Gwendeline realized that it was Lillian and Major St. Audley. She struggled momentarily with her conscience, then allowed the palms to fall back into place and resumed her seat. It was wrong, she knew, but she couldn't resist seeing the outcome of her plan.

Lillian and the major stood silently for a moment. Both appeared nervous. At last, Lillian spoke. "You wished to speak with me?"

"Yes." He stopped. "The thing is, now that we're here, I don't know how to begin."

"Do you find talking with me so difficult, then?"

"Usually no. But what I wish to tell you is so difficult to express."

"Are you going away again, perhaps?" Lillian's tone was unencouraging. "There's certainly no need for you to inform *me*."

"No, confound it. I'm not going away. You would remind me of that awful conversation just at this moment."

"I beg your pardon. I'm not accustomed to being spoken to in such a tone." Lillian moved as if to return to the ballroom.

"Please, Lillian. I'm trying to ask you to marry me."

"Marry you?" whispered Lillian.

"You heard what I said. I've wanted to marry you almost from the moment we met, but I've only just found out that I have the income to support a wife."

Lillian looked shaken. "But you… How can this be? Last year, yes, I would have believed you, indeed I almost expected…but now…"

Seemingly encouraged by these fragmentary sentences, the major began to explain the history of his attachment. He spoke of his hopes of marriage last year, her parents' decision, the reason for his journey abroad.

"Then," he finished, "just this week, my brother took it into his head to review my father's will with me. I remembered nothing of it. It seems I am to be provided with a very good income when I marry. So, you see, your parents' objections are removed."

Lillian did not appear to take this all in. "Your father's will?"

"Yes. I was very young when he died, didn't really

understand it at all. It was kind of Alex to go over it with me, though I must say he was uncommonly gruff about it. And why he suddenly chose to do so… But whatever the reason, it was just in time for me."

By now, Lillian had recovered from her surprise. "You've spoken to my parents then?"

The major's chin rose. "I haven't. I couldn't wait after all this time to ascertain your feelings. I love you, Lillian; will you be my wife?"

Lillian looked at him. "Yes," she said at last.

Major St. Audley smiled broadly and took both her hands. "I swear we'll be the happiest pair in England," he laughed.

"Perhaps," Lillian replied, "though you have a great many bad habits, I daresay, which I shall be forced to correct."

"I'll chuck them all." He waved his arms exuberantly. "Come, let's go speak to your parents." They hurried out.

Gwendeline, in her hiding place, was beaming. It had all come out exactly as she planned. She felt immensely proud of herself and happy for Lillian.

"I'm sorry, Gwendeline," said a deep voice in the palms beside her. "I wouldn't have you hurt for worlds."

Gwendeline jumped and moved quickly out into the room. She was surprised when Lord Merryn followed her. "Where did you come from?"

"I saw my brother come in here, and I followed to speak to him. He was just offering for Miss Everly, so I thought it best not to make my presence known, and I stepped into the palms." He looked at her sadly.

"Isn't it wonderful?" said Gwendeline excitedly. "It went just as I planned."

"Planned?" replied the earl. "But…I thought you were in love with Andrew."

"I?"

"Yes. When you spoke to me about his income, I assumed…"

"You thought that I did it so that I might marry him?" interrupted Gwendeline, aghast.

"It appears I was mistaken."

"How could you think I would do such a thing? I knew he loved Lillian. I planned it all for them."

The earl bowed his head. "I apologize. I'm very sorry I misjudged you." But when he looked up again, he didn't look at all sorry. On the contrary, he looked very happy indeed. "It appears that I'm the only one jilted tonight then."

"Oh yes," began Gwendeline, then she stopped in embarrassment.

The earl raised his eyebrows.

"Adele and the duke were in here earlier. I overheard them, too." She gestured helplessly. "I didn't mean to, but they were talking before I could get away."

Lord Merryn laughed. "This room clearly has a strong influence on its occupants." He moved toward Gwendeline. "Perhaps we too…"

With a sharp cracking sound, glass shattered somewhere nearby, and Gwendeline felt something buzz past her ear, so close that it lifted her curls. Before she could cry out, Lord Merryn had pulled her to the floor behind one of the pillars that supported the roof.

"Are you all right?" He gripped her shoulders painfully.

She nodded as the sound of more glass breaking filled the room. "What is it? What's happening?"

"Some fool is shooting. Stay here. Don't move." The look in his eyes made Gwendeline shrink back against the pillar, and in the next moment, he was gone.

Gwendeline waited in silence for what seemed like hours, peering around the pillar, trying in vain to see what was happening. The room looked oddly peaceful. The candle flames wavered a bit in the breeze coming from the broken window, but otherwise all looked as before. She was just about to rise and go looking for help when another shot rang out, this time outside the conservatory, and she crouched down once more. There was shouting now and the noise of heavy bodies crashing through the shrubbery. Gwendeline suddenly thought of the notes she'd received. Had that shot been aimed at her? She huddled closer to the pillar, wondering where the other guests had gone. She could hear no music or talking, and no one had appeared in the conservatory, though one would have expected the noise to bring them all.

Another silence, even longer than the last, again encouraged Gwendeline to start to rise. She clung to the pillar for support. As she turned and braced herself for a quick dart to the doorway, there was a blast, and glass shattered behind her. Whirling, she found herself face to face with Mortimer Blane.

He shook his head, dazed by his leap through the window, and then looked about him. When he took in the empty room and Gwendeline standing alone before him, he smiled. "How fortuitous," he said. "I shall get *something* out of this, at least." And he raised the gun he was holding to point it at Gwendeline.

Gwendeline's eyes widened, and she put out a hand for support. "Mr. Blane!"

"Yes, the man you harried and ruined, the man your friends hunted across England for sport. You didn't expect to see me again perhaps?"

Gwendeline was too frightened even to shake her head.

"No, I can see that you did not." He sneered. "You thought me safely out of your way, frightened off like a whipped dog." His lips tightened. "But it's not so easy as that." He moved the pistol slightly, directing her attention to it. "I can't be put aside so painlessly. You have been somewhat annoyed by anonymous notes perhaps?" Gwendeline frowned, and he laughed again. "Yes, I sent them. Just as I engaged those bumbling highwaymen who muddled their task and let Merryn escape alive."

"You!" said Gwendeline.

Mr. Blane scowled. "You actually thought I would slink away to the Continent and take no revenge on those who wrecked my life?" His scowl deepened. "You're a little fool, as was your mother. Neither of you had any spirit when it came to the point."

"Are you going to kill me?" asked Gwendeline. She found herself staring at the pistol Blane pointed at her. It was an old-fashioned dueling weapon, and the gleam of the wood mounted along the barrel held her eyes.

"I was," he said. "Tonight was to have been the culmination of my plans. It would have been the perfect revenge. Merryn is obviously besotted with you; one clear shot and I would have had my revenge on both." His grip on the pistol tightened, and he grimaced. "No man ever had worse luck. And now I'm trapped here when I thought to be away long ago."

"You may as well give yourself up."

Blane's head jerked back toward her. "Oh no, I don't think it's come to that just yet. You will get me away from here."

"I?"

He seemed to regain some of his old self-possession. "You," he repeated. "We'll be making another short journey together, my dear." He looked thoughtful. "Or perhaps, yes, perhaps a long one."

Gwendeline watched him, noticing how greatly changed he was from the Blane she'd met when she first came to London. His formerly immaculate dress was crumpled and dusty. His hair was roughly cut. But his eyes showed the most frightening change. They had always been cold, mocking, and supercilious, but they now glowed with a desperate light.

"Come along," he continued. "We'd best be gone." He approached her, and caught her wrist, then grasped her waist. Holding his pistol to her head, he said, "Go."

He propelled Gwendeline out through the archway, across the corridor, and into the ballroom. People were standing about in small groups, silent and nervous, and a collective gasp went up when they saw Gwendeline. Blane pushed her farther into the room and spoke in a clear, carrying tone. "You will excuse us, ladies and gentlemen. We're just leaving. If anyone should be foolish enough to try to stop us, I'm afraid I cannot answer for the safety of the young lady." At this, he moved the pistol so that all could see it. There were murmurs from the crowd, but no one moved.

Blane forced Gwendeline across the ballroom, pressing the barrel of the gun to her temple. The expanse of floor seemed endless to her, and the faces of the guests went by in a blur. She saw Lillian standing with Lady Merryn; their faces were white and strained, and Lillian held out a helpless hand as she passed. They went on; face after face drifted by as in a nightmare. She saw Adele clinging to the duke's arm and the Ameses standing near them. Mrs. Ames looked terribly distressed, but she held her husband's arm, keeping him from leaping at Blane as they neared. Mr. Ames's face was red with rage, and he shook his fist.

They reached the opposite doorway at last—the walk had seemed eternal to Gwendeline—and went down the hall to the outer door. There was no one in this part of the house, and Gwendeline began to wonder what had become of the earl. She was suddenly horribly afraid that he lay dead in the garden.

As they stopped and Blane released her for a moment to grasp the doorknob, the outside door was pushed open. Immediately, Blane regained his hold on Gwendeline, this time with a painful grip, and pulled her back, aiming his gun at the door. Miss Brown walked into the hall.

The older woman stepped forward, holding out her hands. "Gwendeline!" she cried. "Lord Merryn told everyone to stay in the ballroom, but I remembered those notes and I had to go out. I lost sight of the men in the shrubbery, but…" Suddenly, she seemed to take in the whole scene—the gun, Blane, and Gwendeline's terrified eyes. Miss Brown put her hand to her mouth.

Blane gestured with the gun. "We haven't met," he said, "But I've seen you occasionally. As it appears that you will be joining our little party, I must introduce myself. Mortimer Blane." His expression hardened. "And now we'd better go." Pushing Gwendeline toward Miss Brown and the open door he retained an unbreakable grip around her waist, the pistol to her temple once more. Miss Brown lowered her hand and stood rigid. The color had drained from her face, but her expression was resolute.

"You will come with us peacefully and try no tricks or I'll shoot your young friend." Miss Brown flinched but said nothing. "Now shut the door," Blane continued. Miss Brown did so. "Walk ahead of us." She stepped in front of them. In this manner, they traversed the garden, went out through the gate, and walked a little way down the street beyond. There were surprisingly few people about. When they reached a narrow alley just past the house, Blane directed them into it and hurried them urgently along for some time. The way was very dark and twisting, and the air smelled of garbage or worse. Under any other circumstances, Gwendeline would have worried about rats.

Finally, they approached the back of a hackney-coach standing in the alley, and Blane ordered Miss Brown into it. He shoved Gwendeline after her, leaped up himself, and shouted "Drive!" to the cabbie as he slammed the door shut. The cab started with a violence that threw both women together in a heap on the floor, but Blane, hanging onto a roof strap, only laughed and kept the gun trained on them. And thus, Gwendeline found herself once again riding through the darkness in a closed carriage at the mercy of Mortimer Blane.

Twenty-two

THE CAB CONTINUED AT BREAKNECK SPEED, AND constant turns threw the two ladies from side to side. Gwendeline had no idea which way they were headed; lights flashed past the carriage window, then disappeared too rapidly to be identified. She heard the shouts of angry pedestrians as the vehicle nearly ran them down. Finally, the coach slowed, and Gwendeline pulled herself up into the seat, helping Miss Brown up and gripping the side strap firmly. Now that she could see out, she concluded that they'd passed into one of the poorer parts of town. The streets were narrow and filthy.

The jolting and swaying started again on the cobbled road. Gwendeline caught glimpses of the river between buildings, and they finally halted beside one of the docks along the Thames. Blane jumped down, holding the gun on them through the open door. When they'd descended under his direction, Blane slammed the carriage door and threw the cab driver some coins. Soon, the three of them stood alone at the head of the pier. Blane gestured down it toward the open water. "We go this way, ladies," he said, and they moved reluctantly with him in the near-darkness.

The dock was not long; they soon reached the end and stood facing a dilapidated ship moored there. One lantern hung at the top of the gangplank, but otherwise it seemed deserted. Blane raised the pistol and pointed up the gangway. "Up," he snapped.

Gwendeline lifted her skirts and stepped onto the narrow board. It gave with her weight, and she retreated nervously. "Go on," snarled Blane. He cast glances behind them, as if he expected pursuit at any moment.

Miss Brown took a long look at him, then walked forward stiffly and started up to the ship. The plank swayed, but she ignored it after one involuntary tremor. Gwendeline followed her, with Blane close behind, and before long they all stood on deck. A fat dirty man in a torn shirt and dark trousers jumped up from the large coil of rope on which he'd been reclining and spoke to Blane. "'Ere. You never said nothing about no females."

"Hold your tongue," Blane replied. "And tell the captain to get this scow under way. I told you to be ready."

"Scow, is it?" the man said, his tone sharpening.

"Just get us moving," Blane said. He directed the two ladies toward the bow of the ship. The man muttered to himself, then began to shout for his fellow crew members to raise anchor. Blane escorted the women through a short passageway past the main cabin, pushed them into one of the tiny chambers beyond, and locked the door.

As his footsteps retreated, Gwendeline and Miss

Brown sank down on the narrow bunk that extended along the rear wall of the cabin. "I suppose he's headed across the Channel," Miss Brown said. "He cannot mean to stay in England after tonight." She turned and tried to peer out the small porthole behind her. "It's too dark to see anything, but rescue is on the way, I'm certain. We need only keep calm and wait."

"How will they find us?" Gwendeline replied.

"They will," replied Miss Brown positively.

Gwendeline clasped her hands and twisted them together.

The ship was moving out into the river current now. Looking through the porthole, they could see lights on the near shore. The vessel gathered speed in the current, and Gwendeline watched London slip past them. For some time, they sat in silence, listening to the shouts of the sailors and their footsteps on the deck above. Gwendeline couldn't believe this had happened just as everything had seemed to be working out perfectly.

They had been moving for about an hour when Blane returned to the cabin. He looked a little less disheveled and much more complacent. "Well ladies," he said as he stood before them. "Tomorrow we'll be in France, and I will have the pleasure of showing you my house there. A recent acquisition but quite comfortable."

"You must know you can't hold us prisoner," said Miss Brown.

Blane smiled. "Our minds run in the same channels, madam. I've been considering what to do with you. It is a problem I hadn't foreseen, I must admit. But I'm sure we can hit upon some solution."

"Let us go?" cried Gwendeline. "We've never done anything to harm you."

Blane turned to her, his smile widening. "Do you know, that was exactly my thought a few moments ago? I realized that it's Merryn I wish to settle with, not you. I began to remember your mother and how like her you are." His eyes briefly held a faraway look. "Thus, I came to a decision." He stared at Gwendeline; his expression made her shrink back. "I believe we will be married, my dear," he finished.

"What?" cried both ladies at once.

"Don't be ridiculous," snapped Miss Brown.

"I won't," insisted Gwendeline simultaneously.

Blane watched them with some amusement. "It is, of course, a plan that requires discussion," he said. "It's very sudden, I know."

Gwendeline had regained her composure. "I'll never marry you," she said in a tone that left no room for doubt. "I'd rather die."

"Of course you will not," added Miss Brown. "He cannot force you to do so, Gwendeline."

Blane's expression hardened. "This is a rather private matter. I believe Gwendeline and I should talk it over alone." He stepped forward and grasped Miss Brown's forearm, lifting her to her feet. "You will excuse us, I know." He opened the door and pushed her into the passage, addressing someone Gwendeline couldn't see. "Take her to the next cabin and lock her in." And then Miss Brown was gone, and Blane was closing the door once more. He sat down beside her on the bunk. "That's better."

Gwendeline moved to the extreme opposite end,

gathering her skirts around her. Her ball gown was spotted with black stains and torn in at least one place, and her curls hung crookedly about her face, but she summoned all the dignity she possessed and said, "You can say nothing that would make me wish to marry you."

Blane was smiling again. Gwendeline was beginning to hate and fear that smile. "Wish to?" he said. "No, I probably can't make you wish to marry me. But that is beside the point. I think you *will* do so, wishes aside."

"But why should you want to marry me? I don't believe you even like me."

His lip curled. "Not really," he replied. "You are both too like and too unlike your mother. You seem to have inherited all of her mulishness and none of her interesting qualities. I don't wonder Annabella rarely saw you."

"You see, we should never suit," she said.

Blane looked at her incredulously for a moment, then burst into loud laughter. "Suit!" he echoed with amazement. "She thinks we should not suit." Gwendeline watched him uneasily, as he gradually composed himself again. "I wish to marry you for one reason only," he said then, "to get my revenge on Merryn and all of society." He leaned back against the side of the ship. "You've come to symbolize polite society for me," he added thoughtfully. "I shall subjugate you. And Merryn will be helpless, forced to look on and suffer." He clenched a fist exultantly. "It's a splendid scheme. I wonder I did not think of it before."

"But I'll never marry you," said Gwendeline.

Blane turned to survey her, his eyes hooded. "Ah

yes," he said. "There is that little problem." One corner of his mouth went up. "Don't you think these scruples are a little melodramatic, really? You made no demur about living under the protection of Lord Merryn for the season, why pretend to such nicety now?"

Gwendeline stiffened. "I was not living under anyone's 'protection,' as you call it. Lord Merryn was only one of…"

"Surely you're not going to trot out that tired story of 'a group of your father's friends' once more," interrupted the man with a sneer. "It will not wash, my dear. These generous friends do not exist, and I cannot believe you are so naive or so stupid as to think that they do. Don't talk such fustian."

"They do exist," insisted Gwendeline. "They wish to remain anonymous, but they did help me."

Blane smiled. "Anonymous, is it? Very convenient. Why should they wish it? Particularly when Lord Merryn is so open about his aid." He shook his head. "No, even you cannot be so gullible."

The girl set her jaw and looked away from him. "I can't think why I'm arguing with you; after all, I don't care what you believe. And you're mistaken. I talked with one of my benefactors, and he assured me that he had been one of this group."

Blane looked surprised. "Who?"

"Sir Humphrey Owsley," replied Gwendeline triumphantly.

Mr. Blane's face cleared. "Owsley? Impossible. Or"—he paused and looked at her narrowly—"was Merryn there?"

Gwendeline shook her head.

Blane frowned. "No? Well, perhaps he'd gotten to him by then. You should be flattered, my dear. He laid a complicated snare for you."

Gwendeline looked down, letting her disheveled curls fall across her face, and folded her arms to hide the trembling of her hands.

Blane shrugged. He stared at her for such a long time that Gwendeline shifted nervously. "Miss Brown is an estimable lady," he said then. "She is very dear to you, is she not?"

Gwendeline nodded warily.

"It would be a great pity," he continued, "if some accident should befall her." Gwendeline grew cold. "On a journey such as this, for instance, in a ship full of common ruffians, far from all her friends."

"You are despicable!" Gwendeline found herself straining to detect any unusual noises on the ship. She heard nothing.

Blane was unperturbed. "Perhaps now you understand why I believe you will agree to marry me? These other concerns are quite irrelevant. If you continue to refuse, I seriously doubt that your friend will reach France alive."

Gwendeline stared at him, trying to discover some sign of wavering in his face. There was none. "You cannot mean that," she faltered. "Even you could not be so cruel."

"No?" He smiled.

Gwendeline collapsed in the corner of the bunk.

"We'll be wed as soon as we reach the Continent," said Blane, and left, locking the door behind him.

Gwendeline remembered little of the rest of the

voyage. She lay on the bunk, feeling feverish and miserable, for an interminable time. After a while, the ship began to toss and shift from side to side. She thought at first that she would be sick, but then she became accustomed to the motion. It seemed to echo the rise and fall of her emotions as she alternately hoped for and despaired of rescue. She retreated into a kind of tortured dream, repeatedly reliving the ruin of her life.

Hours later, the tossing lessened, and Gwendeline roused herself. She looked out the porthole, and in the predawn light she could see that they had entered a harbor. This must be France.

It seemed to take a long time for the ship to traverse the harbor and tie up at the dock, but even so, the interval was much too short for Gwendeline. When the vessel was moored at last, she turned toward the door of her cabin, expecting to hear Blane approach at any moment. But no one came. She was left alone to pace about the tiny room and worry about Miss Brown. Where was she?

When Gwendeline was on the verge of pounding frantically on the door to attract someone's attention, she heard footsteps at last. She waited tensely as the key turned in the lock and the door opened. Blane entered, a dark garment over his arm. "Here," he said, handing it to her. "You will want this." It was a dark blue cloak. "Put it on," Blane said impatiently. "You must cover that dress. It will attract unwelcome attention." Gwendeline brightened a little at this, but Blane noticed and crushed her small hope. "Miss Brown will remain aboard this ship until we're ready to leave town. The captain has specific instructions concerning her." He took back the cloak and draped it about her shoulders. "You would be well advised not to try anything foolish." He offered her his arm, and she took it listlessly. As long as he held Brown prisoner, she could do nothing, she thought. She was trapped.

They walked out on deck, and Blane helped her down the gangplank. Once on shore, they went swiftly away from the dock and into the town. They did not enter the busy central sector, however, but kept to the poor area near the harbor. Much too soon for Gwendeline, they paused before a small stone church. "Here, my dear, is the site of our wedding," Blane said. "But first we must stop across the way. I regret I cannot leave you for a moment to settle this detail." He led her across the street to a low tavern and pushed the door open. He beckoned to two men drinking within, who responded somewhat sullenly, and returned to the street. "Our witnesses," he remarked in response to her puzzled look. The men came out, and together the four of them entered the church.

A man in vestments awaited them at the altar. A large crucifix hung above him. The chamber was high and dark and smelled slightly of stale incense. Gwendeline paused. "Is this a Catholic church?" she asked before she thought. "I am not Catholic."

Blane looked at her sardonically. "Does it matter?" he replied.

Realizing that the kind of ceremony that joined her to this monster was, after all, irrelevant, Gwendeline subsided.

The man at the altar appeared nervous and gestured for them to hurry. He looked about the room and fingered the book he held. "Come along," he said finally.

"You speak English," Gwendeline remarked in surprise.

The man looked vexed, glanced toward Blane, then nodded shortly. He opened the book to a place marked in it and again gestured to them to approach. They stood before him at the altar, the two witnesses behind them, and he started to read the marriage service.

The forms of the ceremony were a little strange to Gwendeline, but familiar enough to make her heart sink. She'd never expected to hear these words in such circumstances. She nearly choked on her own responses, but the priest remarked neither on this nor on her bedraggled appearance. Blane spoke the phrases firmly and very loudly, it seemed to Gwendeline. She almost imagined that they echoed through the building. Then it was over. They signed a piece of paper, which Blane then put in his coat pocket, and the witnesses returned to their drinks. The priest disappeared through a door behind the altar, and Gwendeline was left alone with her new husband. She felt sick.

Blane observed her despairing expression with sardonic amusement. He held out his arm once more. "Shall we go, Mrs. Blane?" he asked.

Revolted, Gwendeline walked down the aisle and out of the church.

As they came into the street, a seaman from the ship ran up and said a few words to Blane. Blane reacted quickly. Instead of turning back toward the ship, he began to hurry her farther along the street in the opposite direction, and this roused Gwendeline as nothing else could have. "What are you doing? We must go back to the ship and release Brown."

He took her arm in a tight grip. "I've given orders that she be released. Come along."

Gwendeline dragged her feet. "I don't believe you."

"It's the truth," he answered impatiently. "She's free. You didn't think I'd take a chaperone on my honeymoon, surely?" Blane gave her no time for thought but hurried her along the street to an inn a little way ahead. There, he began to speak very rapid French to the proprietress, and before Gwendeline could do much more than marvel at his fluency—for she could understand nothing of what was said—he had been given a key and was urging her up the stairs. She started to protest, but he practically carried her up and across a hallway into a small bedroom, pushed her down on the bed, and strode out, locking the door behind him.

It was too much. It seemed to Gwendeline that she'd been pushed into rooms, imprisoned, and left alone staring at locked doors too many times. A high thin laugh, whose sound frightened her, filled the room then, and it took her a moment to realize that this alien noise was issuing from her own throat. When she did, she covered her mouth with her hand and looked wide-eyed into the mirror on the opposite wall.

The figure staring back at her was not comforting. Her hair was hopelessly tangled; her face was smudged; and her dress a shambles. But her expression was the most unsettling. Out of a white face, dark-circled, green-blue eyes blazed. There was desperation in them.

Twenty-three

GWENDELINE SHOOK HERSELF ANGRILY AND WENT OVER to examine the windows. The room was on the first floor, but they were large and opened easily outward on hinges at the side; the drop was hardly five feet here at the back of the building. Gwendeline climbed onto the sill and jumped.

She landed in a heap, unhurt but tangled in her long skirts and cloak. She got to her feet, shook out her clothing, and surveyed her position. A narrow flagstone path twisted around the corner of the inn, leading to the street, but Gwendeline had no intention of walking that way and perhaps encountering Blane. She faced instead the cobbled alley that ran away from the building at right angles and trudged off holding up her skirts, though they were already so dirty it hardly mattered.

The alley ended in a small street which ran parallel to the one in front of the inn. It went in the right direction, but several people were walking along it, and Gwendeline faltered, afraid to be seen. She pulled up the hood of her cloak and bent her head, then turned and hurried down toward the harbor, avoiding

the eyes of other pedestrians. She hoped nervously
that she could find the ship again. Her chief concern
was for Miss Brown. Was her friend safe? She trusted
Blane not at all, but as she thought over his behavior
after they'd left the church, she was sure something
had gone awry in his plans. Perhaps Brown really was
out of his clutches.

She took some wrong turnings, but at last she
reached the docks, and walked along them until she
recognized the ship. A few sailors shouted remarks as
she passed, but no one offered to harm her, and eventually she came to a vessel which she was almost sure was
the correct one. She'd found that ships look much alike.

She stood behind a stack of wooden crates, watching it for a while. She could see no movement on
the deck, but she wanted to make sure Blane wasn't
about. Finally satisfied, she stepped forward and
mounted the gangplank. There was no one on deck.
Gwendeline walked swiftly toward the cabins and into
the passageway. She passed the room where she'd been
imprisoned. There were three other such tiny cubicles
beyond. None was locked, and all were empty. She
checked the main cabin opposite, but it was also
untenanted. Puzzled, Gwendeline walked back out
on the deck. Where had everyone gone? The ship
appeared to be deserted. Where was Miss Brown?

There was a sudden scraping noise, and Gwendeline
jumped. It had seemed to come from below her feet,
and she crept over to look into the large open hatch in
the middle of the deck. All was dark in the hold, but it
appeared to be empty; she could see the reflection of
some water in the bottom of the boat. Perhaps it was

a rat, she thought nervously. She moved away again, and went to sit on the rail, overlooking the harbor.

She shouldn't stay here. Blane might come at any time. But when she told herself to get up and leave, she found that she didn't know where to go. The sun was setting behind her, throwing her shadow across the waves. In her exhaustion the quiet lap of the water was lulling. Her life was ruined, just as it had seemed that her dreams were becoming real. She shook herself. No self-pity. She must act. But darkness was falling, making the ship seem a safe haven compared to the murky streets. She had no money, and her unconventional appearance would certainly not help her find aid.

A clattering in the darkness startled her. Two men stood with their backs toward her at the bottom of the gangway. Gwendeline gasped. It was Blane and the seaman who had accosted him outside the church. She huddled into a pile of folded sails.

"I say we bolt," insisted the sailor. "The swells snaffled t'other mort hours ago. She'll 'ave opened her budget, or I'm a bag-pudding. Which I ain't."

Blane seemed to have no trouble comprehending these cryptic words. "You may do as you like. I intend to find the girl."

The sailor shuffled uncertainly; he looked around. "What'ud she be doin' 'ere, guv'nor? The big cove, 'e probably nabbed 'er too. Ain't no one aboard this 'ulk."

"I don't believe he had her," replied Blane. "His yacht is still in the harbor. If he'd found the girl, he would have put out. Come, let us search the cabins."

He started toward the bow, and the seaman followed sullenly, muttering, "Females, I knew 'ow it'd be."

The men disappeared into the passage, and Gwendeline dared to raise her head slightly. Could she escape while they were within? But before she could, they were back on deck. "Told ye," said the sailor. "She ain't 'ere."

Blane held the lantern high and peered about the deck. "I was sure she'd come here," he said to himself. "Where else could she have gone?" Gwendeline shrank down as far as possible and tried not to breathe. "Damn!" said Blane finally. "I haven't time to search properly."

"Indeed not," said a voice from the shadows at the top of the gangway. "In fact, I fear you have run out of time entirely, Blane."

Mr. Blane whirled. "Merryn," he snarled, and the earl stepped onto the deck.

"Yes," he replied. "I have caught up with you finally. And I don't plan to have to pursue you again."

"You are alone?" asked Blane.

The earl smiled. "Temporarily. I outdistanced my party in hopes of meeting you first. We have certain things to discuss."

Blane's laugh was ugly. "I daresay you think so. But as there are two of us, and I don't care to remain here, we may have to defer our discussion until another time."

Lord Merryn's smile broadened. "Oh, I have no interest in your friend. I'm quite willing to let him go without hindrance." He stepped away from the plank. "What do you say, my good man?" He gestured toward the shore.

The sailor took one quick look at each gentleman,

then ran for the offered exit. He disappeared down the gangway as Blane shouted, "Come back, you fool."

The earl laughed. "Now," he said. And he started across the deck.

Blane backed away slightly. "What do you mean to do? Mill me down? You'll find yourself out there."

The earl continued to move forward. "Do you think you can best me?"

"Oh no, you are much too handy with your fives for me, but it may not be so easy," cried Blane. He jumped back, reached inside his coat, and pulled out his pistol. As Gwendeline leaped up with a frantic cry, he aimed and shot.

She managed to knock his arm upward, and the bullet went wide. Furious, Blane hit her with the back of his hand, and Gwendeline fell to the deck unconscious.

Twenty-four

GWENDELINE WOKE ON A SOFA IN A SMALL NEAT parlor that seemed remarkably full of people. She looked around her, recognizing Miss Brown, Major St. Audley, and Mr. Ames. What would Mr. Ames be doing here, she wondered hazily. Just then, the door opened, and Lord Merryn strode in, crowding the room even more. She tried to sit up, only to discover that she felt excessively dizzy and that her head ached abominably. She sank back.

Lord Merryn was the only observer of these efforts. He nodded his approval. "That's better. You're not to move around for a while."

As the others turned toward her, Gwendeline put a hand to her head. "Oh, Gwendeline," put in Miss Brown, "I'm so glad to see you awake and safe. Blane is taken by the police; he won't trouble you again."

"He sent those notes to me," Gwendeline said. "And hired the highwaymen who attacked you. He told me so."

The earl nodded grimly. "I know. I've learned a great deal about Mortimer Blane in the last half hour.

He carried out a detailed plan of revenge for his imagined wrongs."

"The man must be mad!" exclaimed Mr. Ames, shaking his fist, and Miss Brown agreed.

But Major St. Audley shook his head. "I don't allow him that excuse. He is a dam…a dashed…" He threw up his hands. "Never mind."

Lord Merryn smiled a little at this and moved farther into the room. "Interesting as it may be to dissect Blane's character," he said blandly, "Gwendeline and I have more important matters to discuss. If all of you would excuse us for a few moments?" He gestured toward the door. The major went directly out, and Miss Brown followed more slowly, looking back over her shoulder anxiously. Mr. Ames hesitated, then also hurried out. The earl closed the door and turned back to Gwendeline. He pulled a chair up beside the sofa and took her hand. "There," he said. "Now we can settle things between us."

"How does Mr. Ames come to be here?" She thought she knew what he wished to say, and she wanted desperately to avoid telling him of her marriage to Blane.

"He forced himself upon me," the earl answered, shrugging and smiling wryly. "He would not allow me to leave that cursed ball without him."

"He is so kind."

"Possibly," said Lord Merryn dryly. "Why do I feel that you are trying to shift this conversation onto trivial subjects? I wish to discuss important matters."

"Important?" faltered Gwendeline.

"Well, the date of the wedding, for example. And whether you wish to go to Paris afterward or would prefer the country. I have a rather good house in Hertfordshire, you know."

"W-wedding?"

"Wedding," he agreed firmly, "our wedding."

Gwendeline burst into tears.

The earl looked surprised. "What have I said?" he asked. "I haven't had much experience making offers of marriage, I admit."

Gwendeline blurted out the story of her marriage to Blane. "So you see," she finished, "I cannot marry you. My life is ruined."

"What a gudgeon you are, Gwendeline," replied the earl indulgently.

Gwendeline sat up straight, only to sink back dizzily once more. "A gudgeon?" she replied hotly, her hand to her head again. "Is that how I seem to you in this horrid situation? You are odious; I am glad I can't marry you."

"Your marriage to Blane is not valid."

"What?"

"No marriage can be legal when one party is forced to it. But even that is beside the point. The man who married you was an imposter. Blane hired him to play a priest."

Gwendeline was stunned and could not take it in at first. "Y-you mean," she began.

"I mean that you are no more married than I, my dear gudgeon. A situation we shall speedily remedy, I hope."

"But…"

"Yes?"

"But you haven't even asked me to marry you…"

"Are you saying that you don't wish to do so?" Lord Merryn asked equably.

"No, but… I mean, yes. There is so much I do not yet understand." Gwendeline set her jaw. "I would like to know, once for all, if you have been supporting me these weeks. Blane didn't think that Sir Humphrey was a party to my rescue."

The earl looked at her with tender amusement. "You never give up, do you? I think perhaps it was your dogged perseverance that first roused my admiration." He sighed. "When I went down to Devonshire to fetch you, I expected to find a child, as you must remember. I'd made no provision for the fact that you might be a young lady. When I saw how it was, I had to revise my plans. I pulled this imaginary 'group' out of the air to satisfy the proprieties and quiet your understandable doubts, I admit. But once I was back in town I did enlist some others, after a hard half hour with Sir Humphrey Owsley, I must tell you. He was incensed that he had *not* been asked to join this mythical group, if you please."

Gwendeline smiled. "Was he indeed?"

Lord Merryn's answering smile was wry. "Extremely. He forced a large sum of money on me to make it true."

"I wish I might have seen him," laughed Gwendeline. She looked down then, and her smile faded. "But before that, you should have told me. It was not right. I…"

"You would have left me the instant you knew," put in the earl. "I couldn't face that when I found that you were the only woman I could ever love." He shook his head. "No fiction or invention seemed too arduous if it kept you near me. How I wished to give you even more! I admit, but I am not sorry." His grip on her hand tightened painfully. "If you knew what I felt when you disappeared! I vowed then that I would never lose you again."

"And so you became engaged to Adele Greene." She looked at him inquiringly.

"She is now safely engaged to the Duke of Craigbourne, as you must remember."

"Yes," said Gwendeline, "but very recently she was engaged to you." She looked at him squarely.

"And you wish to know how that came about?" Gwendeline nodded. "Understandable, I suppose. Well, the base of it was blackmail."

"What?"

"Yes. Adele wanted to marry me, or rather my title and fortune, I believe. She came up to me at a dinner party some time after you had left London and threatened to spread the story she'd heard Mr. Blane tell on our unfortunate country riding expedition throughout the *ton* unless I agreed to become engaged to her."

"Even Adele could not be capable of such a thing."

Lord Merryn shrugged. "Nevertheless, that is what she did. My first impulse was to laugh at her and send her packing. It seemed to matter very little when you had gone, believing the lies Blane had spoken." Gwendeline moved as if to protest this, but the earl went on. "Then, as I thought further, I realized two things. I didn't really want the tale spread. So I gave in, trusting that I could divert Adele, as I did with Craigbourne. I did hope the announcement might make you return to London."

Gwendeline looked away. "I can't imagine why."

"Can you not?" he asked, smiling. "But it did bring you back."

"It did not!" she replied indignantly. "I came back because…because I wished to. And because I'd read the countess's book and found out the true story of my mother. Which you might have told me in the beginning," she added.

"I came to do so on the day you fled London, Gwendeline," he told her seriously. "You gave me little chance to explain."

"I know. I am sorry."

"But my mother's book was helpful. Had I known she was writing it, I would probably not have agreed to become engaged. But she has learned to tell me little about her writing." He grinned. "By the by, she was overjoyed to hear that you are to become a member of the family. She said that your life has provided her with more plot ideas than she ever found in any of her researches. Your latest trials have sent her into ecstasies."

"Have you told everyone that we're to be married then?"

"Not everyone, certainly. Only your particular friends. I must say they were all flatteringly happy to hear it."

"Oh dear," said Gwendeline.

The earl's expression became very serious. "I have come to love you very much, Gwendeline. I hope you don't mean to refuse me?"

Gwendeline looked into his eyes. "No. That is… I hardly know where I am."

"You're with me."

Gwendeline gazed at him. That did seem the most important thing. "Yes, my Lord Merryn," she replied with an impish smile.

Laughing, he swept her into his arms.

*Read on for a sneak peek at the next book
in Jane Ashford's charming series*

A Lord Apart

DANIEL FRITH, VISCOUNT WHITFIELD, SET HIS JAW AS he surveyed the piles of documents and ledgers before him and wondered if he'd ever see the bare surface of the desk again. The estate office in his ancestral home was a study in chaos. It seemed to him that records and correspondence had been flung through the door like stones skipped across water and left to molder where they landed. As with everything else, Papa and Mama had been more interested in visiting far-flung lands than in anything occurring in their own. And so the piles of paper on this desk had grown higher, the disorder had increased, and next to nothing had been done.

His father hadn't bothered to inform him that their estate agent had left some time ago. Whether the fellow had gone out of incompetence or frustration, Daniel didn't know. How could he? If he'd been told that Briggs was gone, he would have found a new agent at least. Wouldn't he? But that was the point, wasn't it? His parents hadn't cared to tell him anything. He'd long ago stopped expecting them to. And so, when the weight of responsibility suddenly

descended upon him with their deaths, it was com-
pounded by this wretched mare's nest. There was so
much information to absorb, so many decisions to
make, while the information needed to do so could
never be found.

Daniel gazed longingly at the green landscape spreading outside the windows. Of course he preferred riding
and shooting and fishing and lively society to tenancy
reports and dry columns of numbers. Didn't everyone?

Brushing aside the suspicion that he wasn't entirely
blameless for his predicament, he picked up another
thick document. Regrets and resentments were a
waste of time. Things were as they were. He should
be working. He began to read.

A familiar irritation rose when he was scarcely three
sentences in. Lawyers didn't want you to understand
what they wrote, he'd concluded some time ago.
They'd created their own twisty, impenetrable language expressly to confuse, so that you had to hire
more lawyers to tell you what the devil the first ones
had meant. He imagined gangs of them tittering in
their fusty chambers, vying with each other to devise
yet more obscure phrasing for some obvious point.
Tontine, they'd cackle. *Partition of messuages lands*. Let's
see what they make of *that*!

Well, they weren't going to defeat him; he was
going to puzzle out this deed of conveyance without
help or additional fees. But as he tried to push on,
his brain jumped to the many other tasks awaiting his
attention. Lists upon lists. The sheer volume made it
difficult to focus on any one job. Particularly when it
was dull as ditchwater and nearly as stagnant. What

the deuce was mortmain? Sounded like some sort of fungus. When he was interrupted a few minutes later by a brisk knock on the office door, Daniel felt only relief. "Yes?"

His stately butler came through. "You wanted to be told when anyone headed for Rose Cottage, my lord. A carriage has been observed approaching the place."

"Indeed." Daniel dropped the document back on its pile and rose. "Thank you, Grant."

Twenty minutes later, Daniel was riding down the avenue of trees at the front of his home and out into the countryside toward a dwelling at the far edge of his lands, once part of them but now separate under his father's will. Finally, a mystery that had been nagging at him for months would be solved.

✦

Dust kicked up by the horses' hooves drifted through the open window of the post chaise, and Penelope Pendleton felt the ominous tickle at the back of her throat that heralded a fit of coughing. She swallowed repeatedly to fight it off, but the cough would not be quelled. The spasms seized her, shaking her shoulders and vibrating through her chest, making her eyes water and her throat ache. There was nothing to do but hang on and ride it out.

Her younger companion shrank away from the paroxysm. "I'm feard you have the consumption, miss. What'll I do if you go and die?"

"Won't," croaked Penelope. She took a swallow of well water from a flask she'd taken care to bring. And then another. A cough tried to rise. She pushed it back. "It's nothing of the kind," she rasped when she could speak again. "This is just a lingering cold, Kitty. That's all." Which was undoubtedly true. She was certain. The smoky mills of Manchester had prolonged the irritation of her lungs. No more. And the coughing was over now, for a while at least. "I'll soon be well here in the country. See how pretty it is."

The Derbyshire countryside rolled away from them, lush and green under the June sun—hills crowned by clumps of trees, neat fields bounded by stone walls.

Her sixteen-year-old maid eyed it uneasily. "Are there bears?"

"Not for hundreds of years, Kitty."

"So there *used to be* bears?"

"Yes, I think so, but—"

"So some might be left, hiding in the woods. Or in a dark cave maybe. Just waiting to jump out and rip your insides." The girl clawed at the air with her hand.

"No." Penelope made her voice authoritative. "They were all hunted down long ago."

"Wolves? With red eyes and teeth as long as your thumb?"

Penelope shook her head. "No wolves." Small, skinny, and addicted to drama, Kitty was a challenging personal attendant. The girl had never been out of Manchester before, and she had a dim view of vegetation. She saw every forest tree as poised to fall and "crush the life out of you." In her mind, undergrowth teemed with monstrous *things* eager to sting and bite and tear. The lack of nearby shops was almost incomprehensible to her. Yet she'd wanted to come along in Penelope's employ. Kitty had an odd sense of adventure that seemed to savor the idea of impending disaster. Her enthusiasm counted for a good deal as Penelope salvaged what she could from the wreck of her family fortunes.

The carriage bounced in a rut. Penelope gripped a strap and held on. The journey from Manchester to Ashbourne, over fifty miles of bad roads, had been exhausting. She couldn't imagine what it would have been like without the indulgence of a post chaise. But all would be well when they reached Rose Cottage, the mysterious miracle that had descended upon her when she'd nearly lost hope. It simply had to be.

They had to stop twice for directions, but at last the chaise slowed, turned, and pulled up before their destination. Penelope pushed open the door and jumped down, her soul awash with gratitude and relief.

Rose Cottage might have been anything. On bad days she'd envisioned a broken-down hovel with gaping windows and rotting thatch surrounded by fever-ridden swamps. But in fact it was a real house, built of mellow stone with a slate roof. The central door promised decent rooms on either side, and a second story showed three windows. There were chimneys at either end. Carved stone lintels suggested age, but the structure looked sound. Yes, it was small compared to what she was—*had been*—used to. But that mattered not a whit these days. The source of the name was obvious. Climbing roses had gone wild in the neglected garden, engulfing one end of the building and filling the air with scent.

Penelope took the key she'd received from the solicitor out of her reticule and hurried up three steps to unlock the door. It opened on a small entry with stairs at the back and bare, dusty rooms on either side. No furniture graced the wooden floorboards. No draperies softened the windows. But Penelope had two wagons coming behind her, carrying all her worldly goods under the care of a crusty old manservant who had tended to her father and then her brother. She would soon have a bed, and other necessities. Penelope smiled. Foyle would spit when he saw this place.

"Smells like old people," said Kitty, coming in on Penelope's heels.

There was also a dead sparrow in the fireplace on the left. But Rose Cottage was an actual house, and it really belonged to her. Penelope had the deeds in her trunk—miraculous evidence, in black and white, of her ownership. Though it was nothing like the spacious mansion where she'd grown up, the little stone building felt like sanctuary. "We will open the windows," replied Penelope. "And scrub it clean."

Kitty groaned theatrically.

Exploring further, Penelope discovered an extension on the back of the house, like the stem of a T, holding the kitchen. A door at one side led out to a small cobbled yard and privy. A neat little barn stood some yards away. Like the house, it seemed in good repair.

She returned to find the postilions setting down one of their trunks by the front door. "Upstairs, please," said Penelope. Looking grumpy but unsurprised, the two men hauled the luggage up the narrow stairs.

"That one goes back here," she said when they

brought in the large hamper of food she'd packed. "In the kitchen."

When they'd set it down, she walked with them back to the chaise and paid them off. Five minutes later, the equipage was rattling away.

"You're letting them go?" said Kitty from the doorway. "Leaving us here all alone to starve?"

Penelope laughed. She couldn't help it. A wild freedom she hadn't felt in ages bubbled through her. "You saw me pack the hamper. I brought plenty to eat. And should Foyle be delayed for some reason, I believe I saw the remains of a kitchen garden beside the barn."

"What's a kitchen garden?" asked Kitty.

"A place where you grow vegetables. Perhaps herbs, too. We can see what we find."

"I won't eat stuff that comes out of the dirt!"

"But that's where vegetables come from, Kitty."

The girl shook her head. "They come from the greengrocer."

"Who gets them from farmers, who grow them in the dirt. We'll wash everything off." Reminded of something, Penelope went back to the kitchen and tried the hand pump beside the stone sink. A bit of pumping produced a stream of water, rusty at first and then clear and clean. She sniffed and then tasted it. "Good," she said. "We won't have to carry water." She removed her bonnet and shawl and set them on top of the food hamper on the floor.

Kitty gazed around the empty room. "Nothing to carry it in," she pointed out.

"Foyle will be here soon with my things. Perhaps

by tomorrow. Let's make a fire. I saw some wood stacked by the barn." The day was warm, but there was something homey and reassuring about a fire.

"I'll get it, miss."

"I can help," Penelope said. She was going to have to learn a great many household skills that she'd never been taught. Carrying wood must be among the simplest.

Kitty held up a hand, palm outward. "It's for me to do, miss." Her features had taken on a stubborn cast. Penelope let her go. There would have to be a good many adjustments, some of which would offend Kitty's intermittent sense of correctness. But not today.

The thud of hooves sounded from the front of the house. Though it couldn't be Foyle yet, Penelope hurried out in hope.

She found a man dismounting a fine blood horse on her doorstep. Stocky, brown-haired, with blunt features and a square jaw, he wasn't classically handsome. But somehow he didn't need to be. He held one's attention by the sheer force of his presence. His expression suggested that he was accustomed to deference and obedience. Penelope took a step back. The last year had made her wary of such men.

The visitor looked her up and down. Was that disapproval? It couldn't be hostility. Unless he'd somehow received word… No. Not yet. Impossible. Penelope wondered if she'd rubbed dust on her face. Her gown was crushed and wrinkled from hours in the post chaise, but it had once been expensive.

"I'm Whitfield," he said.

The name was unfamiliar. Penelope relaxed a little.

He must be a neighbor. She would have preferred not to receive anyone until she was settled, but good relations with the community were important. "Hello, Mr. Whitfield. I am—"

"Not mister."

"I beg your pardon?"

"Rose Cottage was part of my estate until my father willed it to you," he went on. "I'd like to know why."

About the Author

Jane Ashford discovered Georgette Heyer in junior high school and was captivated by the glittering world and witty language of Regency England. That delight was part of what led her to study English literature and travel widely in Britain and Europe. Her books have been published all over Europe as well as in the United States. Jane has been nominated for a Career Achievement Award by *RT Book Reviews*. Born in Ohio, she is now somewhat nomadic. Find her on the web at janeashford.com and on Facebook at facebook.com/JaneAshfordWriter, where you can sign up for her monthly newsletter.

Also by Jane Ashford